D1827113

Friendship

A Pride and Prejudice Variation

by E A Batten

Friendship: A Pride and Prejudice Variation

Copyright © 2017 E A Batten

Cover photo: The Long Water, Hyde Park, London. Courtesy of istockphoto.com

All rights are reserved. No part of this book may be reproduced or transmitted in any form or by any means, electronic or mechanical, without permission in writing from the author.

This is a work of fiction. The characters and events portrayed in this book are fictitious or are used fictitiously. Any resemblance to real persons, living or dead, is entirely coincidental.

Written and Published in the United Kingdom

ISBN-13: 978-1544158259

ISBN-10: 1544158254

Dedication

To my friend Jane, who encourages me every step of the way

"There is nothing on this earth more to be prized than true friendship."
Thomas Aquinas 1225 – 1274

Prologue

"Mr Bennet, *Mr Bennet!*"

Mrs Bennet's cries could be heard throughout Longbourn as she quickly made her way to her husband's study, pulling her reluctant and ungrateful daughter with her.

The gentleman in question could hear his wife approaching, it would have been hard not to. He looked up from the book he was reading and glanced at the closed door, wondering what the latest imagined catastrophe to overtake the Bennet household could be. Mr Bennet shook his head and returned his attention to his book until the door of his study burst open. Raising his head he took in the scene before him. His wife entered the room like a galleon in full sail, pulling their hapless daughter along in her wake.

Mrs Bennet stood before her husband, her countenance full of indignation and her fury palpable. Their second daughter stood next to her mother with her head slightly bowed, but there was still an air of determination in her posture. Whatever Lizzy had done to upset her mother she believed herself to be right and, by the look of her countenance, his daughter had no intention of submitting.

"What has Lizzy done to upset you so, Mrs Bennet?"

"What has she done? What has she done? It is not what she has done but it is what she refuses to do." Mrs Bennet's voice rose as her anger grew. "She refuses to marry Mr Collins. Refuses, I tell you!" Mrs Bennet threw a dark look of indignation at Elizabeth. "Ungrateful child, it is not as though she is likely to receive a better offer!"

With his wife in full flow Mr Bennet knew little would be gained by interrupting her tirade, it was best to allow her to continue for the nonce.

"She refuses to do her duty. What will happen to us when you die if *she* is not made to see sense? I tell you, Mr Bennet, if she will not marry Mr Collins I…I will never speak to her or acknowledge her again." Mrs Bennet turned with exaggerated disdain to cut her daughter from her sight.

Bennet observed his favourite daughter. She reminded him so much of his mother, both in her looks and her love for life. With a gentle tone, he asked, "Now tell me, Lizzy, has Mr Collins made you an offer?"

"Of course he has!"

"I was asking Lizzy, Mrs Bennet. You have had your say, now it is her turn." He returned his attention to his daughter, ignoring his wife's scowl.

"Yes, Papa. But I could not accept him, I just could not. Please, Papa…" Mr Bennet raised his hand and his daughter fell silent.

"Well Lizzy, you now have a decision to make as an unhappy alternative is before you," he said with all seriousness, "as from this day forward you must be a stranger to one of your parents. You will lose your mother's attention if you do not marry Mr Collins, but, my child, you will lose mine if you do."

Elizabeth, never slow in understanding, immediately ran around her father's desk and hugged him. "Oh, thank you Papa."

His wife, realising the implications of his words, cried, "Mr Bennet, how could you be so cruel?" With a glare at her daughter and a swish of her skirts, Mrs Bennet turned and walked quickly from the room, calling for Hill and her salts as she went. The door slammed shut behind her and her cries for Hill became quieter as she went in search of the housekeeper.

Elizabeth bit her bottom lip. "Papa, I am sorry for causing Mama such distress, but I could not marry him. I could never marry a man I cannot like or respect, and I do not believe Mr Collins is a good man. We would make each other miserable."

"I understand, Lizzy, truly I do. I knew on meeting my cousin that he would not do for one of my daughters. Especially not you, my dear; I fear you would be growing foxgloves instead of comfrey for his tea before the year was out."

Elizabeth's lips quivered and laughter bubbled forth. "Oh Papa, I fear you could be right." Her hand covered her mouth as she tried to contain her laughter. The anxiety that her father might agree with her mother and order her to marry the horrid little man had now faded from her mind, replaced with a feeling of deep relief.

Her father told her not to worry, he was old friends with Mrs Bennet's nerves; he was sure that within a week or two all would be forgiven.

If Elizabeth had believed that was the worst of the matter she would be sorely disappointed. A couple of days later two things occurred that greatly agitated Mrs Bennet and her nerves. The first came in the form of Lady Lucas, who came to Longbourn to apprise Mrs Bennet of her daughter Charlotte's good fortune. Charlotte Lucas, spinster daughter of Sir William and Lady Lucas, who everyone believed was firmly on the shelf, was to marry Mr Collins.

Lady Lucas had barely left the ladies of Longbourn before the second event occurred—Jane received a missive from Netherfield. Miss Bingley wrote that following the departure of her brother and Mr Darcy from Netherfield, the whole party was removing to London as her brother's business could not possibly be completed in just a few days. The greatest distress to Jane was Miss Bingley's certainty of her brother's admiration of Miss Darcy, a lady of unparalleled beauty, elegance and accomplishments, whom Miss Bingley hoped with all expectation to call sister.

A second letter from Miss Bingley brought an end to any speculation as to when Mr Bingley might return. Their party, she wrote, was happily settled in London, with Mr Bingley a constant visitor to Darcy House. Miss Bingley assured Jane of her deepest regret that they would no longer be in company, for her brother had no thought of returning to Netherfield before the new year—if ever.

Mrs Bennet, on hearing the news, was distraught.

Chapter 1

31ˢᵗ December 1811, Gracechurch Street

Elizabeth Bennet gazed silently out of the bedroom window, her forehead leaning on the frosty pane. It was still dark outside when she had left the warmth of the bed, but slowly the sky began to lighten as dawn approached. She could see the outlines of the buildings and could hear the crier as he walked up the street telling all it was six o'clock and all was well. If she were at Longbourn she would have been able to see the outline of the trees, but here all she saw was the shape of dark rooves and chimneypots—there was not a tree in sight.

Elizabeth held a thick shawl around her, to ward off the winter chill. There would be no early morning walks. The area around her uncle's home was so different from that of Longbourn. Soon the street would be full of bustling noise, as people went about their daily occupation and costermongers began calling out to sell their wares.

Turning back to the room she looked at the form of her sleeping sister. Today was the last day of the year, Elizabeth wondered if the new year would be any better than its predecessor had turned out to be. Not that it started out that way, oh no, the first eight months were just as they should have been; it was the end of the ninth month, with the arrival of new tenants at Netherfield Park, that things began to change and, unfortunately, not for the better. A short time later a militia regiment arrived in Meryton, bringing handsome young officers in their red coats. Their arrival caused great delight and anticipation for many a lady, both young and old alike. Mrs Bennet became louder, Kitty and Lydia sillier—oh the embarrassment. Colour rose in Elizabeth's cheeks just thinking about their behaviour at the Netherfield Ball; it really was no wonder that Mr Bingley and his party had left the area with all speed, for her mother and younger sisters' behaviour was enough to sour any gentleman's regard for a lady from such a family. Elizabeth only wished that she too had been able to leave Meryton at that same time so that she might have avoided Mr Collins' proposal.

Elizabeth thought of her mother's fury, which had still to abate and hence her banishment to London. Did her mother dislike her second daughter so much that she would willingly tie her to such a man? Poor Charlotte. Elizabeth decided if she lived to be a hundred, she would never understand why her dear friend had accepted him. Surely it would be

4

better to be a spinster than married to Mr Collins, but she could not say that to Charlotte as her friend would not take the words kindly. Mr Collins appeared to be an obsequious little man when in company, but if he thought he was unobserved a different Mr Collins appeared. Elizabeth had seen him the morning of that ill-fated proposal when he believed he was alone in the parlour with Lucy, the pretty young maid who had joined the household just three weeks before. Mr Collins was so intent on the maid that he failed to notice Elizabeth at the door. She had shuddered at the look in his eyes. She had once caught sight of a fox watching a moorhen on a nearby pond, the look in Mr Collins' eyes reminded Elizabeth of that fox. Every night she prayed that Charlotte would be happy and safe in her marriage to Mr Collins.

"Lizzy?" a drowsy voice called from the bed.

Elizabeth watched, in the dim light of dawn, as her sister sleepily pushed herself up. She walked towards the bed, a smile lighting her countenance. "I was just watching the street come to life. I do believe it will be a lovely day. Perchance we could take our cousins to a park."

"We only arrived yesterday. Are you missing your morning walks already?" Jane asked with a laugh. "I am sure, if our aunt is agreeable, we could take the children to a park. Which one did you have in mind, Lizzy?"

"I thought Hyde Park would be nice, if uncle would allow us the use of his carriage. The park is so large Matthew and Frederick would be able to run about, without getting in anyone's way, and also there is the Serpentine. If we took some stale bread our cousins could feed the ducks and fish."

Jane pushed back the bedding and briefly placed her feet on the floor. "Oh, so cold!" she cried as she quickly slipped her toes back under the blanket. "That sounds an excellent idea, but I am sure it is too early for us to prepare for the day yet." Jane pulled the covers up to her neck. The fire had gone out and there was a definite chill in the air. Lizzy crossed the room and was soon on her knees by the grate. "Lizzy, what are you doing?"

"Lighting the fire to give us some warmth, or would you prefer to wait for a maid to light it for us." Jane shook her head and Lizzy laughed. "I thought not," she replied before turning back to continue with her task. Once the paper, sticks and coals were in place, she soon found a matchstick and taper with which to light it. It was not long before a small fire gave some much sought after warmth and Jane reluctantly got out of the bed to dress.

Jane observed her sister in the half light. Something was causing Elizabeth to be thoughtful. "What are you thinking of?"

Elizabeth smiled and let out a small sigh, dear Jane could always tell when she was trying to solve a problem. "I was simply wondering if Mama will ever allow me to return to Longbourn. I fear she will never forgive me, but, if she does not allow me to return when you do, I wonder what I will do."

"Oh Lizzy, Mama will forgive you. Yes, she is angry at the moment, but that will pass. I am sure we will both return to Longbourn before Easter."

"Possibly, I do not know. In any event, I must decide what I will do if I am no longer welcome at Longbourn. I cannot remain here and impose on the kindness of our dear aunt and uncle."

"Surely you are not thinking of employment?" Jane cried, incredulous that that might be her intention.

Elizabeth knew her next words would shock, but there really was little choice in the matter. "I have no money. I must do something to earn my keep. I thought I might be a governess, not, of course, for an older girl; I have not attended finishing school and therefore would not be suitable in such a role. But I would be qualified enough to teach a younger girl, Papa saw to that."

"Please, Lizzy, all will be well, you will see, do not do anything rash," Jane pleaded.

Elizabeth laughed before kissing her sister on the cheek. "My dear Jane, not only do you see the best in everyone, but you also find the best in every situation. I believe everyone should be blessed with a sister like you." Jane blushed and shook her head.

As they prepared for the day, Jane thought of her sister's predicament. She was saddened that Lizzy was only in town because of the depths to which she had fallen in their mother's disfavour, but, if truth be known, Jane was greatly relieved that she had her company. It helped to keep her mind from thinking too much of a certain fair haired young gentleman.

There was a light knock on the door. Fitzwilliam Darcy looked up from the newspaper he was reading and called out for the person to enter. A gentle smile on his lips warmed his eyes as the young lady walked towards him. "Good morning, Georgiana. Did you sleep well?"

"Yes, thank you, William," she softly replied, while appearing to take great interest in the buttons on her brother's waistcoat. Still, after all these months, she could not look directly at his eyes for fear of seeing his disappointment—so she did not see the gentle smile on his face, or it fade as the warmth in his eyes was replaced by sorrow. "I would like to go for a walk in the park, if I may. Mrs Annesley suggests it might be beneficial to me."

"Of course you may go. It appears to be a lovely day and I am sure the sunshine will be good for you, even though it lacks warmth. Wrap up well, Georgiana, and please take Matthews and Bryant with you."

She gave a nod of agreement, thanked her brother as she dipped into a curtsey and turned to leave the room, not once raising her head high enough to look at her brother's face.

As the door closed behind his sister, Darcy sighed. Elbows on his desk, he placed his face in his steepled hands. He was at a loss to know what to do. When Darcy had returned with Georgiana after his surprise trip to Ramsgate he was full of righteous fury. He had never before felt such anger; it almost robbed him of the ability to speak. He wished to kill Wickham for what he had planned and the hurt he had caused his vulnerable sister. He tried to comfort Georgiana after Wickham's parting words had left neither of them in any doubt that he cared only for her dowry and little for Georgiana herself. If Richard had been with him, Wickham would be dead, but Richard was abroad fighting the army of Bonaparte. Not knowing what to do, Darcy had taken Georgiana to the kindest person he knew, their Aunt Gwendoline, Lady Matlock. Aunt Gwendoline had taken Georgiana under her wing and given her the love of a mother. After a couple of months of little improvement, Lady Matlock had advised Darcy to give his sister time and space. "Go and visit one of your friends, do not worry about dear Georgie, she will be all right." So he had taken his aunt's advice and gone to Hertfordshire to help Bingley with the estate he had newly leased. Darcy sighed again as he thought of his time at Netherfield Park. Fine dark eyes, full of life and laughter, came unbidden into his mind. He groaned and banished Miss Elizabeth Bennet from his thoughts; Georgiana was his concern not the daughter of a country gentleman. When he had returned to town with Bingley he had hoped to see an improvement in Georgiana's well-being, but there was nothing. No, that was not true, there was an improvement. She conversed, albeit shyly, with her new companion, Mrs Annesley, and with her aunt and uncle, but not with Darcy. No, with her brother she said nothing, no matter how hard he tried to engage her; she would not even look him in the eye. Now five weeks later, she was speaking to him but she still could not raise her eyes to his. He despaired at how much longer it might be before he had his sister back?

Darcy heard footsteps outside the study; he stood up from his desk, walked through to the library and towards the bay window. Looking out at the street, he watched as Georgiana walked down the front steps to the pavement with Mrs Annesley, he was pleased to see the two lofty footmen follow in their wake. He watched as the party crossed the street and headed into the Park before turning away. In this room he felt his ancestors' presence. What would his father or grandfather say of the mess he had made in caring for his dearest sister; he shook his head and glanced around at the book-lined shelves which surrounded the room.

There was one thing all Darcy males had in common—their love of the written word. It was easy to tell the favourite tomes of each generation as copies of those books could be found in the library of every Darcy residence. When his great-grandfather, Alexander Darcy, had purchased the house on Park Lane, his first change was to knock down a wall which separated a smallish receiving room and, by Darcy standards, an equally unimpressive library. The end result was tolerable for Alexander's requirements. He saw no need for the receiving room as there was another of exactly the same proportions on the other side of the entrance hall.

Darcy began to make his way towards his study but stopped before reaching the adjoining door. There was little point in trying to work when he could not concentrate; he would be better working on some other pursuit like boxing or fencing, something where he could imagine Wickham was at the other end of his fist or blade. Within half an hour Darcy was on his way to Bond Street.

Mr Gardiner's carriage pulled up at the end of Curzon Street. Rogers jumped down from his seat next to the driver and helped the passengers alight. As soon as they entered the park Matthew and Frederick Gardiner ran off, attempting to chase a flock of sparrows which had taken flight from a nearby hedge. Frederick's squeals of delight could be heard all around. Matthew, who was nearly nine, tried unsuccessfully to act more like a gentleman than his younger brother. Their joy was contagious, and soon both Jane and Elizabeth were laughing at the antics of their young cousins. Elizabeth looked down at Patience who held tightly onto her hand, while her other hand was snug and warm in the small muff that hung around her neck. Seeing no strangers in sight, Elizabeth lowered her head and whispered, "Do you wish to run too?"

Patience looked up, glee shining in her eyes. "Oh yes," she replied.

"Come then, let us see if we can catch your brothers." With a laugh, Elizabeth and Patience set off. The girl let go of her cousin's hand and ran as fast as her little legs would carry her. Elizabeth smiled lovingly at the child as she walked quickly, trying to keep up with her, every now and then breaking out into a most unladylike run. Jane shook her head as she and Milly, the children's nanny, followed at a more sedate pace, with Rogers, one of her uncle's guards from the warehouse, following behind. Elizabeth called to Patience to wait for her. Patience stopped, looked at her cousin and then, after giving her cousin the broadest of smiles, ran on around a broad, well foliaged, holly tree that stood majestically in their path.

Suddenly there was a cry and Elizabeth, realising it was her young cousin, picked up her skirts and ran. As she rounded the tree she saw Patience sitting on the ground in front of a young lady. An older lady was holding out her hand to Patience. Elizabeth quickly made her way to her cousin's side and crouched down taking hold of her hand. "Patience, are you well?" As Patience nodded, confirming she was indeed none the worse for her experience, Elizabeth started to rise and looked up to the young lady that her cousin, in her haste, had most likely collided with. "Miss, I do apologise for my young cousin. I trust that you are well and have not been injured?"

"I am well, thank you," the young girl shyly replied.

Patience stood up and Elizabeth bent down to brush the leaves off of her dress. The boys, who had been playing tag around a large rhododendron bush had stopped when their sister had cried out as she fell, but seeing that she was unhurt, and now standing next to cousin Lizzy, they continued their game.

The young lady appeared to be about Lydia's age, while her companion was older and might be about the same age as her Aunt Madeline. Even though they were well wrapped against the winter chill, Elizabeth could tell the young girl was from a social class much higher than her own. Deciding that introductions were necessary, she curtsied. "I am Miss Elizabeth Bennet and this young lady," indicating to Patience, "is Miss Gardiner. She was so intent on catching her brothers that she was not looking where she was going." Elizabeth looked again at Patience and raised an eye brow.

Patience lowered her head and bit her bottom lip. Slowly she raised her head and looked up at the young lady she had nearly knocked over in her rush to reach her brothers. "I am so sorry, Miss…um…"

"Georgiana," the young lady replied softly.

"I am very sorry, Miss Georgiana," Patience said, her eyes brimming with tears.

"I am well," Georgiana quietly replied, "there is no need to worry. It was an accident and accidents do happen."

Realising the ladies were not angry, the child's boldness returned. "I like your name, it is very pretty. I wish I had a pretty name."

Elizabeth could not help herself as her laughter rang out. "Oh Patience, you have a lovely name."

"'Tis not as pretty as Georgiana or Elizabeth," Patience replied with a pout.

"You are most kind, Miss Gardiner," said Georgiana, "I like my name but I also like yours. I have an aunt who is called Patience. I remember looking at her portrait and wishing I could be as beautiful as she when I grew up."

"Really?" Patience looked up, eyes wide, dislike of her name forgotten. Georgiana nodded. "Lizzy says I am named after a virtue and I should try to live up to my name. Is your aunt a virtue?"

The young lady's companion coughed in an attempt to hide the laughter that was threatening to erupt from her; it would not do for the child to think she was being laughed at.

"Do you mean does she take after her name?" When Patience quickly nodded her head, Georgiana continued softly, "I have been told she is the most forgiving and caring of ladies. She married an Italian Count and lives in Venice, I was only a small child the last time she and her husband visited England, so I cannot remember much about her."

As Georgiana was speaking, Jane approached Lizzy. Milly and Rogers both stood back, not wanting to intrude on the conversation.

"Miss Georgiana, this is my sister Miss Bennet. Jane, this is Miss Georgiana and...oh I am sorry I do not know your name."

"That is my fault," Georgiana replied, as she bit her bottom lip.

"No, no," cried Elizabeth, "My cousin has kept us all busy with the discussion of the virtue, or not, of being named Patience."

"Quite so, Miss Elizabeth," the elder lady replied. "My name is Mrs Annesley; I am Miss...Georgiana's companion." Mrs Annesley had seen the brief look of discomfort in Georgiana's eyes and the thankful smile which graced her charges countenance when she had failed to mention the Darcy name.

"We are taking the children to the Serpentine so that they may feed the ducks. Would you care to join us?" Elizabeth asked. Georgiana turned to look at Mrs Annesley, hoping her companion would agree. A warm smile lit up Georgiana's face as Mrs Annesley gave a discreet nod of her head. Georgiana then turned back to Elizabeth. "We would like that very much, thank you."

Elizabeth turned to their guard. "Rogers, would you please gather up the boys and tell them we are going to the lake to feed the ducks." With a quick nod of his head, Rogers made his way to where the boys were still playing.

Patience left Elizabeth's side and went to take hold of her nanny's hand. Milly looked down at the girl and shook her head as she gently picked a couple of stray leaves out of Patience's hair.

As they walked towards the Serpentine Lizzy attempted to apologise for her cousin's impertinence, but their new acquaintances would hear nothing of it.

"It is a pleasure to see such innocent inquisitiveness," Mrs Annesley assured the sisters. "Your cousin is young and has caused no offence." On seeing Miss Elizabeth glance at the two large men following them, Mrs

Annesley decided to waylay any fears the young lady might have. "Have no concern. The men that follow us are in the employment of Miss Georgiana's brother. I would imagine their reason for being here is much the same as your uncle's man."

The rest of the morning passed without any further accidents. The children fed the ducks under the watchful eye of both Milly and Rogers, while the Miss Bennets enjoyed the company of Miss Georgiana and Mrs Annesley. The two footmen stood a few feet away, near enough should there be any danger to their master's sister, but far enough to allow the ladies privacy. The Bennet sisters and Georgiana found they appreciated many of the same things. Elizabeth and Georgiana both took pleasure in reading, and spoke of their favourite authors, while Jane and Georgiana both enjoyed embroidery, they spoke of the stitches and the ones they found most difficult. Georgiana spoke of her brother's estate without actually saying where it was, while Jane and Elizabeth spoke of Longbourn. They discovered they all enjoyed playing the pianoforte, although Elizabeth assured her new friends that she played very ill.

When Patience complained of feeling hungry, Elizabeth realized they had been talking for nearly two hours. There was something about Georgiana that drew out Elizabeth's compassion; she believed that the shy young girl was in need of a friend.

"Lizzy, we must take the children home." Jane's voice shook Elizabeth from her reverie.

"Yes, of course," Lizzy replied. "Miss Georgiana, Mrs Annesley, it has been a pleasure to be in your company. I do hope we will be able to meet again."

Georgiana smiled. "I hope so too. I have enjoyed our time together."

"There are lots of things I would like to do while we are in town, but one is to visit Gunter's. I know it is too cold for ices or sorbets but a cup of hot chocolate with a slice of delicious cake would be very nice. Would you care to join us?" As she spoke Elizabeth's eyes shone in anticipation.

"When are you thinking of going there?" Mrs Annesley enquired.

"We thought perhaps on Monday. Perhaps in the afternoon, which would allow for time to recover from any family twelfth night celebrations." Elizabeth replied. "Would that be agreeable for you both?"

"That would be wonderful," Georgiana said. "We can go, can we not, Mrs Annesley? I'm sure my brother would not mind, as long as Bryant and Matthews are with us."

"That would be ideal," Jane said with a smile. "Your men can keep Rogers company, as I am sure we will not be able to venture to Berkeley Square without our trusted protector."

The ladies walked together as far as Mr Gardiner's carriage, where they said their goodbyes. Rogers climbed up next to the driver, who had been patiently waiting for them, while Jane and Elizabeth got into the carriage with the children and Milly.

Darcy's morning had proved beneficial. He had arrived at 13 Old Bond Street but then hesitated and, instead of entering Gentleman Jackson's club, went next door to Henry Angelo's Fencing Academy. His cousin, Viscount Tansley, was there and, after a good and fair match, they had taken themselves to White's for a light repast and a glass or two of fine brandy.

Tansley knew Darcy was having difficulty with Georgiana, but he had no idea as to why the difficulties had begun or the reason behind them. Had the shy Georgiana Darcy tried to challenge her brother's authority? Darcy was being very tight lipped about it, but any fool could see all was not well. He did wonder if there was more to Darcy's problems than just his sister, he prayed it had nothing to do with that blackguard Wickham. "Why not take her to Derbyshire; surely the peace of Pemberley might improve her well-being?"

"No," Darcy replied, "I do not believe that will help. She would feel isolated at Pemberley, at least in town she has your mother nearby if she wishes her company or advice, and there are plenty of interesting places for her and Mrs Annesley to visit. If your parents retired to Derbyshire then I might follow with Georgiana, but for the nonce we shall remain in town."

"My parents will not leave town anytime soon. Father can get a better supply here than he can in the country," Tansley muttered, so low that Darcy barely heard him. "Speaking of mother," he continued with a more cheery voice, "she received a letter yesterday. Richard should be home as early as next week."

"That, my dear cousin, is the best news I have heard in a long time," Darcy stated.

"Yes," Tansley agreed, "and mother is delighted. From the letter it appears he will have four weeks' leave before he must report to Liverpool at the War Office. I believe mama prays that he will succeed where we have all failed."

Darcy doubted that the countess' wishes would be granted, but did not say so. "I will be glad to see him returned and I would be delighted if he never saw a battlefield again."

"You and I both," Tansley said with feeling. "I think my brother has done his duty for the King and his country."

Darcy raised his glass. "To Richard's good health and peace." Tansley echoed Darcy's sentiments.

Wishing to remove the talk from his family, Tansley inquired after Darcy's friend Bingley and asked if he was enjoying his new estate.

Darcy laughed and shook his head. "Miss Bingley and Mrs Hurst persuaded Bingley to return to town. He found another angel, as is his wont, and his sisters did not approve of the family." Darcy let out a sigh. "Having made the acquaintance of the mother and youngest sisters, I cannot blame them."

"Ah, so let me guess," Tansley said with a chuckle, "you advised him against her and saved your friend from an unsuitable alliance."

"Yes…and no."

"Come on Darcy, it cannot be both. So which is it, yes or no?"

Darcy took another sip of his brandy. "The eldest Miss Bennet is all that a young lady should be. The mother is a loud and unrefined version of any mother in haut ton with daughters to marry off, and will no doubt interfere with the life of any married daughter living nearby. The two youngest girls run wild, if they continue on that track I can see ruin in their path. Their father is a member of the landed gentry but sadly appeared to think more of his books than the behaviour of his wife and children. All this would not matter if I thought Miss Bennet cared for my friend, but I could see nothing. She smiled well enough when in his company, but in the same way she smiled at everyone."

"I see, so the lady may be reserved and not act like those we meet in the ton."

Darcy frowned. "She may," he sighed, hoping his cousin was wrong. "But, Bingley will soon recover and find a new angel, if he has not already. I doubt his intentions towards Miss Bennet were of a serious nature." At least he hoped that was the case.

"Ah, I see. So, if you have not saved him, you may have saved her from untold heartache." Tansley raised his glass. "Drink up, I will buy you another."

Chapter 2

When Mr Gardiner's carriage arrived back at Gracechurch Street, Rogers jumped down and quickly opened the carriage door. The children were so eager to alight that Jane told Milly to go first. Matthew and Frederick ran to the house, followed at a more sedate pace by Milly and Patience. Rogers helped the young ladies alight and then, once he saw they were safely in Mr Gardiner's residence, made his way down the street towards the warehouse.

Mrs Gardiner met her children as they entered the house. "So my dears, did you have an enjoyable morning with your cousins?" While the boys were regaling their mother with their adventures, Mrs Gardiner noticed her daughter walking into the passage looking slightly dishevelled. "Patience, what has happened?"

Before the little girl could open her mouth to reply, Frederick spoke. "Mama, Patience fell over. She was running and bumped into a young lady."

Mrs Gardiner shook her head. "Oh Patience, how many times have I told you, young ladies do not run in public."

Patience looked down at her boots. "I am sorry, Mama," she mumbled.

Elizabeth quickly interceded on her cousin's behalf. "Aunt Madeline, it was my fault. Patience wished to follow her brothers, so we set off after them."

Mrs Gardiner looked from her niece to her daughter and sighed. "Perhaps we should have named you Elizabeth for you are more like your cousin every day," she said in a resigned tone. "Now, children, go to the nursery with Milly, it is time for your luncheon and afternoon rest. But please be quiet," she cried, as the boys noisily began to make their way to the stairway. "Faith is asleep."

The boys immediately quietened and all three children chorused, 'Yes, Mama,' before making their way up the stairs.

Jane and Elizabeth made their way to their room to remove their outer clothing and refresh themselves before returning to the dining room and their aunt's company.

"So tell me, Jane, besides from Lizzy encouraging my daughter to act in an unladylike manner which may have caused injury to a young lady, was the morning's outing otherwise pleasant?"

Jane and Lizzy noticed the laughter in their aunt's eyes. "It was a delightful morning and thankfully the young lady appeared to be uninjured," Jane replied.

"But Patience took quite a tumble, "Elizabeth added, "and I fear she may have a bruise or two."

"I am sure she will survive," their aunt replied, "and perhaps that will make her slow down and behave as a young lady should. You are sure the young lady was well after her encounter with Patience?"

"Yes," replied Elizabeth. "Neither Miss Georgiana nor her companion, Mrs Annesley, suffered any ill. Miss Georgiana must be about fifteen years of age. She is a very shy young lady, do you not agree, Jane?"

"Yes, she was very quiet to begin with and is exceedingly polite. We spent a most enjoyable couple of hours in their company while the children played and fed the ducks."

"From what Miss Georgiana said, I believe her father has passed and she is now in the care of an older brother. Though, strangely, she made no mention of her older sister."

"Perhaps her sister is a lot older than her and married," Mrs Gardiner replied.

"But then surely Aunt, Miss Georgiana would be Miss…" Elizabeth paused. "Oh, neither she nor her companion mentioned her family's name, how strange."

"But you say she is a young lady of quality?"

"Oh yes," Jane replied fervently, "both her clothing and her mien both spoke of quality. I should imagine she is from a family of the highest circle."

"When you meet again on Monday, I am sure you will find that the information was unintentionally omitted and there is no great secret." Mrs Gardiner smiled at her younger niece. "Yes, Lizzy, I know how your mind works, looking for mystery and intrigue where there most likely is none."

The last fortnight for Georgiana had been the happiest for a long time. The afternoon at Gunter's with Miss Bennet and Miss Elizabeth had been delightful, and her friendship with them had continued to grow. The weather had permitted them to meet twice more at Hyde Park. They would make their way to the western end of the Serpentine to the Long Water, where Georgiana and her companion could happily converse with Jane and Elizabeth while the older Gardiner children fed the ducks. Georgiana had felt embarrassed when Miss Elizabeth had asked her about her older sister and she had to confess that there was no older sister, there was only an older brother who was her guardian, a duty he shared with their cousin. Neither Miss Bennet nor Miss Elizabeth had made any remark on learning that she was a Darcy and both assumed that if there were a connection she must be a cousin to the Mr Darcy who had been staying at Netherfield, though Elizabeth did think it quite a coincidence that that Mr Darcy and Miss Darcy's brother both had the guardianship of a younger sister. As Georgiana never mentioned her cousin's proud sister, Elizabeth was convinced that that Miss Darcy must be far worse than Mr Wickham had portrayed. They had met once more at the park and this afternoon Georgiana and Mrs Annesley were to call on the Bennet sisters at Gracechurch Street.

Darcy had been pleased to see the improvement in his sister's well-being. Mrs Annesley had assured him that the young ladies his sister had first met in Hyde Park were genteel and they both appeared to have a positive effect on Georgiana. Although Georgiana still found it hard to look at her brother, for fear of seeing disappointment etched on his visage, she was becoming more talkative and joined in with conversations. Darcy was greatly relieved and, as he hoped one day to meet the young ladies who had helped his sister so much, he had no qualms about allowing Georgiana to be in their company. He had never thought to enquire of their names so was unaware that he already knew both ladies, in fact one still haunted his dreams.

"Miss Darcy and Mrs Annesley," the butler announced.

Elizabeth rose quickly and walked to her friend. "My dear Georgiana, and Mrs Annesley, welcome. May I introduce you to my aunt, Mrs Gardiner?" Elizabeth then turned to her aunt who was now standing beside her. "Aunt Madeline, these are our new friends, Miss Darcy and her companion, Mrs Annesley."

Mrs Gardiner curtsied. "It is a pleasure to meet you, Miss Darcy, and you, Mrs Annesley. My nieces have told me much about you. Please, come, take a seat. Our cook made some delicious Shrewsbury biscuits this morning, I hope you will both join us and partake in some refreshments."

"It would be our pleasure," Mrs Annesley replied.

Georgiana sat comfortably between Elizabeth and Jane on a settee, while Mrs Annesley and Mrs Gardiner sat on chairs nearby. Mrs Gardiner watched Miss Darcy as she shyly spoke with Elizabeth and Jane; by her countenance it was obvious that she enjoyed her nieces' company greatly. But there was something about the young lady which reminded Mrs Gardiner of her youth. "Miss Darcy, I hope you do not mind if I ask, but, are you related to the Darcys of Pemberley?" When Georgiana did not immediately answer Mrs Gardiner continued. "I only ask because I lived in Lambton as a girl, and, if I might say so, you do remind me greatly of Lady Anne."

Georgiana looked keenly at her hostess. "I do?"

"Yes. I only saw Lady Anne a few times, but she was a beautiful lady. Also, from my memory, I believe you are similar in colouring and stature."

"Thank you Mrs Gardiner. Lady Anne was my mother."

Elizabeth listened in shock as her aunt and Georgiana continued their conversation about Pemberley and Lambton. The shy young girl that she and Jane had befriended was none other than the sister of Mr Darcy. Surely not, Mr Darcy was haughty; he would never allow his sister to mix with the likes of the Bennets and their relatives. Besides, Mr Wickham had assured her, Mr Darcy's sister was much like her brother. It was then that Elizabeth wondered if the amiable officer had deliberately misled her. *'Miss Darcy is shy not proud. Have I been erroneous in my judgement of the character? Did my wounded vanity prejudice me so that I would readily believe anything ill about Mr Darcy?'* Elizabeth felt a sickness in the pit of her stomach that she had so readily believed someone so wholly unconnected to her, in fact a stranger in every way.

Jane had also been surprised by the revelation, but when there was a break in the conversation she was determined to behave with good manners to their friend. "Georgiana, forgive me, I had no idea you were Mr Darcy's sister. We met your brother when he was staying in Hertfordshire with his friend Mr Bingley. Miss Bingley spoke often of you. I wish you joy on your betrothal to Mr Bingley, he is a most amiable gentleman." Jane smiled, in an attempt to portray happiness for her friend.

Georgiana was now the one to be shocked. "Mr Bingley?" she cried incredulously. "Oh no, he is my brother's friend. He has no interest in me. Besides, I am not out yet, brother would never allow me to be betrothed to any gentleman before my come out and first season. Fitzwilliam is so good to me...he protects me from those who would harm me." Tears glistened in Georgiana's eyes. With Georgiana close to tears Mrs Annesley decided it was time that they departed, but before she could speak Elizabeth reached for Georgiana's hand. "Georgiana, it is a lovely sunny afternoon, why do we not wrap up warmly and walk in the garden?"

Georgiana nodded in agreement and, once their cloaks and bonnets were donned, Elizabeth quickly led the way outside. Once in the garden she handed Georgiana a fine linen handkerchief.

"Thank you," Georgiana whispered as she patted away the dampness on her eyes. "You must think me so childlike to become upset over something so silly."

Elizabeth shook her head. "Of course not. Mr Darcy is your brother, it is only right you should feel that he is a good protector. There are many times I wish I had an older brother. You are most fortunate."

"You were in the company of my brother when he was staying with Mr Bingley?"

"Yes," Elizabeth replied, "though I do not believe he was very enamoured with our society. He always looked very..." Haughty was the word that came to mind, but she could not say that to her young friend.

"Haughty?" Georgiana interposed.

Elizabeth's eyes widened as Georgiana smiled for the first time since they had come into the garden. "I know my brother," she said with a giggle. "I can well imagine the impression he gave in company. It is a mask you know, as, much like me, he is uncomfortable when in the company of people he does not know. We Darcys tend to be a shy lot. I am told my father was the same." Georgiana let out a deep sigh. "He really is the best of brothers. If not for him I would be lost. I must be such a disappointment to him." Her tears began to fall again.

Elizabeth took hold of Georgiana's hand. "That I do not believe! Your brother spoke most fondly of you when I was in his company at Netherfield."

"He did?"

Elizabeth nodded, gently squeezing her friend's hand before releasing it. "Yes and I am sure whatever has passed to make you believe you have his disapprobation, cannot be that bad."

"Oh but it is. I was taken in by people that I trusted and my brother had to rescue me. So you see if he was distant and preoccupied it was my fault." Georgiana's anguish was palpable.

"No," Elizabeth replied softly, as she noticed tears welling again in the young girl's eyes. "If you were taken in by such people then it is their fault. You are but fifteen and I imagine the people you speak of were much older than you?" Georgiana nodded. "They were of age and, so being, should know better. Believe me, Georgiana, you are not at fault for trusting another."

"That is what William said," she replied. "He said it was the fault of my companion, Mrs Younge, and Mr Wickham."

Elizabeth gasped, surely it could not be, but she had to ask. "Mr George Wickham?"

"Yes, do you know him?" Georgiana's eyes were wide; there was concern in her voice.

"Yes, he is in the Militia and is stationed at Meryton. He arrived in the neighbourhood soon after your brother."

"Oh no! Did they meet at all?"

"I am aware of one meeting. At the time your brother looked very angry, I understand why now, and Mr Wickham looked as though he had seen a ghost."

"I suspect Mr Wickham avoided being in my brother's company after that."

Elizabeth thought back over the weeks that Lieutenant Wickham and Mr Darcy may have been in each other's company. Georgiana was right; Mr Wickham had stayed away from any gathering where Mr Darcy was present. How had she not seen that before? He had been so quick to tell her of Mr Darcy's cruelty, while at the same time saying he could not speak out against the son for love of the father; how could she have so readily believed him. Georgiana was not the only one to be taken in by Mr Wickham's charming manners. What had Mr Darcy said? Something about Mr Wickham making friends easily but had difficulty keeping them. Elizabeth chastised herself, to think she had believed the words of such a charming rogue, although now rogue seemed too mild a word to describe Mr Wickham.

"You are correct," Elizabeth replied. "But, Georgiana, you are not the only one to be taken in by that man." Elizabeth reached out and placed her hand over Georgiana's. "I was too."

Georgiana's eyes widened as she gasped. "Never!" she cried.

"Oh but I assure you, I was. But to understand why I must tell you of the first time I was in the company of your brother." Elizabeth told Georgiana about the fateful night at the assembly and how her brother's words had offended her pride. "So you see, with Mr Wickham's charismatic charm and your brother's behaviour at the assembly, I was too eager to believe his words about Mr Darcy. Now, after listening to you speak of your brother and Mr Wickham, I believe your brother has all the goodness, while Mr Wickham only has the appearance of it."

"I am sure you would never have contemplated that which I nearly did. You would not wish to know me if you knew, I do not know how my brother can forgive my foolishness." Tears of distress slowly made their way down Georgiana's cheeks.

Elizabeth placed her arms around her young friend and held her close. "My dear Georgiana, I will always be your friend. Whatever happened between you and Mr Wickham, there is one thing I am sure of, you are not to blame. He has an abundance of charm, which I am sure no young girl would be able to resist." A terrible thought went through Elizabeth's mind. She stepped back and looked at Georgiana. "Did he compromise you?"

Georgiana shook her head. "No, thank goodness," she whispered. "But he had persuaded me to go with him to Scotland. My companion thought it was so romantic. We were to…"

Elizabeth clasped hold of Georgiana's hand. "Your companion thought it was romantic?" Georgiana nodded. "Oh, that is terrible; she sounds as immoral as Wickham. I am sorry; I should not have interrupted you. So, what happened next?" she asked, keeping a firm hold of Georgiana's hand.

"We were to leave for Scotland the following day, but my brother arrived unexpectedly that evening. I was so pleased to see him. I thought he would be happy for me. It was terrible, Lizzy, William was so angry with both George and Mrs Younge. It was then that William told me about Mr Wickham and his threats." Georgiana told Elizabeth all that her brother had told her. Elizabeth heard about the gambler and rake, the money given in lieu of the living and finally the threat of revenge when more money was not forthcoming.

"I…I do not know how my brother can b…bear to be in the same room…as me," Georgiana stuttered through her sobs.

"Georgiana?" Georgiana raised her eyes to look at Elizabeth, who smiled warmly at her. "Has your brother ever said he is disappointed in you?"

"No, but…"

"Has he ever said he blames you for what happened?"

"No, but I…"

"Then I doubt very much if he is disappointed. Any anger he has will be aimed that those responsible, Mr Wickham and Mrs Younge, not his young sister for whom he cares deeply. He may be worried and concerned for you, but not disappointed. Never that."

"Do…do you really think so?"

Elizabeth nodded. "Yes, I do," she replied, her tone gentle but serious. "You should speak to your brother and tell him of your fears. He will understand." Georgiana slowly nodded, all the while chewing her bottom lip.

Elizabeth and Georgiana returned to the house and Elizabeth took her friend to her room so that she might refresh herself. By the time they returned to the drawing room Georgiana had recovered and, unless under close inspection, no longer had the appearance of someone who had been weeping.

After a further ten minutes of enjoyable conversation Georgiana and Mrs Annesley took their leave, but not before an invitation was extended for the Bennet sisters to join Georgiana at Darcy House the following Monday. A time was arranged, which was to everyone's convenience, and all agreed that they looked forward to their next meeting.

That evening, when dinner ended, Georgiana did not immediately retire to her room, instead she offered to play for her brother and they made their way to the drawing room. Once she had finished on the pianoforte

Georgiana moved to sit near her brother. She took a deep breath. "May I ask a question?"

"Of course, what is it?" The delight Darcy felt that his sister wished to speak with him warmed his heart.

"Am I a great disappointment to you?" Georgiana kept her eyes lowered so she did not see her brother's shocked look.

"Never! Surely you do not think…" Darcy was shocked that his dear sister could ever think sure a thing possible.

"I thought…after Ramsgate…" Georgiana paused and took a deep breathe. "I did not know how you could bear to look at me. You were so angry. You had to be disappointed in my behaviour. I am so sorry…"

"Shhh." Darcy pulled his sister into his arms. Then holding her back slightly, and lifted her chin so that he could look into her eyes. "Yes, I was, and I still am angry at what happened, but not with you, never with you. I blame Wickham and Mrs Younge, and to an extent myself."

"No, brother, it was my…"

Darcy moved his hand to place a finger over her lips. "I hired Mrs Younge, in that I am to blame. I trusted a woman with your safekeeping who was not trustworthy. I am angry with both that woman and Wickham. They tried to manipulate you, a young lady of barely fifteen summers. You had no idea of Wickham's true character…that too was my fault. So you see, my dear, if anything, you should be disappointed in me."

"Never, you are the best of brothers. I think myself most fortunate," Georgiana said with a smile trying to hold back her tears of relief. "Miss Elizabeth said it would be so, she tried to convince me that you might be worried and concerned but never disappointed. She told me to speak to you of my fears."

"I am glad you followed her advice." Then a terrible thought crossed his mind. "Did you tell her about Ramsgate?" Darcy closed his eyes, his sister would be ruined. No one would keep that juicy piece of gossip to themselves.

"Yes, but I am sure she will keep my secret. She said she was ashamed that she too had once believed Mr Wickham's falsehoods."

Darcy was not so sure and wondered how much he would need to pay to ensure Georgiana's 'friend' would keep her secret. "She sounds a wonderful young lady. I should like to meet her one day,"

"Oh but, William, you have already met her. We have spoken about you…though she did have the wrong impression of your character. She thought you were haughty and proud, but now that she knows Mr Wickham's true character I believe she thinks better of you."

While Georgiana spoke, Darcy tried to think who the young lady might be, but no one came to mind. He knew of a few young ladies of the haut ton who were named Elizabeth, but he did not believe any of them had the temperament that Georgiana had described. "What is Miss Elizabeth's family name and whereabouts in London is her home." He inwardly berated himself for not having asked these simple questions before.

"She and her sister are residing in London with their aunt and uncle, her home is in Hertfordshire and her family's name is Bennet." Thankfully Georgianna did not appear to notice her brother's sharp intake of breath at the shock of hearing Elizabeth Bennet's name. She leant towards him and kissed his cheek. "Thank you for being the best of brothers. Goodnight, William."

Darcy wished his sister goodnight and watched as she left the room. He then closed his eyes and sighed. Miss Elizabeth Bennet, of all the young ladies in town Georgiana had been befriended by Miss Elizabeth Bennet. He shook his head, what was he going to do?

He had spent every night since his return from Netherfield trying to forget those fine eyes that haunted him in his dreams, forget the one young lady who tempted him above all others and now he would be in her company again. Then he thought of the marked improvement to Georgiana's wellbeing. Was Elizabeth really so unsuitable? After all it appeared she had been successful where he, Lady Matlock and even Mrs Annesley had failed. His mind continued to cogitate. She was Elizabeth, not Miss Elizabeth. It appeared his heart knew what his mind was refusing to admit; she was his Elizabeth.

A slow smile warmed Darcy's countenance as he took another sip of his brandy. He might not know much about Miss Elizabeth Bennet but he did know she was loyal and honest. He had discovered that much while she lovingly cared for her sister at Netherfield.

If Elizabeth had told Georgiana she would not tell a soul of her near ruination by that blackguard then he would trust that she would keep her word. The next thought that passed through his mind widened his smile.

Perhaps Georgiana should invite her new friends to Darcy House; he would suggest it to her in the morning.'

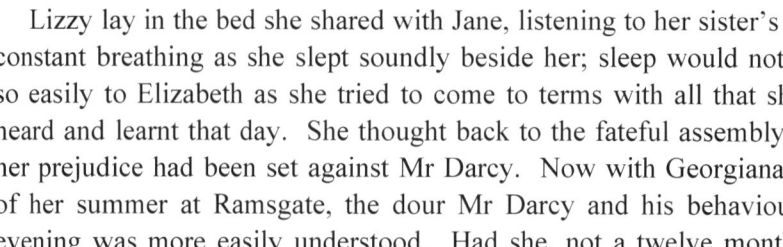

Lizzy lay in the bed she shared with Jane, listening to her sister's gentle constant breathing as she slept soundly beside her; sleep would not come so easily to Elizabeth as she tried to come to terms with all that she had heard and learnt that day. She thought back to the fateful assembly when her prejudice had been set against Mr Darcy. Now with Georgiana's tale of her summer at Ramsgate, the dour Mr Darcy and his behaviour that evening was more easily understood. Had she, not a twelve month ago, behaved in a similar manner? Her mother had chastised her for her behaviour when they had dined at Lucas Lodge. Lady Lucas' sister and her sons were visiting and would remain with the Lucases for a full fortnight. Mrs Bennet, who considered both young gentlemen suitable suitors for Elizabeth, had been furious at the lack of encouragement Elizabeth presented to either Albert or Samuel Wilson and quickly chastised her daughter once they were in the privacy of their carriage. Elizabeth had been too intent with worries about her dear sister, Jane, who was abed at home, quite ill with a cold, to pay any attention to potential suitors.

Remembering her worry for such a minor ailment, Elizabeth could not imagine how much Mr Darcy must have suffered having come so close to losing his beloved sister. Elizabeth felt tears well up in her eyes. What she had learnt about Mr Wickham's character was disturbing. His appearance and charm were all goodness. How wrong she had been. Eventually tiredness overcame her and she fell into a fitful sleep. Her last conscious thought was that her sisters, at least, were safe from Mr Wickham, as the Bennet sisters had little in the way of dowries to tempt such a man as he.

Chapter 3

"I wonder if Mr Darcy will be present."

Elizabeth looked at her sister as their uncle's carriage made its way through the streets of London from Gracechurch Street to Park Lane. "I would think it unlikely," she replied. "I would imagine he would neither have the time nor the inclination to sit with three young ladies while they talk."

Jane laughed. "I expect you are correct. Poor Mr Darcy would become exceedingly bored very quickly."

Georgiana had planned to meet Jane and Elizabeth in the music room, but she changed her mind a few minutes before they were due to arrive. With the help of Mrs Annesley, she took her favourite sheets of music to the drawing room on the ground floor. The room was larger and lighter, and far enough away from the front of the house, separated as it was from the street by a receiving room, to ensure that noise from the street was lessened. The pianoforte in that room was a Wrede. It was wonderful to play and had quite a fine tone to it, though, of course, not as good as the Broadwood that was in the music room. The drawing room also had another advantage, it was closer to her brother's study and, as he had mentioned that he might join the ladies, it seemed the best room in which to greet them. Georgiana walked towards the study door with the intention of informing her brother of the change of venue when a footman spoke her name.

Georgiana turned towards him. "Yes, Greenhill?"

"The master has a visitor with him, Miss."

"Oh. When the caller departs please tell my brother that I will be in the blue drawing room with the Miss Bennets."

"Of course, Miss," Greenhill replied with a bow.

Georgiana placed the sheets of music on the piano, sat down on the stool and began to play a simple tune. Not many minutes had passed when the butler opened the drawing room door and announced her friends. Georgiana jumped up from the stool and quickly made her way towards them. "Jane, Elizabeth, you have arrived. Welcome to Darcy House."

Elizabeth looked around the room as she walked closer to the piano; it was elegant but not ostentatious. "This is a lovely room, Georgiana." Elizabeth then noticed the instrument in front of her. "Oh, you have a Wrede. My aunt has one, it is wonderful to play."

Georgiana smiled as her fingers reverently caressed the keys. "Yes, the tone is excellent." She then reached for the sheets of music. "I hope there is something here you would like to play. If not I have more we might choose from in the music room."

"My playing is very poor. Jane's talent on the pianoforte greatly exceeds mine. I shall simply enjoy listening to you both."

"Oh no, that will not do," Georgiana cried. "I know you are accomplished, for my brother has told me how much he enjoyed listening to you play." Elizabeth's eyes opened wide in surprise. Looking at her shocked countenance both Jane and Georgiana giggled.

Not many yards from where Georgiana was talking to her friends, her brother was sat in his study listening to Charles Bingley talk about his latest angel. Darcy was not surprised Bingley had found a new young lady to admire. Perhaps his cousin was right and he had, unknowingly, saved Miss Bennet from heartache. Having listened to Bingley, for the past half an hour, speak of the unending qualities of a certain Miss Fatherington, Darcy desired to draw the visit to an end. Miss Bennet and Miss Elizabeth may have arrived, he hoped that was the case and by now the ladies would be safely ensconced in the music room with Georgiana. He did not want Miss Bennet to meet Bingley, especially now that his friend's attention lay elsewhere.

"My friend, you simply must come to Lady Bonner's soirée this evening. I have secured an invitation for you. Miss Fatherington is her niece and will be there. She really is the most divine creature I have ever set eyes on."

"I will consider it, Bingley, and will send you word if I am able to attend." Hoping that would satisfy his friend, Darcy stood. "Now I hope you will excuse me, my friend, but I have things I must attend to."

"Of course, of course," Bingley replied, and followed Darcy out of the study. Bingley continued his discourse while they walked toward the front door. "She really is an angel, Darcy. I..."

"Until your next angel," Darcy interjected, wishing to bring Bingley's inane conversation to an end. Darcy would later regret his outburst, for they had just passed the room where the ladies were silently looking through Georgiana's sheets of music.

Bingley stopped. "No, there will be no other. Miss Fatherington is..." he began earnestly.

"Bingley, I believe you said the same about Miss Bennet and before her it was Miss Almeroth. In fact I have lost count of your *angels*."

"This is different, Darcy, you will see."

Darcy bid his friend farewell, and as the door closed he determined to put Bingley out of his mind. He asked Carlton if Georgiana's friends had arrived. On hearing that the Miss Bennets were with his sister in the nearby drawing room, Darcy glanced down the hall to the room; noticing the door was ajar, he blanched. Had Miss Bennet heard their conversation?

Miss Bennet had indeed overheard the gentlemen's conversation. Georgiana, on hearing her brother's voice in the passage, had moved towards the door and opened it a fraction more. Every word spoken was heard clearly by the ladies. Jane's already pale skin, paled further as pain etched her countenance. Elizabeth could hardly believe the words spoken. Surely Mr Bingley loved Jane. He could not be so shallow as to give his affection to another so quickly.

Georgiana stood near the door, her eyes wide with shock at what she had heard. Her heart broke for her friend. Poor Jane, this was much worse than being taken in by a rogue, Jane had been taken in by a sweet and charming ladies' man, someone who was incapable of being steadfast.

Elizabeth was quickly at Jane's side and, holding her sister's hand tightly in hers, she sat down next to her on the settee. "Oh Jane, I am so sorry, I can scarce believe it. I was so sure..." Elizabeth's voice faded, at the increased distress visible in her sister's eyes.

Jane gave a wan smile in an attempt to hide her suffering. "Deep down I always knew I was not good enough for Mr Bingley, despite what our mother might say."

"No Jane, Mr Bingley is not good enough for you. And if Mr Bingley cannot see the good and caring young lady you are, then that is his loss!" her sister declared.

Jane took a deep breath. "I...I feel most fortunate, for I have discovered the truth. I pity the young lady now in Mr Bingley's sight, for I doubt he will remain faithful to her for long." Jane looked at her sister's concerned countenance. "Do not worry, Lizzy. It may take me a little while to recover but I shall be well, I shall not repine at the loss of Mr Bingley."

Jane looked towards Georgiana and saw that Mr Darcy had entered the room and was standing next to his sister.

Darcy watched with concern as Jane tried to push back the sadness that clouded her eyes and smile as she greeted him. "Mr Darcy, it is good to see you again. I hope you are well," she said as she rose from the settee, still holding her sister's hand.

"It is a pleasure to see you again, Miss Bennet, and you Miss Elizabeth. I am sorry…"

"No, no, Mr Darcy," Jane replied. "It is not your fault. I am the foolish one for believing Mr Bingley may have cared for me."

Darcy felt deeply ashamed. How could he have misread Miss Bennet so badly? It was a mask; Miss Bennet had a mask just as he did, to protect herself by hiding her feelings. Bingley had seen through that mask, but he still followed the advice of his sisters and friend. At that moment Darcy made a promise to himself—he would never again give advice of the heart. After all, what experience did he have on knowing a lady's heart? He was the last person on God's earth who should give such advice.

Darcy declared he had some documents that needed his urgent attention, but asked his sister to inform him when the refreshments arrived so that he could join them. With a polite bow he removed himself from the room, leaving the ladies to their own entertainment.

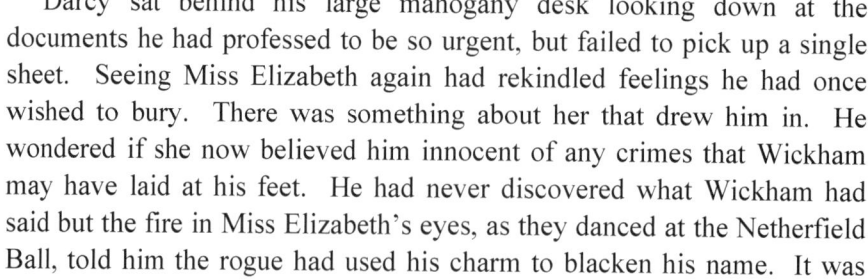

Darcy sat behind his large mahogany desk looking down at the documents he had professed to be so urgent, but failed to pick up a single sheet. Seeing Miss Elizabeth again had rekindled feelings he had once wished to bury. There was something about her that drew him in. He wondered if she now believed him innocent of any crimes that Wickham may have laid at his feet. He had never discovered what Wickham had said but the fire in Miss Elizabeth's eyes, as they danced at the Netherfield Ball, told him the rogue had used his charm to blacken his name. It was not the first time and most likely would not be the last.

For the next hour Darcy's documents sat untouched while he thought about the ladies in the drawing room. When the footman, Bryant, informed his master that the ladies were waiting for him, he took a deep breath and rose from his chair. It was with a nervous anticipation that Darcy left his study to join his sister and her friends.

Darcy was mostly silent while they drank their tea and ate some dainty biscuits; he was so quiet that Elizabeth wondered why he had bothered to join them. He was watching her with the same disapproving manner he had when she stayed at Netherfield. When Jane stood to make her way to the pianoforte with Georgiana, Lizzy rose to follow her but was arrested by Mr Darcy's quiet voice.

"Miss Elizabeth, I wonder if I might have a word," he asked in hushed tones.

Elizabeth was surprised that he had made his way to her side so quickly. "Of course, Sir," she replied as she returned to her seat.

Darcy took a chair close by. Seeing that his sister and Miss Bennet were engrossed, he turned his attention to Elizabeth. "Miss Elizabeth," he said quietly, "I would like to thank you for your help and advice to my sister. She is in great need of a friend and confidante. I know she has spoken to you of…Ramsgate." Darcy took a deep breath. "I worried when she told me that she had confided in another."

"Mr Darcy, I assure you, I will never…"

"I know," he interjected. "I know Georgiana's secret is safe with you and I am grateful for your discretion." Taking another deep breath he prayed his next words would not offend Miss Elizabeth. "I know that Miss Bennet, as well as being your dear sister, is your dearest friend and confidante, but I should be eternally grateful if you were able to keep this secret, even from her. I feel the fewer that know the better."

"Mr Darcy, you do not need to worry. Jane and I are much alike and she would never break your sister's confidence, but, that is of little consequence as I too believe the fewer who know of Ramsgate the better. I have not told my sister, or anyone else, and do not intend to do so." Elizabeth thought the smile that graced Mr Darcy's countenance was a sight to behold. Gone was the disapproving gentleman, in his place was a kind and friendly person. "You should smile more often, Sir, it becomes you," Elizabeth said as the edge of her lips lifted into a small but warm smile.

Darcy laughed. "Why thank you, Miss Elizabeth. I shall endeavour to do so if it pleases you." Darcy saw confusion in Elizabeth's eyes. "Miss Elizabeth, is something the matter?"

"No, it is just I find I am confused. I thought I had completely sketched your character. Then your sister revealed to me the wickedness of one I thought was good. And now...and now you thank me when not five minutes ago I believed you looked at me with disapproval or, at the very least, disdain. Your thanks were so genuine that I wonder if I am mistaken."

Darcy shook his head. "Most definitely mistaken. I have never looked at you with disapproval or disdain, but only with regard and admiration."

"But, surely...not at Netherfield?"

"Yes, even at Netherfield. Your care for your sister, your wit when dealing with Miss Bingley's barbed comments, your kindness to the staff. How could I not admire you? Though I tried to conceal my regard, thinking back to my time at Netherfield, I believe Miss Bingley may have had some notion."

As much as Elizabeth loved her family, she was not blind to their faults and could well understand why Mr Darcy would not wish to be aligned to such a family as hers. "When we first met at the assembly you were not blinded by my charms," she said with a laugh.

All colour drained from Darcy's face. "You heard me?"

Elizabeth tried to make light of the event. "*Tolerably* well, Sir," she said, her eyes sparkling with laughter. "You were, after all, only a few feet away from me."

"Miss Elizabeth, please forgive me. I..." Darcy sighed. "I had not long arrived from London and my mind was still occupied with worry for my sister. I find little pleasure in dancing with strangers and Bingley, much to my horror, was determined I should dance. Believe me, Miss Elizabeth, I soon realized my mistake and until now I was grateful you had not overheard my words. I beg you, please forgive me."

Elizabeth could scarce believe her ears; Mr Darcy was begging her forgiveness. "I do believe, Sir, I shall have to sketch your character once more, for my previous attempt appears to be faulty. Perchance we can both begin again. Mr Darcy, it is a pleasure to meet you, I am Miss Elizabeth

Bennet." Elizabeth gave Darcy such a warm smile that he felt his heart hitch in his chest.

"Miss Elizabeth, the pleasure is all mine."

Darcy stood and offered Elizabeth his arm, which she gladly took before they walked over to join their sisters.

Elizabeth discovered that afternoon that Georgiana was not the only Darcy who could play the pianoforte; Mr Darcy was also quite proficient. Jane and Elizabeth smiled as Darcy and Georgiana, who sat to his right, played Mozart's piano sonata in D for four hands. As the last notes sounded there was silence in the room, until both Jane and Elizabeth applauded eagerly.

"Georgiana, Mr Darcy, you are both truly proficient," Elizabeth said. "I do not think I will dare to play in your company again."

"Oh no," Georgiana cried. "William, did you not say you enjoyed listening when Miss Elizabeth played?"

Elizabeth shook her head as she looked mischievously at Darcy. "My dear Georgiana, I fear your brother's hearing must be faulty. Perhaps he should see a doctor."

"Miss Elizabeth, there is nothing amiss with my hearing," Darcy retorted. "Your playing, although not technically brilliant, is vibrant and has an appeal all of its own. You play with feeling, which is something that comes from within and cannot be taught. I much prefer your style of playing to that of Miss Bingley who, although technically correct, puts little passion into her playing." Elizabeth blushed, while Jane smiled at her sister's embarrassment.

The afternoon passed all too quickly for Darcy, he had enjoyed the time he had spent with the ladies. He was also relieved that although Miss Bennet had been distressed to begin with by Bingley's words, she had not let her sorrow overtake her. He had noticed the occasional look of sadness in her eyes, but it would pass quickly. It was as though she was determined to enjoy herself and not ruin the afternoon for the others. Darcy's admiration for Miss Bennet's fortitude increased greatly that day. He hoped, one day, she would find a gentleman worthy of her.

Instead of calling a cab, Darcy was insistent that his town carriage would take the Bennet sisters home. Darcy then left the ladies to speak with Carlton and arrange the transportation. When he returned, he handed

Jane a sealed missive. "Miss Bennet, I would be grateful if you could give this letter to your uncle. It is an invitation for you all to dine with us on Saturday. I know Georgiana will join me in saying we hope you are able to attend." As he finished speaking he turned his eyes to Elizabeth and gave her a warm smile.

"Thank you, Mr Darcy," Jane replied.

As the ladies departed, Fitzwilliam Darcy came to a decision. He had not been able to totally put Miss Elizabeth Bennet out of his mind since his return from Netherfield, and now he was no longer going to try. He had watched her with his sister; he had not seen Georgiana look so happy and alive for a long time, definitely not since Ramsgate. Why suffer the torments of denying his desire, nay his need, for Miss Elizabeth. What did it matter if she had some embarrassing relatives. In his family there was Lady Catherine de Bourgh, so he was not without a relative whose actions would sometimes make him cringe. The only difference being, his aunt was titled and rich; the ton forgave much for those who were titled and wealthy. He thought of her relatives in trade and then thought of Bingley's father, who he had met once when he and Bingley were at Cambridge. Not all merchants were Shylocks, some behaved in a more gentlemanly manner than a true gentleman; until conversing, it was hard at times to tell if a man was a well-to-do tradesman or a gentleman. Darcy cared little for London and its seasons, and he hoped Elizabeth would be of the same ilk. His mind was decided, Darcy would now pursue Miss Elizabeth Bennet until she agreed to be his wife. She had seen him at his worst in Meryton, now it was time to reveal to her his other side—the side only his family and closest friends saw.

Elizabeth worried for her sister as they made their way back to Gracechurch Street. "Dear Jane, are you well? Hearing Mr Bingley's cruel words must have pained you greatly."

"I will not pretend that hearing Mr Bingley profess his feelings…for his latest love did not hurt. While he was in Meryton, all his actions made me think he cared for me, but then I received Miss Bingley's letter." Jane paused, a wan smile on her lips. "When Georgiana said that there was no arrangement between her and Mr Bingley, my heart lightened, and," Jane's voice lowered to a whisper, "I dared to hope, which was quite silly of me really."

"Oh Jane, I…"

"No, no." Jane interrupted her sister. "While we enjoyed listening to Georgiana play, I thought about Mr Bingley and I have decided I was in love with a dream. So in answer to your question, my dear sister, I shall be well. At present, yes, there is pain, but it shall not last. Now, I will think no more of Mr Bingley and we shall enjoy our time at Gracechurch Street."

Elizabeth admired the determination she could see in her sister's eyes. Her dear Jane, so serene and kind; who only thought good of everyone. Mr Bingley was a fool. Elizabeth wished she could see him, just so that she might tell him what a fickle, undeserving fool he was.

Half an hour after dinner had ended, Jane admitted to feeling fatigued and asked to be excused. As soon as the door had closed behind her, Mrs Gardiner looked at her remaining niece. "Lizzy, what has happened. Jane is trying to hide it well, but I can tell something or someone has upset her. I can only assume it happened while you were at Miss Darcy's home."

Elizabeth looked at her aunt and uncle, their concern evident. She sighed and then relayed to her relatives the happenings of that afternoon that had caused her dear sister such distress.

"Well," Mr Gardiner said, "it sounds to me that she has had a lucky escape. I very much doubt his affection for this new young lady will last, and it will not be long before another 'angel' takes his fancy."

Both his wife and niece agreed with Mr Gardiner's statement, each hoping that no more would be said about the matter. It was a great relief to both the Gardiners and Elizabeth that, when she arrived in the parlour the following morn, Jane appeared to be her normal serene and happy self.

Once the Bennet sisters had departed, Darcy gave his sister a kiss on her cheek and returned to his study. As he walked down the passage, he cursed Bingley under his breath for the hurt that had been caused to Miss Bennet and the distress that must have caused her sister, Elizabeth.

Back at his desk, he looked at the invitation that Bingley had given him to Lady Bonner's soirée and sighed. He had best go. As much as he disliked these sorts of events, it would be discourteous not to attend, especially as Bingley had gone to the trouble of acquiring a personal invitation for him. With luck Miss Bingley would not be present.

Fortune was not with Darcy that evening. He had not long arrived at the Bonners' residence and had barely entered the drawing room, where the entertainment would be held, when Miss Bingley swooped down, like a bird of prey, and her talons gripped his arm.

"Mr Darcy, I could scarce believe it when Charles told me you were to attend." She lowered her voice and raised her fan to prevent others from hearing. "I do not know how you can bear to be in company such as this. I simply had to come to protect my brother. He is so easily led into temptation. I have no doubt you have heard of his latest angel." Miss Bingley gave a dramatic sigh. "She is a sweet young thing but her father is the youngest son of some country gentleman. Mr Fatherington is a vicar, there is no estate, and she, poor girl, is less endowed than the Bennet chits. Such an alliance is unthinkable and could only be detrimental to Charles. He would be better off with Miss Bennet; at least her father owns an estate." The disgust in her tone was evident.

Darcy inwardly sighed; it would be a long night. Normally Darcy would keep his thoughts to himself, but tonight, for some reason, he could not. "I agree, but if your brother is happy surely that is all that matters. After all he would not be marrying beneath him should he decide on Miss Fatherington. As you say, her father is a man of the cloth, which is an acceptable occupation for a gentleman, whereas, your father..." Darcy saw a flush of colour rise in Miss Bingley's alabaster complexion and immediately regretted his forthright speech. "I apologise, Miss Bingley, please excuse me." Darcy removed her tightened fingers from the sleeve of his jacket and with determined steps walked away; looking to see who else was present that he knew. He did not turn around and so did not see the scowl on Miss Bingley's face, nor the look of disgust that entered her eyes.

Miss Bingley was correct. Miss Fatherington was a sweet young thing, but the girl could have been no more than a year or two older than Georgiana and, from what little he had heard of Bingley's conversation with her, she appeared to be very immature.

He did not know what Bingley saw in the young girl, except that she had blonde locks and fair skin like all his angels. *'Conversation with Elizabeth would be much more invigorating.'* Where had that thought come from? Darcy forced his mind away from thoughts of Miss Elizabeth as he slowly made his way towards the refreshment table.

Chapter 4

By the end of the third week of January, George Wickham was starting to become bored with the company in Meryton. Miss King had been sent north by her uncle, she may not have been handsome but her fortune made up for that. The prettiest young ladies in the neighbourhood were the Bennet sisters. The two eldest Bennet girls, who would have proved an exciting challenge for him, remained in town. Miss Mary was too righteous, Miss Kitty was too giggly and had an annoying cough, which only left the youngest Miss Bennet, who, despite being giggly too, was pretty enough to tempt him. But there would be no challenge in that conquest, when the young lady in question all but threw herself at him. So instead of tasting the delights of Miss Lydia, Wickham discreetly seduced three tradesmen's daughters. But even that was losing its thrill. He was, therefore, delighted when a se'nnight later Colonel Forster asked for volunteers to take a package to the War Office. Early Monday morning, he and Lieutenant Denny departed for London. They would not have long in town, as they must return to Meryton that night, but they had some coins and a lot could be done in a short time.

Wickham and Denny left their horses in the stables at the War Office. "Being astride for so long I could do with a walk. Come, we will return in a couple of hours or so for our mounts." The private who had taken hold of the horses' reins, saluted the officers and took his charges into the stables to be cared for. Once they had delivered the package and were once again on the street, Denny looked at Wickham. "Why are we walking?"

"The horses will be safer here than where we are going," Wickham replied. "We will walk a short distance to a busier part of town and hire a cab. "

It did not take long for them to reach the busy thoroughfare. It was thronging with pedestrians and carriages that were barely moving, as there appeared to be a hold up of some sort on the road ahead. Denny groaned.

"Do not worry, Denny, we will find a cab and soon be on our way." Wickham looked around and had no sooner spoken than he saw a large carriage slowly making its way towards them. He was close enough to recognise the livery of the coachman and the man that sat beside him. That livery belonged to the one man he despised above all others.

Although there were many people milling on the pavement, his red jacket would catch the eye and the last thing Wickham wanted was to catch Darcy's eye. Looking quickly at the establishments nearby, he called out to his friend. "Denny, let us go into this tobacconist and see what he might have to offer." So saying Wickham quickly entered the shop with a bemused Denny following behind. The shop had a few customers and Denny walked up to the counter to join the others sampling the tobacconist's wares. Wickham remained near the window. The sun was shining brightly, reflecting on the windowpanes. He was sure the occupant or occupants of the coach would not be able to see him, but, with luck, he would have a good view of them.

The carriage slowly passed by and, once the disbelief had left Wickham's eyes, a slow wicked smile lit his countenance as the vehicle containing his nemesis, and the chit whose dowry should be his, continued on its way. He did not think he had ever seen Darcy look so happy, but then he too would be happy to share a carriage with Miss Bennet and Miss Elizabeth. Whichever of the fair ladies Darcy was interested in, that happiness would soon be a thing of the past; Wickham determined he would see to that and an idea began to formulate in his mind.

Wickham turned to find his friend. His first thought was to return to Meryton immediately and set his plan in motion, but then he thought of Denny's disappointment if they failed to call at Mrs Honeycomb's establishment and decided an hour of gratifying pleasure would not make any difference to the outcome of his grand design.

As Wickham had supposed, Darcy was unaware that he had been seen. He had accompanied his sister and the Miss Bennets to view the latest art exhibition of Joseph Turner's work, now they were on their way to Darcy House for a light nuncheon. Darcy had delighted to see how happy his sister was in the company of the Miss Bennets and, if he allowed himself to think of it, he too was happy in their presence, especially that of Miss Elizabeth Bennet. With his mind favourably occupied, Darcy paid scant attention to anything happening outside the carriage.

When the party arrived back at Darcy House, Darcy was informed that his cousin, Colonel Fitzwilliam, was within. Darcy had seen very little of Fitzwilliam since his return from France and was happy that he had called, but he hoped the presence of his cousin would not reduce the time he would spend in the company of Miss Elizabeth. "Georgie, I will discover what brings our cousin here if you could take our friends to freshen up before nuncheon and I will meet you in the family dining room."

Georgiana was happy to comply and quickly led the ladies up the stairs, while Darcy made his way to his study. The scene that greeted him was of a gentleman in regimentals, lounging on a comfortable chair, his ankles crossed as his feet rested on another chair; a glass of brandy in his hand. "I say, Darcy, this is damn fine brandy you have here. Do the King's customs men know about it?"

"It is quite legal, I assure you," Darcy replied. "It is good to see you, cousin, are you back for long?" he asked as he reached out and knocked Fitzwilliam's boots off of the chair.

"I hope a few months at least." Fitzwilliam straightened himself in the armchair with his feet firmly on the polished wooden floor boards. "Although, if the rumours of unrest in the Americas continue, there is every chance I may find myself in Upper Canada by the end of the year." Fitzwilliam looked up at his cousin. "The chair is free now, will you not sit?"

Darcy glared at his cousin and then gave a slight shake of his head. "That is most kind of you, but I shall remain standing. Georgiana and her friends are waiting for me. Will you join us for nuncheon?"

"You expect me to sit with three young girls, listening to them talk of fashions and lessons?"

"Georgiana will be most disappointed if you do not. She knows you are here."

Fitzwilliam stood up and with a resigned tone replied, "Very well."

Darcy chuckled as he and Fitzwilliam made their way towards the dining room. He believed his cousin would be pleased he had joined them once he met the young ladies.

The two gentlemen quietly entered the room. Colonel Fitzwilliam stopped as he saw Georgiana standing near the table with a young lady on either side of her. His eyes widened—these were not school girls as he had expected.

Darcy looked at his cousin, seeing his surprised countenance the corners of his lips turned up and he patted Fitzwilliam on the back. "Come, Cousin."

On hearing Darcy's voice, the ladies stopped talking and looked towards the doorway. Georgiana ran to greet her cousin. "Richard," she cried. "Oh it is so wonderful to see you again."

"It is good to be here, poppet. Will you not introduce me to your friends?"

Georgiana took hold of Fitzwilliam's arm and walked towards her friends. "Of course. Richard, this is Miss Bennet and her sister Miss Elizabeth." As Georgiana spoke, Richard reluctantly moved his gaze from Miss Bennet to her sister. He missed the rest of his cousin's introduction, so engaged was he with the young ladies before him. It was only when Miss Bennet spoke that he became aware again.

"It is a pleasure to meet you, Colonel. Georgiana has spoken much about you. Your family must be relieved that you have returned to these shores."

Miss Bennet's voice was soft and caring, and Fitzwilliam found himself in a new position, something that had never happened to him before, he was drawn to the young woman before him; it was as though she were a siren calling out to him. For years young women had tried to ensnare him, using all the arts and allurements available to them, after all the younger son of an earl was still a prize worth winning. But never had he felt such an attraction. For the first time in his life Richard Archibald George Fitzwilliam was at a loss for words.

While Richard was trying to get his vocal cords to work, Miss Elizabeth spoke. "Yes, Georgiana has regaled us with tales of your bravery." Her eyes sparkled as she spoke, but the sparkle dimmed as she continued. "We hope, Colonel, your time in England will be of some duration. If only half of what Georgiana has told us is true, I believe you have done your duty for King and country for a while."

Fitzwilliam, whose eyes had once more strayed back to Miss Bennet, was trying to think of a reply when he felt Darcy's boot hit his ankle. "Ah, yes. My parents are glad to have me safely back, but, um, the amount of time I will remain here depends on my general. I shall definitely remain until Whitsuntide, but after that only the Lord and my general know." Fitzwilliam then turned to his boot wielding cousin, as he remembered his original reason for calling. "I wondered if I might rest my weary bones here for a while, if it is convenient. We have persuaded father, for the sake of his health, to remove to Trentavon for a month or two. My parents left this morning and, as I am the only one remaining, it would be sensible to shut the house for that period."

"What about Tansley? I was with him the other day at White's, has he gone to Derbyshire as well?"

"No, my brother has gone south for the nonce. Lord Imber is apparently unwell and Lady Arabella has removed herself from town to her grandfather's estate in Wiltshire."

Darcy quickly looked at his cousin's eyes and stared, as he looked for a tale-tale sign. Suddenly he saw it, so small an action that anyone not knowing Fitzwilliam might have missed it. But Darcy knew his cousin well. Richard Fitzwilliam could never lie. When he was a child the twitch was easy to see, so easy it often got them into trouble, but as the years passed so Fitzwilliam had learnt to control his emotions, but not enough for the twitch to disappear completely.

"I had heard. So Tansley has followed?" Darcy enquired.

"Yes," was Richard's singular reply as his eyes once again strayed to Miss Bennet, but Darcy noticed another slight twitch.

"Are they courting?" Georgiana enquired, bringing Fitzwilliam's attention back to his cousin.

"No, not yet, Tansley still has a long way to go to have any chance of winning her hand."

Darcy chuckled. "It is fortunate that Lady Arabella is on your mother's list of acceptable young ladies."

"Your mother has a list?" Jane asked, at the same time as Georgiana cried, "Aunt Gwendoline has a list?"

"Yes." Determined to get more than a few words out, Fitzwilliam continued. "Mother has been endeavouring to get my brother married since his twenty-fourth birthday, that was eight years ago. Every year, since eighteen hundred and three, my mother has updated the 'suitable' list as young ladies have married. My brother is against a marriage of convenience, having seen too many go sour. Thankfully, our mother has, so far, been in agreement with him, but how much longer that agreement will continue is unknown."

"Lady Matlock must be hopeful now that her list is redundant, or perhaps she will continue the list for you, Colonel?" Elizabeth's eyes sparkled with laughter as the colonel was rendered speechless.

Darcy decided that now was a good time to change the subject, until he could question his cousin. "As to your request, Fitzwilliam, you are welcome to stay. Your usual room is, as always, available for you. Now let us sit and eat."

Fitzwilliam smiled. "Thank you, Darcy." The colonel was delighted to obtain a seat opposite Miss Bennet at the small table.

"I hope your father will find the countryside beneficial and will soon return to good health."

Sadness appeared on the colonel's countenance. "That is most kind of you, Miss Bennet. Sadly my father's…illness is of a long duration. There are days when it is hard to believe he has this problem and others when it is most severe."

"I am so sorry, Colonel," Jane replied wishing she could take back the words she had spoken.

Georgiana, wishing to take the conversation away from her uncle's ill-health, exclaimed. "We are going to the theatre on Saturday; Richard, please say you can come with us?"

"Are you free?" Darcy asked.

"Yes, I have been granted leave and am free of any duties until the seventeenth of next month."

"Excellent," Darcy replied, and then added a tiny morsel he thought would please his cousin. "Miss Bennet and Miss Elizabeth, with their uncle and aunt, will be joining our party on Saturday."

"I will be delighted to join you," Fitzwilliam replied as he smiled at Miss Bennet.

The rest of the Bennet sisters' visit passed pleasantly and Colonel Richard Fitzwilliam appeared to have found his voice again. Though, once they were alone, Darcy took great delight in teasing Fitzwilliam on how a pretty face had struck him dumb.

"You may tease, cousin, but I did notice you were just as enamoured with her sister."

"Miss Elizabeth and Miss Bennet are fine young ladies."

"And the rest of their family?" Darcy sipped his brandy and did not reply to his cousin's question. "Ah, so would I be correct in assuming the rest of their family is not so fine."

Darcy sighed. "There are five daughters. The youngest is but fifteen and yet all five are out. They have little in way of a dowry and, to increase their misfortune, their father's estate is entailed. The heir, a cousin of Mr Bennet's, is Aunt Catherine's vicar."

"That sycophantic fool?" The disgust in Fitzwilliam's tone was evident.

"Exactly. Mr Collins presumed to ask for Miss Elizabeth's hand; fortunately for Miss Elizabeth she is her father's favourite. Although he has more interest in his books than his daughters, he agreed with her refusal to the match. Her mother was incensed and so she found herself in town with her elder sister."

"Why did Collins not apply for Miss Bennet's hand?"

"Because Mrs Bennet was convinced that Miss Bennet would soon be the bride of their neighbour, a young man of five thousand a year, and besides, I believe in Mrs Bennet's eyes, Miss Bennet was too good for the likes of Collins."

"Is Miss Bennet betrothed?" Fitzwilliam hoped not but did not see how any gentleman would pass up that chance.

"No. The gentleman concerned was Bingley."

"Ah."

"Yes! So, my dear cousin, I would ask you *not* to flirt with Miss Bennet. She was deeply hurt by Bingley's inconsistency, especially when she heard from his own mouth that he, after only a few weeks of separation, had found a new angel to admire. You have always let it be known that, as a second son, when you marry your wife must have a substantial dowry. That alone makes Miss Bennet unsuitable for you." Fitzwilliam held up his hand to stop his cousin from speaking further.

"Yes I am guilty of that deception. I watched with horror as you and my brother were hounded by the mothers and debutants of the haut ton—Sebastian for his title and you for your wealth. I am brave enough when it comes to facing Bonaparte's men on the battlefield, but I am a coward when that battlefield moves to the ballroom or drawing room, and I find before me the matchmaking mothers of the ton's elite. So I let it be known that I would only marry a lady of wealth. That removed the daughters of old money and titles from my path, leaving only the newly rich who wished to increase their standing by claiming relationship to an earl's family."

"So that is not your plan?"

Fitzwilliam shook his head. "It never was. Fortunately for me, I am my mother's favourite. When she discovered what I had done she was angry with my deception that I was a poorer second son, but I managed to persuade her to go along with my tale."

Darcy was puzzled. It was common knowledge that, as he had no sisters, Richard would receive the remainder of his mother's dowry on her passing, but, it was also common knowledge that his father had spent a goodly portion of it.

Fitzwilliam, seeing the puzzlement in his cousin's eyes, laughed. "As you know, when I first put on the uniform of an officer in His Majesty's Army, my father had already spent a fair portion of my mother's dowry. He purchased an estate in Staffordshire, which is situated near the village of Longnor. As mother's dowry was used the estate is not part of the entailed earldom, and name of ownership on the property deeds is mine. The steward, Pearce, is a most capable and trustworthy man. The house itself is looked after by the housekeeper. The estate brings in around three thousand a year, a paltry amount compared to Pemberley but not to a poor soldier." Fitzwilliam smiled warmly as Darcy shook his head in amazement. "So you see, cousin, with the estate and the monies I receive from His Majesty for insuring you can sleep soundly in your bed at night, I do not need the remainder of my mother's dowry. Yes, more money from a substantial dowry would make life easier but it is not a necessity. I may be Matlock's spare, but my wealth, or rather lack of it, ensures that I am not eagerly sought after as you. When I meet the right lady, one who can love me for the little I have. Oh do not look so shocked, Cousin, you are not the only one to wish for a spouse who thinks more of you than the comfort your wealth can bring them. When I meet the right lady, I will know and, as long as she does not mind being wed to an active soldier, nor is over zealous on her purchase of lace and the like, we will live comfortably."

As Fitzwilliam finished speaking a wide smile spread across Darcy's features. "I am so pleased Fitzwilliam, in fact I am delighted. I can understand your mother's silence but your father?"

"My father decided to go along with the general belief that Longenaire Estate was part of the Matlock holdings until I reached five and twenty. By that time father was completely under the influence of laudanum, so reliant on it that any thoughts he may have had about my estate were lost in the mists of time."

"Do you think spending time at Trentavon will help him?"

"I would wish it so. We all wish the man that he was back with us." Fitzwilliam sighed. "I arranged for Dr Morgan, who is an eminent physician, to accompany my parents to Derbyshire. Morgan is used to dealing with the addictive effects laudanum has on soldiers and if anyone can help father break his addiction it is he. Only time will tell."

"Now, Cousin, tell me the truth, where has Tansley gone?

Fitzwilliam gave a look of puzzlement; Darcy laughed. "Fitzwilliam, you would never make a gambler; you know you cannot lie. No doubt your poor mother believes he has followed Lady Arabella, but tell me, where is he?"

"He has gone south," Fitzwilliam muttered, as though saddened at his cousin's reluctance to believe his words. Then he laughed. "Tansley is in the New Forest, at Burley, and yes, you are correct, he is hunting four legged prey not his future wife. Although, to be fair, he is well within a day's ride of Lord Imber's estate and may visit."

"Now tell me," Darcy asked as he poured them both a drink, "do you know where you will be sent when you report for duty in three weeks' time?"

"Not for definite, but the general did hint that I would not be leaving the capital for a while."

Darcy smiled warmly. "That is a great relief to hear."

It had been late when Wickham and Denny had returned to camp, but that did not stop Wickham from planning his campaign to ruin Darcy. He had decided it would be safe enough, knowing how gossip worked, in the end no one would know who had started the stories. He doubted Darcy would seriously consider Miss Bennet or her sister, Miss Elizabeth, as his relatives would never approve of such a match. He would one day follow his aunt's wishes and marry his equally dour cousin, the sickly Miss Anne de Bourgh. But by the time Wickham had finished with his character, if

Darcy should ever return to the neighbourhood, Mr Bennet, and the other gentlemen of Meryton, would not give him the time of day.

Lieutenant Walker was a green recruit, barely out of the nursery, who trusted his colleagues implicitly; just the kind of young fool that Wickham needed to aid his cause. Walker had only arrived in Meryton a fortnight ago, so had not met any of the Netherfield party nor the eldest Bennet daughters. Wickham came across as a benevolent gentleman, his handshake was firm. Walker believed, like most young men of his age, that a firm handshake was the key to recognising a gentleman of integrity.

Wickham spent most of the next day with young Walker. He told him of the kind people in the neighbourhood and of the party that had leased Netherfield but were now thankfully departed. By the time Wickham had finished Walker's eyes were wide in horror.

"A villain like that was in the neighbourhood and no one knew of the danger to the young ladies of the area. Wickham, you must tell people. What is his name and how do you know all of this?"

"As to his name, I cannot say. But I know because his father was my godfather. We grew up together as boys on his estate, where my father was the steward. The old man was the kindest of men, sadly the son fooled the father, and when he died he still believed the young man was good and righteous, but I knew differently. His first act of cruelty to me was to refuse me the living his dear father left to me in his will. He has a younger sister who believes her brother can do no wrong, and his relatives know of his character but do nothing to change his ways. They are rich and powerful, and look down on me for my lowly start in life. Between them they would take delight in ruining my life. But that is not the main reason I remained silent. If I speak out his dear sweet sister will believe that I lie; I would not wish to lose her friendship."

"Then I shall speak out for you. What if Mr Bingley was to return to the neighbourhood, that man might come with him and once again turn his attention to Mr Bennet's elder daughters."

"You are right; I should have been braver before."

Walker looked at the regret on his friend's countenance. "You are a good man, Wickham."

"I try to be," Wickham replied with a heavy sigh before concern filled his voice. "But, my friend, you must be careful how you spread this news. It would grieve me greatly if you were injured by this man or his family."

"I will be careful. Mrs Philips is having a soirée this evening and perchance I might mention this man in passing."

Wickham tried to keep his countenance sombre. It would not do to appear too pleased at Walker's words. When Walker departed his room, Wickham waited a full minute before a smile warmed his face and he laughed. If anyone had seen him they would have noticed that the smile did not reach his eyes, they were as cold as ice. When his laughter stopped, the smile continued. *'Vengeance will be mine at last. Ah how sweet that sounds.'*

Chapter 5

Mrs Philips' Thursday evening soirée was well attended. Mrs Bennet was there of course, but Mr Bennet had remained at home in the warmth and seclusion of his study. Mary, Kitty and Lydia were in attendance; although Mary would have preferred to remain at home, she did not wish to incur her mother's wrath. Sir William Lucas and his family were in attendance, as were Mrs Long and her nieces, the Gouldings, the Morrises and the Watsons. There were also a number of officers in attendance from the militia; Lieutenants Wickham and Walker being amongst their number.

Wickham stood near the back wall of Mrs Philips' drawing room. He inwardly smiled as he raised a glass of punch to his lips. Walker was speaking with Mrs Long who, in turn, was sending relieved glances at her nieces. All was going according to plan. Wickham had no doubt that by dusk tomorrow Fitzwilliam Darcy's reputation would be in tatters with the good people of Meryton. Rumours were traitorous things, a person's good character and standing could collapse in a moment, no matter what the truth. Wickham wondered how long it might take for this gossip to spread further afield.

Mrs Philips entered her sister's home early the next morning. It was not yet ten o' clock as she knocked on the front door of Longbourn, much too early for a social call. But this was urgent and Mrs Philips could not wait until a reasonable hour, no the news she had could not wait another minute. Mrs Philips planned to call on Lady Lucas next, by then the hour would be more respectable.

Letitia Philips had missed the departure of her sister and Lady Lucas from her home; she had been too busy listening to the words of Mrs Long. When Martha Long had finished relaying her news, the others had departed, so by the time Mrs Philips rose that morning she was bursting to tell someone the shocking story of Mr Darcy's true character.

"Never, Sister," a wide-eyed Mrs Bennet cried.

"Yes, Sister, I fear it is true. We are so lucky Mr Bingley departed taking that terrible man with him. I know it caused your dear Jane much heartache to lose Mr Bingley. But Sister, what if Mr Bingley is like his friend. After all the apple does not fall far from the tree, I am sure Mr Darcy would mix with people of his own ilk."

"Oh no, Sister, Mr Bingley was a perfect gentleman. He must have been taken in by that horrible man. I never did like him, you know. He treated my Lizzy quite cruelly with his harsh words at the assembly. 'Tis a shame Mr Bingley has been so taken in but I am glad we will never be in Mr Darcy's company again. I should worry about my daughters' safety if he returned to the neighbourhood."

When Mrs Philips left Longbourn for Lucas Lodge, Mrs Bennet hurried to her husband's study. Mr Bennet had little peace for the next hour as Mrs Bennet relayed every sordid detail of the wicked character of the gentleman from Pemberley.

"Are you sure it is Mr Darcy? If no name was mentioned how do you know it is he?"

"But, Husband, who else could it be? The gentleman in question, although not named, arrived in the area at the same time as Mr Bingley's party arrived at Netherfield. It could hardly be his brother, Mr Hurst, for he is a married man!"

Wickham's premonition was not correct. It was in fact several hours *before* dusk when any good name Fitzwilliam Darcy may have had was totally ruined in Meryton, and its surrounding villages and hamlets. Gossip and his brother Rumour had worked hard that day.

Darcy had been looking forward to the evening. He and Fitzwilliam were to accompany the Miss Bennets and Georgiana to the theatre to see Twelfth Night, or What You Will. His party was also to include Mr and Mrs Gardiner, as was only right, and they would all dine at Darcy House afterwards. Although the theatre was the place to be seen—for ladies to parade their elegance and riches before others—Darcy's reason for attending was quite boring in comparison. He knew of Elizabeth's love of Shakespeare's plays and he simply wanted to give her pleasure. Darcy believed that nothing could ruin the evening, so it was fortunate that he was unaware of the defamation of his character in every drawing room and parlour within a three mile radius of Meryton.

Darcy inwardly smiled at his cousin as he led the way into the theatre with Miss Bennet on his arm. Darcy believed Fitzwilliam was as enamoured with Miss Bennet as he was with her sister. He turned and looked at Miss Elizabeth who walked next to him, her dainty gloved hand resting lightly on his arm. Their eyes met and neither could stop the warm smile that quite naturally appeared on their faces. Walking through the theatre to his box was a part of the evening that Darcy normally dreaded, but this evening, with Miss Elizabeth on one arm and his sister on the other, Darcy felt a calmness that he had never known before.

Darcy attempted to steer Mrs Gardiner to the front seats of the box with her nieces and his sister, but the lady declined. "Mr Gardiner and I shall enjoy the evening just as much from these seats," she said as she sat down in one of the chairs in the second row.

Moving to the front row, Darcy was delighted to see that Georgiana had taken the seat between her friends leaving the seating at either end of the row for her brother and cousin. He smiled as he sat down next to Miss Elizabeth, he would have to thank his sister in the morning.

The evening progressed well. Darcy had worried that Bingley and his sisters might have been present, but that concern proved to be fruitless. He saw no sign of them when he made a cursory glance around the auditorium and if they had been present Bingley would have surely approached him. The journey from the theatre had been full of conversation and laughter as they spoke of the actors and their costumes, and how true they had been to the lines of the Bard. Darcy had said little, he was content to simply watch, but Fitzwilliam had joined in the conversation when Miss Bennet spoke. Now the happy party entered a small drawing room in Darcy House, to await their dinner that would be served shortly.

"I enjoyed the play so much. Thank you, Mr Darcy; I shall always remember this evening."

Darcy saw the warm honesty in Elizabeth's eyes and knew, without doubt, she meant every word she had spoken. There was no false flattery as was usually the case with ladies of the haut ton. "I believe we have all enjoyed the evening and it is not over yet, Miss Elizabeth." Darcy felt himself drowning in Elizabeth's smile.

The meal had been delightful, both wine and conversation flowed. There was no separation of the sexes, and they all retired to the drawing room where Georgiana was happy to entertain the company on the pianoforte. Mrs Gardiner and Mr Darcy spoke so passionately of Derbyshire and its dales that Elizabeth expressed a wish to see the beauties of Derbyshire for herself.

"Your uncle and I hope to tour Derbyshire and, if time allows, the Lake District. Would you like to come with us Lizzy?"

"I would love to, Aunt Madeline, thank you so much." Elizabeth's eyes shone and Darcy found his heart beating faster.

"I would be delighted if you would consider staying at Pemberley while you are in the area."

"That is most kind of you, Mr Darcy," Mr Gardiner replied, "but we would not wish to put you or your household to any inconvenience."

"It would be no inconvenience I assure you, Mr Gardiner, you would be most welcome."

"In that case, Sir, I thank you and I will keep you abreast of our plan when the dates are finalised," Mr Gardiner said with a smile before turning to his wife. "Now, my dear, I believe it is time we took our leave. Thank you, Mr Darcy, for a delightful evening; I know my nieces and my wife have enjoyed themselves immensely. Colonel, it was a pleasure to make your acquaintance." Mr Gardiner turned to speak to Miss Darcy but saw that she was deep in conversation with Lizzy and Jane. All three gentlemen looked at the young ladies, each with his own thoughts on the picture before him.

"Jane, Lizzy, are you ready to depart?"

"Yes, Uncle," Elizabeth replied, "we were just making arrangements for our next meeting."

"I thought that might be the case. Goodnight, Miss Darcy, thank you for such a delightful evening."

Georgiana blushed at Mr Gardiner's praise; her shyness overcome with delight as her brother and cousin escorted her friends from the room.

January drew to a close and February arrived bringing with it bright and sunny weather; the coldness of winter was at its peak. Elizabeth much preferred cold sunny days to those that were wet and mild, she could wrap up warm and enjoy being out of doors. During those sunny days Miss Bennet and Miss Elizabeth were often seen in the company of Miss Darcy. More often than not Miss Darcy's brother and cousin would accompany the ladies on their outings. This brought about increased speculation amongst the haut ton as to who the young ladies were. No one was inclined to believe the rumour spread by Miss Bingley; two such fashionably dressed young ladies could not possibly be the eldest of five dowerless daughters born to a country gentleman of little standing. She had also proclaimed they had an uncle in trade, who lived in Cheapside no less, just the thought of it was to be laughed at. Everyone knew that Colonel Fitzwilliam could only marry a lady of wealth and his mother, Lady Matlock, would never approve. And then there was Mr Darcy; such a man as he would not allow his sister in the company of penniless fortune hunters, even more so when they were connected with trade. The matrons of the ton decided that Miss Bingley, who, as everyone knew, had set her cap at Mr Darcy, was jealous of the attention afforded to the pretty Miss Elizabeth Bennet.

Another Bingley was also unhappy. Charles had seen Miss Bennet a couple of times in the company of the Darcys and Colonel Fitzwilliam. The first time had been a se'nnight earlier. He was making his way towards his club, after calling on his tailor, when he noticed Darcy's tall figure a few yards ahead. Bingley had increased his step, to catch up with his friend, calling out as he drew closer. It was then that he realized Darcy was not alone; with him were his sister, Colonel Fitzwilliam, Miss Elizabeth and the lovely Miss Bennet. Bingley could not believe his luck, as he warmly greeted Darcy and his party. He was however bewildered when Miss Bennet blushed slightly and looked at the ground, refusing to lift her eyes to his; nor did she remove her hand from the colonel's arm, if anything she seemed to hold on with a greater firmness. He then glanced at Miss Elizabeth and was shocked, for instead of facing the warm, friendly smile he was accustomed to, he was met with a disapproving demeanour. It was almost as though Miss Elizabeth's eyes held a look of disdain. Suddenly the look was gone, as Miss Elizabeth gave a slight smile, although her eyes did not hold the warmth he was used to seeing. He turned back to Miss Bennet, whose head was still lowered, and noticed the colonel's hand was covering hers. There was no mistaking the look of disdain in that gentleman's eyes. Bingley had been at a loss to understand the reason for the sisters' strange behaviour.

The second sighting was at the theatre. Charles, in the company of his sisters and Godfrey Hurst, had spied Darcy and his party, but made no attempt to speak with them. Bingley had called on Darcy a few days before, it was then he discovered Miss Bennet had overheard his conversation with Darcy the previous month. He had hurt Miss Bennet, no wonder Miss Elizabeth had looked at him in such a way. She must think him a cad. Caroline was furious with her brother when he refused to take her to Mr Darcy's box during the interval; a fury which increased tenfold when she saw Miss Eliza Bennet was not only sitting next to her Mr Darcy, but they were smiling at each other.

Bingley's admiration for Miss Fatherington was starting to wane, especially now he had seen Miss Bennet, angel that she was, on the arm of Darcy's cousin. But there was little hope of regaining Miss Bennet's esteem; he had seen the way she smiled at the colonel and wished that she would smile like that at him again.

March came in like a lion. Gone were the sunny, almost spring-like, days, instead the winds howled and the rain fell. Elizabeth loved England, but there were times when she hated the English weather and the first week of March was no exception. Any plans for walks in the park had to be postponed, but, despite Elizabeth's displeasure at the weather, there was plenty of entertainment. She and her sister enjoyed calling at Darcy House and as time went by their close friendship with Georgiana grew; the fact that Mr Darcy and Colonel Fitzwilliam, when his duties would allow, had also been there pleased both sisters. The Darcys and the colonel also called at Gracechurch Street.

Elizabeth could not understand how she had been so mistaken in her judgement of Darcy's character. During the weeks since they had met again at Darcy House, the friendship between Darcy and Elizabeth grew, as did their feelings for one another, but they were not alone. The budding friendship between Richard Fitzwilliam and Jane Bennet was also progressing at a pace. To begin with both Mr Gardiner and his wife were concerned that the charming officer might merely be flirting with their niece, but the more they watched the more they could see his admiration for Jane was true.

Saturday saw the end of the first week of March, it was the wettest se'nnight Elizabeth could remember, but, despite the rain still pouring down outside, the evening at 5 Gracechurch Street was enjoyable; the Darcys and Colonel Fitzwilliam had come to dine. The intimate meal had allowed congenial conversation and time passed quickly.

When the ladies withdrew to the drawing room, Mr Gardiner and his two guests enjoyed a glass of port.

"So gentlemen, what are your plans for next week should the weather improve? Gardiner smiled, he was sure his nieces would, in some way, be included in any plans the young gentlemen had.

Darcy looked at his cousin; Fitzwilliam had already spoken to him of his plans, so Darcy waited for him to speak.

"I would be grateful, Sir, if I might be allowed a moment or two to speak with Miss Bennet this evening. I greatly admire your niece and wish to ask her if…if she would enter into a courtship with me, with her father's permission of course. If my wishes are granted then I will go to Longbourn on Monday to request an audience with Mr Bennet."

As Edward Gardiner listened to Fitzwilliam, he thought back to his meeting with his brother Bennet, the day before their departure from Longbourn, and to the letter which was securely stored in the drawer of his desk. Realising the colonel was looking at him expectantly he rose from his seat. "Please bear with me, Colonel. I shall just be a moment while I retrieve something which I believe will be of interest to you." Gardiner was true to his word and returned quickly to his seat, placing a sheet of paper on the table so that the gentlemen could read its contents. "Before we returned to town with Jane and Lizzy, my brother wrote a letter. In it he gave me authority, in his stead, should any young gentleman wish to court either of his daughters while they resided under my roof."

Fitzwilliam and Darcy both looked at Mr Gardiner with amazement, then down at the letter of authorisation, which consisted of one short paragraph and Mr Bennet's flowing signature, before turning their attention back to their host.

Gardiner took in their stunned expressions. "Yes, gentlemen, as strange as it may sound, he did just that. I knew he wanted peace from my sister's nerves, but I never expected, when I jokingly asked him what I should do if a young gentleman knocked on my door for Jane or Lizzy, that he would immediately put pen to paper, giving me authority to act in his stead. So you see, Colonel, there is no need for you to ride to Longbourn to seek the permission you require, when a much shorter trip to my study would suffice." Mr Gardiner looked steadily at the young officer before him. "You care for Jane and would see her happy?"

"Yes, Mr Gardiner, very much so."

Gardiner smiled. "Good; then I will allow you to speak to Jane and, if she agrees to courtship, I give my blessing. I will send her to my study, if you would care to wait there. Then I shall not incur my wife's displeasure at hindering our maid from attending to her duties."

Colonel Fitzwilliam beamed. He did not think he could feel any happier than he did at that moment in time. "Thank you, Mr Gardiner, and please call me Fitzwilliam, 'colonel' sounds so official."

Mr Gardiner agreed and then, standing to lead the gentlemen from the room, he turned his attention to Darcy. "I am surprised, Mr Darcy. After watching you with Lizzy, I thought you would be first in line."

Darcy shook his head. "No, Mr Gardiner, I fear, by my own stupidity, I lost your niece's good opinion at our first meeting. As much as I esteem Miss Elizabeth, and wish to court and eventually marry her, I believe it would be best to take things slowly. I would not wish to speak too soon and risk her rejection."

"Very wise, Mr Darcy, but I would suggest you do not wait too long."

When Mr Gardiner and Darcy re-joined the ladies, Jane wondered where the colonel had gone. She was surprised when her uncle asked her to go with him to his study. Gardiner remained just outside of the room, with the door to the study slightly open. A few minutes later the study door opened wide and Gardiner smiled at the happy couple. He kissed Jane's cheek and then ushered them towards the drawing room. The joy in Jane's eyes and the broad smile on Fitzwilliam's face told everyone in the room of their happiness, and the remainder of the evening was one of celebration.

Lord and Lady Matlock had been residing at Trentavon for nearly two months. Dr Morgan, who had accompanied them on the journey to Derbyshire, was still there.

Several years ago, the earl suffered a bad fall while partaking in a local hunt. For over a month he had remained abed, taking daily doses of laudanum to help with the severe pain in his back. Once his body had healed, and he was able to get up and move around, he discovered a small amount of the vile concoction each morning helped. Although he would never admit it, he became reliant on that small glass of laudanum each day. Over the years the amount increased, as Matlock discovered he could not cope with the melancholy that overtook him, when only a little more would ease him. Both his body and mind craved for more.

Lady Matlock became more and more concerned for her husband's welfare. He had hidden his dependency well, blaming his mood changes and shortness of breath on the stresses of estate management and Parliamentary duties. It had been five years since they had shared a bed, so if it had not been for her lady's maid, Clara, Lady Matlock would still be none the wiser.

Five months ago Lady Matlock noticed that her lady's maid appeared to be distracted and worried about something. The countess was fond of Clara, who had been in her service for nearly ten years, and wished to help her with whatever the problem was, if it was at all possible. Clara was at first reluctant to speak to Lady Matlock, but in the end she could not keep something so grave from her mistress. Lady Matlock was shocked beyond belief when she heard that the 'problem' was in fact her husband's valet's worry over his master's addiction to laudanum. Parker had watched and kept his master's secret until he could do so no longer. Lord Matlock needed help or he would not see many more years on God's green earth.

Lady Matlock applied to her son, Sebastian, for help. Tansley could not believe it was true; it had to be a falsity. But when he spoke with Parker any hope of it being a lie was quashed. Tansley wished his brother was at home as he had more experience with people who became dependant on laudanum or opium, but Fitzwilliam was in France and not due home for months. Lady Matlock and Viscount Tansley took it upon themselves to bring the addiction to an end. The family's London physician, Mr Hyde, was called, and sworn to secrecy. With pleading and cajoling, by his wife and eldest son, Lord Matlock promised to stop taking the medication. Not even a se'nnight had passed before he broke that promise. Tansley realized that more help was needed than he, his mother or Mr Hyde could give. The viscount made an appointment to see Lord Liverpool; a month after the viscount had discovered his father's addiction, Tansley's younger brother was on his way home.

On his return from France, Fitzwilliam immediately approached Dr Morgan. Fitzwilliam had seen the good doctor in action and knew he would not give way to any pressure by the earl. After the doctor had made his first assessment of the earl, and left Matlock House to pack his trunk, Fitzwilliam glanced at his brother before taking hold of his mother's hand. "Trust me, Mama. He may seem a hard man, but if anyone can wean father off this vile habit it will be Morgan."

There had been many times in the last seven weeks, since they had returned to their country estate, when Gwendoline Fitzwilliam had broken down. The groans and cries from her husband's chambers, the pleading of a grown man who begged like a small child, together with the sickness and pain he suffered all took its toll on Lady Matlock. She cared deeply for her husband and wanted the man she had married, and grown to love dearly, returned to her.

Lady Matlock was in the process of writing to her sister. Plans had been made many months ago to visit Rosings at Easter; Anne had not been well and the countess wished to see her niece. Now those plans would have to be broken, or at least postponed for the foreseeable future. Dr Morgan had told Lady Matlock in no uncertain terms that a visit, even to family, was out of the question. The earl was improving and the withdrawal symptoms were lessening, but the next few months would be a dangerous time. The earl would have to be watched constantly to ensure he did not acquire any laudanum, it would be too easy for him to slide back into his old habits. He was not free of the drug's hold yet—he may never be.

The family had kept the earl's condition a secret from the haut ton. The servants were loyal to their mistress, who treated them well. The only person to know, besides from her sons, was her nephew Darcy, now she would have to tell her husband's sister. Catherine would be angry that she had not been told, but Lady Matlock hoped she would understand the reasons why.

Lady Catherine de Bourgh read again the letter she had received from her sister.

Trentavon Hall, Derbyshire
13th March 1812

My dear Catherine,

I am exceedingly sorry, my dear sister, but Henry and I will be unable to visit you at Eastertide. Henry has been unwell for some time now and we were advised by a most capable doctor that we should retire to Derbyshire so that my dear husband can receive the care he needs to regain his health.

Dr Morgan has successfully treated quite a few people who have, like Henry, become dependent on laudanum. As you can imagine, we have kept the true state of his ill-health well hidden from the ton to protect your brother's reputation and the family's good name. But I felt it behoved me, and was only right and proper, that I share with you, our dear sister, the true state of Henry's illness.

The doctor assures me that the worst is over, but Henry will still be susceptible to the need of laudanum for some time yet and so must be kept safely guarded from all temptation.

I do hope that Anne is making a good recovery from her latest illness. She is such a dear girl, my heart aches that one so young has been plagued with ill-health for so long. I deeply regret that we are not able to spend some time with you both this Easter, but Richard has returned from France and he has promised to visit you in our stead with our nephew Darcy. I am sure it will cheer Anne to see her cousins.

Perchance when the warmer weather comes and Anne is well enough to travel, you and our dear niece might come to Trentavon for a small holiday. I am sure the change of scenery will do you both good.

I wish you well, Catherine, until we meet again.

Gwendoline

Lady Catherine's anger increased, she was not angry that her sister had taken so long to tell her of her brother's illness. No, her anger was aimed solely at her brother. He was to blame for dear Anne's failing health. She had foolishly listened to her brother and trusted him; she would never do so again.

Lady Catherine stood, walked from the room and made her way to her daughter's chambers. It was late; the tall clock at the end of the passage had just struck the eleventh hour; Anne had retired three hours ago, but Lady Catherine was unable to rest. The letter from Lady Matlock had arrived that afternoon; when she had first broken the seal and read it she had been shocked, but it did not take long for the shock to turn to anger.

Lady Catherine walked quietly into her daughter's bedchamber; the glow from the fire warmed the room and, with the candle she held, gave enough light to see by. She looked at her sleeping daughter, so pale and small in the large bed. As she sat down on the chair next to the bedside a heavy sadness for her daughter overcame her; then anger at her brother rose again. Anne was addicted to laudanum. If she had never listened to her brother it would not be so.

Her mind wandered back to that Easter five years ago. Henry had come on his own; Gwendoline had fallen and sprained her ankle just the day before they were due to begin their journey. Lady Matlock had insisted that her husband continue with their plan to visit Rosings, as she did not want to cause either her sister or niece any disappointment. Worried about Anne's health, Lady Catherine had spoken of her concerns to her brother. His words were still embedded in her brain.

"My dear Cathy, I know just what our dear Anne needs. Many of my friends swear by the goodness a small daily dose of laudanum does for the heart and wellbeing."

"Laudanum? Surely not, Henry."

"Yes, laudanum. Never mind what rumours you may have heard about ill effects. The benefits to one's health way outnumber them. I myself have been taking a small dose every morning, since that wretched riding accident. Trust me, Cathy; it will do her no harm."

Lady Catherine was brought back to the present as her daughter let out a slight moan. *'I trusted you, Henry, trusted you with my daughter's wellbeing.'* Tears slowly fell down her cheeks as she wondered who could help her daughter now.

Chapter 6

The day after dining at Gracechurch Street, Richard Fitzwilliam began his courtship of Miss Bennet in earnest. The day was warm and spring-like as the couple walked in Hyde Park, with Darcy, his sister, and Elizabeth following behind them. Elizabeth watched as Jane, with her gloved hand resting on the colonel's arm, laughed at something he had said. She was so happy for her dear sister; Colonel Fitzwilliam was a good man and he would make Jane a good husband.

"That was a deep sigh, Miss Elizabeth."

Brought back from her musing by Darcy's words, Elizabeth looked at the gentleman who walked by her side. He was looking down at her with concern etching his countenance. She gave him a gentle smile.

"I am sorry, Mr Darcy, I was momentarily lost in thought."

"Nothing sad I hope," he replied.

Elizabeth smiled and shook her head, trying to deny her brief thoughts. "No. I was thinking that the colonel will make an excellent husband for Jane." Elizabeth looked at Darcy's eyes, what she saw there made her believe he doubted that was all she had been thinking.

"I will miss my dear sister very much when they marry. I hope she does not move too far away."

Once Jane was married, if she still did not have her mother's approbation, Lizzy determined she would search for a job as a governess; perhaps Jane's new mother might be able to assist her in the search for a suitable position.

"Well then, Miss Elizabeth, you will be pleased to know that Fitzwilliam intends, once he is betrothed to your sister, to lease a town house." He glanced at her and could not help but see the happiness which glowed from her brown eyes. "Although he has an estate in Staffordshire, he wishes Miss Bennet to be closer to her family if he is sent abroad."

The excitement of Jane living in town was clouded by worry. "Is that likely?" Elizabeth asked. Georgiana remained silent beside them, for she knew it was more than likely; she had overheard her brother and cousin talking about that very fact.

Darcy replied, "I fear so, Miss Elizabeth. That is one of the reasons he does not want a long courtship or betrothal. If all goes according to Fitzwilliam's hopes and plans I can see them betrothed by the beginning of April and married by the beginning of May."

"So soon?" But as she looked at Darcy's eyes she could see the honesty of his beliefs there.

They continued to walk. Georgiana spoke of her excitement of going to Astley's Amphitheatre in Lambeth, but Elizabeth, so lost in her thoughts, barely heard a word and hoped she had replied "Yes" or "No" in the right places. It would appear she had, as her companions made no comment on her lack of attention. Unless her mother changed her mind, Elizabeth would be in employment by June. She inwardly sighed; convinced that Mr Darcy would not allow her to be in Georgiana's company if that was the case.

<hr/>

The next couple of weeks passed quite quickly for Elizabeth; she tried not to think about life after Jane's marriage and concentrated on enjoying the company of her sister and the Darcys. If she was truthful to herself she would admit it was Fitzwilliam Darcy's company she enjoyed the most, but she refused to look too closely and kept any feelings that may be growing towards the gentleman firmly under lock and key. The trip to Astley's Amphitheatre had been a delight; Darcy had arranged a first floor box for their comfort. A young man stood astride on the backs of two beautiful greys, his hands raised elegantly above his head, as the mares cantered side by side around the arena. Georgiana was entranced, her eyes wide with excitement. Elizabeth wished she had been able to bring her cousins; she was sure Matthew and Frederick would have enjoyed the performance immensely.

The date of Darcy's and Fitzwilliam's visit to Rosings drew nearer. Neither gentleman wished to be away from town for too long; their reasons were residing with Mr and Mrs Gardiner at Gracechurch Street. The cousins' plan was to depart town early on the twenty-sixth; it would allow them to arrive at Rosings on the same day at a reasonable hour. They would remain with their aunt for three days, departing for town on the morning of the fourth day. Both gentlemen were optimistic that even if they did not depart before midday, they would, with enough changes of horses, arrive at Darcy House before all the servants had retired for the night.

A dinner was planned at Gracechurch Street the night before their departure; Darcy smiled at the invitation for he had plans of his own for that evening. Darcy asked his sister to arrange a dinner at Darcy House, to which the Gardiners and their nieces were to be invited, for the first Saturday of April. Fitzwilliam had written to his mother, informing her of his courtship and his intention to propose to the lady who had won his heart on his return from Rosings. Lady Matlock's response was just as her son had envisaged.

Darcy and Fitzwilliam sat in Darcy's study. Their trunks were packed for their early departure in the morning and there was still an hour to go before they, with Georgiana, would set out for Gracechurch Street and dinner with the Gardiners and their lovely nieces. They were discussing their up and coming visit to Rosings when the butler knocked and entered the room; he carried a silver platter on which a letter sat. Walking up to the colonel, he bowed. Fitzwilliam, recognising the writing, knew who it was from before he took it in his hand. The butler bowed once more and turned to leave the room.

"Thank you Carlton." Fitzwilliam considered the letter for several seconds before looking at Darcy. "It would appear Mama has replied to my letter."

Darcy waited until Fitzwilliam had broken the seal and had a chance to read the letter's contents, all the while praying that his cousin's marriage to Miss Bennet would meet with the countess' approval. "Are your parents well? What does your mother say of your impending betrothal?"

"I believe she is pleased. Although father is improving, and Dr Morgan is pleased with his progress, Morgan does not believe he is well enough as yet to return to town. Mother, therefore, has decided to return alone so that she might become acquainted with Miss Bennet."

Darcy's eyebrow rose a fraction. "Does your mother say if she will stay here or at Matlock House?"

"No." Fitzwilliam looked at the missive again. "Mother gives no indication as to where she wishes to reside, only that she will arrive by the end of next week. She will leave Trentavon on Tuesday and plans to arrive by Friday."

"I will inform Mrs Carlton that Lady Matlock may wish for rooms," he replied, as he turned in his chair to reach for the bell pull behind him and summoned his housekeeper. "Now, cousin, I believe we should ready ourselves for dinner. I would not like to arrive late at Gracechurch Street."

Fitzwilliam smiled knowingly at his cousin. "I am sure you would not. Neither, for that matter, would I, also I believe Georgiana would be most upset if we were to, in any way, delay her enjoyment."

A curve graced Darcy's lips as he thought of his sister's friendship with Miss Elizabeth, a friendship that he hoped would last a lifetime.

The Darcy carriage pulled up at Gracechurch Street a full five minutes before the appointed time. Darcy hoped their host would not object, but he knew once Georgiana was in the company of Miss Bennet and Miss Elizabeth he would have an opportunity to speak with Mr Gardiner, as long as there was enough time before dinner was to be served. The fates were looking kindly on Darcy and he soon found himself seated in Mr Gardiner's study.

"How can I help you, Mr Darcy?" Gardiner smiled; he believed he had a good idea of the reason behind the young man's request for a moment of his time.

Darcy took a deep breath. "Sir, I wish to seek your permission to ask Miss Elizabeth if she would agree to courtship. I care deeply for your niece, Mr Gardiner. I know she is concerned for her future…"

"She has told you so?"

"No. No, Sir, but I have seen the worry in her eyes when she thinks no one is looking. Miss Bennet has told my cousin that both she and Miss Elizabeth fear Mrs Bennet may never forgive her daughter for refusing the hand of her father's heir. Miss Bennet fears that her sister, so as not to be a burden to your family, will take up employment as a governess."

"What!" This was news to Gardiner, and even though he had long considered that that might be the fate of any of his nieces who did not marry it still came as a shock that Elizabeth was considering such an action.

Darcy continued, "Elizabeth means the world to me. I wish to remove any worries she might have for her future."

"You love her." Gardiner's gaze was fixed on Darcy's.

Darcy gave a brief nod and his lips curled into a soft smile. "It is my dearest wish that Elizabeth will, one day, come to love me…as much as I love her."

Gardiner looked at his pocket watch and then rose from his chair. "I believe there are a few minutes left before dinner. I shall ask Lizzy to join you so that you may speak with her for a moment. The door will, of course, remain open and I shall be in the passage."

Darcy breathed a huge sigh of relief as he watched Mr Gardiner leave the room. Walking to the window, Darcy looked out at the street; he barely saw the people walking by or the costermonger pushing his large barrow.

"You wish to speak with me, Mr Darcy?"

Elizabeth's soft words brought Darcy back to his surroundings. He turned and smiled at the love of his life.

Six hours later, Elizabeth lay in bed staring at the ceiling; the tall clock in the drawing room gave a solitary dong announcing the passing of the first hour of a new day. She could hear Jane's gentle breathing beside her, as her sister slept. But sleep would not come to Elizabeth; her mind was still in turmoil. She could still scarce believe it; Mr Darcy had asked to court her. A smile lingered on her lips as she thought of him. Her eyelids slowly closed as sleep overcame her and brought sweet dreams of a gentleman from Derbyshire.

"At last you have arrived. I expected you hours ago."

Darcy and Fitzwilliam both bowed to the lady who was seated on an ornate brocade chair. "I apologise for our delay, Aunt Catherine," Darcy said. "One of the horses became lame, which unfortunately delayed our journey until we reached a coaching inn and could procure a suitable replacement."

"Humph." Lady Catherine thought the reason for their late arrival was a poor excuse. "I assume you are in want of refreshments?"

Fitzwilliam smiled and agreed. He had wished to stop at the last inn they had passed but Darcy would not entertain any further delay. His growling stomach waited with anticipation as his aunt requested that a cold repast for her nephews be brought to the room.

It was not that late in the evening, as it was still light outside, but Anne was not present. This in itself was unusual; Darcy had never known Anne not be present when he arrived at Rosings no matter what the time of day. Their aunt had for years tried to broker a match between Darcy and Anne, and had them in each other's company as often as was possible.

While waiting for the food to be brought Darcy decided to enquire after his cousin's health. "I trust, Aunt, that you and Anne are both well. You appear to be in good health and I am glad for it."

"I am well, as you see. Anne was weary and retired early."

"My parents deeply regretted their inability to visit Rosings this Easter, but father..."

The anger emanating from Lady Catherine silenced Colonel Fitzwilliam. "Your father," she hissed, "your father is dead to me. He will never be welcome here again." Unable to say more that evening Lady Catherine stood and wished her nephews a brusque good night.

Darcy and Fitzwilliam both stared in stunned silence as Lady Catherine left the room. As the door closed behind her, Fitzwilliam turned to his cousin. "What do you think that was about?"

Darcy shrugged and slowly shook his head; he had no idea as to the cause of their aunt's outburst and knew no good would come of any cogitation that evening.

The following morning both gentlemen rose early. Fitzwilliam rode the estate for an hour, while Darcy spoke with his aunt's steward, Mr Hellyer. They then made their way to the blue parlour to break their fast in the company of their aunt and cousin. When they entered the room it was empty, all but for a servant. Helping themselves to the array of food on the sideboard, the cousins sat at the table and began to eat. Not five minutes had passed when the door opened and Lady Catherine entered. The gentlemen stood.

"Good morning, Aunt," they said in unison.

Lady Catherine acknowledged their greeting with a brief nod of her head and sat on the chair her footman held out for her. The rest of the meal progressed in silence.

Once they had finished their morning repast, Lady Catherine asked her nephews to join her in the study. As they followed in their aunt's footsteps they glanced at each other; perhaps now they would now discover why Lady Catherine had taken such a sudden dislike of her brother.

Darcy and Fitzwilliam listened with growing horror as Lady Catherine told them of her brother's advice and their aunt's increasing fear that a potion which should have aided her daughter was in fact having the opposite effect.

So shocked were they that neither spoke for a while. In the end Darcy broke the silence by asking the question they both wanted to know but dreaded to hear confirmed. "Anne is addicted?"

Lady Catherine gave an abrupt nod.

The three remained in the study for a further hour. Lady Catherine talked openly of her fears for Anne. She feared she was losing her daughter as the laudanum was taking her over.

Her anger boiled over. "How could your father advise such a thing for a niece he claimed to love? How could he do it to her? How could he do it to me? He knew of my wishes for Anne…" She paused and looked at Darcy. "He has ruined the wishes of his sisters…"

Darcy took Lady Catherine's hand. He had put off what needed to be said for a long time, now might not be the ideal time to speak but he could put it off no longer. "Aunt, your wish for Anne and I to wed would never have come about. She is my cousin and in that I respect her, but it could never be any more. Even if Anne had not succumbed to the evils of laudanum, she is frail and could never bear me the heir that Pemberley needs. I will always see to Anne's welfare, if you are unable to, but that is as far as any attachment to Anne will go."

Lady Catherine gave another abrupt nod.

Fitzwilliam spoke of Dr Morgan. Although Lady Catherine was unsure how an ex-military doctor could help her daughter, and balked at the idea of his word being law, in the end she was persuaded to agree. Fitzwilliam would write to the doctor and, as soon as a replacement could be found to care for the earl's needs, Morgan would make his way with all haste to Rosings.

It was two o'clock when Lady Catherine, followed by her nephews, entered the family's dining room. It was smaller than the one used for dinner and allowed for a less formal environment and more intimate conversation. Dinner at Rosings was always a formal affair, no matter how small the company.

Anne had not left her chambers since the arrival of her cousins, but on receiving word from her mother, insisting that she join her cousins for nuncheon, Anne slowly made her way to the dining room. She had slept little that night; waking often and eventually falling into a deep dream-filled sleep just before dawn. Anne woke at midday, grateful to see a small glass containing the dark liquid. She sat up wearily and a small, thin hand reached out to grasp the glass. Although her hand was shaking she managed not to spill a drop before she brought it to her lips and drank the vile potion down. She then closed her eyes and leaned back. Now, as she walked ever closer to the dining room, her thoughts, what little she could muster, turned to those on the other side of the oak door.

Darcy and Fitzwilliam quickly rose from their seats and greeted Anne as she entered the room. They greeted their cousin congenially, but both were concerned for the health of the pale young lady before them.

Fitzwilliam turned and glanced at his aunt as she spoke. "There you are, Anne. Come take a seat so that Broomfield can serve you." He saw the fleeting emotions that passed over Lady Catherine's countenance; if they had not spoken with Lady Catherine that morning he would have been hard put to decipher them, if he had noticed them at all. He turned to Darcy who held the same look of concern that he felt. Anger at his father engulfed him.

Nuncheon progressed as silently as their earlier repast. Fitzwilliam decided now would be as good a time as any to speak of his forthcoming betrothal.

"Aunt, I have some news for you. I am courting a young lady and hope to marry soon."

"Indeed, Nephew, and what does your mother think of your plans?"

"I believe mother is pleased. She is returning from Trentavon next week to meet Miss Bennet."

"Bennet, that name sounds familiar. Who is her father?" his aunt inquired.

"He is a gentleman with an estate in Hertfordshire."

Lady Catherine frowned. "Is she related to the Bennets of Longbourn?"

"Yes. Mr Bennet is her father."

"You wish to marry a girl with little dowry and no standing, and whose family estate is entailed to my vicar? Are you mad, Richard? You have no money. You cannot simply marry where you will."

Fitzwilliam sighed at his aunt's rant. "That is where you are wrong, my dear Aunt. I have an estate, admittedly it is not as large as Rosings or Pemberley, but it brings in a goodly sum each year. More than enough to support a wife and any children we may be blessed with."

"That is beside the point. It is beyond the bounds of propriety to consider marriage to one so far beneath you. You will be the talk of the haut ton." Lady Catherine turned to her other nephew. "And what think you of your cousin's madness?"

Darcy smiled. "I am happy for him. Miss Bennet is everything a young lady should be."

"Ha! More likely she has used her arts and allurements."

"I think not," Darcy replied. Lady Catherine's brow rose but she made no comment. "Miss Bennet is a gentlewoman. She cares deeply for Fitzwilliam and will make him happy."

"It would appear that you too have been blinded by her beauty," the lady said with disdain.

"No, Aunt, not I." Darcy inwardly smiled; this would be as good a time as any to inform his aunt of his news. "I am courting her sister, Miss Elizabeth Bennet."

The clang of Lady Catherine's knife, as it fell from her fingers and hit the plate, resounded around the room. "What!" she cried.

"I spoke with Miss Elizabeth and applied to her uncle the day before our journey here."

"Her uncle? Why not her father?"

"Miss Elizabeth and her sister Miss Bennet are, at present, residing in London with their aunt and uncle."

"Who is this uncle?"

"Mr Gardiner owns a large import and export business. His..."

"Trade! Their uncle is in trade? Have you both lost your senses?" Lady Catherine was incensed by their blatant disregard for propriety. "Whoever heard of such a thing—grandsons of the Earl of Matlock to be the nephews of a tradesman? My father must turn in his grave at such a thought. Are the shades of Pemberley to be so polluted? The ton will condemn you both!"

"She is the daughter of a gentleman, Aunt."

"Yes, but what of her mother?" she demanded.

At Darcy's silence, Fitzwilliam answered in his stead. "Mrs Bennet is the daughter of a younger son who studied law. Her grandfather was a gentleman with an estate in Oxfordshire." Fitzwilliam ignored the surprised look on Darcy's face and continued with a smile. "So you see, my dear Aunt, it is not so very bad."

Lady Catherine silently continued with her meal, refusing to look at either of her nephews.

It was Anne's soft voice that broke the silence as she wished her cousins joy.

Chapter 7

Colonel Fitzwilliam sat at the writing desk in his chamber, ink pot open and nib well sharpened. He wrote two expresses which would be despatched to Trentavon with all haste. The first was for the attention of Dr Morgan, explaining the dire situation he had found his cousin in and asking the doctor to make all haste to Darcy House as soon as a replacement could be found for his father's care; the colonel would then accompany the doctor to Rosings. The second was to his mother, informing her that Dr Morgan was urgently required at Rosings. While Fitzwilliam was at his writing desk, Darcy walked to the Parsonage; he had on his person a letter he needed to deliver to Mrs Collins.

"Mr Darcy, welcome to my humble abode." Mr Collins bowed deeply to the gentleman before him.

Darcy forced back the sigh that tried to escape his lips at the sight of the grovelling man before him. He had had enough of Mr Collins' sycophantic ways the few times he had the misfortune to be in his company in Hertfordshire. But for the sake of his Elizabeth he would smile at the man and greet him civilly. "Thank you, Mr Collins. It is a pleasure to see you and your wife again. Mrs Collins," he said turning his gaze to the lady of the house, "I trust you are well and enjoying your new life in Hunsford?" Mrs Collins smiled and bowed her head as though agreeing with his statement, but remained silent.

Mr Collins ushered their guest into the parlour while bidding his wife to arrange refreshments. As Mrs Collins made to move towards the kitchen Mr Darcy called to her.

"Mrs Collins, before I forget, I have been charged to give you this missive from your friend Miss Elizabeth." Darcy removed the sealed letter from his pocket and handed it to Charlotte.

"Thank you, Sir."

Collins frowned as he watched his wife place the letter in her pocket. He was curious as to what his cousin had written, but far more intrigued as to how Mr Darcy, his revered patron's nephew, came to deliver it.

Mrs Collins returned to the parlour. Mr Darcy sat on a chair near the fireplace, while her husband was sitting on the settee. She smiled at the gentlemen, informed them that refreshments would be arriving shortly and made her way to the spare chair on the opposite side of the hearth.

Mr Collins spoke of his admiration of his patron, allowing little space for any other conversation. Darcy was grateful when a young maid brought in the refreshments as it brought Mr Collins' dialogue to a close.

After enquiring how he preferred his tea, Charlotte poured it and then smiled at their guest as she handed him the delicate china cup from her best service. She wished the visit was over so that she could read the letter which was burning a hole in her pocket.

Once the tea was served, Mr Collins continued with his praise for his patron and her nephews for a further half an hour.

"I am sure that my aunt is most grateful for your diligent service, Mr Collins, but now I must take my leave of you so that you may continue with the care of your parishioners." Darcy then turned to his hostess. "Thank you for the tea, Mrs Collins, it was most welcome. If you wish to reply before the colonel and I return to town, I would be most happy to convey your letter to Miss Elizabeth for you. Just send word to the house and I will collect it before we depart on Monday."

"That is most kind of you, Mr Darcy, thank you. Do you know if Miss Elizabeth and Miss Bennet are well? I believe they are staying with their uncle."

"They are indeed and, yes, they were both well when I last saw them. Colonel Fitzwilliam and I dined with Mr and Mrs Gardiner the evening before last."

Collins could not believe it, surely his ears deceived him. "You dined in the house of a tradesman?" He had not meant to speak the words aloud and was taken aback when Darcy glared at him.

"Mr Gardiner is the son of a gentleman. I see nothing wrong in dining with the son of a gentleman, do you, Mr Collins?"

"Oh no, n...no, of course not," the parson stuttered.

Darcy bowed to Mrs Collins and took his leave. While her husband was escorting Mr Darcy to the door, Mrs Collins walked as quickly as possible to the kitchen and the back door; her destination, the oak stump at the bottom of the garden where she could sit and read her letter in peace.

Gracechurch Street, 25ᵗʰ March

My dearest Charlotte

I do hope this letter finds you well and happy. I think of you often and pray you have found contentment in your marriage. I apologise for my tardiness in replying to your letter and I fear this will not be as long a letter as you are due, but, as I am using Mr Darcy's services to place it in your hands, I cannot dally.

We remain in London with our dear aunt and uncle. Though I believe it will not be long before Jane returns to Longbourn, whether I shall return with her will depend on how the wind blows. We are still enjoying our stay in town. You will remember in my last letter I mentioned our new friend Miss Georgiana, well imagine our surprise when we discovered she is the young sister of Mr Darcy. Yes, dear Charlotte, the very same Mr Darcy who stayed at Netherfield with Mr Bingley and his sisters.

Jane was much touched by your kind words and I am pleased to say she has completely recovered from her disappointment. Truth be told, Mr Bingley was not at all worthy of her tender heart and I am pleased to report that she has met a gentleman who is in all ways far superior to Mr Bingley. He is a military gentleman, who I do believe loves our dear Jane very much. It would not surprise me if he soon made his way to Longbourn to apply to our father for Jane's hand. As much as I will miss my dear sister, I am convinced he will make her very happy; just to see them together lightens my heart. I am sure you would agree he is an excellent choice for Jane.

Charlotte sighed as she continued to read about the dinner they had attended at Darcy House and the delightful performance of A Midsummer Night's Dream they had seen at the theatre. Charlotte was greatly relieved that Elizabeth sounded content, even happy, with her life in London. At the time Charlotte had failed to understand why her dear friend had turned down the eligible suit of her cousin. Now, after being married for nearly four weeks, she understood. Elizabeth Bennet would never have put up with such a marriage. Charlotte wondered how she would reply. Was she happy? Maybe not as much as she hoped she might have been. Was she content? Yes, she was mistress of her own house. The intimate side of her marriage, although sometimes painful, could be born. It was, after all, only once a week that her husband came to her bed; it was over quickly, then he left her alone. And if a child came of it, so much the better, she would have someone to love. Charlotte's mother had warned her that many gentlemen take a mistress; she just had not expected it to happen so soon, after all her husband was a man of the cloth. She had thought that when she was with child he might seek his pleasure elsewhere, but it appeared he had greater needs.

The walls of the parsonage were thin, so it was little surprise that she heard any noise emanating from her husband's chamber at night. The surprise had been to hear the same noises that her husband had made in her chamber on their wedding night, just two nights before. Charlotte had little doubt as to what her husband was doing and, as there was only one live-in maid, fifteen-year-old Sally, she knew who he was doing it with. She was not angry with Sally; she was a timid young girl and would not have the ability to deny Mr Collins. The following day she had noticed Sally's wrist, when one of the sleeves of her dress rode up exposing her thin wrist, and asked the girl what had happened. Sally's frightened answer of "'Tis nothing, Ma'am" did not ease Charlotte's mind, so while her husband called on Lady Catherine, Charlotte went to his chamber, what she saw there shocked her. Now most of Charlotte's time alone was spent trying to think of a way to remove Sally from Mr Collins' grip.

Reaching the end of her letter she sighed again. She folded it and placed it in her pocket. No doubt her husband would demand to read it; nothing was private from his eyes.

Saturday morning dawned bright and Charlotte decided a walk would do her good. She needed to clear her head as tonight her husband would visit her again, but at least Sally could be assured of a night's rest.

As she walked through the groves she could hear the sound of a horse's hooves. It appeared to be getting louder; she stood to the side so that the rider could pass. She was pleasantly surprised when the rider, Mr Darcy, slowed his horse and stopped to speak.

"Good morning, Mrs Collins. It is a fine morning to be out."

"Good morning, Mr Darcy. Indeed it is." A sudden thought entered her mind. *'Could Mr Darcy help with Sally, or would he be like Mr Collins.'*

While Charlotte pondered her thoughts, Darcy watched the different emotions flittering across her countenance. "Is something the matter, Mrs Collins? I would be of help if I am able."

Charlotte looked up at the gentleman and gave a wan smile. "There is a problem which is concerning me greatly. If you are able, Mr Darcy, I would appreciate a moment of your time."

Darcy dismounted, turned his horse and then offered Mrs Collins his arm. "Come, let us walk awhile and you can tell me what concerns you."

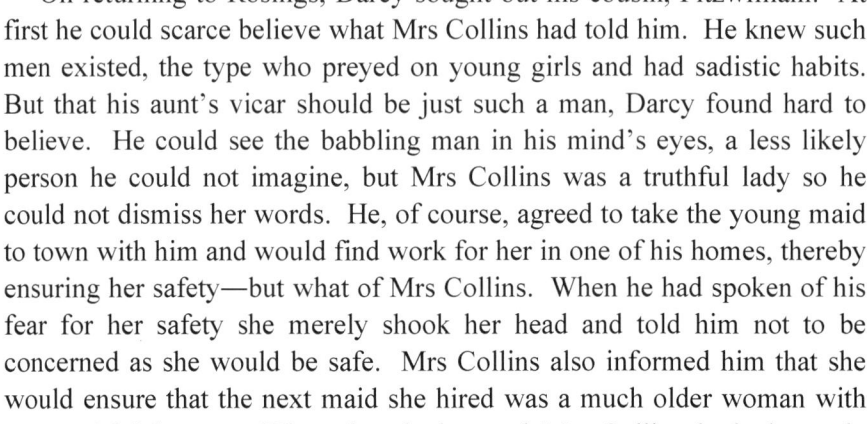

On returning to Rosings, Darcy sought out his cousin, Fitzwilliam. At first he could scarce believe what Mrs Collins had told him. He knew such men existed, the type who preyed on young girls and had sadistic habits. But that his aunt's vicar should be just such a man, Darcy found hard to believe. He could see the babbling man in his mind's eyes, a less likely person he could not imagine, but Mrs Collins was a truthful lady so he could not dismiss her words. He, of course, agreed to take the young maid to town with him and would find work for her in one of his homes, thereby ensuring her safety—but what of Mrs Collins. When he had spoken of his fear for her safety she merely shook her head and told him not to be concerned as she would be safe. Mrs Collins also informed him that she would ensure that the next maid she hired was a much older woman with no youthful beauty. When they had parted Mrs Collins looked greatly relieved, as though a great weight had been lifted from her shoulders. They had agreed it was best the girl not be told until the Sunday. Darcy thought it ironic that Collins observed the Lord's Day so both the girl and Mrs Collins were spared his company. Darcy watched anger infuse his cousin's countenance as he relayed Mrs Collins' tale.

"Are you sure it is wise to leave Mrs Collins alone with such a man?"

"Mrs Collins assured me she would be well. But I believe we should speak to Aunt Catherine. She should be aware so that a watchful eye can be kept on the situation."

Fitzwilliam agreed and the two set out to find their aunt.

Lady Catherine was in the library; she had just started to read a book by a Lady entitled Sense and Sensibility. Although a novel was not normally her choice of reading, it had been recommended by her neighbour, Lady Hitchley, and was apparently much superior to the normal romantic hogwash printed these days. She had not quite finished the second chapter when the door opened and her nephews walked into the room. Lady Catherine found this distraction both a relief, as she was becoming annoyed with the weak Mr Dashwood who would treat his father's widow so poorly, and a disappointment, as she wished to read on to see if there was any hope of compassion in the gentleman. Any annoyance she had with the fictitious Mr Dashwood gave way to outrage that a vicar, under her patronage, should act in such an abominable way to both his wife and his servant. She informed her nephews of her determination to sever his tenure immediately.

Darcy pleaded with his aunt. "No, Aunt Catherine. But, think, if Mr Collins leaves here under a cloud, Mrs Collins, who will have to go with him, may be in greater danger."

"Humph," was her only reply.

"Please reconsider, for Mrs Collins' sake." Fitzwilliam added his entreaty to his cousin's.

"May I suggest," Darcy continued, "inviting the Collinses to join us for dinner on Easter Sunday? If there is a separation after the meal, Fitzwilliam and I will speak to Collins."

"Yes," added the colonel with a smile, "I am sure we will be able to make him see the error of his ways."

"Fitzwilliam," Darcy glared at his cousin, "Collins must not know that we are aware of his indulgences. Also, I believe it would be best if the girl is removed to safety before Collins and his wife return home."

"Indeed. And we should arm Mrs Collins with a plausible reason for the maid's absence."

Lady Catherine, who had remained silent up to that point, interrupted her nephews' conversation. "I will invite the Collinses to dinner. That way I can speak with Mrs Collins without her husband realising she is aware of his infidelity." She looked directly at Darcy. "You must speak with Mrs Collins. The young maid must pack and be ready to leave the parsonage while her master and mistress are dining here."

Darcy gave a slight bow of his head in agreement. "I will arrange for my coachman to retrieve the girl."

"Thank you, Nephew. I will speak with Mrs Snell regarding a bed for her, as soon as I have discussed tomorrow's sermon with my vicar." Lady Catherine rang for her butler, Diplock, who soon ensured that a message was sent with all haste to the parsonage, requesting Mr Collins to call on Lady Catherine at his earliest convenience.

When Diplock had departed, Darcy stood and smiled at his aunt. "Thank you, Aunt. I believe I shall go for a walk, as it appears to be a pleasant kind of day. I shall call at the parsonage to see if Mrs Collins has a letter for me to take to her friend."

Ten minutes after Mr Collins departed for Rosings in answer to the summons from his patron, Mr Darcy was announced by the maid.

"Mr Darcy, this is a surprise. I am afraid you have just missed my husband, he has gone to call on Lady Catherine."

"I see. Never mind. I was passing and thought I would call to see if you have finished your letter to Miss Elizabeth."

"That is most kind of you, Mr Darcy, but I fear I have not. I hope to have it finished by tomorrow. Might I bring it to church with me and give it to you then?"

"Of course, or if you require more time my aunt has issued an invitation to you and your husband to dine with her at Rosings tomorrow evening; you could bring the letter with you then."

"Thank you, Mr Darcy. Would you care for some refreshments?"

Darcy shook his head and started to rise. "That is most kind of you, Mrs Collins, but I believe I should be on my way. There is more of the park I wish to see and we shall be leaving early on Monday." He walked towards his hostess and lowered his voice, so as not to be overheard by anyone. "My coachman will collect the girl while you are dining at Rosings. She will be cared for, do not worry."

Mrs Collins smiled at Darcy. "I shall ensure that my…letter is ready for you. Thank you, Mr Darcy."

Darcy was glad when the Easter Sunday service was over. It had been longer than any normal service due to the sermon. As he had watched and listened to the vicar preach to his congregation, Darcy wondered why such a man had taken Holy Orders. He was also eager to return to town; tomorrow could not come soon enough.

Anne had attended the service and, as she felt a little better that day, remained with the company until after dinner. Lady Catherine kept country hours and at five o'clock the carriage, which had been sent to the parsonage, pulled up at Rosings and the Collinses alighted. Mr and Mrs

Collins hurried into the entrance hall, eager to get out of the rain which had been steadily coming down since the middle of the afternoon. Relieved of their outer wear, they were soon escorted to the drawing room where everyone was gathered.

Mr Collins bowed deeply to his patron. "Oh Lady Catherine, it is such an honour you grant to my humble self and my dear wife. Is it not, Charlotte?"

Mrs Collins smiled as she rose from a curtsey. "Thank you, Lady Catherine, for your kind invitation and for the use of your carriage."

"Oh yes, my Lady, your kindness was…"

Lady Catherine interrupted her parson's words. "You have arrived just in time; I believe we shall be called to dinner at any moment." After what she had heard from her nephew, Lady Catherine felt little need to listen to the man. If not for her nephews' wishes, and of course Mrs Collins' welfare, she would have found a way to rescind the living immediately.

The meal seemed to last forever; what little conversation existed was strained. Every time Mr Collins made any kind of utterance, Lady Catherine changed the subject and asked a question of one of the others. If Mr Collins tried to answer in his wife's stead, his patron glared at him before saying, "Thank you, Mr Collins, but I wish to know Mrs Collins' opinion," or, "Mr Collins!" which, accompanied by a look enough to mute the bravest of men, was sufficient to ensure his silence on the matter.

Darcy looked at Fitzwilliam as Lady Catherine rose from the table and indicated that the ladies should follow her. Mr Collins was delighted to be spending some time drinking port with such fine gentlemen.

Once the port was passed and the decanter placed in the middle of the table, Richard Fitzwilliam took a sip and sighed. "I am looking forward to returning to town tomorrow. I miss my dear Jane."

"You are betrothed, Colonel?" A note of surprise caught in Collins' voice.

Fitzwilliam sighed again and slowly shook his head. "No, not yet, but I am courting Miss Bennet. Tomorrow I hope she will do me the honour of agreeing to be my wife. If she agrees I will ride to Meryton on Tuesday and request an audience with her father."

"M…Miss Jane Bennet?" Collins' stammered, his eyes widening. Surely the colonel could not be talking about his cousin!

"I believe you are her cousin," Fitzwilliam replied.

"B...but, that is impossible," the vicar stuttered. "When I was at Longbourn, Mrs Bennet assured me that Cousin Jane was soon to be betrothed to their neighbour, Mr Bingley."

Fitzwilliam laughed. "Fortunately for Miss Bennet, she saw the real Bingley before it was too late. I doubt he would have remained faithful; Bingley falls in and out of love too easily." Fitzwilliam regretted blackening Bingley's name, he knew hardly anything about the man, except for his ability to fall in and out of love with ease. "You, as a man of the cloth, must realize the importance of fidelity in a marriage. For when we marry, do we not agree to forsake all others? I do not intend to lie when I marry Miss Bennet, for that is a sin against God and one of His commandments."

"Quite so Cousin," Darcy agreed, "and I believe there should be another commandment that every decent gentleman would wish to obey—Thou shalt not cause any harm to those under your protection, be they servant or wife, but care for them and ensure their wellbeing."

Collins silently drank his port while Darcy and Fitzwilliam continued to talk about the depravity of some so called gentlemen, and what they would do if someone like that injured anyone they knew. He began to feel fear when Fitzwilliam stated, "If I ever discovered a friend of Miss Bennet was in the clutches of such a man, I would do all in my power to bring that man to justice. How about you, Darcy?"

"Absolutely! Do you not agree, Mr Collins?" Collins gave a quick bobbing nod of his head but said nothing.

Fitzwilliam smiled. "Now let us speak of pleasanter things. Darcy, I have seen the way you look at my soon-to-be sister, Miss Elizabeth. I suppose it will not be long before you will also request an audience with Mr Bennet. I am sure Mrs Collins will be delighted if that comes to pass, for did you not say that Miss Elizabeth and Mrs Collins are dearest friends?"

"They are indeed," Darcy replied. "Miss Elizabeth's happiness is paramount to me. I know she worries about the happiness of those she loves." He then looked directly at Collins. "But I am sure, Mr Collins, Miss Elizabeth has no need to worry about the happiness of *your* wife."

Collins noticed the hardness on Darcy's countenance; he turned to the colonel and observed the same expression. "No...no, of course not. My dear wife's happiness is of the utmost importance to me. You may rest assured, gentlemen, if it is in my power to prevent it, no harm or upset will ever befall my dear Charlotte." Collins felt the sweat rise on his brow; he knew without question, these gentlemen would make formidable enemies.

The Collinses departed and Anne, with the aid of her companion, retired for the night. Once Anne had left the room Darcy said, "We too should retire, Fitzwilliam, as we have an early start tomorrow."

Fitzwilliam agreed but Lady Catherine requested they remain for a while. "I wish to speak with you both before you retire. As I am sure you will depart with the dawn chorus, I thought it best to speak this evening."

"Of course, Aunt," Darcy replied and the gentlemen returned to their chairs.

Once seated, Lady Catherine continued. "Mrs Collins is now aware that she can call on me for help at any time, should her husband's behaviour require her to do so."

"I believe Mrs Collins will be well. Fitzwilliam and I left Mr Collins in little doubt as to our opinion of his sort of behaviour."

"Good," their aunt replied, in a no nonsense tone. "Now, tell me, when will I meet your young ladies? I believe you will have to bring them here, for I cannot leave Anne or Mrs Collins alone."

When Mrs Collins retired that night, it was with a great deal of relief. Sally was safe at Rosings and would soon depart for a better life in the service of Mr Darcy. Lady Catherine's words that evening had given Charlotte both comfort and hope. She had not expected her husband's patron to be so understanding of her concern for the maid. The relief she felt, following their conversation while the gentlemen drank their port, was beyond words. As sleep overcame her, Charlotte knew she was indebted to Lady Catherine for her kindness that evening.

Chapter 8

Preparations for the cousins' departure from Rosings began before dawn. Within an hour of the sun rising, young Sally Linwood found herself seated in an elegant carriage with Lady Catherine's nephews. Darcy and Fitzwilliam were not the only ones to rise early that day. Mr Collins knew that his patron's esteemed nephews would be leaving Rosings early that morning. Determined to demonstrate all respect to the fine gentlemen, especially after their discussion last night, Collins ensured he was properly attired and standing by the gates to bid the gentlemen farewell when the carriage passed by.

The sound of horses' hooves on the hard earth alerted him to the carriage's approach, but when he saw who was seated in the carriage, and the countenance of the gentlemen within, Collins' shock was so great that his mouth fell open and he completely forgot to bow deeply to Mr Darcy and Colonel Fitzwilliam. Collins, eyes wide with confusion, watched the carriage until it rounded the bend in the lane and disappeared from view. So shocked was he that he wandered into the road and began to walk in the direction the carriage had taken. Why was Sally in the carriage? Collins then thought back to the conversation of the evening before and remembered the look the gentlemen had given as they saw him standing by the roadside. *'Oh my, oh no, they know. They are taking Sally because they know and if they know...then Lady Catherine...'* William Collins continued to walk, totally unaware of his surroundings or where he was going, his mind in turmoil.

When Charlotte Collins descended the stairs and made her way to the dining room, she was surprised that her husband was not already at the table. She knew that Mr Darcy and the colonel had intended to leave Rosings soon after dawn and she hoped they managed to get away before her husband rose for the day. No doubt, if not, Mr Collins would soon be demanding to know why their servant had left with the gentlemen. When Charlotte finished her meal there was still no sign of Mr Collins, so she made her way to the kitchen to speak with cook; it was Monday and the meals for the week must be decided.

As time passed so Charlotte's concern as to the whereabouts of her husband grew. Charlotte was sitting in the parlour mending one of her husband's shirts when, at just past eleven o'clock, there was a knock at the parsonage door. Having no maid, now that Sally was gone, Charlotte rose and walked quickly to the front door. She was surprised to see the local apothecary and barber, but assumed he had come to see her husband.

"Mr Bexley, I am afraid Mr Collins is not at home."

"I have not come to see your husband, ma'am. May I come in? I am afraid I am the bearer of bad news."

Mrs Collins led the way to the drawing room, concerned as to what the bad news might be. "Would you like some refreshments, Sir?"

"No, that is most kind of you, Mrs Collins, but no, thank you." Bexley also refused a seat, but once Mrs Collins was sitting down he took a deep breath before speaking. "Mrs Collins, I am afraid there has been a terrible accident. Mr Collins was walking along the London road; he must have been deep in thought because it would appear he did not hear the stage coach approaching. When the driver rounded the bend at Lopcombe Corner, he was shocked to see a gentleman walking in the road. There was no time to pull up the horses, which were going at a fair rate, before they were upon the gentleman."

"Is my husband dead?" Charlotte asked slowly.

"Yes, Mrs Collins. I believe he died instantly."

"Then he would not have suffered?" *'Unlike poor Sally.'*

"No my dear lady, you can take comfort in that. Is there anything I can do to assist you before I leave?" Charlotte shook her head. "Then I will leave you in peace and make my way to Rosings to inform her ladyship." Mr Bexley bowed and quietly left the room. He felt so sorry for Mrs Collins, the vicar's wife was obviously deep in shock. She did not say a word to acknowledge his leaving; she just sat there, staring at nothing. *'She must have loved her husband deeply,'* he mused.

Once the door closed behind Mr Bexley, Charlotte looked towards it and sighed. There was no justice in this world. A man who caused suffering to another had died in an instant, like a candle being snuffed out—no prolonged suffering—where was the justice in that. Charlotte now looked to God; surely He would ensure that such an evil man spent eternity in the fiery pits of Hell.

Not one person shed a single tear on the passing of William Collins.

Sally was safely in the care of Mrs Carlton. Darcy's physician had been summoned and once she had been examined, and pronounced well, work would be found for her below stairs. After hearing of the poor girl's treatment at the hands of her previous master, Mrs Carlton decided that no matter what Dr Jowett said, young Sally would not work that day—she would have the remainder of the day to settle in to her new home. The young girl had cried with relief once left alone in the room she would share with two other maids, and made a silent vow to never set foot in Kent again. The doctor gave instructions for a salve to be made up for her, but time would be the best healer. Four years after arriving in London Sally would meet a young man, who would think the world of her and love her as every young woman should be. Their wedding night, six months after they met, would finally exorcize the ghost of William Collins from Sally's mind as her husband gently revealed to her the pleasures of the marriage bed.

Darcy and Fitzwilliam were eager to make their way to Gracechurch Street, but both wanted to refresh themselves after the journey first. Hot water was called for and while the gentlemen bathed, Darcy's valet and Fitzwilliam's batman saw to their attire. Once the gentlemen were ready, Darcy's town carriage was called for. But before they could depart, an express arrived from Rosings.

Fitzwilliam looked at Darcy with concern. Anne's death would mean mourning for three months, which would prevent him marrying Miss Bennet by the end of April.

Darcy broke the seal and quickly read the missive. "You can breathe again, Cousin. It is not Anne but Collins who has died." Darcy heard the whoosh of air as Fitzwilliam exhaled. "It would appear that the sight of Sally in my carriage shocked Mr Collins and he wandered into the path of the Ramsgate stagecoach as it rounded a bend. His body is too mutilated to lie in rest at home." Darcy paused for a moment and frowned.

"What is it, Darcy?"

"It seems that Mrs Collins will be moving into Rosings. Aunt Catherine is sure she will be a great help with the care of Anne, as well as company for herself."

"Really?"

"I believe it will only be a temporary position. Our aunt needs the parsonage for a new incumbent, but Mrs Collins does not wish to return to her father's home yet to act the grieving wife, so our aunt has offered her a temporary solution to her problem. With Lady Catherine, Mrs Collins will not need to pretend."

Darcy slipped the letter into his coat pocket. "I must tell Miss Elizabeth and Miss Bennet of their cousin's passing." Fitzwilliam blanched. "There is no need to worry, Fitzwilliam. He was their cousin in the looser meaning of the word; I believe it was their grandfathers who were first cousins."

"Enough Darcy! No more frights, I beg you. Now let us depart for Gracechurch Street before Miss Bennet believes I have forgotten my promise."

Elizabeth Bennet let out a sigh. The afternoon was passing and there was still no sign of Mr Darcy. Not paying attention to her needlework, she poked the needle into the handkerchief just missing one of her fingers that held the cloth.

"Oh Lizzy, put that poor handkerchief down. You have been pretending to embroider the lavender on it for at least an hour, but have not made even one decent stitch. They will be here soon. I am sure Mr Darcy or the colonel would have sent an express if they were delayed in Kent."

Mrs Gardiner smiled at her nieces as Elizabeth replied. "Dear Jane, you have so much more patience than I. I know you are correct, but I had expected them to call by now and you know patience is not one of my better qualities."

Voices were heard in the passage; the gentlemen had arrived.

"Well Lizzy," Aunt Gardiner said laughingly, "I believe your waiting is over." Elizabeth blushed and, picking up the handkerchief, needle and silk, began to stitch. Mrs Gardiner shook her head and smiled.

As Darcy entered the room his eyes immediately fell on Elizabeth. To his mind she was a picture of loveliness as the sunbeams through the window danced on her chestnut hair. He could well imagine her sitting in the conservatory at Pemberley delicately stitching as she was now. When she looked up and her eyes met his, his heart jumped for joy at the pleasure of seeing him that shone clearly from her eyes. A cough from Mrs

Gardiner caused him to look around and he noticed his cousin had been similarly affected by the sight of Miss Bennet.

"It is a lovely day," Mrs Gardiner announced. "My nieces have not ventured outside as yet today, so have not had a chance to partake in the warm spring air. Perhaps you should all take a walk in the park. I am sure in such an open space you will be able to chaperone each other."

The young people quickly agreed with Mrs Gardiner's suggestion. Ten minutes after entering the Gardiners' residence in Gracechurch Street, Darcy and Fitzwilliam escorted Elizabeth and Jane out of Mr Gardiner's home.

Mrs Gardiner watched from the doorway as her nieces walked towards the small park at the end of the street. Each walked next to her young gentleman with her hand resting on his arm. She smiled; both young men would make excellent husbands. Mrs Gardiner then turned back to the house, closed the door and made her way up to the nursery to see how her children fared.

Elizabeth always had been a faster walker than any of her sisters, so it was not surprising that within a short time of them entering the park Darcy and Elizabeth were quite a way in front of Fitzwilliam and Jane. The former couple did not realize the gap had grown so wide, while the latter did not mind.

Once he felt that he and Jane were out of hearing distance from his cousin and Miss Elizabeth, Fitzwilliam slowed his pace. "Miss Bennet, I know we have not been courting for many weeks, but…" Fitzwilliam sighed and wondered why he was so nervous. He had commanded men in battle and yet standing here, preparing to ask the most important question in his life to the young woman who meant the world to him, was more terrifying than facing the enemy with a bunch of raw recruits.

A slight frown marred Jane's countenance as she looked at the colonel's face. She was confused and also slightly concerned at his discomfort. Then sorrow began to creep into her heart as one possible reason for his behaviour entered her mind.

Seeing the sudden worry in Jane's eyes startled Fitzwilliam. "Oh no, Miss Bennet, Jane, I did not mean to worry you, it is just…well, you see, I have never found myself in this position before and…" Deciding he was starting to sound like a babbling drunk, he took a deep breath and reached out to take hold of Jane's gloved hand. "Miss Bennet, you are a wonderful young lady and deserve much more than I can offer, but, I love you, Jane, and will care for and protect you for as long as I live if you will have me." Fitzwilliam was looking at Jane's hand, securely wrapped in his large one, so he did not see the smile that graced her lips or the look in her eyes. "What I am trying to say is…Miss Bennet, will you do me the honour of being…" At that moment he looked up and saw what he could only describe as love shining in Jane's eyes. His throat closed so he could barely whisper, "my wife."

Jane's countenance lit up even more if that was possible. "Yes. Oh yes." Then she lowered her tone to a whisper. "I love you too…Richard."

Fitzwilliam lifted Jane's hand to his lips and gently kissed it. "If we were alone, I would take you in my arms and kiss you. Then, my dearest Jane, there could be no doubt as to how much I care and how happy you have made me."

Jane blushed. "I believe we should continue with our walk, Sir, or my sister will wonder what has become of us."

Richard placed Jane's hand on his arm and covered it with his. "Darcy knew of my intentions this morning, so I am sure he will have reassured Miss Elizabeth of your safety and my honourable intentions."

They continued their walk through the park, a deep contentment in each other's company, in the direction his cousin and her sister had taken. They noticed the pair, deep in conversation, about five and twenty yards ahead of them.

The joy that Jane was feeling reduced slightly when she was close enough to make out her sister's countenance. "Lizzy, what is the matter?" Jane cried, for something obviously was concerning her sister.

"I am worried for Charlotte."

"Charlotte? Why?"

"Has not Colonel Fitzwilliam told you?" Elizabeth asked.

"I am afraid that is my fault," said the colonel. "I was so intent on asking Miss Bennet to be my wife that I forgot."

Elizabeth beamed, all thought of Mr Collins' demise fled from her mind. "Really?" she cried. Jane blushed and gave a shy nod of her head. "Oh that is wonderful." Elizabeth rushed up and hugged her sister. "I am so happy for you."

The colonel smiled at his beloved before saying, "I intend to ride to Longbourn on Wednesday. I would do so in the morning, but unfortunately there are things I must do first."

When Colonel Fitzwilliam woke on the following day, he felt he must be the happiest man alive. He could barely believe his good fortune, his dearest Jane had agreed to be his wife. Today he would visit his family's solicitor; the marriage settlement must be written and made ready for Mr Bennet's approval, Fitzwilliam wished to take the document with him to Longbourn. He also intended to approach another doctor he knew, who was at present on Home Duty, but before he had a chance to leave Darcy House another express arrived. This one was from Lady Matlock.

The letter was short and to the point. Richard was to call at Matlock House and inform the housekeeper her mistress was returning to town, without the earl as he was suffering from a severe spring cold and not well enough to undertake the long journey. As planned, she hoped to arrive before the end of the week and looked forward to meeting the young lady her son had decided to marry, as soon as it could be arranged. His mother suggested Fitzwilliam bring Miss Bennet to Matlock House on Friday afternoon to take tea with her. Dr Morgan was on his way. He would call at Darcy House as soon as he arrived in town. The doctor had arranged for a colleague, Dr Nicholls, who had been on leave in the neighbouring county of Nottinghamshire, to take over the care of the earl as his treatment continued. Lady Matlock stated that Dr Morgan had assured her that his colleague was more than capable; he had dealt with people with the same complaint successfully and therefore had no concerns on leaving the earl in Dr Nicholls' care.

Darcy looked at his cousin after reading the missive. "I assume your plans for today will change? I believe you intended to find a replacement for Dr Morgan, but it appears he has beaten you to it."

"Yes, I am relieved that is one less thing I need to do. Now my only port of call will be Lincoln's Inn to make arrangements for the marriage settlement." Richard sighed as another thought crossed his mind. "I do not want to, but perhaps I should remain in town until Morgan arrives."

"No Richard, you go to Longbourn as planned. I doubt the doctor will reach town that quickly. But whenever he arrives, I will be the one to escort the gentleman to Rosings. I am sure you will have other more enjoyable things to do than spend time with our aunt. And besides, Miss Elizabeth will be grateful for the opportunity to see Mrs Collins. I will take a maid to act as chaperone for Miss Elizabeth, possibly Sally. The young girl had no chance to say farewell to any family she may have in the area and, with Collins gone, there is no fear for her safety now."

Once Fitzwilliam left to make his way to the stables, Darcy returned to his study. Documents had arrived from Pemberley the previous day which he needed to look at, and that was how he intended to spend the next few hours. Georgiana would be with her companion until luncheon and he did not expect Richard to return before their repast, so there would be no disturbance.

Darcy completed only half of the work he intended by the time Richard returned to Darcy House. He secured the documents in his desk drawer and joined his sister and cousin for a light luncheon before the three of them left for Gracechurch Street to call on the Miss Bennets.

Fitzwilliam was pleased with his morning's work; Mr Wells assured him the marriage settlement would be ready for him to collect at eight o'clock on the following morn. Darcy offered Fitzwilliam the use of one of his carriages for his journey to Hertfordshire, it was old but had recently been refurbished and re-sprung, and should ensure that he would not be completely covered with the dust of the road when he arrived at Longbourn; for that would not give his future father a favourable first impression. Although Fitzwilliam would have preferred the freedom of being astride his stallion, he could see the logic in Darcy's suggestion and gladly accepted.

Wednesday morning came quickly enough and Fitzwilliam departed early; only Darcy was downstairs to wish his cousin a safe journey to Longbourn. Even with stopping at the solicitor's chambers on the way, Fitzwilliam was hopeful he would arrive at Mr Bennet's home well before luncheon.

An hour after the colonel's departure, Carlton knocked on his master's study door. Darcy, who had returned to the estate business outstanding from the previous day, was surprised when his butler announced the arrival of Dr Morgan.

"Doctor, welcome to Darcy House. We had not expected you to arrive so quickly, my aunt's express only arrived yesterday morning."

"The colonel's letter spoke of urgency. Miss de Bourgh, I believe, is in a bad way, so it behoved me to make my way to town at the earliest opportunity, Mr Darcy."

"Thank you, doctor." Darcy rang the bell. "My housekeeper will show you to a room for your convenience. If you would care to refresh yourself after your journey and then join me and my sister for our morning repast, you would be most welcome. My sister knows little of our cousin's illness, so, you understand, I would appreciate it if we could wait until after our meal before discussing Miss de Bourgh and our journey to Kent." Darcy then noticed the weariness in the doctor's eyes. "Or if you would prefer to rest for a while after your long journey and take a light repast in your rooms, I will arrange for a tray to be sent up to you."

"A short rest sounds wonderful. If it is no trouble I would appreciate that very much," the doctor replied.

Mrs Carlton led the doctor to a bedchamber in the guest wing, while promising hot water and a tray would be sent up to him immediately.

Colonel Fitzwilliam relaxed on the well-padded comfort of his cousin's carriage, grateful for the loan of such a finely sprung vehicle—this really was the way to travel. It was just after midday when he arrived. Alighting from the carriage refreshed and ready to meet his darling Jane's father, he left the wellbeing of Darcy's prime horses to Longbourn's groom who assured him the beasts would be well cared for.

From the description Jane had given him, Fitzwilliam assumed it was the housekeeper, Mrs Hill, who answered his knock. While he waited to discover if Mr Bennet would grant him an audience, he could not help but hear the voices that came from further down the hall—no doubt Jane's younger sisters and some gentlemen from the militia. It was not long before Mrs Hill returned and Fitzwilliam found himself standing in a study being welcomed by the master of the house.

"Colonel Fitzwilliam, please take a seat. What can I do for you, Sir?"

Fitzwilliam reached into the pocket of his greatcoat, which hung over his arm, and retrieved a letter. He then sat, holding the letter like a talisman in his hand. "I had the greatest privilege to meet your daughter,

Miss Bennet, soon after she arrived in town with her sister, Miss Elizabeth. We have spent much time in each other's company and have got to know one another well. I care…I love and admire your daughter greatly. And with your permission, Sir, I would like to spend the rest of my life loving and caring for her."

"What sort of life would my Jane have being married to an officer in His Majesty's Army? I imagine she would have to move from place to place with you."

"No Sir. I would not want Miss Bennet to face any danger. I intend to resign as soon as the troubles with France and the Americas are over. I am a second son and therefore will not inherit my father's estate, but, I have no sisters and my parents in their wisdom provided for me. I have an estate in Staffordshire, it is not large but it brings in three thousand pounds per annum. I shall also receive the remainder of my mother's dowry, but I hope that will not be for some time yet. I have been frugal, saving as much as possible of my army pay and the profit from my estate. I have seen too many officers and gentlemen squander their money, wasting it on excessive gambling and the other pleasures of life. There are two things I am determined; my wife shall want for nothing, nor will she have any cause to repine the day we marry. I have enough to buy a modest town house…"

"Yes, yes. I believe you have expressed your wishes and desire quite admirably. As you are here and she is not, I am correct in assuming you have yet to ask my daughter?"

"No, Sir. I asked Miss Bennet if she would do me the honour of being my wife last evening."

"I see. What of courtship, or is that a thing of the past?"

"No, Sir, of course not. Mr Gardiner gave his permission for courtship last month. Miss Bennet and I were most grateful that you had granted your brother permission to act in your stead."

"Permission?"

"Why, yes, Sir. I saw the document myself. It was dated the twenty-eighth day of December last year."

Mr Bennet cast his mind back. "Oh yes…, I remember now."

"Miss Bennet gave me a letter for you, should you require confirmation of her acceptance and happiness." Fitzwilliam stood and held out the letter he had held so firmly in his hand to the gentleman he hoped would one day be his father. By G_d, this was harder than going against the Little Corporal's men in battle.

Fitzwilliam remained standing while Mr Bennet broke the seal and read the letter from his eldest daughter. A few minutes passed as Mr Bennet read and re-read the letter. Trying not to let a sigh escape, Bennet looked at the young man in front of him. "Jane appears to care for you very much."

Fitzwilliam smiled. "Yes, Sir. I am a most fortunate man."

"By the sounds of her letter, you are planning a short betrothal. I doubt Mrs Bennet will be happy." Mr Bennet suppressed a groan at the thought of Mrs Bennet's wailing.

"Miss Bennet did fear as much. But, Sir, I have it from the War Office that it is more than likely I will be sent to Upper Canada in the summer. Jane, I mean, Miss Bennet and I wish for as much time together, as man and wife, as is possible. If you approve, Sir, we hope to marry by the end of the month." Fitzwilliam suddenly remembered Mr Collins. "Miss Bennet assured me that Mr Collins was a distant cousin so there would be no need for a prolonged mourning period for your family."

Mr Bennet was considering his wife's response to the wedding of their eldest daughter in less than a month's time when the colonel's final words penetrated. "Collins is dead?"

"Yes, Sir. Have you not received word yet? My cousin and I visited my aunt for Easter, we returned to town on Monday. In a letter from my aunt, she mentioned that Mr Collins had had an unfortunate accident and died. His widow is staying with Lady Catherine for the nonce."

News of his heir's demise was of little concern to Bennet, but knowledge that the colonel was related to that reprobate, Darcy, did.

"You speak of your cousin. Would that be Mr Darcy, by any chance?"

"Yes, Mr Bennet," Fitzwilliam replied, at a loss as to what Darcy had to do with anything.

Mr Bennet thought of all he had learnt about Mr Darcy's character. The colonel did not look like a rake, but then neither had Mr Darcy. "Do you have a mistress?"

Fitzwilliam's mouth dropped open. "I beg your pardon, Sir?"

"You heard me. Do you have a mistress?"

"No, Sir, I do not!" Fitzwilliam emphatically replied. "Nor do I intend to ever keep a mistress or take a lover. I wish to marry your daughter. She is already my life—my everything—I would never treat her so poorly." Fitzwilliam could feel his anger rising and needed to take a deep breath to calm himself before continuing, "I shall be faithful to my wife for as long as I live."

Bennet hoped the colonel was truthful. "Very well, Colonel, you have my permission and blessing, but you will have to win over Mrs Bennet regarding the date of the nuptials. What do your family think of your plans?"

"My mother is aware that I intended to ask Miss Bennet to be my wife and she is happy. She has yet to meet Miss Bennet as my parents are at the family estate. They retired there in January for my father's health." Fitzwilliam made a mental note to ask his mother, as soon as possible, if his parents would be able to attend the wedding. He then reached again into the deep pocket of his greatcoat and retrieved the marriage settlement.

"Where is your family's estate?" Mr Bennet asked, curious as to who his parents might be.

"Trentavon Hall in Derbyshire is the family seat of the Earl of Matlock. My estate, at Longnor in Staffordshire, is less than a day's ride from my father's estate, which is near Barrow on Trent."

"You say you have an older brother, are there any others?"

"No, Viscount Tansley is my only brother and is three years my elder. He is a good man and will make a fine earl, when the time comes." Fitzwilliam then held out the document. "This is the marriage settlement which I asked my solicitor to prepare. I hope it meets with your approval, Sir."

Mr Bennet stood and took the document from Fitzwilliam's outstretched hand. He opened the package and quickly read the content. "This appears to be quite generous towards Jane, and any future offspring, considering your income and occupation. I will read it most thoroughly later." He then folded the document and placed it on his desk, before walking around it to stand next to the colonel. "We had better pass the happy news on to my wife. I suppose Jane warned you of her mother's exuberance?"

Fitzwilliam smiled and nodded. "Do not worry, Sir, I am prepared."

"Excellent. Well, let us go to the drawing room where I believe we will find my wife and younger daughters entertaining some officers."

Fitzwilliam followed Mr Bennet down the passage; with every step they took the sound of voices grew louder. Mr Bennet opened the drawing room door and indicated the colonel to walk ahead of him. Fitzwilliam entered and looked around at the people sitting there. He had a warm smile on his face until his eyes lit on an officer, who was lustfully eyeing the blonde girl sitting next to him. From Jane's description the girl was the youngest Bennet daughter, Lydia. Fitzwilliam froze on the spot. He clenched his fists and jaw. His face was red with the anger that marred his countenance. Mr Bennet wondered what had caused such an instantaneous response in the colonel. Before he could bring their presence to the attention of his wife he discovered the reason.

Chapter 9

"Wickham," the colonel growled. "What are you doing here?"

Wickham, on hearing his name, turned his attention from Lydia. When he saw who had spoken, he blanched, stumbled to his feet and ran from the room. Before anyone had time to recover from the shock and speak, Wickham was mounting his horse and riding back to camp as though the hounds of Hell were chasing him.

Mrs Bennet's eyes were round, she was unsure as to what had just occurred. In the middle of her drawing room stood a very angry officer, though why he should be so angry she had not the slightest idea. Lieutenant Denny and Captain Chamberlaine, who had also been sitting near Kitty and Lydia, jumped to attention; they saluted the officer, thanked Mrs Bennet for her kind hospitality, made their excuses and left Longbourn with nearly as much haste as Wickham.

With the departure of the officers Lydia found her voice. "You...you brute, how dare you abuse poor Wickham so!" With that she ran from the room and out of the front door, hoping that dear Wickham was still in the grounds.

Fitzwilliam looked at Mr Bennet. "I am sorry, Sir." He then turned to Mrs Bennet. "Ma'am, please accept my apologies for interrupting your company. I fear it was the shock of seeing that...man." Returning to Mr Bennet, Fitzwilliam continued, "Sir, for the safety of your daughters, I must warn you of Mr Wickham."

"Yes, well, perhaps we had best return to my study."

Fitzwilliam bowed to the ladies before following Mr Bennet from the room, leaving a bewildered Mrs Bennet to wonder who the officer was and what he could possibly know about dear Mr Wickham. *'Surely it cannot be that bad, Mr Wickham is such a handsome and dear young man.'*

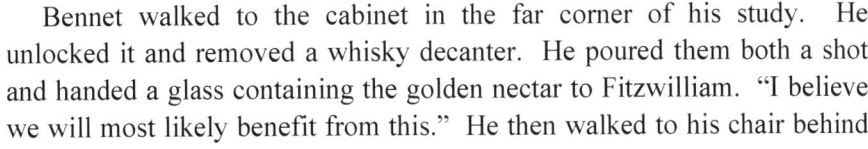

Bennet walked to the cabinet in the far corner of his study. He unlocked it and removed a whisky decanter. He poured them both a shot and handed a glass containing the golden nectar to Fitzwilliam. "I believe we will most likely benefit from this." He then walked to his chair behind his desk and sat down.

Fitzwilliam took a sip of the whisky and then another, before lowering the glass.

Mr Bennet watched as differing emotions flickered across the colonel's face. Bennet prided himself on being a good reader of a man's character, but he was sometimes wrong. He had a disturbing feeling that his judgement of Wickham's character was one of those times; if so, this would be the second time, in not so many months, that he had failed to read a gentleman's character correctly. He had believed Mr Darcy to be a proud and haughty kind of fellow who would never dally with a lady, but Mr Walker had said it was otherwise. And now, no doubt, Wickham would not be the harmless ladies' man Bennet had thought him to be.

Fitzwilliam started to speak, bringing Bennet back from his musings. "My dealings with George Wickham go back many years."

Bennet felt his heart sink as he heard about the steward's son, who had received many advantages in his life. Godson to the master of the estate, his education had been paid for by the gentleman, but, instead of making the most of such opportunities, the ungrateful boy wasted his time at university on wine, women and gambling.

"A book was started while George was at Cambridge, to see who could bed the most maidens in a term. George won," Fitzwilliam said grimly, "and I do not believe his record has been beaten since. I began to wonder if there would be a single virgin left in the area, by the time he completed his studies."

The more Bennet heard, the worse he felt. Maybe it was not Mr Darcy that Lieutenant Walker was talking about, but his fellow officer, Wickham, instead. For surely their small community could not have harboured two such blackguards.

"When his godfather died, Wickham was left an inheritance. *If* he took Holy Orders he would, when the position became vacant, become the vicar of Kympton. My cousin was not overly worried when Wickham asked for money instead of the living; he knew George would not be a good shepherd for the souls of Kympton. He gave him three thousand pounds in lieu of the living, as well as a gift of one thousand, stipulated in the will. Three years later the living became vacant. Wickham heard of incumbent's death and returned, requesting the living that his godfather had bequeathed him. When this was refused he threatened revenge on my cousin. Last year he was nearly successful, but that is not my story to tell."

Bennet took a larger sip of his whisky. "I believe Mr Wickham may have continued with his revenge against your cousin." Mr Bennet told the colonel of the stories, damning Mr Darcy's character, which had spread since that gentleman's departure from the area.

"He obviously spoke of himself."

"It was not him," Bennet replied. "A young, and I fear very impressionable, officer was his vessel. He was clever. No name was mentioned, only enough information that it could be no one else."

"Sir, anyone who knew my cousin would know without a doubt that it was a lie. Heavens it would not surprise me if Darcy was still a virgin. My uncle instilled a strict moral code into his son." Fitzwilliam looked up at Mr Bennet and saw a look of disbelief. Unsure which part of his rendition had caused it, Fitzwilliam continued. "If you would like confirmation of both my cousin's and Wickham's characters, I am sure my mother would be happy to oblige."

"No, no, Colonel. I believe you. I am just shocked that so many have been taken in by such a man."

"Many have in the past and, I am sure, many will in the future. Mr Wickham makes friends easily, whether he can keep them is another matter."

"Now that you know he is here, what will you do?"

"I will call on his colonel and warn him. It does the militia no good to have someone of his ilk in their ranks."

"Colonel Forster will be the man you wish to see. He is renting a house on the other side of Meryton, it is quite large and I am sure anyone will be able to point it out to you."

Fitzwilliam stood. "Thank you, Sir, and thank you for granting me your permission to marry Miss Bennet."

"Ah yes, I think before you leave we had best inform my wife. You have still to get her permission for the date." Bennet laughed at the look of trepidation that crossed the countenance of the, no doubt war-hardened, colonel.

As they walked out of the study, Mrs Hill was walking along the passage. "Is my wife still in the drawing room?"

"Yes, Sir, and Mrs Philips, who arrived a few moments ago, is with her."

"Excellent. Thank you, Mrs Hill." Bennet turned and whispered to his visitor, "This could prove very fortuitous for your cousin's good name. My wife's sister, Mrs Philips, is the best gossip in the whole of Meryton. Once she hears of Wickham's infamous behaviour and lies, I can guarantee the whole of Meryton will know before the day ends."

Mrs Bennet was busy telling her sister of Mr Wickham's sudden departure, when the door opened and Mr Bennet entered the room; the officer, who had been so angry earlier, followed behind him.

Lydia scowled, she may like officers in general, but she did not like this one; he had been mean to her dear Wickham. Her mother and aunt both looked at the gentlemen with eager expectation. Both ladies hoped they might discover what had caused the earlier outcry.

"Mrs Bennet, this is Colonel Fitzwilliam. Colonel, this is my wife, Mrs Bennet, her sister, Mrs Philips, and my daughters, Mary, Kitty and Lydia."

Fitzwilliam bowed to the ladies. "It is a pleasure to meet you all." Lydia's scowl deepened. "Mrs Bennet, I am very sorry for my behaviour earlier. I hope you are able to forgive me."

Before Mrs Bennet could say a word in reply, her husband spoke again. "My dear, you will remember I gave our brother Edward permission to act in my stead, while the girls were under his roof." He doubted she would, as he himself had forgotten about the missive written in jest. "Colonel Fitzwilliam has been courting our Jane and today he came to ask for her hand in marriage."

"Jane? To be married?" she squealed, as her hand rose to briefly cover her mouth. "Oh my!"

Mrs Philips smiled at the gentleman, who would soon be her nephew. Mary and Kitty both smiled and congratulated the colonel, but Lydia continued to scowl. She had hoped to be the first married, but now it looked as though her plans would come to naught.

"Colonel, you must stay for luncheon."

"That is most kind of you, Mrs Bennet, but I must call on Colonel Forster before returning to town."

"Colonel Forster?" Mrs Bennet enquired.

"The colonel needs to speak with Colonel Forster. It would appear, Mrs Bennet, we have all been taken in by a practiced liar and rakehell of the worst kind." Bennet then looked at his daughters. "Girls, I believe it is time you went to your rooms."

Lydia pouted and frowned. "Why, Papa? I want to hear what this officer accuses dear Wickham of, I am sure if anyone is lying it is he. He is jealous of poor Wickham."

Fitzwilliam shook his head at the seductive powers Wickham had over this child. "Mr Bennet, if I might suggest, perhaps your daughters should be allowed to hear what kind of man they champion. It may protect them from his like in the future."

As much as Mr Bennet wanted to shield his daughters from hearing such words as would be spoken that day, he had to admit, Fitzwilliam might be right on the matter. "Girls, you may stay if you wish, but, do not say a word." Mr Bennet turned to his visitor. "Colonel, I believe you should tell my family what you told me earlier." Mr Bennet sat down in his comfortable chair and waited for the colonel to speak.

Fitzwilliam retold his tale, omitting all mention of the infamous betting book at Cambridge. When he had finished, Mrs Bennet and her sister had both paled. Mary was shaking her head; Kitty looked startled, while Lydia looked fit to burst with indignation but before she could utter one word, her mother cried out, "Surely not!"

"I am afraid so, Mrs Bennet," her husband replied. "And, I fear, that we will not be the only ones to be so deceived."

Colonel Fitzwilliam added his voice in agreement. "Indeed not, Sir. If Mr Wickham has been true to his nature, I fear, many of the traders in Meryton will be owed substantial sums of money and, no doubt, he will have compromised more than one young girl."

Lydia stamped her foot. "You lie," she cried. "Wickham would never act like that. He cares for me, he told me so."

Fitzwilliam looked at Lydia sadly and shook his head. "I am sorry, Miss Lydia, but you have been deceived. Wickham cares for no one but himself. He will tell a young lady what she wants to hear. He will speak of love and marriage, but, once he has her virtue, he will move on to his next conquest."

Lydia refused to listen to anymore. She jumped up from her chair and ran from the room for the second time that day, slamming the door behind her. The sound of her running up the stairs and the crash of her bedroom door could be heard by those remaining in the drawing room.

Mrs Philips broke the silence. "Oh, I have just remembered…, I am so sorry, Fanny dear, but, I must away." Mrs Philips kissed her sister on her cheek, said goodbye to her nieces and brother, smiled at the colonel and quickly made to leave. Mr Bennet looked at Fitzwilliam while Mrs Philips said her farewells, he smiled as his eyes silently said, "I told you so!"

As Mrs Philips left the room, Kitty glanced at her mother and pleaded, "May I go to Lydia?"

"Yes, yes, and I shall come with you." Kitty quickly left the room, expecting her mother to follow.

"Mrs Bennet," Fitzwilliam said, "before I leave, I would like to talk to you about the date for my marriage to your daughter. Jane and I would like to marry before the end of April."

Mrs Bennet, whose nerves were slowly recovering from the shock of Mr Wickham's true character, startled at his words.

"But, Colonel," she cried in alarm, "that is less than a month away. It is impossible. Why, there is Jane's dress to be made and…"

"My mother is returning to town. I am sure she will wish to take your daughter to visit her modiste, Madame Marron, in New Bond Street. Mother was so excited that one of her sons was, at last, to wed and give her a long awaited daughter, she insists on purchasing the wedding dress.

Mrs Bennet's mind had yet to grasp that another woman would be choosing her daughter's wedding apparel. She was still processing the fact that the modiste his mother favoured was situated on New Bond Street.

"New Bond Street?"

"Yes, Mrs Bennet."

The next fact to penetrate was that the colonel had said *sons,* which meant he had at least one brother. "You have brothers?" she hopefully enquired.

"Only one, Mrs Bennet." Understanding the way Mrs Bennet's mind worked, when single young men were involved, Fitzwilliam quickly continued. "He is an older brother and although not yet married, the family has great hopes that his friendship with Lord Imber's granddaughter, Lady Arabella, will bloom into a love match." Fitzwilliam nearly smiled at the disappointment which crossed Mrs Bennet's countenance.

Finally, Mrs Bennet realized, with growing horror, that if the colonel's mother had her way, she would have no input on her daughter's wedding dress. That could not be borne. "Oh but, I must make sure that dear Jane's dress is suitable for the occasion."

"My dear Mrs Bennet," her husband drawled, "I am sure that the countess will be aware of the latest fashions and will ensure that our Jane is suitably attired."

"Countess?" Who is the countess?

"My mother," replied Fitzwilliam, hoping to bring the conversation to a close. He did after all need to see Colonel Forster before returning to town. "My parents are the Earl and Countess of Matlock."

"Oh." Mrs Bennet's eyes widened, her hands clasping and unclasping in an agitated manner. "Oh, Mr Bennet, my dear Jane is to be the daughter of an earl." Then she remembered the proposed date for the wedding, no that would not do—it would not do at all. "I suggest the late summer, Colonel. No, no, yours must be a wedding befitting an earl's son, it cannot be organised in less than six months. Your mother, I am sure, would be horrified if it was anything else."

"I am sorry, Mrs Bennet, but there is a good reason for an earlier date."

Mrs Bennet gasped at his words. "You have not, surely not!" she cried.

"No, Mrs Bennet, you misunderstand my meaning; I assure you, your daughter's virtue is safe with me. No, what I meant was…" Fitzwilliam sighed. "I have only two or maybe three months before I expect to be sent abroad. Our dearest wish is to marry and spend some time together as husband and wife before we are parted. If you insist on a later date, then I fear the wedding will have to be postponed for an indefinite period. And before you worry about my mother, I can assure you, Mrs Bennet, she will understand."

"I suppose, if it must be so, then we will have to do our best. But Jane must return home as soon as possible. There is much to be done."

"Of course, Mrs Bennet, I shall inform your daughters that they must return to Longbourn with all haste, once Miss Bennet has visited Madame Marron."

Mrs Bennet's eyes darkened with anger. She managed to hold back the words she wanted to say and merely replied, "Only dear Jane need return. It would be better if Lizzy were to remain with my brother and his family for the nonce. Now, you must excuse me, I must go and speak with Hill. Luncheon will be served shortly; I trust you will stay to partake in refreshments, Colonel."

Fitzwilliam watched Mrs Bennet leave the room.

"My wife has not yet forgiven Lizzy. Mrs Bennet had planned that Lizzy would marry my heir, but my daughter had other ideas. When Mr Collins proposed, she adamantly refused. Lizzy is my favourite and I could not bring myself to force her. Mrs Bennet was, and still is, very annoyed, especially as Mr Collins married our neighbour's daughter. It had been planned for Jane to stay with my brother's family after Christmas; for peace and harmony, Lizzy joined her. I do not know when my wife will allow her to return."

Fitzwilliam was shocked. He knew of the estrangement between mother and daughter, but for Mr Bennet to profess that Elizabeth was his favourite and yet allow his wife to treat her so abominably was beyond his understanding. "But surely, once she is aware that Collins is dead Miss Elizabeth will be forgiven."

"Ah yes, but what if Mrs Collins is with child? No, until it is known if Mrs Collins carries Longbourn's heir, I doubt my wife will forgive Lizzy."

"Perhaps, Sir, if Miss Elizabeth were to have a rich suitor, matters would change."

Bennet laughed. "I suspect you are right, Colonel."

Little did Mr Bennet know, but his daughter did have a rich suitor; Fitzwilliam, however, had no intention of enlightening the gentleman.

If Colonel Fitzwilliam had known of the speed at which Wickham would return to camp, he would have spent less time trying to pacify Mrs Bennet's nerves regarding her eldest daughter's wedding and called on the Militia's commanding officer with all haste.

Denny hurried to catch up with his friend, leaving Chamberlain to make his own way back to camp.

As soon as he was in hailing distance, Denny shouted, "I say Wickham, are you well?"

Wickham slowed his horse's pace a tad, turned and smiled at Denny. "Yes, yes. It was just a surprise to see the Earl of Matlock's son in Mr

Bennet's home. Fitzwilliam is much like his cousin Darcy, dour and proud. He does not believe that a steward's son, despite being his uncle's godson, should be an officer. But I shall not let his prejudice affect me any longer. Come Denny, let us return to camp, I have better things to do than be in the company of one such as he."

They parted company at the cordwainer's in Meryton, where Denny had an appointment. When Wickham neared the large house where he and his fellow officers were billeted, Walker was striding towards him.

"Wickham," he cried, "you have an express. I was about to come to Longbourn to ensure you received it quickly."

Wickham jumped down from his horse, thanked his young friend and tore open the seal. He cared little for what it said; his mind was already working out how he could use it as his ticket out of Meryton. It was from Susanna Younge. It appeared he would be fathering another bastard, but Susanna would not accept that and demanded that Wickham make an honest woman of her as soon as possible. With his mounting debts and Richard Fitzwilliam appearing in the area, this news was yet another reason why it would be best for him to disappear.

Lieutenant Walker, concerned for the welfare of his friend, enquired, "I say, Wickham, are you well? You have gone a might pale."

The meeting with Colonel Forster went much as Fitzwilliam thought it would. Forster was shocked. The more Fitzwilliam told the colonel, the paler the gentleman became.

"Knowing Wickham as I do, Colonel, if his debts become too great, or if he should get some young innocent in the family way, then I believe he will simply disappear." Fitzwilliam sighed as he thought of the meeting with Wickham at Longbourn. "Unfortunately, I met Wickham a short while ago in the drawing room at Longbourn. My shock at seeing him was so great that I could not contain my displeasure. If he believes I will be able to cause trouble for him, he may have already packed his belongings and departed."

"I see," the colonel replied, shaking his head. "Let me enquire as to whether Mr Wickham has already left the camp."

"Left the camp?"

"Yes, Colonel Fitzwilliam. It was not much more than half an hour ago when a distraught Wickham entered my office. An express arrived for him this morning. It contained sad news regarding his mother's only brother. He came to ask for a se'nnight's leave. His aunt, Mrs Younge, had written that his uncle was near death and she begged Wickham to attend his bedside before it was too late. Of course I granted the man immediate compassionate leave."

Fitzwilliam, who was stunned to silence, shook his head at the colonel's foolishness in believing Wickham. Forster rang for his adjutant, who quickly attended the colonel and after a few short words departed again.

"Colonel, while we wait, might I ask a question?" Fitzwilliam gave a nod of his head and Forster continued. "Why did Mr Darcy not warn the residents of Mr Wickham's character while he was staying in the area?"

'A Good question,' thought Fitzwilliam. He could never mention the Ramsgate affair, for to do so would risk the ruin of his young cousin's reputation. Before he could answer, Forster spoke again.

"I believe Wickham's first complaint of Mr Darcy was of an inheritance and was made while the gentleman was still at Netherfield. If that was a falsehood, why did your cousin not denounce the accusation as such?"

"I cannot answer for my cousin. To know his reasons you would need to ask him. But I *can* say Darcy is a gentleman down to the tips of his toes. He would never slander another; no matter how justified others might believe the action to be. I am certain he also remembers the time when he and Wickham were friends. As young boys at Pemberley they would play together. I believe it was my cousin's dearest wish that his erstwhile friend had joined the militia with the intention of mending his ways."

Fitzwilliam was saved from any further questioning, or being required to give any more explanations for Darcy's dour behaviour, by the arrival of a young officer.

"Ah, Captain Braithwaite, thank you for joining us. Please close the door; what I have to say requires discretion. Has Lieutenant Wickham left yet?"

"Yes, Sir, he departed immediately."

"Colonel," Fitzwilliam interrupted, "I believe there is little point in asking the captain any further questions regarding Mr Wickham, for I would be very surprised if you ever see the man again." Captain Braithwaite looked shocked but Colonel Forster merely sighed.

"Let me guess, Colonel," he said with resignation, "he has no uncle."

"No, and Mrs Younge's connection to Wickham is much more carnal than that of an aunt. I would be surprised if *Mrs* Younge was ever married, I believe she uses the title for respectability's sake at the boarding house she runs in Islington. Do you know that the express was definitely from her?"

"I only saw the express held tightly in his fist." The colonel then looked questioningly at his captain.

Braithwaite shook his head. "Lieutenant Walker was with him when he opened it, he might have seen its contents."

"Well do not just stand there!" Colonel Forster roared. "Go and find out."

Braithwaite returned ten minutes later and reported his findings. Walker did not see the whole message but as Wickham went to fold it, he did see the beginning of the last line. The words 'I need you' were quite clear; so was the signature of Susanna Younge.

"Well, as I said, Colonel, I do not think you will see Wickham again. He has been in the neighbourhood for about five months?" Colonel Forster gave a nod of agreement. "Then he has had plenty of time to accrue quite a few debts, not to mention debts of honour. I appear on the scene and then he receives a letter from Mrs Younge, making some demand, which gave him the opportunity to quit the area. Yes I believe our bird has flown. Unfortunately, because of his cleverness, he cannot be classed as absent without leave until the ninth of April, by which time he could be anywhere."

Fitzwilliam had seen the look of dismay on Braithwaite's face. "I am afraid, Mr Braithwaite, there never was much chance of you getting any money owed to you back from Wickham." Fitzwilliam turned his attention back to Colonel Forster, perhaps he could give the young officer some small glimmer of hope. "Colonel, can you discover the amount Mr Wickham owes to his fellow officers from his time at the tables. There is a possibility that my cousin will purchase his vowels."

Fitzwilliam thanked the colonel for his time and quickly made his way to the bookshop where Mr Bennet was waiting for him. Mr Bennet had agreed to accompany Fitzwilliam when he called on the tradesmen that Wickham might have had dealings with, as Fitzwilliam wished to know the full amount that Wickham owed in Meryton. Mr Bennet had decided that the bookshop was the best place to loiter while Fitzwilliam spoke with Colonel Forster.

As they began to call on the merchants of Meryton, Fitzwilliam could see the chance of an early return to town disappearing before his eyes. *'Damn Wickham.'*

Chapter 10

The church bell struck the third hour as Fitzwilliam and Bennet walked out of the tailor's shop. There were still two more shopkeepers to call on as well as the publican, Fitzwilliam had no doubt that was where the largest debt would lie. The number of bills owing was increasing with every premises they entered; the amount owing in Meryton alone would be enough to put Wickham in a debtors' prison for the foreseeable future. The thought of Wickham in a place like Marshalsea brought a faint curve of a smile to Fitzwilliam's lips before he continued to think of his plans for the rest of the day—plans that now made returning to Darcy House that day highly unlikely. *'Damn Wickham!'*

"Are there rooms for rent at the White Horse?"

Bennet frowned. "Yes."

"I believe it will be too late for me to return to town today before darkness falls. I must also send an express to Darcy and another to Miss Bennet; I would not like either to worry about my delayed return."

"You must stay at Longbourn. My wife would never forgive me if she learnt you spent the night at Mr Snelgrove's establishment."

The thought of spending the evening in the company of Mrs Bennet and her silly younger daughters did not appeal, but he reminded himself the lady would soon be his mother and therefore deserving of his consideration. "Thank you, Mr Bennet," he replied with a smile. "I am grateful to accept your hospitality."

"Let us briefly return to Longbourn. You can write your missives and while you do I will inform Mrs Bennet that you will be our guest for the night."

Darcy had decided they would not depart for Rosings until the following morning. Dr Morgan's journey had been long and tiring; he had the look of a man who had not slept properly in days. The doctor needed a good night's rest before arriving to deal with his new patient. This would also give Elizabeth, and Georgiana who had insisted on accompanying them, plenty of time to pack the little that would be needed for a brief stay at Rosings. He had called on Elizabeth that afternoon to make arrangements for the journey, now he was back at Darcy House making preparations for their departure. Just as he was about to leave his study to join Georgiana for their evening meal an express arrived. He was not best pleased with either the contents or the fact that he would not have a chance to speak with Fitzwilliam until he returned from Rosings.

The following morning Darcy informed his butler that the colonel should return to Darcy House that day and asked the man to inform his cousin of his and Georgiana's whereabouts, and his intention to return as soon as possible, hopefully the following day. Then with his sister at his side, and Georgiana's maid and the doctor following behind them, he helped Georgiana into his carriage so they could be on their way to Gracechurch Street before continuing on to Kent. The journey would not be rushed for the sake of the ladies. Darcy did have some concerns; the main one being what would his aunt's response be to Miss Elizabeth? While Darcy watched his sister and the woman he hoped to marry converse so warmly he made up his mind; if his aunt did not treat Miss Elizabeth Bennet with the respect due to her, their visit to Rosings would be very short indeed.

Thursday 2nd April

Colonel Fitzwilliam's return to London was again delayed. Originally he had planned to be away soon after dawn, but the evening spent in the sole company of his host had been fruitful. As soon as they had broken their fast the gentlemen had called on Mr Philips, in his role as Mr Bennet's solicitor, to witness the signing of the marriage settlement.

Fitzwilliam eventually arrived at Darcy House to discover he had the house to himself. He ordered hot water for a bath and a light repast to be brought to his room. Once bathed and refreshed from the journey he would make his way to Gracechurch Street without any further delay.

Jane had been disappointed when she received the letter from Richard. Yes he had assured her that her parents were pleased with their betrothal, but gave no indication as to the reason for his delay in returning to town. She was relieved that her father had given his blessing, but she would still worry until she had a chance to speak to Richard. Jane suddenly let out a light laugh, which caused her aunt to give her a quizzical look.

"I fear, dear Aunt, that if my thoughts are anything to go by I am starting to suffer with my mother's nerves." Both ladies laughed at that thought.

"If Milly is available to accompany me, do you think the boys would enjoy a walk in the park while Patience and Faith have their nap?"

"I am sure they would, if you really wish to take them," her aunt replied. At Jane's smile and slight nod of her head, Mrs Gardiner left the room to find Milly and prepare her two eldest children for a trip to the park. That was where Richard Fitzwilliam found his dear Jane nearly an hour later.

"Colonel Fitzwilliam," cried Matthew with joy, "have you come to play with us?" Frederick squealed and, clutching the reins of his hobby horse tightly in his hand, ran as fast as he could to the colonel's side. Jane turned around on hearing Matthew call out. A wide smile instantly appeared on her face and she too made her way to the man she loved.

Colonel Fitzwilliam met Jane's smile with one of his own, just as bright, just as heartfelt. "I am delighted to see you again, Miss Bennet."

Jane's eyes twinkled with warmth. "I am pleased to see you too, Colonel. I trust your journey was uneventful?"

"Indeed, thank you. Your parents were well when I left and both send you their love. Your mother is eager for you to return to Longbourn with all haste, but Mrs Bennet was persuaded that you should remain here for the nonce as she agreed that having your wedding gown made by the modiste of the Countess of Matlock was an opportunity not to be missed."

"Mama did not mind that she would have no say in my gown?" This did not sound at all like her mother.

Fitzwilliam laughed. "Ah well, not exactly, but with a little persuasion she agreed that the choice of a countess would be all that is fashionable."

Matthew and Frederick stood nearby; both tried to be patient while their cousin and the colonel spoke, but Frederick was finding it harder and harder. The skirt surrounding the frame of his hobby horse swished in the breeze as he started to jump up and down. Jane looked in his direction and smiled. Fitzwilliam also glanced at the young boy and quietly sighed, there would be no more conversation between them until two small boys had run off their energy; he remembered those days of his youth, impatiently waiting for adults to finish their conversation so the games could begin. He looked at Jane once more, smiled and then turned back to the boys.

"Those are fine horses you have, gentlemen." Both boys jumped to attention as he spoke.

"Thank you, Colonel," replied Matthew. "We saw a hobby horse with the Morris Dancers last summer. Papa, with Mama's help, kindly made us one each. Papa's friend, Mr Miller, made the heads for us. He is a fine carpenter."

"Yes, I can see he is. They are very fine hobby horses indeed."

The boys were delighted at the praise their horses received from the colonel.

"Gentlemen, I believe it is time we put these fine steeds through their paces."

While Colonel Richard Fitzwilliam was commanding his newest recruits, much to their young delight and Jane's admiration, his mother was entering Darcy House.

Lady Matlock had decided to call on her nephew and son before going to Matlock House. She was most disappointed to be told by the ever efficient Carlton that the Darcys were away from home and not expected to return until the next day, or the day after.

"And my son? Has the colonel accompanied his cousins?" Lady Matlock thought that most likely the case. The disappointment she felt at not meeting Miss Bennet until her son returned from Rosings disappeared like a morning mist at Carlton's reply.

"No, my Lady. I believe the colonel has gone to Gracechurch Street to call on Miss Bennet."

After enquiring as to the number of the house in Gracechurch Street, Lady Matlock thanked the butler and walked back to her carriage. "Matlock House, Martins."

The coachman touched his hat and once her ladyship was seated, and the door to the carriage firmly closed, Martins flicked the reins and the horses began the final short journey to the town house of the Earl of Matlock.

Once refreshed, Lady Matlock sat at her bureau and wrote a short note. She dried the ink, folded the missive neatly and sealed it, before calling for a servant to arrange its immediate delivery. When the note was safely on its way she called for her housekeeper and cook to attend her.

Fitzwilliam enjoyed calling at the Gardiners' residence. He liked the couple immensely. Gardiner had a dry humour and could easily be mistaken for a gentleman of the ton. He clearly loved his wife and family; Fitzwilliam could tell it was the Gardiners' influence on the lives of Jane and Elizabeth that had helped to mould them into the kind and caring young ladies they were. On their return from the park, the now exhausted children went immediately to the nursery. Mrs Gardiner arranged for refreshments, while Jane and Fitzwilliam entered the drawing room. Once assured that they were alone, Richard held out his arms to Jane. She moved closer to him and his arms surrounded her, moulding her to him. He bent his head and kissed her forehead; she let out a soft sigh and rested her head against his firm chest. "It is truly settled?" she asked.

Fitzwilliam was in heaven. The woman he loved was in his arms and they would marry by the end of the month. "Yes, my love. We will marry on the twenty-seventh. Your father was going to call on the vicar of St John's after I departed this morning to secure the date of the wedding and arrange the reading of the Banns."

"Poor mama, she must be so disappointed that I am not there, though I am sure that will not stop her calling on the neighbours to share our good news."

Fitzwilliam heard footsteps in the passage. Planting another soft kiss on his beloved's forehead he released her and took a step back before the door opened. Mrs Gardiner entered with a maid following closely behind. She placed a tray containing refreshments on the small circular tea table, bobbed a quick curtsy and left the room closing the door behind her. Mrs Gardiner raised an eyebrow slightly as she looked at the colonel but made no comment; instead she invited the colonel to sit and poured him a cup of tea.

When Jane asked why he had been delayed in returning to town the previous day, Richard could not lie as much as he wanted to protect her from the evils of the world. Both Jane and Mrs Gardiner were horrified and shocked to hear of Wickham's behaviour, and Fitzwilliam was glad when he could change the subject and talk of pleasanter things. The conversation had just turned to the imminent arrival of Lady Matlock to town when the butler entered the room.

"Excuse me Ma'am, but there is a letter for the colonel."

Fitzwilliam stood and took the missive from Davies' outstretched hand, thanking him as he did so. He looked at the writing and smiled, shaking his head as he returned to his seat.

"It would appear my mother has arrived."

He broke the seal and unfolding the letter, lifted it to read. A muffled laugh escaped his closed lips. "Jane, my mother is so eager to meet you that she asks me to invite you, along with your uncle and aunt, to dine with us at Matlock House this evening. There will be just the five of us as mother is tired from her long journey, but she writes, '*I cannot wait another day before meeting my future daughter.*' As it is such short notice, Mrs Gardiner, I am sure my mother will understand if it is not convenient."

"Of course we would be delighted to dine with Lady Matlock. I will send a note to my husband to make sure he does not tarry this evening."

"Thank you, Mrs Gardiner. I know my mother will be delighted." He stood before continuing. "Now I had best leave so that you can both rest before this evening." The look he sent Jane's way pleaded with her to walk with him to the door. But Mrs Gardiner stood before Jane could rise from her seat or say anything.

"I will leave Jane to see you out, Colonel. I must write to my husband informing him of this evening's engagement." She gave a slight curtsy and walked quickly from the room.

Fitzwilliam took Jane's hand in his. "Have I told you how much I like your aunt? She is a wonderful woman."

Jane laughed lightly, her eyes smiling with joy, as Fitzwilliam pulled her once again into his embrace for one last sweet kiss before they parted.

With two lengthy stops, to rest the horses and allow those riding in the carriage time to refresh and partake in some light refreshments, the journey to Rosings took longer than usual for Darcy. Not that he minded. It was in fact the most enjoyable journey to Rosings he could ever remember.

Dr Morgan spent most of the journey with his eyes closed, though Darcy doubted the man slept unlike Georgiana's maid who, within five minutes of the carriage moving, fell into a restful sleep like an infant being rocked in a cradle. The sun was still in the sky but lower in the west, as

Darcy's carriage rolled through the ornate gates and made its way up the long driveway towards Rosings.

"Good afternoon, Aunt," Darcy said as he walked into the drawing room. Walking up to his aunt he bent and gave her a light kiss on her cheek. "Lady Catherine, may I introduce Dr Morgan?"

Lady Catherine turned to look at the gentleman who stood a few feet away. He was not what she had expected. "Dr Morgan?"

"Yes, my Lady."

"I expected someone older." Her voice was laced with scorn.

"I assure you, Lady Catherine, I have had many years of experience in my chosen profession. One and twenty to be precise."

Lady Catherine glared at the doctor's impertinent response. "That is as may be. But, are you any good at your occupation? My nephew, Colonel Fitzwilliam, assures me that you are quite competent and will be able to help my daughter." It was a statement but Morgan understood a question that lay beneath.

"I will do my best, Lady Catherine. Though I must warn you," compassion filled the doctor's voice, "your daughter's condition will worsen before it improves. The opium contained within the laudanum is extremely addictive. Depending on how long the young lady has been under its influence, how much she consumes each day and therefore how reliant she is on it, to withdraw the drug, no matter how slowly, will cause the patient distress." At Lady Catherine's gasp, he continued quickly before she could utter any words of dismissal. "It is unfortunately a necessary distress, for to continue on this current path will without doubt lead to more distress when your daughter's life is snuffed out. And," Morgan said with a sigh, "the opium will not allow a peaceful death."

Lady Catherine said nothing as she gave a sharp nod of her head. A moment later she enquired, "Do you wish to refresh from your journey, or would you like to see your patient first?"

"I should like a few minutes to rid myself of the dirt of the road, then I would be pleased to meet Miss de Bourgh."

With another nod Lady Catherine rang the silver bell which sat on the small table beside her chair. A footman immediately entered the room and on receiving his mistress' instruction turned to the doctor. Dr Morgan bowed before following the servant from the room.

"And you, Nephew." Lady Catherine turned her gaze to Darcy. "Will you remain a day or two, or are you back to town immediately?"

"I will remain for the night at least, as I have brought Georgiana and Miss Bennet with me."

"Georgiana *and* Miss Bennet?" the lady admonished. "Miss Bennet?"

"Miss Elizabeth Bennet, the young lady I am courting. Georgiana, on hearing of Anne's ill health, expressed a wish to see her cousin. Miss Bennet was greatly concerned for her friend Mrs Collins and wished to see with her own eyes that the lady is well. She feared for her friend on her marriage to Collins and believes herself responsible for any distress Mrs Collins may have suffered."

"How could Miss Bennet possibly be responsible for any fate that befell Mrs Collins?"

"Miss Bennet refused her cousin's offer of marriage." Darcy shuddered at the thought of his Elizabeth being tied to such a man.

"Sensible girl," Lady Catherine muttered, not meaning for her nephew to hear her words.

"Quite," he replied.

"So where are Miss Bennet and my niece?"

"Mrs Snell took them to a chamber so they could refresh themselves after the journey, while rooms are prepared for them. They will join us in a moment I am sure."

It was not many minutes later when the door open and the butler, with his gravelly voice, announced, "Miss Darcy and Miss Bennet, my Lady."

Darcy turned from his aunt; a broad smile warmed his countenance as the young ladies entered the room. He walked up to them and offered his arm to Elizabeth. Georgiana smiled at her brother and then walked up to Lady Catherine, curtsied and greeted her aunt. Darcy walked Elizabeth to where his aunt was sitting. "Aunt Catherine, may I introduce Miss Elizabeth Bennet?"

"Miss Elizabeth, this is my mother's sister, Lady Catherine de Bourgh."

Elizabeth dropped into a neat curtsey. "Lady Catherine," she said, lifting her head as she rose.

Lady Catherine's bright blue eyes examined the young woman in front of her. First the doctor and now this buxom chit; Miss Bennet was not at all what Lady Catherine had expected. She had had plenty of time, since her nephews told her of their courtships with the Bennet sisters, to decide on what kind of woman had trapped her sister's son, the nephew she had hoped beyond all else to one day call son. Her mind had imagined a pretty young thing, classically beautiful, a Lady in every way. Instead the young girl in front of her barely reached her nephew's shoulders. The long imagined blonde with china blue eyes, a faultless porcelain complexion and slender proportions, faded at the reality. Lady Catherine looked at the lively brown eyes that held her gaze. The young woman her nephew had chosen would never be called a beauty in the eyes of the ton, she was too short and her figure too shapely. But Lady Catherine saw the intelligence and determination in the depths of those brown eyes and knew what had drawn her nephew to Miss Bennet.

"Miss Bennet, I believe you and my nephew are courting?"

"Yes, Lady Catherine."

"You are not what I expected."

Elizabeth's brow rose slightly, but her eyes danced as her mind pondered on whether to be flattered or annoyed at Lady Catherine's remark. Darcy frowned at his aunt.

"Oh do not look so disapproving, Darcy." Lady Catherine's eyes moved back to Elizabeth.

"Do you play, Miss Bennet?"

"A little, my Lady, although not as well as my sister Mary."

"Do you embroider, Miss Bennet?"

"Yes, I do. But not so well as my sister Jane. She has more patience than I, so her stitches are much neater than my humble attempts."

"Do you paint, Miss Bennet?"

Elizabeth decided to bring an end to Lady Catherine's enquiries about her accomplishments. "No, Lady Catherine. My sister Kitty is the artist in our family. I like to broaden my mind with extensive reading." She glanced at Darcy and smiled. "I also enjoy a game of chess with my father."

"Chess!" Lady Catherine cried. "How extraordinary."

"Extraordinary, my Lady? I had not thought it so, for it is only a game of tactics. I enjoy pitting my wits against another. I believe the exercise will bode well when dealing with people from all levels of standing. I am grateful for the varied education my father has allowed me. It may have not been conventional, my sisters and I did not have a governess, but if any of us wished to broaden our horizons my father gave us the books and encouraged us to read."

"That kind of education is of no use to a Lady."

"I fear I must disagree, Lady Catherine," Elizabeth replied. "All learning is of use. A fondness for reading, if properly directed, must be an education in itself. My father simply wished to broaden our education so that his daughters would be able to converse on a variety of subjects. My mother ensured that my sisters and I knew how to lay a good table and all the other necessities for running a household successfully. She was determined that no gentleman would regret having one of her daughters as the chatelaine of his home."

"You are decidedly outspoken for one so young!" Lady Catherine retorted.

Elizabeth simply smiled, making no comment. Then, much to Darcy's surprise Lady Catherine turned to him. "I see you have chosen to court a young lady who knows her own mind."

Darcy's lips curved up in a smile as his eyes met Elizabeth's. "Indeed, Aunt."

"Humph," was all that Lady Catherine uttered as she picked up the silver bell to summons her butler.

"Diplock, it is time for refreshments. Ask Mrs Collins to join us; the doctor as well, if he is able. I believe they are both with Miss de Bourgh." Lady Catherine then turned her attention back to Elizabeth. "Have you seen your friend yet, Miss Bennet?"

"No, Lady Catherine, but I am eager to do so."

When Elizabeth retired that night she sat on a chair by the window and, looking out at the moonlit garden below, thought back on the day.

Charlotte was well. Elizabeth had not spent much time with her friend but the little time she had spent had alleviated her most pressing concerns; she hoped to spend more time in Charlotte's company on the morrow. Elizabeth was grateful that Lady Catherine had given Charlotte shelter at Rosings. Her friend was happy to help with the care of Miss de Bourgh and she was happy to become a second companion even though it would only be for a short time, while Miss de Bourgh was under Dr Morgan's care. Elizabeth had been shocked when she had met Anne de Bourgh; the young lady looked so ill that Elizabeth wondered if she would ever be well.

She may not have been what Lady Catherine expected, but, by the end of the evening, Elizabeth decided that Lady Catherine was not what she had expected either. Charlotte had written about the advice that her husband's patron constantly gave her. Darcy had told Elizabeth of his aunt's wishes regarding the uniting of Rosings and Pemberley and her desire to have her way in all things. Elizabeth let out a small laugh has she thought of Georgiana's words. *'Aunt Catherine is a tyrant, but she must never know I said that.'*

'Lady Catherine is not a tyrant,' Elizabeth mused as she thought back on their conversations. *'She is a Lady who knows her own mind. She has her opinions and is not afraid to speak them. I believe she wants the best for her daughter, which sometimes causes her words or actions to upset others. She called me opinionated, but so is she. I wonder if her mother ever called her impertinent when she was a young girl.'*

The clouds slowly masked the moon and its clear light dimmed. Elizabeth stood and made her way to the bed. Feeling the chill of the night air, she wrapped the blankets around her and soon fell into a deep sleep.

Chapter 11

Edward Gardiner was one of the most prominent traders in London. His import and export business thrived, and his yearly income now greatly surpassed his expectations. The house in Gracechurch Street was becoming too small for his growing family and Gardiner was in the process of purchasing a new home for his wife and children in a more fashionable area, more suitable for the gentleman he hoped to be one day. For Gardiner's long-term plan, which was progressing much better than he had ever envisaged, was that by the time he reached the age of five and forty he would sell his business and purchase an estate—preferably near his dear wife's beloved childhood village of Lambton.

As his carriage conveyed them to Matlock House, Gardiner spent the time worrying. Jane's father might be a gentleman, but he was not in the higher circles of the ton. Would having an uncle in trade be too much for the Countess of Matlock to bear, no matter what her son's wishes might be?

Gardiner's concerns started to ease when, as they entered a charming room and the colonel introduced Jane to his mother, the lady in question smiled warmly at his niece and cried, "My dear Miss Bennet, it is such a pleasure to meet you." She then turned her attention to the Gardiners. "Mr Gardiner, and Mrs Gardiner, welcome to my home and thank you so much for agreeing, at such short notice, to join me this evening."

"The pleasure is ours, Lady Matlock," Mr Gardiner replied.

Dinner was an enjoyable event and although Fitzwilliam did not wish for a separation, his mother would not hear of forgoing the tradition. He knew the reason had nothing to do with 'tradition' but everything to do with speaking to Miss Bennet away from his company. Fitzwilliam reluctantly agreed when his mother had broached the subject earlier. The countess wanted time alone with Jane to be able to converse without her son's interference and as Fitzwilliam wanted his mother's approval of his future wife, he found himself sitting at the table with Jane's uncle when the ladies made their way to the drawing room.

As the gentlemen drank their port, conversation turned to that of houses. Fitzwilliam was interested to hear of Gardiner's own search, especially when he mentioned that there were a couple of decent properties for rent or sale in the area of Russell Square. On hearing that Gardiner had already put in an offer for one of them, Fitzwilliam decided to view the other and asked Gardiner for the Duke of Bedford's agent's directions. The thought of owning a house nearby to Jane's favourite aunt and uncle pleased him greatly; it would be gratifying to know that she was not far from the Gardiners when service to his country took him abroad.

It pleased Mr Gardiner too, so he offered to accompany Fitzwilliam to the agent's offices and to the property if he so desired. Fitzwilliam was pleased to accept the older man's offer and they lost no time in arranging to meet the following morning.

In the drawing room Lady Matlock was enjoying herself. For the first time, in what felt like a very long time, her mind was occupied with things other than her husband's continued ill-health and the burden that placed on her eldest son, said son's inability to find a wife and the constant strain of keeping her husband's true illness a secret. Fitzwilliam had told her that the two elder Miss Bennets and their relatives, the Gardiners, were aware of what really ailed Lord Matlock; he also assured his mother that the secret was safe with them. Lady Matlock knew that was true as although both Mrs Gardiner and Miss Bennet had said how sorry they were to hear that Lord Matlock had been struck down by a nasty summer cold, neither made any mention of the real reason her husband remained at their country estate.

Although Fitzwilliam had told Jane repeatedly that his mother would adore her, she had worried that Lady Matlock may not think her a suitable bride for the son of an earl. Jane had been quiet at the beginning of the evening but Lady Matlock's warmness helped calm her worries and, by the time the gentlemen re-joined the ladies, Fitzwilliam was greeted with the sight of the three ladies deep in conversation.

As he and Gardiner walked up to the ladies, Fitzwilliam overhead his mother saying, "But of course the boy dawdled so much that he has lost out to another." Lady Matlock looked up at that point and saw her son and Mr Gardiner. Noticing the questioning frown on her son's countenance she realized he probably did not know. "I am afraid, Richard, your brother took so long to decide if he would offer for Lady Arabella that the Marquis of Riding beat him to it. Sebastian returned to Trentavon three days before I departed; he will remain there for some time, as there is much to do in the way of estate business." Lady Matlock turned back to Jane. "He is looking forward to meeting you, my dear, but fears it will not be until the

.

wedding. But," she said as she glanced back at her son, "he wishes you both joy. Now I think it is time for a nice cup of tea before we make arrangements for a visit to my modiste. As Mrs Gardiner insists that she and your uncle will pay for your wedding gown, I insist that I am allowed to purchase your ball gown."

"Ball gown?" questioned Fitzwilliam.

"Why yes, of course," his mother replied. "Jane will need a new gown for the Ball I am organising to celebrate your marriage. Jane and I decided two days after your wedding would be a good date. I can then leave for Derbyshire early on the Thursday and will arrive at Trentavon before the Sabbath."

Fitzwilliam heard a quiet laugh behind him, turned and saw Gardiner's smiling eyes.

The rest of the evening passed enjoyably. Jane was nearly asleep by the time her uncle's carriage arrived back at Gracechurch Street.

As they entered the house Mr Gardiner told his wife and niece of his plans for the following morning. Jane's sleepiness fled as she took in her uncle's words. The thought that she and Fitzwilliam might have a town house within walking distance of the Gardiners new home thrilled her immensely.

"Will you have need of the carriage," Mrs Gardiner inquired of her husband.

"Do you need it, my dear? If so I can easily take a hackney."

"That would be most kind if you do not mind. I have told Lady Matlock that Jane and I will call for her tomorrow morning."

"Ah yes, of course, your visit to Lady Matlock's modiste. I am sure you will have a lovely time, Jane, but please try not to bankrupt me in the process." His niece was about to retort that she would never dream of such a thing, when she was halted by the teasing gleam she saw in her uncle's eyes.

Madame Marron's establishment was situated in an advantageous position in New Bond Street. It was eleven o'clock when the Countess of Matlock entered the shop with Jane and Mrs Gardiner close behind her.

"Lady Matlock, welcome." A lady in her late forties, elegantly dressed and quite handsome, walked into the room. The curtain separating the front of the shop had swung back into place after she had passed through it. Two assistants stood close by. Madame Marron looked at Jane as Lady Matlock introduced her soon to be daughter and Mrs Gardiner to the modiste.

While Lady Matlock and Mrs Gardiner discussed fabrics with Madame Marron in a secluded area, Jane sat on a chaise longue with a large book of patterns beside her. She slowly turned the pages, entranced by the beautiful designs before her. The bell above the shop door rang causing Jane to glance up. Her breath caught as she watched Miss Bingley and Mrs Hurst enter the room. One of the shop's assistants walked quickly to the ladies. Jane wondered how much more uncomfortable the day could become.

The young assistant hurried off and Mrs Hurst followed her sister further into the room, nearly colliding with Caroline as she suddenly came to a halt.

"Why Miss Bennet, what a surprise," Miss Bingley cried, the tone of her voice gave credence that it was indeed a surprise, though not necessarily a pleasant one. "Have you been in town for long?"

"Just a few months, since the new year, but time has passed so quickly, Miss Bingley, that it hardly seems possible." Jane's confidence and her ability to see others for what they really were had grown considerably since meeting the colonel. His mother had only added to that confidence. "I trust your family is well. Have you returned to town for the season, Miss Bingley? I had heard you were in Yorkshire."

Miss Bingley briefly wondered where Miss Bennet had garnered that information from. "Yes, we were visiting friends in the country. I suppose you must be staying with your uncle in Cheapside?" Her voice dripped with disdain. "I am surprised to see you in this establishment."

Having decided on a selection of fabrics that they believed would suit Jane well, Lady Matlock and Mrs Gardiner made their way back to Jane so that a final decision could be made on the fabric and pattern before the tedious task of measuring began.

Miss Bingley only noticed the middle-aged woman walking towards Jane, and not the elegant older lady who followed.

Neither Miss Bingley nor Mrs Hurst had ever met the Countess of Matlock. As much as Miss Bingley wished to be part of the upper echelons of the ton, she was not. It was only her brother's friendship with Fitzwilliam Darcy that had permitted her to dip her toes into the sea of London's haut ton. So it was that Miss Bingley was unaware that the lady, who she disregarded along with Mrs Gardiner, was the dear aunt of the gentleman she was planning to marry.

Lady Matlock looked between the young women and her soon to be daughter; it did not take her long to see the hostility that the younger woman had towards Jane and her aunt. "Jane, my dear, will you not introduce your friends to us?"

Caroline Bingley looked at the woman she had dismissed as no one of any importance, but both the tone of her voice and her deportment spoke of breeding. No sooner had that thought penetrated her mind when Caroline dismissed it as impossible, for how could Miss Bennet and her relatives of Cheapside know anyone of importance. So lost was she in her ruminations that she failed to hear the beginning of Jane's introduction. It was only her sister's gasp that brought her back to the present.

"…Gardiner, may I introduce Miss Bingley and Mrs Hurst? They are the sisters of Mr Bingley, the gentleman who leased Netherfield Park, an estate near my father's, last Michaelmas."

"Ah yes, my son told me about that young man." Lady Matlock turned her hard gaze to Miss Bingley and her sister, but said nothing more. With the swish of the curtains Madame Marron entered. "Miss Bingley, Mrs Hurst, good morning. My assistant tells me you wish to see me. As you can no doubt see I am busy at present, but if you would care to return in an hour or so, I am sure I will be free to serve you then."

Caroline's mien radiated anger, but before she could open her mouth to complain Louisa took hold of her arm. "Yes, Madame Marron, I believe your suggestion would be an excellent one. We will depart so that you can continue to serve Lady Matlock's party.

As her sister's words registered, Caroline let out a gasp. No, it was impossible.

"Lady Matlock." Louisa curtsied and, not loosening her grip on her sister's arm, forced Caroline to curtsey with her. "Miss Bennet, it was a pleasure to see you again," Louisa continued. "Mrs Gardiner." She bowed her head to Jane's aunt before half guiding and half pulling her sister out of the door.

"Oh Caroline, how could you?" Louisa cried, once they were away from the modiste's salon. "How could you openly cut Lady Matlock so?"

"How was I to know? Mr Darcy has not yet introduced us to his aunt." Her tone indicated that that error lay firmly with the gentleman. "Why would a countess be in the company of Miss Bennet and her *Cheapside* relation, when everyone believes she and the earl are at their country estate? How did Miss Bennet manage to worm her way into such company? Surely Mr Darcy does not approve. We will have to call at Darcy House; it has been an age since we have been in the company of Miss Darcy and Mr Darcy, I am sure they will be delighted to see us. Come, Louisa, do not dawdle." Caroline turned and walked quickly to their carriage.

It really was not Miss Bingley's day. When their carriage arrived at Darcy House they discovered that the knocker was not on the door. Caroline Bingley fumed all the way back to the Hursts' town house. Caroline decided that she would need to question her brother; he was Darcy's friend after all and so would be sure to know where Mr Darcy was and when the Darcys were likely to return to town. There too she would be disappointed, for although Charles knew of Darcy's visit to Rosings with his cousin, he had no notion as to where Miss Darcy might be.

After the departure of Mrs Hurst and Miss Bingley, Jane started to enjoy the day again. She eventually decided on the designs for both her wedding gown and her ball gown; her aunt, Lady Matlock and Madame Marron all approved of her choice. Lady Matlock was particularly pleased at Jane's ability to know what would suit and complement her to the best advantage. Mrs Gardiner had brought some swatches of silk with her and when Jane had been unable to find the colour she wished for, Mrs Gardiner had pulled out the small fabric squares from her reticule. Madame Marron commented on the fineness of the silks and how well the delicate colours would suit the young lady. On enquiring where Mrs Gardiner had acquired them, the modiste was surprised that they came from Mr Gardiner's warehouse. With the decision made that the silks for the gowns would come from Mr Gardiner, there were only the measurements left to be taken before the ladies could depart to a nearby tea shop to partake in well-earned tea and pastries. By the time Jane left the salon, she felt as though she had been measured to within an inch of her life.

As they sat drinking tea, Lady Matlock and Mrs Gardiner both praised Jane for her choice of gowns and fabrics.

"Your wedding gown is so stylish, with a slight alteration to the mull cape you will be able to wear it as a ball gown in the future," Lady Matlock commented.

"I do not know what Mama will say when she sees it. I fear she will not be happy."

"Why ever not? It will be a lovely gown," the countess exclaimed.

"I agree, Lady Matlock, but my sister is a great believer in lace," Mrs Gardiner said and then smiled at her niece. "Your mother will recover from her disappointment. I believe your choice is the right one. You will make a beautiful bride."

"Indeed," Lady Matlock agreed, "and my son will fall in love with you all over again." Lady Matlock and Mrs Gardiner laughed, as Jane dropped her eyes to her plate and blushed.

When Darcy woke the following morning he was sure that both Georgiana and Elizabeth would be happy to depart as soon as they had broken their fast. He felt without doubt that now Elizabeth had seen her friend and knew that Mrs Collins was well, she would want to return to her uncle's house and the company of her sister as soon as might be. So he was somewhat taken aback—nearly choking on his coffee—when he had broached the subject with Elizabeth and she replied with all innocence that she wished to spend more time with her friend Charlotte; she felt it would be discourteous to depart when not even a full day had passed since their arrival. Darcy had no time to argue the point before the door opened and his aunt walked into the room.

"Nephew, I am surprised to see you here. I thought you would have been away at dawn, now that your *duty* is done."

"No, Aunt. Although we will need to leave promptly tomorrow morning as I am hosting a dinner in the evening, Miss Bennet wishes to remain a while longer. I will use the time to speak with Hellyer again, unless there is anything else you wish me to do?"

Darcy was surprised by the frown on his aunt's brow as she replied, "No, by all means spend the time with my steward." Lady Catherine then turned her gaze to Elizabeth. "And, Miss Bennet, what do you intend to do with yourself."

Elizabeth smiled. "I would like to spend some time with Charlotte, if it is at all possible. I realize she will be busy with Miss de Bourgh, and I would not wish to take her away from your daughter's needs, but I am hopeful there might be some time when she and I will be able to converse. I would also like to spend some time with you, my lady, if you are agreeable. Family is very important to me and you are Mr Darcy's aunt, part of his family. If things should progress the way they usually do in such circumstances then I will also be part of that family."

Seeing the stern look in Lady Catherine's eyes, Elizabeth wondered if she may have said too much. So she was astonished when Lady Catherine's countenance softened.

"I would like that Miss Bennet. I must speak with my housekeeper but perhaps we could meet in the parlour at eleven o'clock. That should give you time to see Charlotte before Dr Morgan requires her. It appears to be a nice morning, you and Charlotte should take a stroll in the gardens, I am sure the fresh air will do you both good. Anne's maid can stay with her in the meantime."

Elizabeth was not the only one surprised by Lady Catherine's reply, Darcy was too. He could scarce believe that his aunt, who up until now had been adamant that Darcy would marry her daughter, had not only agreed to spend time with Elizabeth but had spoken cordially to her.

"Where is Georgiana?"

Darcy looked to his aunt at her question. It was a good question—where was Georgiana? But before he could make a reply, Elizabeth answered.

"I looked in on Georgiana before coming down. She was still sleepy, so I suggested that she broke her fast in her room and joined us later."

Darcy looked at Elizabeth and attempted not to smile. *So my sister would have been your second argument if I had not complied with your request.*

Elizabeth glanced at Darcy and, seeing his lips firmly shut but his eyes alight with laughter, she smiled brightly. "As I have finished, Lady Catherine, and if it is agreeable with you, I will search out Charlotte and suggest we stroll in your beautiful gardens."

Lady Catherine gave a nod of agreement, so Elizabeth curtsied and quickly made her way out of the room.

Elizabeth decided that walking around the garden, arm in arm with her dear friend, was just what both she and Charlotte needed. They spoke of Mr Collins; Charlotte refused to let Elizabeth feel any guilt for her marriage to the man.

"No, my dear Eliza, you had more sense than I. As much as I do not wish to speak ill of the dead you saw Mr Collins for what he truly was, whereas I refused to believe you when you tried to warn me. No Eliza, you must not worry. Besides it is all over. Mr Collins is dead and I am happy in my new position with Lady Catherine. She has been most kind and understanding of my wish not to return, as yet, to my father's house. At Easter she discovered what kind of man my husband was and does not expect me to mourn him deeply, if I returned to Lucas Lodge it would be expected and I would feel hypocritical to pretend that I grieved for a man I had no respect for. Now let us speak of more pleasant things, like your courtship with Mr Darcy." Charlotte smiled warmly at her friend. "Eliza, you simply must tell me all, your letter at Easter was not detailed enough."

Elizabeth laughed and started to tell Charlotte all about her meeting Georgiana, learning the truth about Mr Wickham and her subsequent meeting with Mr Darcy. They spoke for over an hour, until Elizabeth looked up at the sky and noticed the position of the sun. "Oh, I must return to the house. I promised to meet with Lady Catherine at eleven o'clock. What will she think of my tardiness?"

Elizabeth was quite out of breath when she entered the parlour.

"Ah there you are, Miss Bennet. Why you look quite flushed. Are you well?"

"Yes, Lady Catherine, but I feared I was late for our meeting and so walked quite quickly. Charlotte and I had such a pleasant time walking the gardens that I am afraid that time got away from me."

Darcy had hoped to be away from Rosings early on Saturday morning. He did not want Elizabeth to be too fatigued from the journey that evening, when she, Jane and the Gardiners would dine at Darcy House. He wanted Elizabeth to have plenty of time to rest. In the end, it was approaching midmorning by the time they had said their farewells.

While Darcy, Georgiana and Elizabeth were bidding farewell to Lady Catherine, a note arrived from Dr Morgan requesting to speak with the Lady. The tone of the missive did not give the Lady any comfort, so she requested that her family remain with her. Elizabeth had made to leave the room, after all she was only being courted by Mr Darcy and was not a member of the family, but Lady Catherine had stopped her retreat with a request that she remain.

The next half an hour proved very difficult for Lady Catherine. Dr Morgan had thoroughly examined Miss de Bourgh and his diagnosis was not good. He informed Lady Catherine, as gently as he could, that her daughter's addiction to laudanum was minor compared to her other ailments.

When Dr Morgan had questioned Mrs Jenkinson and the Rosings housekeeper, Mrs Snell, he had learnt of the illnesses his patient had suffered as a young girl which had left her body weakened and her heart damaged. The ever-changing physicians employed by Lady Catherine, with their constantly changing treatments and remedies, had not improved Miss de Bourgh's health but only worsened it and the weakness now encompassed her heart. So distressed was her state that he intended to only slightly reduce the amount of laudanum ingested by his patient for the nonce, and with a special diet he hoped for an improvement in her wellbeing. Dr Morgan did not believe in giving the family false hope and so when Darcy asked if his cousin would recover, Morgan gave a negative reply.

"I am afraid the young lady's chances of recovering are exceedingly slim," he replied gravely. "As to how long Miss de Bourgh will remain with you, I cannot say. It may be weeks, months or even a year. Even when the body is failing, a person's will to live is a strong defender of life."

Lady Catherine remained stalwart while she thanked the doctor. Elizabeth could see that Lady Catherine was close to breaking down and so she asked a shocked Georgiana to find her aunt's maid. Georgiana removed herself from the room with all speed. Elizabeth took hold of Lady Catherine's hand and placed a handkerchief in it. That one small act of kindness was enough that Lady Catherine broke down and wept for her daughter.

As the carriage made its way on to the road leading to London, the passengers were each deep in their own thoughts. All were saddened by the fate that awaited Miss de Bourgh. Darcy took a deep breath and decided it was time for conversation or the journey would be a melancholy one. He asked Elizabeth how, apart from the sad news of his cousin's health, she had enjoyed her stay at Rosings.

"I enjoyed it very much, Mr Darcy. Your aunt was most kind and I enjoyed the time I spent with her and my friend. It is a great relief to know that Charlotte is well."

Georgiana looked at Elizabeth, her eyes wide. "You enjoyed my aunt's company? I find her quite terrifying."

Elizabeth laughed. "Oh, my dear Georgiana, you should not fear her. Lady Catherine means you no harm."

"I know, but…she is so stern. Although…" Georgiana paused. "Last night at dinner she was almost merry in your company."

"Our aunt likes Miss Elizabeth."

"She does?" cried Elizabeth, astonished by Darcy's comment.

"Do not sound so surprised, Miss Elizabeth," Darcy replied. "I believe you understand our aunt well."

Elizabeth smiled at the gentleman seated opposite her. "I would like to believe that is so. Although Lady Catherine appears to wish everyone to agree with all she says, in truth I believe she enjoyed our discussions."

"I do not know how you managed to speak your point of view so forcefully. Just one look at Aunt Catherine's eyes silences me," Georgiana said, while her brother noted the admiration in her tone.

"Ah but you see, you only have an older devoted brother, whereas I have four sisters. I learned at an early age that if I wished to have my share of the conversation I had to speak out." Elizabeth took hold of Georgiana's hand. "You are still young, Georgiana, and, quite rightly, you treat your aunt with the respect due to her. As you get older you will find that your confidence will grow. I am sure Lady Catherine will enjoy having discussions with you. You will find that you learn a great deal through debates with family and friends."

"I do hope so." Georgiana then turned her attention to her brother. "But…how do you know that Aunt Catherine likes Elizabeth?"

"Because Aunt Catherine told me so," he replied, smiling at the young ladies before him. Seeing both his sister and Elizabeth with curiosity etching their features, but both being too polite to ask what was said, he continued, "Lady Catherine also said that you could learn much in Elizabeth's company." Darcy watched his sister's delight in their aunt's approval of her friend, while he mused on the rest of his aunt's words. *'You have chosen well, nephew. Miss Elizabeth stands up for what she believes in, she will make a fine mistress of Pemberley. Her background could have been better, but she is a gentleman's daughter so at least in that you are equal. With her intelligence and wit, I am sure given the right tutorage she will do well in the haut ton.'* Darcy was unsure that Elizabeth was in need of tutorage; he liked her just as she was. But after giving the situation some thought, he decided to speak with Lady Matlock; but first he would speak with Elizabeth as he did not wish to anger her by making a decision that she might be unhappy with.

Chapter 12

Darcy felt his frustration mounting. By his calculations it was thirty-six miles from his aunt's home to Gracechurch Street and, even allowing for only the briefest of stops to change the horses and take some light refreshment, the journey would take six hours. Darcy was sure that his sister would join her maid and sleep for some of that time, which would enable him to speak privately to Elizabeth. But no, his normally introvert sister had found her tongue and she chatted with Elizabeth for nearly the whole six hours. Their conversation varied from their delight at Jane and Richard's betrothal to distress at the doctor's prognosis for Anne. Georgiana was not close to Anne, as she had not been in her company that often, but she was none the less distressed that there was no hope of recovery for her cousin. Now with only a few miles left of their journey, even if Georgiana succumbed to sleep, time had run out for any significant conversation with Elizabeth. They could not remain at the Gardiners' home for any length of time as it was nearly four o'clock and they must reach Darcy House with all speed, so that he and Georgiana could prepare for the dinner that evening.

Although the evening was enjoyable, Darcy still felt a certain amount of frustration. It had been an intimate gathering and he had been unable to acquire any quiet conversation with Elizabeth. Colonel Fitzwilliam had not wanted Jane to be too overwhelmed, as when the dinner was arranged he had believed it would be her first meeting with his mother, so the only people attending were the Earl and Countess of Eversleigh and two of their children, Viscount Kettly and Lady Henrietta Farleigh. Lord Eversleigh's estate was half way between Pemberley and Trentavon, and the three families had been friends for many years; the earl and countess were like a dear uncle and aunt to the Darcy and Fitzwilliam children. There was not much of an age difference between Viscount Kettly, Viscount Tansley, Fitzwilliam and Darcy, which meant the four boys had become firm friends—a friendship that had lasted through the passages of youth and would continue for the remainder of their lives.

Lady Matlock's delight in her son's choice of bride was soon conveyed to all those present and when the ladies left the gentlemen they soon convened in a comfortable group in the drawing room. Elizabeth was delighted to see that Lady Matlock and her friends took Jane to their hearts. Lady Henrietta, the Earl and Countess of Eversleigh's youngest child, was enjoying her second season. She was a great friend of Georgiana and it soon became clear that she wished for the same friendship with Jane and Elizabeth.

Lady Henrietta was most disappointed to hear that Jane would soon be returning to Longbourn. "Oh please stay in town longer, just a se'nnight or so, *please*."

"I wish that I could, Lady Henrietta, I really do, but Mama has expressly bid that I return to Longbourn with all haste. There is much to do for the wedding and she wishes me there."

"But surely, as your mother will be attending to the details with your housekeeper and cook, you do not need to be there." Lady Henrietta pouted slightly as she pleaded with Jane.

"Indeed Jane," Lady Matlock pondered. "You cannot leave town immediately, you must at least have another fitting with Madame Marron. I suggest that you return to Longbourn on Saturday and I will arrange with my modiste for a fitting the day before."

"Thank you, Lady Matlock. I shall write to Mama, I am sure she will agree it is for the best."

Elizabeth caught her sister's attention and raised her eyebrow a fraction. Jane blushed slightly and looked away; not even Jane was so naive as to believe their mother would calmly accept a delay in her return to Longbourn.

"Will you return to Longbourn with your sister, Miss Elizabeth?"

"No Lady Matlock, I will remain in town for the foreseeable future," Elizabeth replied.

"That will please my nephew," Lady Matlock said with a smile.

"Will Richard follow you to Hertfordshire?" Lady Henrietta looked at Jane enquiringly.

"Yes, I believe so," Jane replied. "If not on the same day, then we hope within a day or two. Richard has business to attend to in town which might prevent his immediate departure."

Four sets of enquiring eyes looked at Jane; the only ones not intrigued were Elizabeth and Mrs Gardiner. Glancing around at the ladies, she blushed and continued quietly, "Richard is in the process of purchasing a house off Russell Square."

"Oh that is marvellous news," cried Lady Matlock, hoping that would mean her son would retire from the army and sell his commission.

"What is marvellous news, mother?"

Lady Matlock looked up and watched as her son walked towards her with Darcy at his side and the other gentlemen following close behind. "Why your purchase of a town house, of course."

"Ah yes. I wanted Jane to live close to her Aunt and Uncle Gardiner, and not be stuck on my estate in Staffordshire when I am away. Mr Gardiner is purchasing a house in Russell Square for his family, our house," Richard smiled at Jane, "is just around the corner in Bedford Place. I hope we will be able to see it before you return to Longbourn, my love, so that you can begin to decide on decoration and furnishings. Perhaps, Miss Elizabeth, you would care to join us, I am sure Jane would enjoy your company."

"Oh yes, Lizzy," Jane cried. Elizabeth smiled and happily agreed with the plan.

"Not a bad area, my boy," said the Earl of Eversleigh, "and the buildings are not that old. There should be little draught or damp. 'Tis leasehold?"

"Yes, Sir," Fitzwilliam replied. "Ninety-nine years, so a goodly length of time should we wish to sell it at a future date."

"We attended a Ball at Bedford House, I believe it was a year or two before the duke had it demolished. Do you remember, my dear?" the earl asked his wife.

"Indeed, but, if I remember correctly, it was in '95, so a few more years ago than you recollect."

"Was it really, my dear? Hmm, where does the time go?"

"As we get older it goes too quickly, my Lord," Mr Gardiner replied.

"Quite so! But Gardiner, enough of this 'my Lord' business, you must call me Eversleigh."

Mr Gardiner smiled at the earl and bowed his head in acquiescence.

Lady Matlock sat quietly; any joy she felt at the news had quickly dispersed at her son's words and the realisation that Richard had no intention of leaving the army. Lady Matlock was not the only one affected by his words, Jane too felt sad at the thought of separation, but she loved Richard Fitzwilliam and she would not change the man that he was. If she had to share him with his King and country so be it.

On Sunday Darcy and Georgiana remained at Darcy House, while Fitzwilliam spent the day at Matlock House with his mother. It proved to be a long day for Darcy and his cousin without the company of the Bennet sisters, so it was not surprising that the distant bells of St Mary-at-Hill had barely proclaimed the eleventh hour on Monday morning when Davies announced the gentlemen's arrival. Fitzwilliam wished to spend as much time as possible with Jane, for he knew that once she returned to Longbourn their time together would be very limited.

There were a few clouds in the sky but the chance of rain was slim, so Mrs Gardiner allowed the gentlemen to accompany her nieces to the nearby park. They walked as a cheerful group, conversing freely.

"I have written to Mama to inform her of my intention to return home on Saturday and the reasons for my delay." Jane sighed and smiled weakly, she knew her mother would not be pleased.

Fitzwilliam squeezed the hand that lay on his arm. "Do not worry, my love, I will be there, and will persuade your mother that the fault lies with me and my determination that we marry soon. Now let us talk of pleasanter things. I sent a message early this morning to Bedford's agent, inquiring as to the possibility of taking you to view our home even though the documents are not yet complete. I received a reply just before we left Darcy House. Mr Burton has suggested tomorrow at two o'clock, would this be convenient? One of his men will meet us there with the keys."

"Oh yes, tomorrow would be perfect."

"Miss Elizabeth, Darcy, would you be able to join us?"

Both agreed willingly and Jane, delighted at the prospect of seeing her new home with her sister, said she would ask her aunt if they might all enjoy a light luncheon before departing for Bedford Place.

On reaching the entrance of the park the couples parted slightly, allowing enough space so that they could hold private conversations without being overheard by the others.

Darcy and Elizabeth walked for a while in silence. A cloud had masked the sun, which seemed to remove any warmth in the air; Elizabeth shivered.

"Are you cold, Miss Elizabeth?"

"No. Perhaps someone has walked over my grave," Elizabeth replied, her eyes twinkling with laughter.

Darcy shook his head and then laughed. "I hope not." He took a breath before continuing. "There is something I would speak with you about." Darcy looked questioningly at Elizabeth. She smiled and gave a small nod of her head; he gratefully returned the smile. "My aunt, Lady Catherine, approves of our courtship."

"It did surprise me when you said as much the other day," Elizabeth exclaimed. "I did not think that your aunt's desire of a marriage between you and her daughter would ever fade."

"Neither did I, and I was greatly relieved of her acceptance of my choice. But her words have given me cause for thought. I know we are not betrothed yet, but, if our courtship progresses in a way that you are happy with the conclusion, it is my intention to apply to your father for your hand when my cousin marries Miss Bennet."

Elizabeth smiled. "So what are these words that have given rise to such consideration? Tell me what your Aunt said."

"Lady Catherine said I had chosen well and that you would make a fine mistress of Pemberley. She believes that, with your intelligence and wit, if given the right tutorage you will do well in the haut ton."

"You cannot say Lady Catherine made no comment of my lowly background. Now come, Sir, tell me the whole."

Darcy smiled and shook his head. "I would rather not." He looked at Elizabeth's raised eyebrow and sighed. "But if you insist, my aunt said your background could have been better, but you are the daughter of a gentleman and so in that we are equal. I am sorry, Elizabeth."

"Do not be. Your aunt speaks the truth and she told you nothing that she did not tell me. I did not say anything because I thought I should wait; after all a lady should never presume that a gentleman will offer marriage."

Darcy took hold of her hand and raised it to bestow a gentle kiss on her gloved knuckles. "I will speak with Lady Matlock. I believe she intends to remain in town until after the ball for Miss Bennet and Fitzwilliam. She will know, much better than I, the conduct expected of a discerning young matron of the haut ton."

"I would be most grateful, as would Jane. Do you think Lady Matlock might agree to meet with us before my sister returns to Longbourn? I realize that she has a lot to do and not only for the ball, but I would, and I am sure Jane would too, greatly appreciate her guidance."

"I am sure she will be delighted to help, my love." Elizabeth's heart fluttered on hearing the endearment slip from Darcy's lips.

The cry could be heard throughout the house. Mrs Bennet had received a letter from her daughter, Jane. Instead of the expected news that she was returning home forthwith, Jane would not be returning until Saturday. It was not to be borne. Mrs Bennet wanted her daughter to return to Longbourn well before the first reading of the Banns, so that she would have two or three days to boast of her daughter's forthcoming wedding before that first reading. Fanny Bennet was still unhappy that the colonel had talked her into agreeing that his mother would see to Jane's wedding gown, but now there was a new home to view as well. How could Jane possibly make decisions without her mother's guidance and to only have so short a time to take her daughter to call on the neighbours—how could Jane treat her mother so infamously.

Half an hour after the initial cries and shouts, Mr Bennet opened his study door. He saw Mary walking along the passage towards the door with a book in her hand. "Ah Mary, my child, come here." Mary obediently followed her father into his inner sanctum.

"Now tell me, what has your mother's nerves so irate this morning? They appear to be blustering as much as the breeze outside."

"Mama received a letter from Jane."

"Ah, I see. And I assume, by the wailing and gnashing of teeth, she is not returning home immediately?"

Mary hid the smile that threatened. "No, Papa. Jane will remain at our uncle's home until Saturday. Lady Matlock insists that further visits to her modiste are necessary before she can return home. Jane is also having a ball gown made for her, as Lady Matlock is holding a ball to celebrate the wedding. Mama said that she should be in town assisting Jane at this time and not Lizzy, as Lizzy has no idea what is suitable."

"I thought Lady Matlock was advising Jane, not Lizzy?"

"Yes Papa, I believe that is the case. But…" Mary fell silent.

"Your mother does not like to be left out of the decisions," her father said with a wink. "I fear that the next few weeks leading up to the wedding will be a trial for your mother's nerves." Mr Bennet looked out of the window. The clouds were starting to build up, as was the breeze. He turned and looked at his middle daughter, a book held firmly in her hand. "The sun has gone and I expect it will be chilly outside. You may remain here if you so wish, Mary, and read your book in comfort."

Mary could not hold back the surprised look on her countenance; usually only Elizabeth was allowed to read in their father's study. "Thank you, Papa, I would like that."

Father and daughter had barely made themselves comfortable when Mrs Bennet's cries for her husband echoed around the room as the study door flew open.

"Mr Bennet, Mr Bennet, I must away to London. I am needed at my brother's house."

"How so, Mrs Bennet?"

"Jane requires my assistance and advice."

"But, Mrs Bennet, I was under the impression that Jane was returning at the end of the week."

"Yes, that is true, but I could read between the lines of her missive. It was a plea for her mother's help."

"Is that so, Mrs Bennet? Well, I hate to disappoint you or our daughter, but the horses are not available today, so the earliest you can leave is tomorrow. I am sure Jane will understand if you write to her."

"But that will be Wednesday."

"Yes my dear, today is Tuesday, so tomorrow will be Wednesday."

Mary sat quietly in the corner, away from her mother's notice. *'Poor Mama,'* she thought, *'to be ridiculed so.'* The more Mary had heard her father aim his wit at her mother over the years, the more she became resolved that if this was what marriage was about then she would have none of it.

"Tomorrow then, I shall leave first thing." Mrs Bennet turned and quickly left her husband's study calling for Hill.

"Do you believe your mother has the right of it and Jane wishes her presence?"

"No Papa. When Mama read the letter out it appeared that Jane was enjoying herself with Lizzy. She said that both Lady Matlock and Colonel Fitzwilliam were most attentive to her needs. And before she returned she hoped that she would be able to visit the town house that the colonel was purchasing for them. But the main reason for remaining in town until the eleventh is the further visit required to the countess' modiste for Jane's wedding gown and ball gown."

Mr Bennet sighed. "I see. It is not only the amount of lace on Jane's gowns that concerns your mother, but also the house the colonel is purchasing. Your mother would be most disappointed if she did not have a say in its suitability. I believe I will send a missive to Gracechurch Street, we would not wish your mother to suffer any discomfort if she were not expected."

'Poor Jane,' Mary thought as she heard the nib of her father's pen scratch its way hurriedly across the parchment.

On Mrs Gardiner's enquiry, as to how her niece found her soon-to-be new home, Jane replied enthusiastically, "It is perfect, Aunt Madeline, simply perfect. The décor is most acceptable. There are no furnishings, but Richard and I intend to go shopping for the bare necessities tomorrow and possibly again on Thursday. But I am not concerned if we do not find exactly what we want before I return to Longbourn, as Mr Darcy," Jane smiled warmly at the gentleman, "has said that we may live at Darcy House until our new home is ready for occupation."

"That is most kind of you, Mr Darcy," Mrs Gardiner said.

Darcy smiled. "It is my pleasure, both Miss Bennet and my cousin know that they are most welcome to stay at Darcy House for as long as needs be."

Conversation about the house continued until the maid entered the room. "I am sorry to disturb you Ma'am, but this express has just arrived for you." The girl handed the letter to Mrs Gardiner, curtsied and quit the room.

Mrs Gardiner opened the missive and began to read it. Her shock of what she read was revealed on her countenance, causing Elizabeth to cry out, "Is something wrong, Aunt?"

Madeline Gardiner looked at her nieces. "It is from your father but do not worry for all is well at Longbourn. Jane, your mother believes that you are in need of her advice and assistance. She will be arriving tomorrow. Your father had told your mother that the horses were not available today or she would be arriving much sooner."

Both Jane and Elizabeth paled at their aunt's words.

"Oh Jane, Mama will insist on more lace on your beautiful gowns. What are we to do?" Elizabeth closed her eyes to stop the tears that threatened. Jane's wedding gown would be perfect as it was, and any interference from their mother would surely ruin it. The ivory silk under-dress was covered with a long cape style covering of the finest semi-transparent peach satin mull. The satin stitches of orange blossom would complete the outfit, peach satin stitches on the ivory bodice and the front of the dress where the cape opened, and ivory stitches on the mull.

When Elizabeth opened her eyes and looked at Jane, she spied a solitary tear running down her dear sister's cheek.

Fitzwilliam took hold of Jane's hand as he sat next to her on the couch. "Do not worry, Jane. I have a plan but I must speak with my mother first." He then stood. "I will return as soon as may be." The colonel then bowed to the company and left the room.

"Do you have any idea what the colonel means, Mr Darcy?" Elizabeth looked at Darcy questioningly.

"I am not sure. I believe so, as he has gone to speak with his mother, but I cannot be sure and do not want to raise any hopes." Darcy then turned to Jane. "But please, Miss Bennet, do as my cousin bids and do not worry. I am sure he will be back in a trice with a plan of action."

Darcy and Mrs Gardiner tried to keep the conversation going on happier topics, but both knew it was a losing battle against the concern that Jane and Elizabeth felt with the impending arrival of their mother.

Three quarters of an hour later a beaming Colonel Fitzwilliam entered the drawing room. He walked up to Mrs Gardiner and handed her a missive. Mrs Gardiner opened the letter. She read it and, looking up at her soon-to-be nephew, smiled.

"An excellent plan, Colonel." Mrs Gardiner's smile remained as she looked at her nieces. "My dears, Lady Matlock has invited you both to stay with her, as she wishes to introduce you to some of her friends who are in town. The countess has also invited us all to dine with her on Friday evening. Jane, she suggests that you return home with us after the dinner so that you might prepare for your journey to your father's home on the following day. But Lizzy, if you are happy, she begs you to stay with her for a while longer, for a se'nnight or two." Mrs Gardiner turned her attention back to the colonel. "It is most gracious of Lady Matlock to extend this kind invitation to my nieces, Colonel. I am sure that being under your mother's guidance will help them both with their future lives."

The gentlemen took their leave, so Jane and Elizabeth could spend the next couple of hours seeing to the packing of their trunks. They promised to return later with Georgiana for dinner and at that point, if the sisters had finished their packing, Darcy's carriage would take the trunks to Matlock House, before returning to Gracechurch Street.

Much later that evening, after an enjoyable meal, Mr and Mrs Gardiner watched as the carriage carrying their eldest nieces, the Darcys and Colonel Fitzwilliam made its way down the street; soon it turned the corner and was out of sight. Once Jane and Elizabeth were safely ensconced with Lady Matlock, Fitzwilliam would continue on with his cousins to Darcy House as his mother would not hear of him residing under the same roof as his betrothed.

Edward Gardiner led his wife back into their home. "I fear my sister will not be happy when she arrives tomorrow."

Mrs Gardiner laughed at her husband's understatement. "Oh my dear, your sister will be furious! But do not worry, Edward, by the time I have finished telling Fanny of the wonderful opportunity the countess is affording Jane, our sister will be appeased. I hope…"

"I believe it is best not to mention Thomas' letter."

"I agree," his wife replied. "And also, as our brother is not aware of Lizzy's courtship, it would probably be best not to mention that either."

Mr Gardiner shook his head as he embraced his wife. "Oh, my love, what a tangled web we weave." He leaned down and gently kissed her forehead.

Chapter 13

It was just before midday when the carriage carrying Mrs Bennet arrived at her brother's home. She came without her lady's maid. Johanna, the maid that saw to the needs of all her daughters, had accompanied Jane and Elizabeth to town, so Mrs Bennet left her maid at Longbourn to continue seeing to her three youngest daughters. Johanna could easily see to her needs as well as her two eldest. Although Mrs Bennet did not realize it, the fact that she would have a maid at all to see to her needs was thanks to Lady Matlock. The countess relayed in her missive that she had maids aplenty to assist the young ladies and it might be prudent if their maid remained at Gracechurch Street in case Mrs Bennet had need of her.

Mrs Gardiner welcomed her sister. "Fanny, what a surprise, we were not expecting you."

After kissing her sister on her cheek, Mrs Bennet made her way to a comfortable chair. "Yes well, after I received dear Jane's letter, I knew that she needed me here."

"Oh." Mrs Gardiner endeavoured not to smile or shake her head in amusement at her sister's words.

"No, well your children as still so young, but as the years go by you will comprehend your children's desires without them having to put their needs in so many words. Now where is the bride to be, my beautiful Jane?"

"Jane and Lizzy are not here, Fanny."

"Not here?" Mrs Bennet cried. "Why not? Where is Jane?" Fanny Bennet's agitation grew and she reached into her reticule for her smelling salts.

"Oh my dear Fanny," Mrs Gardiner crooned, "Jane has been highly honoured. The Countess of Matlock, the colonel's mother you know, invited both Jane and Lizzy to stay with her. It would have been just Jane, but Lady Matlock realized how close the sisters are and she included Lizzy in the invitation. The countess wishes for Jane to be aware of her role when she becomes the daughter of the Earl and Countess of Matlock, and so Lady Matlock is introducing Jane to her friends in the haut ton. Edward and I are humbled by the kindness that the countess is affording our niece."

Mrs Bennet's mouth slowly dropped open as she listened to her sister. Her thoughts a jumble, she was at a loss as to what to do. She could not call at the home of the countess uninvited, but she could be at the modiste's establishment in New Bond Street and accidently meet her daughter then. Now all she need discover was when Jane's next appointment would be.' "Yes, a great honour indeed, sister. How is the wedding gown progressing, do you know when Jane's next appointment is with the countess' modiste?"

"Not exactly but I do believe it will be later in the week. Oh, and I have more news. It has been arranged that Jane will return here on Friday evening, so as to prepare for her return to Longbourn on Saturday, but we have been invited to dine at Matlock House with Lady Matlock and her family that evening before we bring Jane home. I am sure the countess will be agreeable to us bringing an extra guest. I shall write to her and tell her of your arrival."

"Then Lady Matlock will surely invite me to her home," Mrs Bennet cried with a happy smile.

"I know the countess has many visits planned; I expect them to be quite busy." Mrs Bennet's smile vanished and a dark frown filled her countenance. Mrs Gardiner continued before Mrs Bennet could make any complaint. "Mr Gardiner has agreed that I might have a new gown for the dinner, I am sure he would be agreeable for his dear sister to have one too."

The mention of a new gown had the desired effect that Mrs Gardiner wished for. All talk of calling on Lady Matlock disappeared; instead it turned to patterns and fabrics, and when they would visit Mrs Gardiner's modiste. Mrs Gardiner suggested that her sister rest for an hour or two while she wrote a note to her modiste. "You must be tired after your journey. You should rest, my dear, for you will need to be refreshed before we shop this afternoon." Mrs Bennet agreed that she was feeling a little tired and happily followed her sister as she walked up the stairs to the room which, unbeknown to her, her daughters had occupied until the previous day.

"Now rest and I shall return shortly with some refreshments for you."

No sooner had her sister left the room than Mrs Bennet lay down and within minutes was fast asleep; dreaming sweet dreams of fabrics and lace.

As Mr Gardiner made his way home from his warehouse for luncheon an empty carriage passed him. It needed no more than a quick glance to tell him it was his brother's carriage, as the man on top was Bennet's groom, Harding. When Gardiner entered his home he had expected to hear his sister complaining about the girls' absence, but silence greeted him.

Entering the parlour, he noticed his wife but there was no sign of his sister. "Where is Fanny, my dear? I thought I saw my brother's carriage as I walked home."

"Fanny is resting. She was fatigued from the journey."

Mr Gardiner looked at his wife with shock before walking with her to the dining room. They helped themselves to some of the repast laid out on the sideboard, then taking a seat next to his wife Gardiner continued to enquire about his sister. "She was not upset?" he probed; hardly able to believe that might be the case.

"No, I mean, yes, she was upset, but only to begin with. Edward, she cared nothing of where Lizzy might be." Mrs Gardiner shook her head in disgust. "So I spoke mainly of Jane and the opportunities residing with Lady Matlock afforded her, but the turning point of Fanny's ire came when I mentioned the gown that I was having made for Friday's dinner at Matlock House and how I was sure you would wish your dear sister to have a new gown too."

Mr Gardiner, who had been taking a sip of his coffee while listening to his wife, choked. Mrs Gardiner patted her husband on his back as he coughed and spluttered. "A...new gown?"

"Yes, my dear husband. Surely a new gown for Fanny is worth the peace that will come with it. Eliza has been working on a new evening gown for me for the past fortnight, as I knew I would need more than one decent evening gown now that our nieces had met such fine young gentlemen."

"I know Miss Riseam is talented, but can she make a gown for Fanny at such short notice?"

"Not from scratch, no, that would be asking far too much of her. But, when one of her clients is in a hurry, she always has a few simple evening and day gowns on hand that only need a day or two of work on them for completion."

Mr Gardiner sighed. "Very well, my love. When do you intend to call on Miss Riseam?"

"I plan to take Fanny there later this afternoon. I have sent a note and I am just awaiting a reply to indicate what time is best for us to call."

Jane and Elizabeth enjoyed their stay with Lady Matlock; the days were full and both Jane and Elizabeth believed they had learnt a lot from the countess.

While Mrs Bennet and her sister Gardiner were admiring the skeleton gowns, and deciding on various trimmings and embroidery to complete a gown fit to wear when dining with a countess, Jane, Lizzy and Lady Matlock had collected Georgiana and were now sitting in the drawing room of Eversleigh House in Grosvenor Square. As they alighted from the carriage Lizzy had looked longingly at the beautiful park that the square surrounded and wished that she might escape, just for a half an hour, to the seclusion of that wooded area.

Lady Eversleigh's other daughters, who were in town with their husbands, were visiting their mother that afternoon. Lady Anne had been named after two people who were very important to Lady Eversleigh; the first was her mother, Lady Randall, and the second was her dearest friend, Lady Anne Darcy. Lady Anne Farleigh first met her husband at her come out ball, but it was weeks later before he won her hand. The Honourable Peregrine Rutledge was the 'spare' of the Earl of Quantock. The earl, not wanting his second and only other son in any danger, had given him one of the lesser estates of the earldom. Rutledge had attended the season for the last four years as his mother wished to see him wed, but he had no intention of being leg shackled too soon. He was enjoying life and had not yet met any young lady who tempted him in the least to give up his lifestyle. Of course, that was before Lady Anne Farleigh's ball. Once he had danced with the young lady he intended to retire and find some action elsewhere, that idea flew out of the window by the end of the first set and Rutledge found that his plans had suddenly changed.

Lady Sophia was two years younger than Lady Anne, and had made a most advantageous marriage last year to the Marquis of Worthington. The marquis had not come to town when Lady Sophia made her debut in 1810, as he was in full mourning following the death of his beloved mother. When he attended Lady Armitage's ball at the beginning of the following season, he set eyes on Lady Sophia and was lost.

Lady Eversleigh had been delighted with both of her daughters' choices and now she had high hopes for her youngest daughter's happiness. That afternoon's visit proved to be an enjoyable time for all the young ladies and was the beginning of a lifelong friendship, which they would pass on to their children.

The first two mornings were consumed with shopping for Bedford Place, while Friday morning saw Jane's appointment with Madame Marron. The afternoons were spent calling on friends of the countess and the evenings, when not dining with said friends, were spent quietly at Matlock House. Darcy and Fitzwilliam, along with Georgiana, if she was not already there, would arrive in time for dinner and not leave until the ladies wished to retire. The days flew by and it was not long before Friday arrived, and the impending arrival of Mrs Bennet and the Gardiners at Matlock House.

As the afternoon drew to a close, Elizabeth began to worry. They had returned home early that afternoon after calling on the Countess of Mansfield, for Jane to oversee the packing of her trunk and for all the ladies to rest before dinner that evening. Lady Matlock wondered what was worrying Elizabeth, she could see it in the girl's eyes, and intended to get to the bottom of it.

Elizabeth sat on the window seat, starring out at the garden beneath her, when a sharp knock on her door brought her back from her musings. Thinking it might be Jane requiring her help Elizabeth called out for whoever was there to enter. The smile on her lips froze and surprise crossed her countenance as Lady Matlock entered the room.

Smiling, the countess walked up to the window seat and joined Elizabeth. "It is a lovely view from this side of the house, is it not?"

"Indeed, my Lady," Elizabeth replied. "It is a most peaceful outlook."

"So, with all this peace and tranquillity before you, what is it that has you worried, my dear?"

Elizabeth's mouth dropped open briefly before she started to deny that there was anything troubling her.

"Now, now, Elizabeth, please, I know a troubled face when I see one and, as your mien has changed as the afternoon has progressed, I can only assume that it is the dinner this evening that is making you anxious. Though why that should be, I have no idea. On Wednesday evening we dined with the Eversleighs and that did not trouble you, so what is it that makes this evening such a terrifying prospect."

Elizabeth sighed. "My mother, she can be a little loud at times and...well it is her nerves, they cause her to get over excited. Sometimes she says things that..."

"And you are worried that I may take offence? Oh Elizabeth, do not concern yourself. I am sure your mother is no worse than many a mother of the ton."

"Jane is Mama's favourite and I was my father's."

"You speak in the past tense, are you no longer his favourite?"

"I do not know. Papa wants a peaceful life, surrounded by his books." Elizabeth then went on to tell Lady Matlock about the happenings of the previous November at Longbourn. "As Papa made no objection to Mama's decree that I be banished from Longbourn, in answer to your question...I do not know."

"I understand, my dear. Are your parents aware of your courtship with my nephew?"

"No, Lady Matlock. Before my uncle brought Jane and I to town, my father handed authority to him. Although Colonel Fitzwilliam did ask my father for Jane's hand in marriage, he could have, just as legitimately, asked my uncle again, as he did for their courtship."

"I see. Well in that case, your mother shall not hear of your good fortune from me." Lady Matlock had liked Mr and Mrs Gardiner, and was surprised to hear that Mr Gardiner's sister was insensitive to her daughter's happiness. Lady Matlock reached out and took Elizabeth's hand. "Now, my dear, I suggest you rest. It will be a long evening for you and you will want to be at your best." She then leant forward and kissed Elizabeth on her cheek. "I will see you at six o'clock in the receiving room." Lady Matlock rose and left the room. Elizabeth smiled as the countess left, closing the door quietly behind her and then let out another sigh. In a small way Elizabeth envied Jane her soon to be mother, but, if Mr Darcy did one day ask for her hand she would have the countess as her aunt, that thought pleased her greatly.

The butler opened the door of the receiving room and announced, "Mr and Mrs Gardiner, and Mrs Bennet, my Lady."

"Thank you, Harris. Welcome to Matlock House, Mrs Bennet. Mr Gardiner, Mrs Gardiner it is a pleasure to see you again. Mrs Bennet, I believe you have met my nephew, but not my niece, Miss Darcy."

Georgiana curtsied. "It is a pleasure to meet you, Mrs Bennet."

Mrs Bennet looked at the tall and willowy young girl standing next to Mr Darcy. "Miss Darcy, Mr Darcy," she said as courteously as she could, pitying the poor child for being related to that dour and haughty gentleman; it was little wonder she had spoken so quietly.

As soon as they had entered Matlock House, Mrs Bennet had been in awe of her surroundings. Now in the presence of the Countess of Matlock, she found herself at a loss for words.

"Can I interest you in a small glass of Madeira before dinner?" Lady Matlock asked her guests.

By the time Elizabeth said goodbye to Jane, and watched as the carriage taking her mother, sister and the Gardiners back to Gracechurch Street, disappear from view, she felt a great relief that the evening was over. Lady Matlock gently patted her arm. "Come, Elizabeth, let us return to the drawing room. I am sure a nice glass of sherry would be welcome, and it will help you sleep tonight."

The carriage bearing the Darcys and Richard Fitzwilliam had left at the same time as the Gardiners' carriage, so it was just the countess and Elizabeth remaining at Matlock House.

"I believe my mother is still angry with me," Elizabeth said with a sigh, after taking a sip of the sweet sherry she had been handed in a small crystal glass.

"Do not worry Elizabeth. I do not know your mother well, but I am sure she will soon come around once she realizes you have captured Mr Darcy." This brought a welcome chuckle to Elizabeth's lips.

Those words were also spoken as soon as the gentlemen retired to Darcy's study. "I do not know Mrs Bennet well, but I am sure she will soon come around and forgive Miss Elizabeth, once she realizes her daughter has captured the wealthy Mr Darcy," Fitzwilliam said, trying to pacify his furious cousin.

Darcy let out a snort. "No doubt! But, in all honestly, there should be nothing to forgive. How could she expect Elizabeth to willingly accept the hand of that...that...that ludicrous individual? And to ignore her own daughter while dining in a house where she is a guest was beyond the pale. If she were a man..."

"Yes, Darcy, I know. But be calm. I believe you will have some apologising to do to your sister in the morning. The poor girl was scared to speak on the journey home."

"What? Surely not?"

Fitzwilliam slowly shook his head. "Darcy, you have no idea how intimidating you look when you are angry." He stood and patted his cousin's shoulder. "Now I am off to bed. I must finish packing."

"Tell Carlton when you have finished and he will see that your trunk is taken to Gracechurch Street first thing."

"That is much appreciated, Darcy."

"Have you settled your accommodation for while you are there?"

"Yes, indeed. I am staying at a coaching inn just outside of Meryton; it is barely four miles from Longbourn."

There was a haze in the air as Darcy watched his cousin ride away from the stables. Fitzwilliam's trunk had left a half hour earlier in one of Darcy's carriages; the same carriage would then take Jane and Mrs Bennet to Longbourn. It was an unmarked carriage and although Jane knew it belonged to Mr Darcy and not the colonel, her mother did not.

Darcy had broken his fast with Fitzwilliam and then the two gentlemen had walked out to the mews behind Darcy House, where the colonel's large grey stallion was housed. The head groom, knowing the colonel wanted to be away by nine o'clock, had saddled Talos and walked him out as he heard the gentlemen approaching.

Fitzwilliam mounted and smiled down at his cousin. "So, Darcy, I will see you in three weeks?"

"Absolutely! And as soon as I have spoken with Bingley, and discovered if he still holds Netherfield's lease, I will contact you. But whether Netherfield is available or not I shall arrive in Meryton on the same day as Miss Elizabeth. Even though her aunt and uncle will be there,

I do not wish Miss Elizabeth to return to Longbourn without being close by."

"I shall keep my fingers crossed that Bingley is still having the difficulties you spoke of. But do not worry, cousin, if Bingley has disposed of Netherfield and, heaven forbid, if there is no room left at the inn you can share with me," Fitzwilliam replied with a laugh. Then, giving his horse a light tap with his heels, he set out for Gracechurch Street, leaving a bemused Darcy shaking his head as he smiled at the colonel's retreating back.

Darcy turned and walked back to the house. He had some documents that needed to be seen to, hopefully that would be finished before Georgiana rose. Once he had apologised to his sister, he would make his way to Matlock House. He wanted to see Elizabeth; he needed to reassure himself that she was well.

Chapter 14

The next three weeks passed quite quickly for Elizabeth. She remained at Matlock House for a further se'nnight before returning to her uncle's home. During that time Lady Matlock continued to introduce Elizabeth to her friends; usually it was just the two of them unless they called on Lady Eversleigh, then Georgiana always accompanied them.

The highlight for Elizabeth occurred six days before her return to Longbourn. In the company of Lady Matlock and Mr Darcy she arrived at the Sadler's Wells theatre, where they met Lady Henrietta and their hosts of the evening, Lord and Lady Eversleigh. Before arriving Elizabeth was sorely disappointed that her uncle and aunt had been unable to accompany her because of a prior engagement, but now Elizabeth felt the burning excitement of a five-year-old waiting for a promised treat when she discovered the play they were about to see was a new production of The Talisman, starring Joseph Grimaldi. In the box Lady Henrietta sat on Elizabeth's left, which allowed for easy conversation between the friends, while on her right was Mr Darcy. Elizabeth enjoyed the play immensely but her attention was not totally absorbed by the actors on the stage, as there was always a part of her that was very aware of the close proximity of Mr Darcy. It was without doubt, she decided later when alone in her bedroom, a perfect evening.

The three weeks between Jane's departure and when they would be reunited were so full that Elizabeth had no time to feel lonely, or miss her sister too greatly. She did think of Jane, in those moments between laying her head on her pillow and sleep claiming her; but as the days progressed her thoughts swayed from Jane to Mr Darcy.

Those three weeks were also very busy for Jane, but sometimes not as enjoyable.

"Jane, Jane, hurry girl. Oh my nerves. Do not tarry so, Jane."

"But Mama," Jane tried to reply, but Mrs Bennet had closed the door as quickly as she had opened it and was now heading down the stairs calling for Hill. Jane sighed; she was not expecting Richard for at least another half of an hour. She was sure her sister was not having this problem with their aunt or the countess. Jane smiled weakly at Johanna, she was very grateful that their maid had returned to Longbourn with them. "We had best hurry then, Johanna."

"Yes Miss," the girl said with a giggle.

And this became a routine of sorts. Mrs Bennet's nerves would be all a fluster, but once Jane was in the parlour, and the colonel was with her, Mrs Bennet's nerves would settle until the next day.

It was just a se'nnight before the wedding when Mrs Long called at Longbourn. The four sisters and Mrs Bennet were in the parlour, awaiting the arrival of Colonel Fitzwilliam. Mrs Long entered the room in great excitement. "Oh Mrs Bennet, I have such news."

When Mrs Bennet heard that Netherfield was being prepared for occupation again, her nerves got the better of her. She slumped back into her chair, fanning herself with her lace handkerchief while weakly calling for her smelling salts. Mary jumped up and ran from the room, calling for Mrs Hill, while Lydia and Kitty giggled as they whispered about the return of Mr Bingley. Mrs Long made a hasty retreat from Longbourn, promising to call on her dear friend again in the morning.

"Just think, Jane will have two beaux," Kitty said dreamily.

"I wonder if they will fight over her," Lydia giggled.

Kitty sobered at that thought. "I would like just one. Maybe Mr Bingley will turn his affections to me."

"Do not be so silly," Lydia retorted. "If Mr Bingley turns his attention to anyone it will be me."

While Kitty and Lydia bickered, Mrs Bennet wailed, "Oh Jane, what will Mr Bingley think? He has been barely gone a six-month and you are betrothed to another."

"Mama, calm yourself. It is not Mr Bingley."

"How...how can you be so sure?" Mrs Bennet asked between coughs, as she inhaled deeply from the small bottle Mary had placed in her hand.

"Because, Mama," Jane replied softly, trying her best to reassure her parent, "if Mr Bingley still had the lease for Netherfield, Mr Darcy was going to ask his friend if Colonel Fitzwilliam could make use of the estate before his wedding."

"Mr Bingley has no intention of returning?"

"No Mama." Jane smiled at her mother.

Mrs Bennet did not know whether to believe her daughter or not. She hoped Jane was right but when the expected hour of the colonel's arrival came and went with no sign of the gentleman, Mrs Bennet's over active mind thought of all sorts of situations—Mr Bingley distraught with love for Jane, Mr Bingley and the colonel fighting a duel, both gentlemen dying and Jane left with no one. There was no rest for Fanny Bennet or her nerves as she worried her handkerchief; it was nearly a rag by the time Hill announced a smiling Colonel Fitzwilliam.

"Ladies, my apologies for my delay, but I have some good news. My batman arrived late last night with a letter from Darcy and this morning Corporal Jones assisted me in moving into Netherfield."

Mrs Bennet collapsed back into her chair in a dead faint. Mary picked up the small bottle that lay limply in her hand on her lap and began to flitter it under her nose. The colonel looked enquiringly at Jane, who merely gave a weak smile and gently shook her head. "Lydia, call for Mrs Hill, we will need help to get Mama to her chamber. I believe Mrs Long's visit and now the colonel's news has been too much for Mama."

Once Mrs Bennet was safely ensconced in her room, Jane and Fitzwilliam took a walk around the garden. Mary, their ever present chaperone, followed discreetly behind them at just the right distance so that any conversation between them was private.

"Mr Bingley was happy for you to stay at Netherfield? I assume as you are there now, he still holds the lease."

"He did hold the lease, but that is in the process of changing hands."

"Oh, so your stay there might be cut short." Jane wondered why he had moved there at all if the leasehold was changing ownership.

Fitzwilliam shook his head. "No. I will remain there until our wedding. I will tell you what has happened, in so much as I know it." Jane whispered her thanks.

"Darcy met with Mr Bingley at his club. He did not want to risk the possibility that Miss Bingley might invite herself to Darcy House, should they meet there. Bingley still had the lease for Netherfield. Much to his frustration he had been unable to find anyone willing to take on the estate for such a short amount of time."

"It is only till Michaelmas?" Jane enquired.

"Yes. If he simply gave it up without someone to take on the lease for the remaining months, he would get no come back on the monies paid in advance. Darcy said his friend was quite despondent, it appears his younger sister is eager for him to get an estate in Derbyshire."

Jane could not withhold the laughter that bubbled up inside of her. "I am sure she is. Poor Mr Darcy."

"Yes," replied the colonel. "He did find himself in a bit of a quandary. My cousin admitted that readily in his letter. If he took on the lease of Netherfield he would be giving Bingley the possible means of leasing another estate closer to his home, but he did not like to see his friend in such a fix. So they came to an agreement, Darcy would take on the lease of Netherfield but Bingley agreed not to rush into leasing another estate just to please his sister. Darcy told him to be his own man, to be strong and not to bow to his sister's demands."

"Do you think Mr Bingley will take Mr Darcy's advice?"

"I would hope so, for his own sake."

"But what use is Netherfield to Mr Darcy? He already has an estate."

"True, but Darcy sees Netherfield as a contingency plan. Should Mrs Bennet, as we hope she will, allow Miss Elizabeth to remain at home once you are safely wed, Darcy would not wish to be too far from her."

"So he would move to Netherfield!"

"Yes, along with Georgiana and Mrs Annesley, and any others of his household who would be required for my cousins' comfort."

"Now that you have the use of Netherfield, will the countess come to Meryton when my sister returns?"

"Indeed. With Darcy's letter was a missive from my mother. The plan, as far as I can make out, is for mother to join Darcy and Georgiana, and they will travel with Miss Elizabeth and your relatives. Mother has arranged for her modiste, with her assistant, to arrive on Saturday for the final fitting of your gown. Her assistant will return to town once the gown is complete, but Madame will remain until the wedding service begins. Mother insists that her modiste be on hand in case her expertise is needed. My brother intends to leave Trentavon early on Friday morning and journeying for two long days should arrive by nightfall on Saturday."

"I look forward to meeting the viscount. Will your father attend?"

"Sadly no. Although Sebastian has the doctor's assurance that father will be fine without his presence, he does not believe him to be well enough to spend much time in unknown company."

"And you would abide by the doctor's advice."

Fitzwilliam nodded. "Dr Morgan, who now sees to my cousin, Anne, and his colleague, Dr Nicholls, both excel in their profession. I would trust either man with my life, and the lives of those I love."

Jane smiled and gently squeezed Fitzwilliam's arm. Their turn about the garden was coming to an end as the manor house once again appeared in front of them.

Friday morning arrived all too soon for Elizabeth. She left the warmth of her bed and slowly made her way to the window. It was a cloudy day. Rain could be felt in the air, not a good day for a journey or for the people busily going about their business on the street below.

Elizabeth remembered the morning after she and Jane arrived at Gracechurch Street. It had been the last day of the old year and she had stood at this very window contemplating all that had happened over the last few months of the old year and wondering what the new year would bring. Elizabeth let out a laugh; never in her wildest imagination could she have envisaged the dear friendships she had made since arriving in town, *'Or,'* she mused, *'to be betrothed to the most wonderful gentleman it is my honour to know.'* It was a very new betrothal; Darcy still had to speak to Mr Bennet. After dinner the previous evening Darcy had asked permission to speak with Elizabeth in private. When they returned from her uncle's study, no more than five minutes later, the smiles on the young couple's faces left the Gardiners in no doubt of their niece's good fortune. Elizabeth gazed out of the window, looking at nothing in particular as her thoughts took her back to the previous evening, when her happiness had known no bounds.

The door to her uncle's study remained open; anyone passing would be able to see in clearly. Darcy took her small hand in his. He remained silent for some moments, simply looking at their joined hands.

Elizabeth's dearest hope was that he wished to ask for her hand, but as his silence persisted she was beginning to wonder if she had it wrong.

"My dearest Miss Elizabeth." Darcy lifted his eyes from their hands to her face, but did not loosen his hold. "My dearest, loveliest, Elizabeth, these few months we have spent in each other's company have been the happiest of my life. During that time my feelings for you have nurtured and grown. I must tell you how much I ardently love and admire you. You have become my dearest friend. I adore your intelligence, wit and kind nature. My greatest wish is to love and cherish you for the rest of our days, if you will allow me that honour. My dearest Elizabeth, I beseech you to accept my hand and become my wife."

Elizabeth, her heart full of joy, had barely uttered her words of acceptance before Darcy wrapped an arm around her and held her close.

"May I kiss you?" he whispered. She gave a slight nod and he lowered his head, his breath caressing her cheek before his lips found hers.

Elizabeth shook her head as memories of that first kiss warmed her being. Moving away from the window her thoughts turned to Longbourn. Would she be able to stay at Longbourn after William speaks to Papa, or would Mama still insist she returned to London? Elizabeth sighed and then smiled, and, as she removed her travelling gown from the wardrobe, she suddenly realized that she really did not mind. As long as wherever she was William was nearby, that was all that mattered. By the time she made her way down the stairs to the dining room to break her fast, she had finished packing her trunk. Although it may well be coming back again after Jane's wedding, but only time would tell.

Mrs Gardiner was busy giving last minute instructions to the servants before going to the nursery for one last time before they departed.

Only the Gardiners' eldest son, Matthew, would be accompanying them as it was felt that the others were too young and would put too much of a strain on Mrs Bennet's nerves. Matthew's excitement grew as he watched the horses pulling his father's carriage come to a stop outside of their home. His eyes widened as a second carriage stopped outside. "Lizzy! Mr Darcy has arrived."

Elizabeth joined her cousin at the window. Darcy's carriage had pulled up behind her uncle's. They watched as Darcy got out, spoke to someone within, closed the door and stood back as the carriage pulled away.

"Is Mr Darcy travelling with us?"

"I believe so, Matthew. Come let us greet him." Elizabeth walked with her cousin out to the hall and smiled as her uncle greeted Darcy.

Mrs Gardiner walked quickly down the stairs. "I hope I have not kept everyone waiting."

"Indeed not, Mrs Gardiner. I have only just this moment arrived."

It was a further fifteen minutes before they all boarded the Gardiners' carriage. The driver had instructions to go to Matlock House and, once Lady Matlock's party were aboard her carriage, Mr Gardiner's coachman led the way to Meryton. Darcy's carriage had left Matlock House well ahead of the others, ensuring that Lady Matlock's and Miss Darcy's lady's maids were settled at Netherfield well before the main party arrived. Darcy's valet remained at Darcy House; he would only journey to Netherfield if his master did not return after the wedding.

Georgiana would have preferred to travel with her brother and Elizabeth, but instead she sat next to her aunt, listening to Lady Matlock's conversation with Mrs Annesley.

The Lady turned to her niece and smiled. "I know, my dear, you would prefer to ride with Elizabeth, but I suspect Mr and Mrs Gardiner will wish to discuss certain matters with Elizabeth and your brother before they arrive at Longbourn. When we stop for refreshments I intend to inquire if Master Gardiner might like to ride with us for a while." Seeing the inquiring look on her niece's countenance, she continued, "I believe any conversation they wish to have would be best said without that young man's presence."

The stop was not truly necessary as it was only thirty or so miles from Matlock House to Netherfield, but the coaching inn at Southgate Green was a good distance between those two places, and the inn was renowned for its wholesome fare for travellers and excellent stables. When the carriages pulled away from Ye Olde Cherry Tree, three quarters of an hour after entering the courtyard, Master Gardiner was seated between the countess and Miss Darcy, and enjoying the ladies full attention.

"It was most kind of Lady Matlock to offer to entertain Matthew, Mr Darcy."

"My aunt is very fond of children, Mrs Gardiner. I can guarantee that, if my cousin and Miss Bennet are not careful, any children they are blessed with will be terribly spoilt by the countess. She will be without doubt a doting grandmamma."

Conversation continued smoothly until the subject changed to their arrival at Longbourn. Elizabeth's countenance suddenly clouded when her uncle asked Darcy what his plans were for speaking with Mr Bennet.

Mrs Gardiner took hold of Elizabeth's hand, gave it a gentle squeeze and smiled at her niece. "All will be well, Lizzy," she whispered.

"I will see how the land lies before deciding when to approach Mr Bennet. I hope he will look favourably on my suit, but I do not wish to tempt fate. This was another reason for wishing to stop at Netherfield. Besides from allowing my aunt and sister to rest before meeting the rest of Miss Bennet's family it will allow me to ascertain from Fitzwilliam how things are at Longbourn, especially regarding Elizabeth's return." Darcy then looked directly into Elizabeth's eyes. "I will be close by, Elizabeth, and I will not allow anyone to harm you in any way."

"Do not concern yourself on that front, Darcy, Mrs Gardiner and I will also see to Elizabeth's wellbeing."

Darcy gave a grateful nod of his head. He was glad, nay relieved, that Elizabeth had relatives such as the Gardiners.

Lady Catherine looked down at the letter on her desk, which had arrived not half an hour ago—her nephew Fitzwilliam Darcy was betrothed. She picked up the letter and placed it in the pocket of her gown with the letter she had received from Richard nearly three weeks before. As she stood Lady Catherine straightened her shoulders and made her way to her daughter's chambers.

The sun's dappled rays shone through the window, warming the pale skin of Miss de Bourgh's face. Anne sat on a comfortable chair close to the window. She was wrapped in a blanket to ensure her warmth while she listened to Charlotte read. Anne liked Charlotte Collins, she was good company and being the same age she was more of a friend than a companion.

There were times when Anne wished she could just go to sleep and not wake up. The pains and sickness she felt were sometimes more than she could bear. Dr Morgan was kind enough, but she was sure he did not truly understand what she was going through—no one could. Now that the amount of laudanum she drank each day was reduced, the only difference she felt was that her mind was clearer and so she was more aware of the pain, discomfort and sickness. Some mornings she would have scarcely finished her first meal before she was wretchedly emptying the contents of her stomach into the spare chamber pot.

Today she did not feel too bad; her headache was not as severe as it had been the past couple of days and her morning meal had remained where it should. Dr Morgan had smiled when she had told him and said he was pleased she was feeling a little better. Charlotte Collins' smooth voice and the warmth of the sun were slowly relaxing her to such an extent that her eyes began to close; her eyelids were just too heavy. Just as she started to drift off to sleep, the sudden opening of her sitting room door startled her.

"Ah, there you are Anne."

Anne smiled weakly at her mother. *'Where else did you expect me to be Mama,'* she silently mused.

Charlotte closed the book she was reading, placing her finger in it so as not to lose her place and began to rise from her seat.

"No, no, Charlotte, remain where you are," Lady Catherine declared. On Charlotte's removal to Rosings, Lady Catherine had insisted on calling her by her Christian name, omitting all mention of Collins, which Charlotte was truly grateful for. "I am sure my news will be of interest to you too. I have received a letter from William, he has proposed to Miss Elizabeth and she has accepted him. He has still to ask her father, but that is just a formality. No father in his right mind would refuse Fitzwilliam Darcy." Lady Catherine looked expectantly at her daughter. "Well, have you nothing to say. I know you must be disappointed, Anne. It was always my deepest wish that you and William would one day marry, but you are not strong enough and Fitzwilliam needs a wife who can bear him sons."

"I am not disappointed, Mama, I am pleased for my cousin. From the little I saw of Miss Elizabeth, and from what I can remember, I believe she and my cousin will suit each other well."

"Miss Elizabeth has a mind of her own, would you not agree, Charlotte?"

"Indeed, Lady Catherine. Eliza is definitely no simpering miss." Charlotte tried hard not to laugh, while she gave thanks that Mr Darcy's aunt appeared to approve of her nephew's choice.

"No she is strong and just the kind of wife that William needs. Hopefully, Anne, if you are well enough, we will be able to attend their wedding. He does not say when they plan to marry but I imagine it will be in two or three months hence."

Anne doubted she would be well enough to attend when her cousin wed Miss Elizabeth, but then thought of her other cousin. "You should attend Richard's wedding, Mama. I know they would be delighted to see you."

"I cannot leave. You are not well enough Anne."

"I will be fine on my own. Not that I am on my own, for I have Charlotte's company, Dr Morgan to see to my wellbeing and all the staff. Please, Mama, go," she begged. "When you return you can tell me all about it and it will be almost as though I was there."

Lady Catherine frowned and looked down towards the letters that were in her hands. Richard had written that his father was unable to attend. As Lady Catherine had still not forgiven her brother, and had no wish to be in his company, this would not be an impediment for her attendance.

"I will make sure nothing happens to Miss de Bourgh, Lady Catherine."

Lady Catherine looked purposely at Charlotte Collins and then nodded. "Very well, I shall send an express to Netherfield so that Richard knows that I shall attend. If I leave directly I can spend tomorrow at Matlock House and continue on to Meryton early on the Monday. I will spend Monday night in town and return on Tuesday." Lady Catherine then looked closely at her daughter. "Are you sure, Anne?"

Anne smiled at her mother, attempting to hide the pain she felt. "Yes. Have a pleasant trip, Mama, and please give Richard and Miss Bennet my very best wishes for their future happiness together."

Chapter 15

Sunday evening was a quiet affair at Longbourn. The colonel and his relatives had returned to Netherfield soon after seven o'clock. The countess had thanked Mrs Bennet for a delicious meal but had said that, with the wedding on the following day, Jane's mother must have a hundred and one things she wished to be doing and entertaining the Fitzwilliams and Darcys was not one of them. The front door had no sooner closed than Mr Bennet and his brother Gardiner removed themselves to the gentleman's study. Mrs Gardiner, wanting a word in private with her sister, suggested that they all retire to their chambers as there was a busy day ahead of them.

Kitty and Lydia giggled as they ran from the room and noisily made their way to the bedroom they shared. After wishing their aunt and mother a good night, Jane, Elizabeth and Mary left the drawing room at a more sedate pace. When they reached the door to Jane's room, Mary turned and placed her hand on her sister's arm.

"Jane, I wish you every happiness in your marriage. The colonel is a good man and…and I am sure he will be a good husband to you." Mary's voice lowered. "I much prefer him as a brother to Mr Bingley."

"So do I," Elizabeth said, as she and Jane both giggled.

Jane hugged her younger sister. "Thank you Mary. I believe the colonel and I will be very happy." Jane kissed Mary's cheek. "I hope, my dear sister, one day you will meet someone as kind and caring as he is."

Mary blushed at Jane's words. Regaining her composure, Mary wished her sisters a good night and continued on to her room.

Opening the door Jane glanced back. "Please spend some time with me, Lizzy. I find I am not at all fatigued." Elizabeth agreed willingly and the two sisters were soon ensconced in Jane's bedroom.

"Now, Lizzy, tell me, when will Mr Darcy speak with Papa?

Elizabeth blushed. "I…I…"

"Oh come. I see the way he looks at you," Jane teased. "And the way you look at him when you think no one is watching. Mr Darcy has the same look in his eyes that I see in Richard's when he looks at me. Now, no more procrastinating, sister dear, I promise your secret is safe with me."

The sweet ring of laughter filled Jane's room. "Oh Jane, you know me too well. William asked me on Thursday just past and will ask Papa's permission tomorrow, after your wedding. We would do nothing to diminish what is solely your day."

"Lizzy, your happiness means everything to me. Learning of your betrothal would do nothing to lessen any happiness on my part, if anything it has increased it."

As the sister's embraced they could hear their mother's raised voice; both turned and stared at the fireplace. Their mother's chamber was next to Jane's. The two rooms shared a chimney and the divide between the rooms at that point was thin. The unseasonably warm weather meant there were no fires in the grates, so there was no burning logs or coals to mask the voices in the next room.

Elizabeth blanched and felt tears well up in her eyes at the sound of her mother's voice.

"I do not care, Madeline. That girl has caused me nothing but trouble since her birth. She refused to marry a perfectly good man."

Elizabeth and Jane could not hear their aunt's reply clearly, as she did not raise her voice, so they sat in silence and waited.

"Love, ha, what is love against a roof over our heads!"

They heard the gentle murmurs of their aunt.

"He might be dead, but if that ungrateful girl had done her duty then I would not be waiting to hear that I will be evicted from my home by Mrs Collins' son when Mr Bennet dies."

Jane gasped. "Is Charlotte with child, Lizzy?" Her sister merely shrugged her shoulders in way of a reply. Elizabeth did not need to see her mother, from the tone of her voice she knew Mrs Bennet's anger had not diminished in the slightest.

"Of course she will be with child." They heard their mother shriek. "Otherwise why has she not returned to her father's house? They were married for three months before Mr Collins passed away, plenty of time for him to get her with child."

Jane stood from the bed where she was sat with Elizabeth, picked up a clean handkerchief from the drawer of her dresser and pressed it into her sister's hands as she sat down again.

"Madeline, I do not care what you say. You will take that ungrateful Miss back to London. She is not welcome here as long as I am mistress. Now please leave me..." Their mother's voice lowered so the remainder of her words to their aunt were lost in the chimney. They heard a door shut, followed by footsteps as Mrs Gardiner walked down the passage.

Another room that shared that chimney was the master's study, which was directly below Jane's room. Jane and Elizabeth were not the only ones to here Mrs Bennet's tirade, her husband and brother did as well.

When his sister's voice quietened Mr Gardiner sighed. "Bennet, you must do something about your wife."

"She is your sister!"

"True but for the last three and twenty years she has been your responsibility, how can you let her treat Lizzy so."

"Believe me it is much easier to simply let her have her way. Fanny will come around, no matter how much she argues to the contrary. If my Lizzy marries well, Mrs Bennet will want to have her share in her daughter's good fortune. I can hear her now bragging to her sister of Mr Darcy and his ten thousand a year."

"Ah so you have seen the way he looks at Lizzy."

"One would have to be blind not too," he replied. Then, almost as though thinking to himself, he said, "I am surprised he has not asked for courtship yet."

Edward Gardiner shook his head. "But he has. Surely you have not forgotten, again, your request that I act in your stead." He let his words sink in before he continued. "When he speaks to you I believe it will be regarding marriage rather than courtship. I gave my consent to their courtship weeks ago."

When Thomas Bennet did not say anything his brother rose from his seat and placed his empty whisky glass on the table. "Thank you for the drink, it was a fine whisky. I will tell Madeline that Lizzy will be returning with us after the wedding. I hope you are able to sleep well tonight, Bennet."

Lady Catherine departed from Matlock House for the final stage of her journey early on the Monday morning. Even Harris, who had been the butler at Matlock House for over twenty years, was surprised to see her ladyship descend the stairs at such an early hour; that was something that rarely happened these days. Her early departure meant that her carriage pulled up to the entrance of Netherfield Park a good hour and a half before the ceremony was due to begin.

As Lady Catherine entered the house the first person she saw was her nephew, pacing the entrance hall. When he turned and saw his aunt, Richard stopped pacing and quickly walked to her side bestowing a kiss to her cheek. "I am so glad you could come, Aunt Catherine."

"Anne insisted. Perhaps when you return to town, Richard, after introducing your wife to your estate, you might bring her to Rosings for a few days. Anne would be pleased to meet her."

"If time permits, before I get my new orders, Jane and I will visit."

The Netherfield housekeeper, Mrs Robinson, came forward and offered to escort Lady Catherine to the room which had been prepared for her use. Once his aunt had turned the corner at the top of the stairs, and was out of view, Fitzwilliam once again began his pacing. He had not been this nervous when going into battle. Suddenly he felt hands take hold of his arms. Looking to either side he saw his brother and cousin.

"Come brother, we cannot have you wearing the floorboards away. I suggest you join us in the study and we can indulge in a little of Darcy's fine brandy. I am sure it will be just the thing to steady a bridegroom's nerves. Would you not agree, Darcy?"

"Absolutely."

An hour after her arrival Lady Catherine made her way down the stairs, the front drawing room door was open and she could hear voices emanating from that room. Entering she saw Lady Matlock and Georgiana, but there was no sign of her nephews.

"Catherine, I am so glad you are here."

"Thank you, Gwendoline." Lady Catherine looked at her niece. "You look very happy, Georgiana. You obviously approve of your brother's choice of wife." Georgiana's smile widened as she gladly agreed with her aunt. Looking back to the entrance hall Lady Catherine asked, "Where is your brother, I expected to see him here."

"William has gone on to the church with Richard and Sebastian."

Lady Catherine shook her head, with only the slightest lift of her lips showing her amusement. "Are my nephews worried that the nervous groom might get lost on his way to the church without the two of them to guide him?"

In Longbourn the morning passed with a maddening frenzy. Mr Bennet remained in his study, attempting to shut out the noise surrounding him. Pushing all thoughts from his mind that today might well be the last day that both Jane and Elizabeth resided under his roof.

When Mrs Gardiner had entered Elizabeth's bedroom she had expected to find her niece preparing for her sister's wedding, instead she found her packing the last of her things, as best as she could, into her already overfull trunk.

"Oh Lizzy." Madeline Gardiner felt such sorrow for the dear girl.

Elizabeth looked up, a wan smile on her countenance. "I know I shall never return. It seems that Mama forgot that Jane's room is not only next to hers but the shared chimney gives nothing for privacy if voices are raised."

"You heard everything?"

Elizabeth did not bother to reply, she merely nodded her head as she tried to hold back the tears.

Mrs Gardiner took Elizabeth into her arms. "I am so sorry, my dear. I do not understand your mother, or, for that matter, your father's response. But remember, Lizzy, your uncle and I love you dearly, as does your Mr Darcy. Soon you will have a new life, one filled with happiness and joy. Then you will be able to remember the past only as it gives you pleasure."

Madeline lifted her niece's chin. Tears flowed unheeded down Elizabeth's cheeks as she tried to smile at her aunt. It was a wobbly smile which soon collapsed as sobs racked her body. Her aunt once more held Elizabeth in a firm embrace, while rubbing her back in round soothing strokes.

The wedding itself passed without incident. Much to Mrs Bennet's displeasure Jane kept firm with her insistence that Elizabeth would stand up with her, so it was Elizabeth, not Lydia, Mrs Bennet's choice, who led the way up the aisle in front of Jane and her father. Darcy was seated with his sister and aunts in the first row of the pews, opposite were Mrs Bennet and her remaining daughters. As the organ began to play everyone turned to watch the bride walk up the aisle, everyone except for Darcy whose eyes were firmly fixed on Elizabeth. What he saw did not make him happy. He could tell, even with the distance between them, that Elizabeth had been crying. Something, or rather someone, had upset her. His gaze turned briefly to Mrs Bennet. He would find out what had happened as soon as the ceremony was over.

To Darcy the service appeared to last for ever, such was his impatience to speak with Elizabeth. He watched with relief as Fitzwilliam and Jane walked back down the aisle, both radiating happiness. Behind them walked Elizabeth, her hand resting on Tansley's arm. As soon as they had passed he walked out into the aisle, placed Georgiana's hand on his arm and followed after them. He did not care if he broke with etiquette by walking in front of his aunts or Mr and Mrs Bennet; he wanted to get to Elizabeth's side as quickly as possible.

Whispering to his sister, as they made their way towards the door, he told her of his intention to walk back to Longbourn with Elizabeth and asked if she would come too, to protect Elizabeth's reputation.

Darcy congratulated Fitzwilliam and his new cousin, he then turned to Elizabeth. "Miss Elizabeth, it is such a fine day that Georgiana and I wonder if you would care to walk with us to Longbourn?"

"I would like that, Mr Darcy, thank you."

Glancing towards the church porch he could see his aunts and Elizabeth's parents making their way towards them. "Excuse us, please," he said to his cousins, and then offered one arm to his sister and the other to Elizabeth and purposely made his way out of the church grounds.

By the time they had walked the mile and a half back to Longbourn, Elizabeth had soaked her handkerchief, Darcy's handkerchief and the spare handkerchief Georgiana held in her reticule for emergencies. Georgiana was horrified that her dear friend's parents could treat her so. Darcy was furious.

Darcy, Elizabeth and Georgiana were the last of the wedding party to arrive at Longbourn. As they entered the already crowded drawing room, Darcy glanced around looking for Mr Bennet. When he eventually saw the man conversing with Sir William Lucas he turned his attention to locating

Mr Gardiner. Darcy then informed Elizabeth and Georgiana of his need to speak with Mr Gardiner before he requested an audience with Mr Bennet. "Will you be all right if I leave you here for a moment?"

"Of course," Elizabeth replied, placing a bright smile on her face. "I see Lady Catherine is talking to Lady Lucas, we will join them." Elizabeth turned to Georgiana. "I do not believe you have met Charlotte's mother."

They soon joined Lady Catherine, but Elizabeth was distracted as she watched Darcy and her uncle slip out of the room.

When Darcy and Gardiner returned to the room, Mr Gardiner went to speak quietly with his wife while Darcy walked first to Fitzwilliam. Standing close to his cousin he whispered, "I am going to speak with Mr Bennet. He may insist that I leave. If he does, I will be taking Elizabeth and Georgiana with me."

"Jane has told me of last night. Do what you must," Fitzwilliam replied and clasped his cousin on his shoulder.

If Darcy hoped Mr Bennet would see him immediately he was to be sorely disappointed. It would be over an hour later before the gentlemen spoke.

Darcy spent the time in the company of Elizabeth and Georgiana, and anyone they were conversing with. He avoided Mrs Bennet; Darcy had no intention of speaking to that woman now. He did not want to be the cause of a scene and possibly ruin Jane's and Fitzwilliam's day. It was while he was listening to Sir William extolling Jane's virtues and the loss to the county of such a jewel, as the happy couple had just departed, that he suddenly realized Mr Bennet was no longer in the room.

'Damn the man, he will not avoid me.' Darcy made his excuses to Sir William and went in search of Mr Bennet.

Thomas Bennet sat in his study. His eldest daughter had just left and soon his Lizzy would be going too. He picked up the glass of whisky he had liberally poured himself and downed it, coughing as it burnt its way down his throat.

At the sound of a knock on the study door, Bennet knew who was there. He poured himself another whisky and called out for Darcy to enter. Thomas Bennet looked at the young man before him and offered him a whisky. Darcy tried to keep the anger and disgust out of his tone, as he reasoned with himself that he needed this man's agreement to marry Elizabeth.

"Take a seat, Mr Darcy. My brother Gardiner told me that you and Lizzy were courting and I should expect you to want to speak with me." Mr Bennet held Darcy's gaze. "I know you dislike me, Mr Darcy, and I cannot blame you. There are times when I dislike me too."

Darcy remained silent, unsure of where this line of speech was going.

"I would like to tell you a story. It is something I have told no other living soul."

Darcy glanced at the wall clock, its pendant ticking the seconds away.

"Do not worry. Lizzy will be safe enough in the company of your aunts. My wife would never malign her least favoured daughter in front of Jane's new mother."

Mr Bennet took another sip of whisky. "My family line has occasionally been blessed, or in my case cursed, with twins. So when we discovered Fanny was expecting our second child and she grew so large, I was not surprised when the midwife said she suspected my wife was carrying twins. When Elizabeth and Thomas were born they were such tiny little things. The vicar came when they were only a few hours old and privately baptised them, and for that both Fanny and I were grateful, because although Lizzy was a fighter, even then, her brother sadly did not survive his first night." Bennet raised his glass to his lips again.

"Then came three single births, Mary, Kitty and Lydia, and we hoped that was a sign, an end to begetting twins. Mrs Bennet came with child again, but a few weeks or so after she felt the quickening she went into labour. They, of course, were much too small to survive and our sons died within the hour—with them went all hope for an heir."

Noticing the puzzled look on Darcy's countenance Bennet said, "You are wondering why Lizzy never mentioned her brothers?" Darcy nodded. "That is because none of my daughters know. The only person to know of my wife's condition was Fanny's sister, so when my wife went into labour I packed the girls off to their aunt in Meryton. They were told their mother was ill and needed peace and rest to get better.

"Not only did I lose my sons but I also lost my wife that day. We were both so wrapped in our individual grief that we did not see the other's suffering. Mrs Bennet never recovered to the caring woman she had been.

Instead of taking comfort from our remaining daughters she blamed Lizzy for the death of our first son. By the time I sufficiently came out of my grief ridden state to see what was happening, it was too late. My dear wife had changed and nothing I could do would alter that.

"I am a weak man, Mr Darcy, instead of persevering I retreated to my study, taking Lizzy with me when I could. It was on the pretext of teaching her, as she had indicated an interest in books and the world, but in truth it was to protect her from my wife." Bennet sighed and took another swig of his whisky.

"That was fine while she was a child, but as she grew into an independent young lady so did the differences with her mother. It became harder. For the last six years or so my two eldest daughters have spent more and more time with their uncle and aunt in London. Lizzy and Jane were always close, so I saw no harm in them both having a respite from their mother. When that fool Collins proposed, everything got out of hand. Our home became a battlefield. Mrs Bennet was demanding that Lizzy be banished from Longbourn, so when my brother offered to take her I readily agreed.

"I am to blame for my wife's behaviour. I should not have distanced myself from her when dealing with the boys' deaths. If I had acted differently all those years ago perhaps our lives would be different now. So you see it is only right that I should suffer."

"But not Elizabeth!" Darcy could remain silent no more. "You could have protected her, no matter how unpleasant it might have been for you."

"So you would have me demand that Lizzy remain at Longbourn? I cannot be with her always," he argued. "And my daughter, independent as she is, would not want to be constantly in my shadow. I know my wife, in these past eleven years she has changed from a loving mother and wife, who although prone to worrying had a joy for life, into a harsh, nervous woman whose mind has twisted into believing Lizzy is the root of all our ills." Bennet sighed. "I love my children, Mr Darcy, though it may not always seem so to others. I know I am not the best of fathers, but I try to do what is best given the circumstances. I cannot go back in time. You can have no idea how much I wish I could. If you love my daughter, take her from me and make her yours. I believe that is your reason for being here. You wish to marry Lizzy?"

"Yes, I do. Elizabeth means the world to me."

"Then take her with my blessing, but also heed this warning. Share your sorrows as you share your joys. Do not make my mistake. Never grieve on your own. You and Lizzy will be two made one, share everything in the comfort of each other's arms and love."

"I will, of that you can be sure." Bennet gave a nod of his head in satisfaction. "But might I ask, why did you not tell your daughters of your loss? Surely that knowledge would have helped them to understand their mother's actions and behaviour, especially Elizabeth."

"You are the first person I have spoken to about our loss."

"Not even your brothers, Gardiner and Philips?"

Bennet shook his head before lowering his gaze to his now empty whisky glass.

"Perhaps you should talk to someone."

Bennet looked up and saw in Darcy's eyes his unspoken words.

"You would have me tell Lizzy?" Darcy's gaze did not falter. "Yes, I believe you are right. She of all people deserves to know. Will you ask her if she could spare her father a few minutes before she departs?"

Darcy stood up. "I will bring her to you and then wait in the passage for her."

As he reached the door Darcy turned. "I will let you know when and where the wedding will be held. I am sure you would wish to give your daughter away." Not waiting for a reply Darcy turned and left the room.

Chapter 16

Richard had wished to journey to town with his bride and so they had the use of Darcy's carriage. This left Talos. Richard trusted his horse with his cousin and it had been arranged that Darcy would ride beside the Gardiners' carriage, while the maids would travel with Lady Matlock, but that was before Mr Bennet had spoken with his daughter. When Elizabeth walked out of the study Darcy gathered her into his arms, propriety be damned. She was in shock. "I never knew. I had no idea," was all Darcy heard her murmur.

As lovingly and carefully as he could, Darcy walked her out of the house and to the waiting carriage. Mr Gardiner stood by the drawing room door and as soon as he saw the couple exit Longbourn he returned to his wife and son. "Come my dear, it is time we departed; Lizzy is waiting for us. Goodbye Fanny, it was an excellent repast you provided for Jane and her husband. Do not bother coming out, I am sure there is a lot that still needs your attention."

The first stage of the journey was only as far as Netherfield, where Tansley and the other ladies were preparing for their departure. When Darcy had taken Elizabeth to her father, he had returned to speak briefly to his aunts before returning to take up his guard outside Mr Bennet's study. Lady Matlock had then gathered her son and niece, and with Lady Catherine, they had said their goodbyes to the bride's mother before departing Longbourn. Mrs Bennet immediately found Mrs Philips and, still in awe of having such noble persons at Longbourn, was busy reciting to her sister every word the noble ladies had uttered.

Tansley was not dressed for riding, but seeing the sadness in Miss Bennet's eyes, he quickly agreed to Darcy suggestion. He borrowed his cousin's greatcoat and mounted Talos, as his mother and young cousin boarded the Matlock coach with their maids and Mrs Annesley.

It was a very pleasant spring afternoon and so much to his delight Matthew was allowed to sit beside the coachman. Gardiner had been surprised that Darcy had suggested the treat for his son and equally surprised that Darcy wished to sit next to Elizabeth, but as the journey progressed he soon understood Darcy's reasoning and the need for private conversation. While telling the Gardiners all that had happened while he was ensconced with Mr Bennet, Darcy held Elizabeth's hand securely in his.

"I had no idea," cried Mrs Gardiner. "Did you, Edward?"

"No, but it explains a lot."

"Indeed," Mrs Gardiner agreed.

"Tomorrow I will see my solicitor to arrange the marriage settlement. Mr Bennet has agreed that you might sign the document in his stead, Mr Gardiner, so I will arrange a copy to be sent to you as soon as it is drafted, for your approval. I would also like to start introducing Elizabeth to the ton as my intended." Darcy then turned to Elizabeth. "My love, I know we have not discussed a date or a place for our wedding, but I was thinking of about six weeks from now if that is not too soon for you."

To Darcy's relief Elizabeth smiled. It was the first genuine smile he had seen grace her lips that day. "That would be mid-June," she replied. "I think that is ideal, if you are happy, Aunt. For then we can return to Pemberley before the heat of the summer arrives."

Darcy smiled warmly. "My thoughts exactly, Elizabeth."

"I had always thought I would marry from Longbourn, but I can see that is no longer an option."

"I believe you have spent much time at Gracechurch Street and the vicar of St Mary's must be used to your company. Would you be happy to marry at St Mary's? Or if you would prefer a completely new environment, we could marry at St George's in Hanover Square. The choice is yours, my dear."

"Thank you, I believe St Mary's would be perfect. Oh, but I forgot, we will no longer be living at Gracechurch Street. What is the nearest church to Russell Square, for I would wish to marry from my uncle's house?"

"Of course, and so St George's, Bloomsbury, it will be," Darcy said, smiling warmly at his intended. "It is a beautiful old church with its ornate colonnades and, I believe, was Hawksmoor's last great design."

The Gardiners' carriage stopped again at Southgate Green. This allowed the horses to rest while the travellers partook in some light refreshments. Matthew had a large cup of hot chocolate to warm him. When they set out again for the final stage of their journey to Gracechurch Street, Matthew joined his parents in the carriage. It was not long before the warmth of the chocolate and the rocking of the carriage sent the young man to sleep. He sat between his cousin and his mother, with his head gently resting on his mother's lap. The boy slept soundly until they stopped at Darcy House. Darcy thanked the Gardiners for driving out of their way, kissed Elizabeth's hand and, with a promise to see them all on the morrow, entered Darcy House to write some missives, which he would personally deliver before calling on Elizabeth. The first was to his solicitor, while the second was to The Times announcing his betrothal to Miss Elizabeth Bennet, daughter of Mr Thomas Bennet of Hertfordshire.

Fitzwilliam kissed Jane's hand and left her as she walked through the door to her chamber to prepare for her wedding night. Jane, lost in thought, remembered Richard's whispered words to her when she had first viewed the house. "These are your chambers, my love, but I hope your bedchamber will be obsolete and you will spend your nights with me." She could feel the heat rising up her neck just at the thought of his words, when a small cough brought her back from her musings.

"Polly," she cried with delight. "I did not expect to see you here."

"Mrs Fitzwilliam, ma'am." The maid curtsied; a bright smile covered her small face. "Lady Matlock told me to come and see to your needs, ma'am. My Lady knew you would not have your own maid as yet, so I am here for as long as you need me."

"Lady Matlock may come to regret her generosity, Polly," Jane said with a gentle laugh, as she thought back to how well Polly had looked after her and Elizabeth during their stay at Matlock House.

"I have prepared a bath for you, ma'am, if you should wish it."

"Oh thank you, Polly. That would be wonderful."

Half an hour later Jane sat at her dressing table, clothed in a ruby satin night gown, its fit was perfect and Jane was delighted with the present from her new mother. Polly was brushing out Jane's long fair locks when there was a knock at the door which led to the master's chambers. As the door slowly opened, Polly put down the brush, curtsied and quickly left the room. Jane slowly stood up from the stool and turned to face her husband. The look she saw in his eyes made her heart skip a beat.

Richard hoped he had given his new wife enough time. He had bathed and was now wearing a pair of clean britches and a silk dressing gown, which partly covered his bare torso. On hearing her response to his knock, he opened the door of her chamber. He hardly noticed her maid; his eyes were fixed on his wife's back, the thin straps of her nightgown with its hollowed out back covered little and his breath hitched as he took in her beauty. Then she rose and turned towards him, and his breath caught in his chest. Jane, his beautiful wife, was all his and tonight he would truly make her his. As he stepped forward he held out his hand. Jane smiled and reached out. He clasped her hand and pulled her into his embrace.

Richard breathed in the sweet scent of the rose oils she had bathed in. "My beautiful wife, how much I love you."

Jane pressed a kiss to the patch of bare skin on his chest where his robe parted. "As I love you, my dearest husband."

Gently scooping her up into his arms, Richard quickly made his way back to his bedroom and the beginning of their life together.

Viscount Tansley, the Honourable Sebastian Fitzwilliam, known simply as either Sebastian or Tansley to his family and his friends, had intended to return to Derbyshire immediately after his brother's wedding. Two things put a stop to that plan. The first was his brother's horse. Tansley pondered on his journey to town, as he sat astride the great brute, on why his brother had brought Talos to Hertfordshire in the first place. Instead of his carriage returning north with him, it was at present journeying south to London with his valet and his brother's batman enjoying its comfort. The second was a much more compelling opposition—his mother!

Before the wedding, in what little spare time she had, the Countess of Matlock had been planning a ball to celebrate the marriage of her second son and Miss Bennet. The countess' London servants were well trained. The housekeeper ran a tight ship and Colonel Fitzwilliam always claimed she would be a formidable general if women were ever allowed to serve in His Majesty's Army. The countess' presence was not really necessary in the planning, for she knew her directives would be carried out to her exact requirements.

Lady Matlock wished for her eldest son to attend the ball and no one, especially the viscount, would go against the wishes of the countess. Instead of travelling to Derbyshire his plans were delayed and now he found himself helping his mother with the last preparations for the ball being held that evening.

"No, no, Sebastian, not there, it just does not look right. Try placing the arrangement on the table over there," Lady Matlock said as she pointed with her hand to the opposite side of the entrance hall.

Tansley sighed, walked to the small occasional table, which stood close to the entrance, removed a Ming vase and replaced it with the flower arrangement. He did not like to say that that was the table he had suggested in the first place, a suggestion his mother had rejected. He had been walking the large arrangement of flowers around the hall for over a half an hour, while his mother decided where to best place them; although where his mother had acquired such beautiful blooms at this time of year he had no idea, obviously one of her friends had a well-stocked hothouse.

"There, Mother, are you happy now?" On seeing his mother's lips rise into a smile he continued quickly. "Good. Now I suggest we retire to our rooms before preparing for the evening. I am sure your maid will have your trunks packed but I must still see to mine if we are to leave for Trentavon in the morning." Sebastian moved to escort his mother to her chambers. "At what hour will Richard and his wife arrive in the morning? I assume you have already arranged a time with him."

"No. I intend to speak with both Richard and Jane this evening about our journey tomorrow." Lady Matlock, who was looking ahead as she ascended the stairs, did not see her son roll his eyes as he slowly shook his head.

In the Gardiners' home in Gracechurch Street, Elizabeth was also preparing for the ball. When Mr Darcy had started to court her, Mrs Gardiner had insisted that her niece would need new gowns. As Lady Matlock had purchased Jane's ball gown, Mrs Gardiner insisted that they would purchase one for Elizabeth. As she looked at herself in the mirror Elizabeth could barely believe her eyes at the young lady staring back at her. Her chestnut locks were elegantly coiffured, with a few ringlets gently caressing her neck. Her gown was pale green, made of the finest silk, with a delicate dark emerald green lace half covering the bodice. But what finished the outfit perfectly were the emeralds that adorned her neck, her ears and her wrist, even her hair was decorated with diamond and emerald pins. The emeralds had arrived at Gracechurch Street late that morning. Darcy had called on Elizabeth and in his hands had been a velvet covered box. When Darcy had said it was a betrothal present for her, Elizabeth had demurred, for she already wore his ring—a beautiful platinum ring adorned with small diamond and aquamarine forget-me-nots—but Darcy had insisted, saying it would match her gown perfectly. Reluctantly Elizabeth had accepted the box. She had gasped when she had looked at the earrings, necklace, bracelet and hairpins nestled within it; now she looked with astonishment at her reflection, barely recognising herself.

When Darcy arrived at Gracechurch Street, to escort Elizabeth, along with her uncle and aunt, to Matlock House, he was speechless as his eyes rested on his Elizabeth. Then a broad smile broke out as he walked to her and raised her gloved hand to his lips. "My dearest Elizabeth, you will be the most beautiful lady at the ball this evening. I am so proud to have you by my side."

Although very little truly frightened Elizabeth, she found this evening she was a little apprehensive. Tonight was the first night she would be seen in public as Mr Darcy's intended, the future Mrs Darcy. "I hope I will not disappoint you."

Darcy held her gloved hand tightly in his grasp as he took in the look of concern which flooded her eyes. "Never! Elizabeth, you could never disappoint me, no matter how hard you tried. No doubt there may be a few disappointed matrons and their daughters there; I have been open game on the marriage market for quite a few years. But I have made my choice and I chose you…remember that." Kissing her hand once more, as he lowered it he whispered, "I love you, Elizabeth."

Elizabeth smiled, determined she would worry no more. *'He loves me and I love him, all will be well.'*

When Darcy's carriage pulled up outside Matlock House, Darcy and Gardiner helped their ladies alight. With Elizabeth on his arm and the Gardiners walking behind them, Darcy led the way in to Matlock House to join the receiving line. As they made their way to the front, Elizabeth smiled warmly as she watched her dear sister greet the people before them. Jane looked so happy. *'Married life is obviously agreeing with Jane,'* Elizabeth mused. She was then brought back to the present as Lord Tansley greeted her and Darcy. Tansley bowed over her hand, before begging Elizabeth to save him a dance.

Lady Matlock greeted her warmly with a kiss to the cheek. "My dear, the Darcy emeralds suit you well. They could have been made for you." Elizabeth thanked the countess before moving on to her new brother.

Fitzwilliam kissed her hand and also asked for a dance. When she moved on to Jane, tears gathered in Elizabeth's eyes at the sight of her sister radiating with happiness. "My dear Jane, you are enjoying life as Mrs Fitzwilliam?"

"Indeed I am," Jane replied as she embraced her sister. "I can highly recommend the institution."

"Jane, you look so beautiful. The gown suits you so well." Jane's satin ball gown of pale cerulean blue, paid justice to Jane's fair complexion, and the drop diamond necklace, of gold and diamonds, that plunged into the wide V-neck of her gown complemented her ensemble.

Richard leant towards his wife and whispered something which made her glance about. "Oh dear, I believe we are causing quite a queue, Lizzy." Jane smiled as Darcy placed Elizabeth's hand on his arm and walked her into the ballroom.

The orchestra warmed up and soon the call was made for the first dance of the evening. Richard had requested a waltz but his mother had refused to have such a scandalous dance performed at a ball held in Matlock House. Richard led Jane on to the floor, Darcy and Elizabeth joined them, as did Lady Henrietta partnered by Lord Tansley; the last couple to make up their group were the Rutledges. Soon the music began for the first quadrille of the evening.

The rooms were ablaze with candles, flowers adorned every corner. Darcy, determined to sit next to Elizabeth at supper, had requested the first, supper and last dances of the evening. While Elizabeth was delighted with that thought, she had insisted that he dance with others; he was not to stand at the side of the room and merely stare out as he had at the Meryton Assembly. Darcy looked at the determination on Elizabeth's countenance and acquiesced.

It was a small gathering by the standards of the haut ton with just under two hundred in attendance. Lady Matlock had been careful with the invitations; to receive one of the embossed cards was felt to be an honour and the invitations were most sought-after. Fitzwilliam's general and his wife were invited, along with some fellow officers who were close friends of her son. Only two of the eight officers invited had wives, so Lady Matlock had ensured that there were enough single young ladies among the invited guests to even up the numbers. Of the single young ladies in attendance with their parents, many had long desired to be the next Mrs

Darcy. Fitzwilliam Darcy may not have had a title but he was the grandson of an earl, he was handsome to look at and, more importantly for the ladies of the ton, he was wealthy, possibly the wealthiest eligible gentlemen in the whole of England. A lady would put up with a lot to marry such a man.

The first young lady of this ilk who Darcy escorted on to the dance floor was Miss Helena Jannings, the eldest daughter of Sir Edmond and Lady Jannings. Miss Jannings delight knew no bounds. She was honoured to be the first young lady Mr Darcy asked to dance after his compulsory dances with the sister of the bride and the bride, as well as the daughters of the Earl of Eversleigh who everyone knew were very close friends to the Matlocks and the Darcys. Miss Jannings wore an angelic smile on her face, which briefly turned into a smirk when she looked at her friends Miss Harwell and Miss Ingham. The first thing Helena noticed was that Mr Darcy appeared to be glancing around at the other couples on the floor, as though searching for someone. Deciding conversation was needed, she looked around the room searching for inspiration.

"Your cousin looks to be very happy with his new wife. Have they known each other long?"

Darcy turned his attention back from Elizabeth, who was partnered with Colonel Brisco, to the young lady opposite him. "Since the beginning of the year," he replied. "Mrs Fitzwilliam and her sister, Miss Bennet, are friends of my sister."

"Ah yes, Miss Darcy. Will she be making her come out soon? She must be eagerly awaiting the day when she can attend balls such as this."

"Miss Darcy will make her come out proper next year but, if we are in town for the little season, she may attend some family events then."

Miss Jannings eyes lit up with pleasure and as soon as the dance allowed them to converse again she said, "It would be wonderful if you are in town for the little season. It is so nice to have familiar faces around." Darcy's next sentence burst Miss Jannings' happy bubble.

"It will depend on the wishes of my wife."

"Your wife?" Her eyes widened in astonishment. "I did not realize that you had married, Mr Darcy."

Darcy smiled. "I have not, as yet, but my betrothed and I will be wed by the autumn. The announcement of our betrothal will appear in The Times tomorrow."

"I see." Miss Jannings fixed a smile on her face. "I wish you and Miss…"

"Miss Bennet." The smile on Darcy's countenance as he mentioned her name was startling. Helena did not think she had ever seen the gentleman smile so.

"I wish you and Miss Bennet much joy, Mr Darcy."

"Thank you, Miss Jannings, that is most kind of you."

When the dance finished Darcy led Miss Jannings from the floor and, as she requested, escorted her to her friends, Miss Harwell and Miss Ingham. After leaving Miss Jannings, Darcy made his way to his aunt's side.

"There you are William. Now tell me, are you enjoying the ball? I believe that Elizabeth is."

Darcy followed his aunt's gaze to where Elizabeth was now in deep conversation with her sister and Lady Henrietta. "I am, Aunt. Though I should tell you I have just danced with Miss Jannings. You can see she is now conversing with a group of her friends. During our dance talk turned to the little season. Miss Jannings was pleased to hear that I might be attending, but I believe her pleasure diminished somewhat when I explained it would depend on my wife's wishes. I have no doubt she will tell her friends of my betrothal to Elizabeth."

"Ah, I see." Lady Matlock replied, as she glanced to where Miss Jannings and her friends appeared to be in deep conversation. "Well, it would seem, Nephew, the news of your betrothal is spreading as we speak." She turned towards Darcy, a warm smile gracing her countenance. "Now I suggest you make your way to Elizabeth, it will be time for the supper set soon." *'I would not like any of the disappointed young ladies to say anything untoward in her presence,'* she thought silently as Darcy bowed and made his way around the crowded room to where Elizabeth stood smiling with her sister as they listened to something Fitzwilliam was saying.

The eyes of the ton followed his progress, noting a slight curve grace his lips as he neared the lady in question. Mothers and daughters alike sighed with regret at the loss of one of the haut ton's most eligible gentlemen.

In a seedy part of town, a man sat in a dimly lit corner of a public house. He held a battered tankard in his hands and sipped slowly. South of the Thames, Jacob's Island was a notorious rookery. The man knew he was safe here from the two men he hated the most, as neither of those gentlemen would think of searching in this decrepit hole where the scum of humanity resided. The cards had been in his favour of late, and although he had more than enough coins in his pocket to fill his tankard again he would not waste them. Fifteen minutes passed before a scrawny young lad, of no more than eight summers, entered the house; he was filthy as were the rags he was wearing. The boy quickly made his way to the gent's table, whispered something and all but snatched the farthing from the man's hand before leaving as quickly as he arrived.

The man stood and drained his tankard of the remnants of ale it still held. He was soon out on the grimy street and heading towards another public house on the outskirts of the rookery. Perhaps luck would be with him this time. To gain the revenge due him he needed money. *'If I cannot win it I shall have to think of another way of lining my pockets.'*

Chapter 17

Mr Bennet was weary of listening to his wife's woes and complaints. If it was not Lizzy for failing to tie herself to his fool of a cousin, it was Charlotte and the heir she must be carrying, for why else had Mrs Collins not yet returned to Lucas Lodge. She must be with child, the same infant that would no doubt evict his wife while playing with his favourite toy. The previous evening he had told Mrs Bennet that she should call on Lady Lucas and enquire about Charlotte's health, instead of moaning and wailing about something that might never be. But instead of seeing the sense in his suggestion, his wife had ranted for a full quarter of an hour. Even when he had escaped to his book room, Mrs Bennet's loud tirade could still be heard quite clearly through the oak panelling. This was, to Thomas Bennet, the last feather that broke the horse's back. The following morning, as soon as it was a reasonable hour, Mr Bennet made his way to Lucas Lodge to call on Sir William.

"Bennet, it is good to see you. How is everything at Longbourn; you must miss Jane and Eliza."

Bennet nodded; he did not wish to speak of Longbourn and thought of a way to enquire about Charlotte. "I do miss their company. It seems all sense has fled Longbourn. Is it the same for you here, with Charlotte remaining in Kent?"

"Ah yes. From my dear Charlotte's letters it would appear she is holding up quite well after the death of Mr Collins, but I am sure she must still be devastated by the loss of her husband so soon after their marriage."

Bennet said nothing as his mind turned to the babbling fool of a man that had been his cousin.

"Lady Lucas wanted Charlotte to return to our home, but Charlotte is determined to remain at Rosings and care for Miss de Bourgh."

"Is Lady Catherine's daughter unwell?"

"Yes, and from what I can gather it is an illness of some years."

"Some years? But my cousin, when he was with us last year, informed me of Miss de Bourgh's betrothal to Mr Darcy." Although he knew this was untrue, Bennet was curious as to what might ail Miss de Bourgh; surely Mrs Collins would not nurse the young lady if her complaint might cause danger to an unborn child.

"Reading between the lines of Charlotte's letter, I think any betrothal is highly unlikely. Miss de Bourgh sounds a frail young lady, and if that is the case, surely her mother would not wish her to marry for fear of losing her daughter to childbirth."

Deciding no more information would come from Sir William, Bennet took the direct approach. "Was your daughter fortunate enough to fall with child before Collins departed this world?"

"No. And I believe that must be a blessing. Charlotte has not inherited anything from her husband, and a little one would be an extra mouth to feed. But Bennet, I have been meaning to ask, what of the entail? Is it now broken, or who is next in line after Collins?"

Thomas Bennet thought for a moment and then shook his head. "No, the entail will not break for another generation. I am not sure who is next in line to inherit. I shall have to look back over the family's history. I know somewhere in my book room is the family bible, that should be an aid to discovering who it is. Perhaps it will be an eligible young man who will wish to marry one of my daughters. That should ease Mrs Bennet's nerves."

"I do not think I will ever understand ladies, Bennet."

Mr Bennet gave his friend a wry smile. "Sir William, the working of the female mind is one of the greatest mysteries of the known world."

As Lady Lucas passed the closed door of her husband's study she was surprised to hear laughter emanating from the room.

Thomas Bennet returned to Longbourn just before noon. Mr Hill informed him that Mrs Bennet, along with Miss Kitty and Miss Lydia, had gone to call on her sister, Mrs Philips. Taking advantage of the peace, Bennet retired to his book room to search out the bible.

The Longbourn family bible was a large tome, printed in the early 17th century. The names of all family members, from the marriage of his great-great-grandparents and all their descendants to the present day Bennets, were written in the book. Thomas Bennet had only ever written in it once, as his father had been the master of Longbourn at the time of all his children's births except for Lydia. After carefully wiping off any dust from the top of it, the bible now lay open on his desk. Bennet took his pen, dipped its nib in the ink well and carefully entered his daughter Jane's marriage to Colonel Richard Fitzwilliam, son of the Earl and Countess of Matlock and the death of William Collins. He looked at the entry for

Collins' parents and noted that their deaths were not recorded. That, of course, was his fault. Once his father had passed, it had been his responsibility to keep the family records up to date, but there was nothing he could do about it now for he had no memory as to when his cousin, or indeed his cousin's wife, had died.

Once the ink was dry, he turned the pages to reach the first entries; that was the marriage of his great-great-grandfather, William Bennet to Augusta Colley in 1664. As Thomas looked at the entries recording the births and deaths of their children, he could not help but feel sorry for the loss his ancestors endured. He had thought the loss of his sons was bad, but William Bennet had sired eight children with only one surviving infancy; his heir Matthew.

Matthew Bennet and his wife had three children; Ambrose in 1715, and Susannah and Mary in 1717. Their mother died just three days after the girls' were born. Susannah Bennet had married Jeremiah Collins. Thomas checked the rest of Susannah Collins' line for any other male descendants, but according to the entries made by previous masters of Longbourn, the late William Collins had been the only surviving male descendant of that lady.

Bennet's grandfather had started the entail. His father, Matthew, overcome with grief at the death of his wife, turned to drink and gambling as a way to cope with his loss. By the time Ambrose Bennet inherited Longbourn it was nearly half of its original size. Ambrose, determined to save his beloved home from any future wasters, set up a three life entail, which would cover the lives of his son, grandson and great-grandson. Only his great-grandson, or the great-grandson of one of his sisters, would be able to end the entail at his death.

Thomas Bennet turned his attention to Mary Bennet's line; she had married a man named Butterworth and had given him six daughters. The eldest, Joanne, married a Mr Lange; Bennet laughed aloud as Joanne had followed her mother and also produced only daughters. The eldest died before leaving the nursery, the second married a gentleman from Saint Albans but had no offspring. Bennet's lips curled as he read the entry for the third daughter. "Oh my," he chuckled aloud. "I wonder what Fanny will think of that young man now."

It was nearly six years ago when young Samuel Goulding had knocked on the door of Longbourn clutching a posy of wild violets for Jane. They were both sixteen at the time. Fanny Bennet had been horrified; any chance of that young love surviving had soon been squashed by Mrs Bennet's outcry. Bennet had watch from his study window as the forlorn young man had left Longbourn. For many weeks after that day Samuel had avoided Mrs Bennet. Now Thomas looked at the entry for Juliette Lange, third daughter of Joanne Butterworth and George Lange, and her marriage to Mr Jacob Goulding. Underneath that entry was the birth of her son, Samuel Goulding.

Thomas Bennet had not looked at the family bible since the day he had recorded Lydia's birth, even then he had not bothered to look at any other entries. Following Collins' death he thought he had best look soon, but, with his wife's insistence that Mrs Collins was with child, there seemed little point in the exercise.

About to close the old bible, Bennet stopped his action and turned back to the page containing his children's births. They were all there, except the twins. Bennet briefly closed his eyes in an attempt to hold back the sorrow he still felt. He straightened and took a deep breath. Determined to right a wrong he picked up his pen, dipped the nib in the inkwell again and began to write. *Matthew Douglas and Edward Alfred born 18th January 1800, died 18th January 1800 – suffer little children to come unto me.*

Putting the old tome back in its place high in the bookcase, he returned to his desk, sat down and began to write to his solicitor, informing him of the name of the new heir to Longbourn. He trusted Mr Philips would in turn inform Mr Samuel Goulding that he was now the heir presumptive to Longbourn Estate.

It was early on the Thursday morning for those of the haut ton, not so early for others; the driver of the hired hack that pulled up at Matlock House had been awake for over three hours and this fare was his fourth of the morning. As soon as the carriage stopped, Fitzwilliam, not waiting for the boy to jump down from the box, opened the door, alighted quickly and then turned to help down his wife. The boy clutched the carpet bag he had retrieved from the boot of the carriage, but, as he moved to walk behind the colonel, Fitzwilliam turned and removed it from the boy's hands. Having paid the driver, he took a coin from his pocket and gave it to the young lad before escorting his wife to the door. Their trunks had been delivered an hour before, in the care of Jane's lady's maid and Fitzwilliam's batman.

Polly and Corporal Jones would travel to Trentavon with their trunks in a second carriage, along with Lady Matlock's maid and Viscount Tansley's valet.

It really was not surprising, given the lateness of the night before, to find that the occupants of the Earl of Matlock's carriage had succumbed to the gentle rocking, as the horses steadily made their way north. Within half an hour of departing Matlock House, the countess, her two sons and new daughter had all drifted into slumber.

Two long days later the carriages entered the gates of Trentavon Hall and slowly wound their way up the driveway towards the large house in the distance. Jane's eyes widened as she saw the grand structure looming in the evening twilight ahead of her. Lady Matlock smiled at her daughter.

"I understand your feelings, my dear. I can still remember the first time I came to Trentavon as a new bride. The house does have an intimidating look about it, but it is a home none the less and I hope you will be comfortable here before you and Richard continue your journey to your estate."

Jane thanked the countess and then glanced at her husband who was beside his brother on the seat opposite her. His warm smile gave her all the courage she needed.

The exterior of Trentavon Hall may have appeared austere and foreboding nonetheless the inside was anything but. The entrance was airy and inviting, every servant Jane met made her feel welcome. From the warm smiles and murmurs of congratulations from the Housekeeper and Butler, when Fitzwilliam had introduced her as his bride, to the obvious attentiveness of the cook enquiring of her favourite dishes, Jane felt welcome. Rooms had been prepared for them, as now he was married Richard would no longer occupy the chambers of his youth, and the housekeeper quickly led them to the suite of rooms which would be theirs whenever they stayed at Trentavon. Jane thanked Mrs Pritchard for her kindness as the housekeeper opened the door to their chambers and informed them that hot water was prepared in their dressing rooms and a light repast laid out in their sitting room, with a carafe of red wine, for their refreshment.

The housekeeper shook her head at Jane's thanks, informing her it was no trouble as she was sure all they wished for after such a long journey was the ability to rest. After reminding the colonel to pull the cord if he or his wife required anything further, Mrs Pritchard departed.

Half an hour later, after washing the dust of the road from their hands and faces, and changing from their travelling attire, they partook in the delicious array of foods laid before them. Once any hunger was satisfied, Fitzwilliam said, "I know you are fatigued my love and would most likely wish that we both retire with all haste, but I would see my father, if you do not mind."

"Of course I do not mind, Richard. Would you like my company?"

"That is most sweet of you, but, no. I believe it is best if, at first, you remain here while I assess his health. If he is greatly improved, as I hope, then I am sure that you will be able to meet him tomorrow."

Jane gave her husband a gentle smile as she willingly agreed. "While you visit the earl, I shall prepare for the night. I will endeavour to remain awake until you return, but do not think too poorly of me if I should fail in my attempts."

Fitzwilliam knocked on the door of his father's chambers, at the sound of a voice he entered. Sebastian was already there. "Well, Father, it appears I win the bet." Tansley grinned at his brother.

Walking further into the room, Fitzwilliam enquired, "What bet is that?"

"Father believed you would prefer to spend the remainder of the evening with Mrs Fitzwilliam."

"Ah, I see." Fitzwilliam turned to his father. "Well, Sir, as you can see I am here. What do you owe my brother for my diligence?"

The earl gave a dramatic sigh. "It would appear I have lost a bottle of my best brandy."

"I trust you will share it with me, brother dear. After all it is my presence that has ensured your success."

Tansley groaned and Fitzwilliam laughed, while the earl looked on smiling warmly at his sons. He was delighted to have them both at Trentavon, well worth the loss of some fine French brandy.

Fitzwilliam looked towards his father and his laughter died in his throat as he caught sight of something he had not seen in a very long time; there was an unmistakable twinkle in the earl's eyes. He quickly glanced at his brother and noticed the warmth in his countenance. Fitzwilliam smiled broadly at the earl. "It is good to see you back with us, Father."

"It is good to be back, Son."

"Will you return to the House before the summer recess?"

The earl shook his head. "Not yet, Richard. There are still days when there is nothing I want more than a good swig of laudanum. Dr Nicholls advised me against returning to town too soon. I would be a fool to go against him. I am so fortunate to have a caring family and count myself blessed to have a second chance."

"You have come far, Father," Tansley interjected. "It has not been an easy path for you, but you have succeeded. We are proud of you, Sir."

"Indeed we are," Fitzwilliam agreed.

The earl whispered his thanks as a tear edged its way out of the corner of his eye and slowly slid down his cheek.

"I wish I had never given your aunt my ill-judged advice regarding Anne's health. I will never forgive myself for the pain it must be inflicting on her and my poor niece. I only hope that one day they will forgive me." The earl's remorse was evident.

Tansley and Fitzwilliam gave no response; both knew that would be another difficult path for their father, which would weigh greatly on his conscience.

Fitzwilliam quietly closed the door as he walked into the chambers he and Jane had been allocated. The table in the sitting room, now clear of all the detritus from their repast, was the home of a solitary candle which sent a dim glow around the room. It had burned down and only an inch or so of the candle remained, but it was enough light to aid his way to their bedchamber. With the candle holder firmly in his grasp he slowly opened the bedroom door, all the while praying the hinges were well greased.

Another candle spread its light from its position on the bedside table. He quickly doused the candle in his hand before entering the room fully; he did not wish to wake Jane.

Fitzwilliam stood by the bed for a full minute, looking down in admiration at the sleeping form of his wife. *'How did I get so lucky? She is so beautiful, both in and out, a veritable angel. Hmmm. Bingley, you are a fool and I thank you.'*

He rubbed his hand over his chin. He would never have been classed as a handsome man; he had taken after his father. The earl had had a title to help him when he was looking for a bride, but Richard was the second son—no added incentive there. Now, as his hand passed over the scar on his cheek, he could not understand how he had won the hand of such a beautiful, kind and caring young woman. He held down a chuckle, she had even called him handsome—poor Jane obviously needed spectacles.

Smiling as he undid his jacket, Fitzwilliam was soon down to his breeches and boots. Sitting on a nearby chair, so as not to disturb Jane, he attempted to remove his boots; not the easiest of things to do quietly when there was no help available. After struggling, for what felt like an age, he heard a sleepy voice murmur, "Do you need help, my love?"

Fitzwilliam looked up from his task to see Jane leaning on an elbow as she smiled across the bed at him.

"I am sorry, Jane. I was attempting to be silent so as not to disturb you."

"Well now you know you can make as much noise as you wish. I am sure a good grunt or groan will see to the speedy removal of your boots."

To Fitzwilliam's frustration his dear wife was correct and he was soon free of his boots. By the time his breeches followed them Jane had turned down the sheet and blankets, and was patting the mattress inviting her husband to join her.

As she lay contented in her husband's arms Jane asked if the earl was recovering.

"Yes, thank the Lord." Fitzwilliam went on to tell her of the meeting and how pleased he was to see the improvement in the earl's well-being. "You will meet father in the morning, and before you say anything, I am sure he will love you."

Chapter 18

"Lizzy, you have a letter. By the handwriting I would say it is from Jane."

Elizabeth looked up from the handkerchief she was endeavouring to embroider. Smiling widely at her aunt she immediately put down her embroidery. Taking the letter she looked down at the elegant writing. "Thank you, Aunt. I do hope she is well."

"I am sure she will be," her aunt replied. "Now I must have a word with cook, so I shall leave you to read your letter."

Elizabeth returned to her seat and quickly broke the seal.

Longenaire, Longnor, Staffordshire
4th May

My Dearest Sister,

We arrived at our estate this afternoon and I cannot begin to describe how beautiful it is or how happy I am. Mrs Pearce, the housekeeper, is a dear and reminds me greatly of Hill. While I write, my husband, I cannot say how pleased I am to write that, is with his steward. We are only here for a se'nnight or so and the colonel feels it behoves him to spend as much time with Mr Pearce as he may. As you may have already surmised our housekeeper and steward are wed, and we could not ask for a more conscientious couple caring for our home.

But before I tell you more about Longenaire, I must tell you of our time in Derbyshire. The journey was long, as we expected, but comfortable none the less. Poor Lady Matlock was quite exhausted by the time we arrived and immediately retired to her chambers. The colonel was eager to see his father to ascertain the state of his health for himself, but I did not meet the earl until the following day.

Lord Matlock made me feel most welcome. He even apologised for not attending our wedding. I have to say, Lizzy, if I had not known of his illness I would never have guessed. Both my husband and the viscount seemed well pleased with their father's health. The countess remarked that she was delighted to see her husband so well.

Although our visit was exceedingly short it was very enjoyable and I hope it will not be too long before we are able to enjoy the hospitality at Trentavon again, but next time for a longer period.

We departed early this morning, breaking our fast while the horses rested at a coaching inn at the market town of Ashbourne. The journey to Longnor was much less arduous, but slow at times because of the numerous hills and dales. Our horses had truly earned their rest by the time we arrived at Longenaire.

Longnor appeared to be a good sized village, possibly even as large as Meryton, and is conveniently situated between Bakewell and Macclesfield. I doubt I would need to go often to those towns, as we passed a goodly number of shops in the village. I am sure I will be able to acquire most things I might need right here. A mile or two from the village the driver steered the horses to the right and we left the road we had been travelling on. A few minutes later the horses made their way through a stone archway. As we drove into the estate I had a clear view of the surrounding land, and in the distance the house lay nestled in the shade of a nearby hill. Lizzy, there was grass as far as the eye could see with the occasional oak tree peppering the horizon. Sheep grazed contently on the pasture, and drystone walls kept them from straying. I have to admit I was in awe of the tranquillity and beauty of the vista. My husband laughed at my eager appreciation and was quick to inform me that I had not, as yet, seen inside the house. I informed him that did not matter. I loved the land already, so I was sure the house would be perfect too.

Now what can I say of the house. It is indeed perfect. I wish we could remain here, though I would miss you, my dear sister, far too much. It is an old manor house built I am informed in the reign of good Queen Bess. As soon as I had refreshed from our journey, my husband and dear Mrs Pearce took me on a tour of the house. I believe it is slightly larger than Longbourn as the main rooms on the ground floor appear to be quite spacious. From what my dear husband had told me of Longenaire I had formed a picture in my mind, but as I alighted from the carriage and looked up at the house I realized the picture I had envisaged was a very poor substitute for the real thing.

My husband informs me that Mr Darcy's estate is not far from here, only twenty miles or so across the county border. Just think, Lizzy, when you marry Mr Darcy we shall be within easy distance to visit each other.

My dear sister, I trust that you and everyone at Gracechurch Street are well, and the move to Russell Square is proceeding according to plan.

There is no point in sending a reply to this letter to Staffordshire as I fear we will be on our way to town before any reply could arrive here. But do not think that I do not wish for a letter from you, for it is quite the opposite. If you have time in the next few days to write then send it to Bedford Place, I will greatly enjoy reading it when we arrive there.

Now I must bring this letter to a close as I wish speak with cook. In anticipation of meeting our tenants in the next few days, I shall ask cook to make some toffees for the children. I have no doubt they will enjoy them as much as we and the children of Longbourn's tenants did.

I look forward to being in your company again. Please give my love to our aunt and uncle. I miss you all greatly.

Your loving sister,

Jane Fitzwilliam

Looking at the carriage clock on the mantelpiece, Lizzy quickly rose and went in search of her aunt. She had nearly an hour to spare before William would arrive, enough time to share Jane's letter with her aunt and perhaps begin a reply.

Darcy looked at his pocket watch; he opened the drawer of his desk and placed the documents he had been reading within it. He was about to rise and call for his carriage to be brought around from the mews when his butler knocked and entered the room.

"An express has been delivered for you, Sir."

"Thank you, Carlton. I shall be leaving to call on Miss Bennet shortly."

"Of course, Sir. I shall arrange for your carriage immediately."

Darcy did not hear his butler leave the room, he was looking at the express and wondering what could have caused his aunt to send such a missive. He broke the seal, read the few short lines and sighed. Rising from his desk, he walked quickly out of the room.

Seeing his butler, Darcy called out, "Ah, Carlton. I shall be leaving for Rosings as soon as I return from Gracechurch Street. Speed is of the essence, so ask Higgins to start packing immediately. Also I would be grateful if Cook could put together a basket for the journey, for I do not wish to dally at coaching inns. I do not know how long I will be away."

"Do you wish Higgins to accompany you, Sir?"

"Yes. Now I must see Miss Darcy, is she in the music room?"

Carlton affirmed he believed that to be the case; he had barely finished his sentence before his master turned and quickly made his way up the stairs.

Fifteen minutes later than planned Darcy was in his carriage on his way to Gracechurch Street. He deeply regretted that his visit would be short and worse he did not know when he would next see Elizabeth.

Darcy walked into the drawing room of Gracechurch Street and was greeted by the warm smile of his beloved. That smile vanished as Elizabeth took in Darcy's countenance.

She walked quickly to his side. "What is the matter, my love?" Concern etched her face.

"I am afraid I must away to Rosings. I do not know when I will return."

"Is it Miss de Bourgh?"

Darcy gave a nod of his head. "Yes, I have received an express from my aunt. Anne's condition has worsened."

"Oh, poor Lady Catherine. How terrible to have to watch her only child fade away. Of course you must go and quickly, but I would like go with you."

When Darcy made to object she continued, "I might be of some help with the care of Miss de Bourgh, or offer some companionship to Lady Catherine in her time of need."

"Georgiana has also imparted her wish to accompany me. But, Elizabeth, I must warn you, the journey will not be like our previous visit to Rosings. We will not be stopping at inns for more than the barest necessities."

"Of course, I expected as much. And as Georgiana is to accompany you I can see no reason why I too should not join your party. I assume Georgiana's maid will attend her?" Darcy gave a quick nod of his head and she smiled. "Good, then there will be three ladies to one gentleman, well within the bounds of propriety, my virtue will be safe.

"Two gentlemen, my valet, Higgins, will also travel with us. But as you say, it is well within the bounds of propriety. Can you be ready within the hour?"

"Of course, sooner if needs be. But, before you return to Darcy House we should tell my aunt."

It was in fact a little less than an hour later when the Darcy carriage pulled away from Gracechurch Street with Miss Elizabeth, Miss Darcy, Miss Darcy's maid, Mr Darcy and the gentleman's valet aboard.

Darcy's coachman had his instructions. He was to stop at the coaching inn at Bromley where the horses would be changed, a groom had been sent on ahead to ensure there was a private parlour for the Darcys and Miss Bennet.

They were not far into their journey when Elizabeth spoke of receiving a letter from Jane that morning. She spoke of Jane's delight at her new home in Staffordshire, and also told Darcy and Georgiana of the improved health of their uncle.

"That is good news indeed. I have been praying for my uncle's recovery."

"So have I," said Georgiana. "Do you think we might be able to go to Derbyshire soon? I miss Pemberley."

"I miss the quiet of Pemberley too, but no, Georgiana, we shall not return until Elizabeth and I are wed." Darcy turned his gaze to Elizabeth. *'I would not wish to be so far away from you, my love.'*

Elizabeth smiled at her betrothed and a look of understanding passed between them, as though he had spoken the silent words.

It was a long and tiring journey, and all were relieved to eventually arrive at their destination.

"Good evening, Diplock. Where is my aunt?"

"Lady Catherine is in the family drawing room. Please follow me, Mr Darcy."

Darcy turned to Georgiana and Elizabeth. "I will attend my aunt, but I am sure you both will wish to refresh from your journey before joining me."

"No," replied Elizabeth, "I would like to join you, even if it is for only a short while before I change in to more comfortable attire." Georgiana quickly added her agreement.

When Diplock announced her visitors, Lady Catherine rose from her chair. She was relieved to see her nephew but surprised that her niece and Miss Elizabeth had accompanied him. "Fitzwilliam, thank you for coming so quickly. Georgiana, and Miss Bennet, I did not expect you to join my nephew."

"Lady Catherine," Elizabeth replied, "when Mr Darcy told me of your message I could not stay away. I hope that I might be of some assistance with Miss de Bourgh's care, or company for yourself. I trust you do not think me presumptuous."

"I wished to be here too, Aunt," Georgiana whispered meekly.

Silence ensued and Elizabeth was beginning to think she had over stepped the mark with familiarity when Lady Catherine smiled. "Thank you Miss Bennet, and you too Georgiana, I am pleased to have you both here. Now I am sure you all wish to refresh after your journey, but do not tarry. I will inform Cook to hold back dinner until six o'clock."

Elizabeth rose from her bed and walked over to the window, it was well light outside but still early; a glance at the small carriage clock on the table nearby confirmed that. It was too early to break her fast and she was sure the remainder of the family would still be abed. Dressing in a day gown which needed no help from a maid, she then put her hair into a simple bun before quietly making her way from her room to the one occupied by Miss de Bourgh.

Opening the latch as quietly as possible, Elizabeth peeped around the oak door and saw her friend Charlotte sitting by Miss de Bourgh's bedside. Entering, and as silently as possible closing the door, she softly made her way across the room.

Charlotte turned in her chair, away from the sleeping Miss de Bourgh, to see who had entered. A wide smile warmed her countenance as she saw her friend walking towards her. Charlotte rose and took a couple of steps before they embraced each other.

"It is good to see you, Eliza," Charlotte whispered. "I knew Lady Catherine had written to Mr Darcy, but I did not expect to see you, my friend."

"I could not stay away when I might be of help. Have you been with Miss de Bourgh all night?"

"No. A maid sits with Anne until just after sunrise and then I take over. You do not need to worry about me." Charlotte lowered her voice to a whisper. "Dr Morgan set out a rota, so that no one is so weary that they cannot care for Miss de Bourgh properly."

"Dr Morgan sounds an eminently sensible gentleman."

"He is." A gentle blush rose in Charlotte's cheeks as she replied.

Elizabeth's eyes sparkled. "Ah, so that is the way the wind blows," she whispered with a light giggle and then immediately regretted her words. The look of sadness in Charlotte's eyes was heart-breaking.

"No Eliza. I admire the doctor greatly, but it can be no more than that. I am newly widowed, little more than a month, and can be of no interest to a gentleman such as he."

Elizabeth hugged her friend once more and then softly asked, "How is Miss de Bourgh?"

Charlotte spoke quietly to Anne's lady's maid, who was standing nearby, before suggesting to Elizabeth that she join her in Anne's sitting room. There they would not be overheard.

"It is so sad. The grave illness she endured as a young child has prevented Miss de Bourgh from enjoying life. Her heart is weak and the constant taking of laudanum over the years has not helped her constitution, and now even the simplest of illness, which would usually not affect a person greatly, worsens Anne's already frail health.

"Dr Morgan tried to persuade Lady Catherine to wait a day or two before contacting Mr Darcy, and now that Anne's breathing has improved he does not believe her passing is imminent. The discomfort she suffers is great at times, so, as well as a little laudanum, different medications, such as Willow Bark, are being used to ease her suffering.

"Dr Morgan has explained to Lady Catherine that no one is at fault. The blame, if it lies anywhere, is with the frailness of our human bodies. The laudanum has not speeded her death, if anything it may have given her some comfort from the pain and constant fatigue she has suffered since childhood."

"How much time does the doctor believe she has?" Elizabeth thought of the young lady lying in the next room. 'She is but five years my senior, 'tis no age at all.'

"He cannot be sure. It may be days, but more likely it will be weeks or perhaps a few months."

Elizabeth attempted to hold back a tear, but it was no good. She could not hold back the sorrow she felt, not only for Anne de Bourgh but also for Lady Catherine for no mother should witness the passing of her child. Silent tears flowed unabated down her cheeks.

When Darcy entered the dining room he discovered it was empty, except for Elizabeth. "Good morning, Elizabeth. I see you are breaking your fast alone. I hope you do not mind if I join you."

Elizabeth looked up and attempted to put on a happy face. "Of course not, William, I am glad of your company."

Darcy quickly made his way to Elizabeth's side. "Elizabeth, tell me, what is the matter?" He was shocked to see her red rimmed eyes. "What, or who, has made you cry so?"

Elizabeth glanced quickly at the maid who was standing next to the sideboard before returning her attention to her betrothed. "Might we go for a walk once we have broken our fast? I feel in need of some fresh air."

"Of course, my love. We shall go as soon as you wish."

The fresh morning air was exactly what Elizabeth needed. As they walked silently across the lawn towards the shelter of the groves, Elizabeth could feel a weight lifting. She was still sad at heart and wished more than anything that something could be done to help Miss de Bourgh, but the deep bone wrenching sorrow that had overcome her was gone.

Darcy said nothing, he knew Elizabeth was troubled but he would have patience and wait until she felt ready to speak of it. When eventually she told him of her conversation with Charlotte, Darcy gently gathered her into his arms and softly stroked her back.

"Life is so unfair," she muttered into his jacket.

"I know," he replied. "Anne has had every affordable comfort but not the health to enjoy it. When the time comes I shall mourn my cousin, but I shall be glad for Anne's sake that her suffering has passed."

Darcy released her and they continued their walk. "When we return to the house I shall speak with the doctor and then sent an express to Trentavon. I do not know if they will be able to come and I do not know if Aunt Catherine would welcome her brother here."

"But, now that Lady Catherine knows that her daughter's early demise was inevitable, surely she will no longer solely blame the earl?"

"I cannot say, but it might be best for some time to pass before they meet again. I will also send an express to Fitzwilliam, though I am not sure as to the best place to send it. I am uncertain of when they intend to return to town, it may pass them on the road but it is a risk I will take."

"Perhaps if you send your missive to Longenaire and I shall quickly finish my letter to Jane, informing them of Anne's condition, then it can be sent to Bedford Place."

"That is a sound proposition. Are you feeling restored enough to return to the house?"

Elizabeth smiled lovingly at him; his care and concern for her wellbeing touched her greatly. "I am well. Returning to the house would be an excellent idea."

Darcy finished his letters and after he had collected Elizabeth's missive to her sister he sought out his coachman and gave him instructions to take the letters with all speed to Maidstone. With enough coins in his pocket, Johns was to ensure that the three missives were dispatched with all haste. Darcy did not expect his uncle or aunt to appear at Rosings. Lady Matlock had only recently returned to Derbyshire, and he was sure the earl must feel some guilt for Anne's condition. As he walked from the stables towards the house, Darcy thought of his Fitzwilliam cousins. *'Tansley may come south, if his father's health allows—Mrs Fitzwilliam's letter to Elizabeth gives hope on that score. Fitzwilliam was here not long ago and has so little time with Jane before his next orders arrive. As much as I would like his company, I hope Fitzwilliam will not cut short their time in Staffordshire to rush to our cousin's side.'*

Having spoken at some length with Dr Morgan, Darcy included the doctor's prognosis in his letters.

...The doctor believes there may be more of these periods, when Anne's health wanes before appearing to recover again, before the end comes. It may be some weeks away yet, but he does not believe she will still be with us at the end of the summer.

Chapter 19

Mr Hunt, the new vicar of Hunsford, was much like his predecessor in his manners to his patron, but that was where any similarity ended. The rotund gentleman was in his early forties and had an equally rotund wife. When not in the company of Lady Catherine, or her exalted nephew, the couple were of a cheerful manner, showing kindness to everyone they had contact with. Elizabeth discovered the true characters of the vicar and his wife quite by accident.

On the second day of her stay at Rosings Elizabeth rose early. She found sleep impossible as much was going through her mind, thus allowing for little rest. After dinner, the evening before, Lady Catherine had questioned her about Jane; no not questioned, it was more like an interrogation, as if Lady Catherine wished to know everything about her sister. As Elizabeth walked through the parkland she thought back on the conversation.

"So, Miss Bennet, tell me of your sister. Your parents must be delighted that their daughter has captured the son of an earl."

"I believe my parents are content that my sister is happy in her marriage," she replied, *while thinking in the case of her mother even ecstatic was too mild a word. "She loves the colonel and I believe he loves her in return."*

"Humph. Love is not a sentiment required in a marriage, especially not one of the haut ton."

"That might be the case, my Lady, but both Jane and I pledged a long time ago that we would only marry for love. A marriage of convenience, no matter how fortuitous it might be to our family, was not something we wished for."

"No, I believe you refused your cousin. A marriage to your father's heir would have given security to your mother and unmarried sisters." Elizabeth could scarcely believe Lady Catherine's words, had she forgotten Mr Collins' character? *"But of course,"* the Lady continued, *"hindsight has revealed you to be most wise in your steadfastness. I wonder if your sister would have been had she been the object of Mr Collins' desire."*

"The outcome would have been the same, Lady Catherine. Had my sister any mercenary tendencies she would have married the young man who offered for her five years ago. He wrote the most appalling poetry, but he was the eldest son of a viscount, my sister had she been so inclined could have been a viscountess one day."

"May be it was the idea of being the *chatelaine* of a large estate, which decided her against him."

"No, Lady Catherine. My mother has taught all her girls well. We all know the importance of household accounts, setting a good table, seeing to the welfare of our tenants, as well as all the other accomplishments a lady would need to ensure that her husband and his estate were well cared for."

"Your elder sister called on your father's tenants?"

"Yes, and in a letter I received, but a few days ago, from Jane, she was looking forward to meeting her husband's tenants at Longenaire over the next day or two. She was instructing her cook to make some of our grandmother's soft toffees, which she intends to give to the tenants' children."

Elizabeth was abruptly brought out of her musing as she walked around some thick bushes in the copse and found herself on a well walked track, right into the path of a woman walking towards her. Elizabeth had not expected to meet anyone and had not realized how far she had walked. She apologised profusely to the woman.

"I am so sorry. I am afraid I was in a world of my own."

"It is of no concern, there is no harm done," the woman replied kindly.

"I appear to have walked farther than I intended. Can you tell me where I am?"

"Of course, Miss. That house that you can just see through the trees is the Hunsford vicarage."

"Oh, my friend lived there." *'If not for Papa it would have been my home.'*

"You are a friend of Mrs Collins?"

"Yes," Elizabeth replied with a slightly quizzical look; she wondered if this woman had been a friend to Charlotte.

"I do hope she is well and recovering from her loss. Not that it is much of a loss, if you ask me. Oh I am sorry, Miss, I should not have spoken so."

"Do not trouble yourself, Mrs …"

"Partridge, Miss."

"Mrs Partridge, do not trouble yourself for I am in agreement with you. I am Miss Bennet and Mr Collins was my cousin. You knew him well?"

"Yes, I am the cook at the vicarage. It is not a large house and therefore little happens that escapes my attention."

Elizabeth wondered about the new vicar, but could not ask if he was a good man. "Is the new incumbent settling in?"

Mrs Partridge smiled; she guessed the young lady's concerns.

"Mr Hunt and his dear wife are excellent people. It is a pleasure to work for them." Seeing the look of disbelief on Miss Bennet's countenance she quickly continued. "I know what you are thinking. He is much like Mr Collins with his bowing and subservience to her Ladyship, Mrs Hunt is the same, and I am sure that if her Ladyship was not so worried about poor Miss de Bourgh, she would be very pleased with her new vicar. But what they are like in the presence of her Ladyship is where any similarity ends. They are a happy and jovial couple behind the walls of the parsonage, kind to their servants and caring to Mr Hunt's flock. Beggin' your pardon, Miss, but Mr Collins was a bad apple. The folk of Hunsford are in much safer hands now."

"That is good to know, Mrs Partridge. I shall tell Mrs Collins, I know she will be relieved to hear it."

The following morning, after the Sunday service, when Elizabeth spoke with both Mr and Mrs Hunt, she was pleased to agree with Mrs Partridge's estimation of the couple.

The next few days followed in much the same way as the previous two. Georgiana and Elizabeth spent time with Anne, who was confined to her bed chamber, sometimes together and sometimes separately. This allowed Charlotte more free time; Elizabeth was pleased to see that her friend was beginning to lose her fatigued appearance, which had worried Elizabeth when they first arrived. Time was also spent with Lady Catherine. Elizabeth was relieved that after a second day of questions regarding her sister, Lady Catherine rarely spoke of Jane. When she did it was in general conversation, usually relating to her nephew, Colonel Fitzwilliam. Elizabeth and Darcy did manage some time alone. It was usually early in the morning, before Lady Catherine and Georgiana rose for the day, that

Darcy and Elizabeth could be found walking around the grounds. Elizabeth found this time enjoyable, and she hoped they would be able to continue with this routine when they were wed and living at Pemberley.

As Darcy and Elizabeth walked towards the grove on Thursday morning, he remained silent for longer than was his usual wont.

"William, is there something troubling you?"

He turned and smiled. "No, there is nothing for you to be concerned about. I was just thinking over my aunt's conversation last night."

Elizabeth remembered Lady Catherine's request to speak with her nephew before he retired. "The conversation you had before you retired?"

"Yes." Darcy sighed and then drew Elizabeth towards an old tree stump. He took off his greatcoat and laid it over the stump. "Rest here, my love, and I will tell you about my conversation with Lady Catherine. But, what I tell you must remain just between us for the nonce."

By the time Elizabeth left Anne's room it was mid-afternoon and she had thought much about what William had told her that morning. Of course, *now* Lady Catherine's questioning made much more sense. She hoped, for Jane's peace of mind and the colonel's safety, that Colonel Fitzwilliam would agree to his aunt's demands.

Elizabeth made her way down the stairs in the hope of getting some refreshments. She heard voices coming from the direction of the entrance way and so peeped over the banister to spy the figures below.

"Jane!" she cried, as she hurriedly made her way down the stairs.

Jane walked quickly to the foot of the stairs. As soon as Elizabeth's feet touched the floor Jane reached out to embrace her sister. "Oh Lizzy, it is so good to see you."

"You look well Jane. I see married life is suiting you."

Jane blushed as they walked towards the others. Elizabeth then noticed that Viscount Tansley was standing with his brother and Darcy. As soon as they reached the gentlemen Elizabeth curtsied.

"Lord Tansley, Richard, it is a pleasure to see you both again."

"It is a pleasure to be in your company too, Miss Bennet. I trust you are well?" Tansley asked.

"I am indeed, thank you, my Lord."

"Oh no, Miss Bennet that will not do. You call Richard by his given name."

"But he is now my brother, my Lord."

"Well, unless I have been misinformed, you are soon to be my cousin. I am Sebastian or Tansley amongst family."

"Thank you, Sebastian. If that is the case then I believe Miss Bennet is far too formal amongst soon-to-be cousins. Please call me Elizabeth or Lizzy."

"Elizabeth. A delightful name for a delightful lady." Tansley looked at his cousin's dour expression and laughed. "Do not worry, cousin. I assure you your lady is safe with me."

"Should we not pay our respects to Lady Catherine?"

"You are right as always, my dear Jane," her husband replied. "Diplock, this beautiful lady is my wife."

"It is a pleasure to meet you, Mrs Fitzwilliam. Colonel, I wish both you and Mrs Fitzwilliam every happiness."

"Thank you, Diplock. I am indeed a fortunate man. Now tell us, where might we find my aunt?"

"Her Ladyship is in the drawing room, Sir." Diplock began to walk towards the room.

"Diplock." The butler stopped and turned towards the colonel. "There is no need to announce us."

Diplock bowed, taking a step back, and Fitzwilliam set off with his cousin and brother while the ladies linked arms and walked behind them.

Lady Catherine looked up from her book; she was pleasantly surprised to see both her Fitzwilliam nephews and new niece enter the room.

Richard and Sebastian walked quickly to her side, leaving Darcy with the ladies. Each kissed their aunt's cheek before she had time to rise from her chair.

"We came as soon as we received Darcy's express. How fares Anne?" Richard asked.

Lady Catherine saw the look of concern in their eyes as the brothers looked down at her. "I believe *as well as can be expected* would be the doctor's reply." Lady Catherine paused for a moment. "I must thank you, Richard, for insisting Dr Morgan attend to Anne. I know the outcome will not be the one I would wish for, but I am well aware that he has done everything in his power to ensure her comfort. Moreover, I know what little time my dear Anne has left he will ensure she is well cared for."

Her nephews stepped away as Lady Catherine rose from her chair and looked at Jane, who was standing next to her sister. "I had not expected you to make the journey, but I am pleased to see you, Niece."

"Lady Catherine." Jane curtsied. "I insisted on accompanying my husband. I hope I might be of some help with the care of Miss de Bourgh. I may not have met your daughter but she is now my cousin. I would like to be of assistance."

"Very well, Jane, but my daughter would wish you to call her Anne, not Miss de Bourgh. I am sure your assistance will be much appreciated." Lady Catherine turned back to her nephew. "Richard, once you have refreshed from your journey I would have a private conversation with you. I will await you in the study. Do not dally."

Both Fitzwilliam and Tansley stared after their aunt as she left the room. Worry etched Jane's countenance but neither Darcy nor Elizabeth could say a word, not to ease Jane's concern or the brothers' curiosity as to what Lady Catherine was about, it was not their place to do so.

The door to the study opened. Lady Catherine glanced at the carriage clock on the desk then looked at her nephew as he walked towards her.

"I am glad to see you, Richard. It is fortuitous that you arrived today, otherwise I would have been forced to write to you." Richard's eyebrows rose at his aunt's comment. "I can see you are curious so I will get straight to the point. But before I do, sit down, you are much too tall."

Fitzwilliam sat, facing Lady Catherine over the large oak desk.

"I had once wished that Anne would marry William, and have a long and happy life. I realize now that will never happen. For every day she is with us is a blessing."

Fitzwilliam opened his mouth to speak but Lady Catherine raised her hand. "No, there is no need to say anything. Dr Morgan has been brutally honest with me, and I would have it no other way. Anne's days are few. It will not be long before she joins her father.

"I have decided to make a new will. As I said it is fortuitous that you arrived today, for my solicitor will arrive tomorrow to write down my instructions.

"I have decided to leave Rosings to you." Lady Catherine raised her hand to ensure her nephew's silence. "*But* there are conditions, and I would have you remain silent while I list them."

Fitzwilliam looked at Lady Catherine warily, wondering what his aunt was planning.

"Firstly, you will resign your commission immediately. You will write to your general. The letter will be sent by express today. Secondly, you and your wife will take up residence at Rosings as soon as is possible. I suggest you sell your house in Bedford Place as the de Bourgh town house will be available to you. Brook Street is a great improvement on Bedford Place. I am not insensible to the fact that a house cannot have two mistresses. I will remain as Mistress of Rosings for as long as Anne lives. During that time your wife will prepare for the role she will assume at Anne's demise. When Anne is no longer with us I will hand over the care of Rosings to Jane. I will remove myself to either the Dower House or the de Bourgh town house.

"I do not expect you to give me your answer now. In fact I encourage you to speak with your wife. After all it will be both your futures. You have until Mr Whetherington arrives tomorrow to give me your answer."

"What if I decide against one of your conditions?"

"If that is the case, Rosings will go to William."

Fitzwilliam stood. "Whatever my decision, I would thank you for your generosity. I never for one moment believed Rosings might be mine."

Darcy was waiting as he walked out of the study. Fitzwilliam shook his head and frowned at his cousin. "You knew!"

Darcy smiled. "I hope the conditions do not put you off accepting our aunt's offer."

"It is not me I am concerned about. Believe me, Darcy, it would be no hardship to resign my commission. I would miss the camaraderie but not the mud and mire of the battlefield with all its blood and gore. The uniform might be appealing to some but war is not. No, it is Jane that is my concern. She has been her own mistress, not for very long I admit but nevertheless she has been the mistress of my home. If I accept the conditions laid down by Aunt Catherine then Jane will no longer be mistress of her own home."

"It will not be for long."

"You cannot say that. Only the Almighty knows when Anne's time will come."

"No, Fitzwilliam. You have not seen Anne since Easter. Her health has declined. As I wrote in my letter, Dr Morgan believes it is a matter of weeks and I am inclined to agree with him. He has promised our aunt he will remain at Rosings until the end, although really there is little he can do. He would not have made such a promise if he did not truly believe the end was nigh.

"Speak with your wife. I am sure Mrs Fitzwilliam would prefer to live under Lady Catherine's rule and have you safe at home rather than be her own mistress with you fighting on some foreign soil."

Fitzwilliam knew Darcy would be correct in his assumption, and he was. Jane cried with relief at Lady Catherine's generosity. Her husband would no longer risk life and limb protecting his country in the theatre of war.

Richard gathered her into his arms. "You would be happy living at Rosings?"

"Yes," she murmured into his chest. Slowly Jane lifted up her tear stained face and looked into her husband's blue eyes. "I would be happy living anywhere if you were by my side."

"In that case, my love, there is little else to say. Now dry your tears. We will find Lady Catherine and give her our answer. Tonight I will write out my letter of resignation. Tomorrow I shall journey to town and request a meeting with the general. I shall take Jones with me. Hopefully we shall return the following day, if I can persuade him to leave His Majesty's service and remain in mine."

"I should be grateful if you would take Polly too. I will give her a list of things at Bedford Place that I would have with me here. I am sure I will survive without her attention for a day or two."

Chapter 20

George Wickham could not believe his ill-fortune. He had been so sure he had the winning hand. He was lucky to still have the clothes on his back, but what use were they when his pockets were empty. He needed money and the need was urgent. Those he was in debt to would not wait patiently if he could not pay up within the allocated time. They would be more likely to take a pound of flesh—his flesh.

He had come north of the river two days ago as rumour had it there were easy pickings around Blackfriars. The truth had been far different. Instead of a cove with more money than sense, it appeared he was not so ripe for the picking and the game of chance was lost.

Wickham made his way through the dirty streets while bemoaning his fortune. *'It is all Darcy's fault. If I had received that to which I was entitled as the old man's godson I would not be walking through the slums with only the clothes on my back.'*

Remembering his old friend's aversion for the season, Wickham wondered if he had already departed town. *'Tomorrow I will take a walk in the park. If the house is shut up it will be easy pickings. The servants are so set in their ways. If Darcy is away it will be too easy, just like before.'*

Happy that he may have a solution to his current financial problems he began to whistle a pleasing little ditty as he continued towards Eastcheap.

Mrs Honeycomb ensured that all the windows and doors were secured. The last client had left and the girls had all retired for the night. It was not that she did not trust her neighbours; she just preferred to err on the side of caution. With candlestick in hand she had barely placed one foot on the bottom stair when there was a hammering at the front door.

Annoyed at whoever was calling at this time of night but never willing to turn away a paying customer, Mrs Honeycomb walked to the door, unbolted it and opened it a fraction.

"Sarah, my love. Are you pleased to see me?"

Sarah Honeycomb gave a most unladylike snort. "What do you want?"

"Ah Sarah, I just need a bed for a night or two. You would not leave your Georgie out in the cold and damp, would you?"

With a sigh Mrs Honeycomb opened the door to allow George Wickham entry. "Two nights and no more!"

"Of course, my love. After two nights I will be out of your hair."

Wickham took the candlestick from her hand and placed it on the occasional table which stood against the wall at his back. His face was shaded from the faint, flickering light of the candle.

"Now, my dear," Wickham said as he reached out and pulled Mrs Honeycomb to him. "How about giving your old George a proper welcome. Hmm, I have missed you and your delectable body."

The coach made its way out of Hunsford and headed for the road to London. "I thought to make this journey with just Jones and Polly for company. I was surprised to see you both." Fitzwilliam smiled at his two companions.

"I thought I might accompany you as there are matters that need my attention in town," his cousin responded.

"And what is your reason, brother?" the colonel asked.

"Once I discovered that both you and Darcy intended to be away from Rosings, I decided to join you. I spent some time sitting with Anne last evening. I was saddened to see her so wan and if I thought my presence would aid her recovery I would not hesitate to remain at Rosings. Our dear Aunt has the company of Mrs Fitzwilliam, Georgiana and Miss Bennet, and has little need of me. She was most understanding of my need to return to town, for Lady Catherine knows I cannot hope to find a wife while rusticating in the country. I will rely on you, brother, to inform me if Anne's condition deteriorates significantly, otherwise I will come to Rosings at the end of the season for a few days before returning to Trentavon."

"Do you think you will find a wife?" Fitzwilliam asked after promising his brother that he would be kept informed of Anne's condition.

"I doubt it, but I shall have fun trying." This response amused the gentlemen, but caused poor Polly to blush.

The colonel, taking pity on his wife's maid, turned the conversation to his cousin. "How long do you envisage remaining in town, Darcy? I hope to return to Rosings tomorrow, I do not wish to wait until Monday if I can avoid it."

"My business will not take long. If all should go according to plan, what time do you wish to depart tomorrow?"

"No later than noon, if possible. It will all depend on when I can meet with the general, and if Polly and Jones have everything readied for departure by then. Of course, depending on the length of the list that my wife entrusted to Polly, I may need to hire a second carriage."

It was early afternoon when Darcy entered his home in Park Lane.

"Mr Darcy, Sir, welcome home. Is Miss Darcy with you?"

"No, Carlton, Miss Darcy remains at Rosings for the nonce. Please tell cook that I hope to be dining out this evening. Inform Thomas there will be a letter for him to deliver to Gracechurch Street, I will let you know when it is ready." Darcy, who had started to make his way to his study, suddenly turned back. "Oh, and, Carlton, do not put the knocker back on the door. I am not at home to callers and will be returning to Rosings tomorrow if all goes well."

The remainder of Darcy's day did indeed pass well and he hoped his cousin was meeting with equal success. The visit to his solicitor's office at Lincoln's Inn had been worthwhile. The marriage settlement was ready, as was Darcy's new will which was signed in the presence of Mr Harwood and his senior clerk. When Darcy returned to his house, a reply to his missive to Mr Gardiner was awaiting him inviting him to dine at Gracechurch Street.

"Mr Darcy," Gardiner stood up from his desk and greeted his caller with a wide smile which turned into a grimace. "You will have to excuse the state of turmoil that surrounds us but we plan to move to Russell Square tomorrow."

"I would not wish to cause any inconvenience to Mrs Gardiner, perhaps it would be best if I dined with your family another evening after Miss Elizabeth and I return to town."

"And disappoint my wife? I think not. It is no inconvenience at all; we have to eat. What is one more place setting at the table?"

Darcy smiled and acquiesced, while hoping that Mr Gardiner was correct in his wife's expectations.

"I have to say," Gardiner continued, "I was intrigued when I received your missive this afternoon. The marriage settlement I could understand and I imagine you have it with you." Mr Gardiner glanced at the satchel the gentleman held.

"Indeed, Sir. I hope you will find it all to your satisfaction."

"I am sure I shall. But firstly, what is the good news you wrote. Is Miss de Bourgh recovered?"

"Sadly no."

With lips pursed, Gardiner shook his head. "I am sorry to hear that, Mr Darcy. I hope Lizzy is able to be of some assistance."

"I can honestly say my Aunt appreciates Elizabeth's presence. I know Mrs Collins is grateful for the time she and Georgiana spend with Miss de Bourgh, and now that Mrs Fitzwilliam has arrived..."

"Jane and the colonel are at Rosings?"

"Yes. With Miss de Bourgh's failing health I wrote to Fitzwilliam and Lord Matlock. Lord and Lady Matlock were unable to make the long journey to Kent, but Viscount Tansley came in their stead. He arrived at Rosings yesterday, as did Colonel and Mrs Fitzwilliam."

"Lizzy must be pleased to have Jane's company again."

"Yes she is. Elizabeth was also delighted on hearing the news that I can now share with you, for although Mrs Fitzwilliam is not the principal, it affects her greatly."

It had been an enjoyable evening with the Gardiners as the dinner had turned into a celebration. On hearing that Fitzwilliam was also in town, Gardiner sent a note to Bedford Place requesting the colonel's company for dinner if he was able.

Mr Gardiner was pleased to hear of Fitzwilliam's inheritance, but his pleasure was nothing to that of his wife—Mrs Gardiner was overjoyed. Her joy was not so much for the grand estate her niece would be mistress of, but that Richard Fitzwilliam would no longer be at risk fighting for King and country. Darcy was not surprised when she confirmed what Elizabeth had told him many days before.

As she wiped the tears of joy from her eyes, Mrs Gardiner smiled at Fitzwilliam. "I know Jane was dreading the day when you would be sent abroad, to face unknown terrors. I cannot adequately express how delighted I am that that will never come to pass."

It was approaching eleven o'clock before Darcy returned home. He was not surprised to find Carlton waiting for him. After greeting his butler, Darcy enquired if the rest of his staff had retired for the night.

"Bryant is on duty and there is a maid in the kitchen, Sir, should you require refreshments."

"Thank you, Carlton. I am going to my study before retiring. I will require nothing further this evening. Send the maid to her bed, and I suggest that you and Bryant follow her example."

"Yes, Sir. Good night, Mr Darcy."

Across town in Eastcheap Mrs Honeycomb was about to prepare for bed; it had been a quiet evening and the last customer had just departed. She was tired and was grateful that Wickham had retired two hours earlier, he would be asleep and she would be free of his advances for tonight. The sight that greeted her as she opened the door to her bedchamber was not what she expected. "Why are you dressing, George? Where are you going at this time of night?"

"I have an appointment."

"An appointment? At this time of night? George Wickham what are you up to?"

"'Tis nothing you need to concern yourself about, my dear." Wickham smiled seductively.

Unmoved by his enticing charm, she declared, "Well just make sure you do not bring the magistrate to my door. I run a respectable establishment and I shall not let you ruin it for me, or the girls who work for me."

"You worry too much, Sarah. I will be back before you have time to miss me." Wickham blew her a kiss and, with a wink and a smile in her direction, he walked out of the bedroom, closing the door firmly behind him.

Wickham knew, without doubt, this night would solve all his problems. He would give a small portion of his ill-gotten gains to Sarah before purchasing a ticket to America; he had heard good things about New England. His reconnaissance to Park Lane early that morning had given him all the information he needed. The knocker was off so the family were definitely not at home, but how far from home were they? Was there a chance Darcy might return soon? It was a young scullery maid he had come across in the back alley who put his mind to rest, convincing him of success. It did not take long to charm the gullible girl and he was soon in possession of all the information he needed. The family, along with Georgiana's companion, had removed to the country in the last few days. Although the young girl could not say if the Darcys had retired to Pemberley, Wickham was convinced that was the case. As far as he was aware, Georgiana rarely accompanied her brother to Rosings. The one time she had, during Mrs Younge's tenure, her companion did not accompany her. He was sure this could be no different. Miss Darcy's companion had accompanied the young mistress therefore Pemberley must have been their destination.

The one important piece of information Wickham failed to learn was that although Miss Darcy's companion had travelled in one of Mr Darcy's carriages, it was not the same carriage as her young charge nor was it even travelling in the same direction. Mrs Annesley had been granted time to visit her sister who lived in Surrey, who sadly was not in good health. Miss Fretwell was fifteen years Mrs Annesley's senior and had no other relatives to call on.

Wickham made his way through the still busy streets, carrying with him an old lantern which shed little light but would be good enough for his needs. In his pocket he carried a tattered bag, which could be used as a cover for the lantern should it be necessary, and a newly acquired set of lock picks. He hoped not to use the lock picks but it had been five years since he had last broken into Darcy House, then he had entered by means of a faulty window in the scullery. The window had been in a state of disrepair for many years, but there was every possibility that it had, by now, been mended making that means of entry no longer available to him.

He did not know what items he might find, but he was sure they would be objects of worth. Old Mr Darcy's strong box was sure to house some treasurers that would make the risk all worthwhile. From the outside it looked like a bench seat in front of the bay window. But once, from the safety of the library, a much younger Wickham had spied the old man as he opened it and retrieved a velvet box; he had then heard Mr Darcy ask a servant where his wife might be. Young Wickham should not have been in the library so, using the servants' stairway for his getaway, the boy made haste to remove himself before anyone discovered him.

Walking past St Paul's he was halfway up Ludgate Hill when he heard a town crier calling the eleventh hour. Wickham picked up his pace. *'At this rate I will be at Darcy House a quarter of an hour before midnight. Excellent. All the servants will have retired and be asleep in their beds.'* Wickham smiled to himself as he continued on to Fleet Street.

Darcy looked up from the documents he was reading and glanced at the large carriage clock which sat on the mantelpiece. He let out a deep breath; it was a quarter to midnight, if he wished to return to Rosings on the morrow it was time to retire. He placed the documents from his steward that he had been reading in the desk's drawer and returned the signed marriage settlement to his satchel. Tomorrow the settlement would be returned to his solicitor for safe keeping; tonight he would keep it with him, for having the document nearby made him feel closer to Elizabeth.

He stood and walked over to the window, taking the candelabra with him, leaving a solitary candle burning on the desk. Reaching out he pulled back the drapes, placed the candles on an occasional table nearby and snuffed them out. There was no smog or fog to hide the moon and its light shone brightly into the room, enabling Darcy to see clearly without the need of a candle.

Leaving the curtains open he made his way back to his desk, picked up the remaining candlestick and the satchel, then made his way to the door which connected his study with the library. He had promised Elizabeth that he would bring back with him a copy of Robert Southey's Poems. Not wishing to risk forgetting it, he decided to retrieve it now.

Closing the door behind him, he walked towards the bay window and looked out at the moonlit park. It was so peaceful at this time of night. Gone was the bustle of the day. There was little noise from the street outside, just the occasional clop of horses' hooves and the rumble of carriage wheels as people returned to their homes.

In a fleeting moment he remembered a previous time when he had stood at this very window as his sister and Mrs Annesley made their way to the park. *'How much has changed since that day when Elizabeth and her sister freely gave their friendship to Georgiana. Thanks to Elizabeth and*

Jane, Georgie has gained confidence, enabling her to recover from the terrible events of last summer. Fitzwilliam is now happily married, and Elizabeth and I soon will be.' A warm smile brightened his mien as he thought how the young lady who was at present his dearest friend would soon be his beloved wife.

Turning away from the window he made his way to the shelves that he was sure held the book he wished to retrieve. He placed the satchel on the floor next to him and began to look along the shelves. It took him a few minutes to locate it; he reached out to take hold of the book when he heard a noise. It was faint, but at this time of night when the house was asleep all sound magnified. Darcy was sure it had come from his study.

Placing the candle, book and satchel quietly on a small table, he slowly made his way in the dim light that the candle afforded him towards the door which led to his study. If a thief was searching his desk he might, with luck, be able to enter the room without the person noticing as the adjoining door was behind his desk.

Slowly he opened the door. Now the noise became clearer. Whoever was in the room was muttering and he could hear what appeared to be metal scraping against metal. Darcy frowned, wondering how many people were in the room and what they were up to. Opening the door a little further he peeped around the edge but he still could not see anyone. The large oak desk, which sat a few feet away, blocked his view forward.

Darcy inched his way around the door, entering the study as stealthily as he could. The carpet, which had been replaced two years ago, absorbed the sound of his foot fall. Two steps gave him a clear view of a solitary man kneeling on the ground in front of the old strong box.

Darcy's expression hardened. A few more discreet footsteps brought him around the desk. His anger increased as he slowly and carefully made his way forward until he was within four or five feet of the man. Clenching his fists, Darcy angrily hissed his nemesis' name. "Wickham!"

Chapter 21

Getting into Darcy House had been no trouble at all. Wickham smiled and had to hold back a chuckle as the scullery window opened with ease. He soon found himself walking slowly through the silent, dark house towards the master's study.

Wickham stealthily opened the study door. Not that there was a need for absolute silence, the servants' quarters were three floors up, there was no one around to hear him, but old habits die hard. He had wondered if Darcy might have employed a night watchman, but the darkness that greeted Wickham as he made his way out of the kitchen firmly dismissed that possibility.

Closing the study door behind him, not quite as silently as he had opened it, Wickham made his way to what appeared to be a box seat under the window. He placed the lantern on the floor close to the lock. Its cheap tallow candle burnt dimly, but would give enough light to work by. After removing the lock picks from his coat pocket and placing them on the floor next to the lantern, he took off his coat and jacket. These were dropped to the floor before Wickham knelt down, facing the object of his desire. He grasped hold of one of the picks and began to work on the lock.

Patience was not something that Wickham possessed in abundance. He soon began to mutter to himself.

"Damn lock. Surely something this old should not be a difficulty to open." He scowled at the lock, before concentrating once more on the task before him.

So focused was his concentration that he failed to hear anyone approaching until a voice, he never expected to hear, hissed, "Wickham!"

Darcy's voice startled him. Turning his head to look up at Darcy, Wickham tried to rise quickly but was unable to before Darcy reached out, grabbing hold of the front of his shirt. Wickham found himself off balance as Darcy dragged him to his feet, but that mattered little as a moment later he hit the floor again with some force as Darcy's fist connected sharply with his jaw.

"Ouch." Wickham rubbed his jaw and attempted to rise again to fight off his foe. Half way into rising from the floor, once again Darcy's fist connected with his face; this time it was his nose which took the brunt of the punch. Blood gushed forth and Wickham decided to remain where he was. "You broke my nose," he complained.

"You should not have attempted to steal from Darcy House," came the grim reply. "By the by, what did you expect to find in this strong box?" Wickham remained silent as he held a blooded handkerchief to his nose. "Well," Darcy continued, "I can assure you, whatever you had thought to find there, you would have been most disappointed. The chest has been empty for many years."

"I do not believe you!"

"It matters little whether you believe me or not." Darcy turned slightly; he reached for one of the window sashes and began to rip it away from its holding. Wickham, noting an opportunity, rose quickly and threw himself at Darcy, knocking him off his feet.

The fight that ensued was in the end one sided. Punches were exchanged but it was not long before Darcy got the upper hand, although he did not come away from the skirmish unscathed. Once Wickham's hands were bound behind him and his ankles trussed together, Darcy went to wake Carlton, leaving Wickham, a bruised and blooded mess, sitting on the floor near where he had found him.

It was a further two hours before Darcy was able to retire for the night. Three runners had arrived from Bow Street, two removed Wickham from the premises while the third questioned Darcy as to what had occurred. Despite his exhaustion, sleep did not come easily to him. Tomorrow he would write to Elizabeth, informing her of what had happened. He could not return to Rosings as planned, for he would need to meet with the magistrate and see to the charges that would be brought against Wickham.

Darcy thought long and hard into the night. He held enough bills and promissory notes that Wickham had accrued, but failed to pay over the years, to put the man into Marshalsea for the remainder of his life, but Darcy's conscience battled with him. Before sleep finally found him, Darcy prayed to God for his father's advice.

It was dark, so very dark, then daylight began to fill the room. It was not very bright so it must be a gloomy day. He stood staring at the carpet, it was an old carpet, and he recognised it but could not place it. Then he felt someone beside him, it was his cousin, Richard. He then remembered where he was and more importantly why.

"Now boys," a deep voice said, "do you know why I have called you here today?"

Both nodded their heads. Darcy could feel a tear in the corner of his eye. "I am sorry, Papa, we did not mean to destroy Mama's favourite blooms."

"That my boy is beside the point. You were playing in the orangery, a room that you are forbidden to enter without the company of an adult."

"It was raining outside, Papa, and the orangery is like a jungle. We were playing explorers. But we should not have been there. I promise, Papa, I will never enter a room forbidden me without first asking your permission."

"Hmmm. Explorer games should be played out of doors, not in the house. Richard you may go." Darcy felt his young shoulders droop as Richard smiled.

"Thank you, Uncle. I am exceedingly sorry."

"Oh do not thank me yet, boy. Carlton will escort you home. He has on his person a letter for your father."

"Oh."

"Oh indeed," Mr Darcy replied, lifting an eyebrow as he stared down at his young nephew.

Once the door closed behind Master Richard Fitzwilliam, George Darcy looked again at his son.

"I do not enjoy punishing you, Fitzwilliam, but you have done wrong, and those who commit a wrong must be prepared to accept their punishment when they are caught. All wrong doers are eventually caught. You have admitted your fault and know you have done wrong. I trust you will learn your lesson today.

"When passing punishment for a misdemeanour you must always take into account the regret of the wrongdoer. Is that regret honest? Is it truthful? Words are easy to say. It takes nothing to say three little words in an attempt to avoid punishment. I would like to believe you are truly sorry and, when you say you will not enter the orangery again without permission, I trust you to keep your word as a gentleman.

"You will apologise to your Mama. You will not leave the house for a fortnight, and you will not ride your pony, or any other mount, for one *month. Should you break your promise, I promise you, Fitzwilliam, next time your punishment will be severe.*

"When you are older you will come to realize that it is prudent that punishment, for any wrongdoing you are likely to preside over as Master of Pemberley, matches both the culpability and repentance of the person involved. If a person repeatedly offends, be they a servant or our peer, they must be dealt with accordingly. You cannot protect a person from the consequences of their crime. I know you are still young, Fitzwilliam, but remember my words my son..."

Darcy woke with a start. His father's words still echoed in his mind. How old had he been? Five, maybe six, he had forgotten all about that summer. Now it was embedded in his brain. Darcy closed his eyes and smiled. It was still early but the sun was rising. He quickly left his bed, put on some breeches and a shirt, and barefoot made his way down the stairs to his study. He entered the room, walking over to a portrait which hung on the wall behind his desk.

He looked up at his father and smiled. "Thank you, Father, for reminding me. I am sorry I had forgotten your wise words. How I wish I had remembered them before Ramsgate. But now I know what I must do. Wickham will not harm another living soul. I promise you."

Darcy returned to his room without encountering any of the servants. Deciding there was little point in returning to his bed, he rang the bell and requested a jug of warm water so that he could prepare for the day. He had much to do. A letter to Elizabeth was a priority, as was a note to Fitzwilliam.

Elizabeth returned to the house. Despite her love of walking, a solitary ramble through the groves without William at her side no longer held the delight it had. Elizabeth walked towards the family dining room, hoping that either Lady Catherine or Jane might be present, even though it was a full fifteen minutes before the allotted time. Yesterday had brought a slight improvement in Anne's well-being, allowing her to feel strong enough to join the others for a light nuncheon. Dr Morgan carried her down the stairs where a Bath chair waited for her; he then pushed his patient to the dining room.

The Bath chair was a new acquisition that Dr Morgan had requested to be made for his patient soon after his arrival; it had been delivered to Rosings that very morning. Anne was delighted; she was too weak to walk far but now with the chair, if she was well enough, she had the ability to escape the confinement of her chambers and join the company.

The family dining room was at the back of the house and the view from the window was unhindered across the lawn to the lake. Elizabeth was admiring the view when the door opened. Turning she smiled as Jane entered, but her smile faded as she took in her sister's weary mien.

"Jane, are you unwell?" Elizabeth asked as she quickly made her way across the room to her sister's side.

Jane gave a weak smile as she shook her head. "No, Lizzy. I am well." Elizabeth responded with a disbelieving frown. "Truly I am," she continued, "I did not sleep particularly well last night." A blush rapidly made its way across Jane's cheeks and down her neck, embarrassed, she lowered her gaze to the floor.

"You miss your husband," Elizabeth stated. "I miss Mr Darcy. I do not understand the reason, as when I am at our uncle's home I am quite content if I do not see William for a day or two.

"Perhaps it is that your heart knows Mr Darcy is not far away and could be with you in a trice if you needed him. But enough of bemoaning the loss of our gentlemen, God willing they will return today."

Georgiana and Lady Catherine then joined the sisters, allowing conversation to turn to other things.

When the ladies retired to the morning room, Elizabeth was delighted that Anne felt well enough to join them. Charlotte accompanied her, pushing the Bath chair into the room.

On asking the whereabouts of her cousins, Anne listened intently as Lady Catherine informed her of her wishes regarding Rosings. "I am not getting any younger and you are frail, I have come to accept that now. Neither of us knows how long we have left on this earth before we join your dear father. I wanted to secure both the future of Rosings and the safety of your cousin."

"I am pleased, Mama. It was never my desire to marry William. I am glad that Richard will have Rosings to care for." Turning to Jane she continued, "Will this mean that you and Richard will live here with us?"

"I believe so," Jane replied. "Although I am sure we will also spend some time at our estate in Staffordshire and our town house, but, at present, I would be delighted if Richard and I could spend the majority of our time here at Rosings so that we might enjoy one another's company."

"What of you, Charlotte?" Elizabeth enquired. "Are Sir William and Lady Lucas content for you to remain here?"

Charlotte Collins sat next to Anne, dressed in muslin of a dark brown hue. It was at Lady Catherine's insistence that Charlotte wore the sober colours of half-mourning, instead of the more sombre colour that in general adorned a newly widowed lady. She had stated quite adamantly that Mr Collins did not deserve any more. Charlotte had set about dyeing one of her gowns black before Lady Catherine's edict, now the only time she wore it was to church services.

"Thankfully, yes. I have little desire to return to my father's house. I am content and, as long as Anne and Lady Catherine are also content with my presence, I will remain." Charlotte turned to Jane. "That is of course if you and the colonel are happy with the arrangement."

"Of course we are, dear Charlotte."

Charlotte smiled, she was greatly relieved. There were two reasons for her relief. Firstly, her parents simply would not understand her lack of propriety for not mourning her late husband and, secondly, she found that she enjoyed the company of Dr Morgan. He was a wonderful doctor; both in understanding and caring for the needs of his patient. Charlotte was no fool, she knew nothing could come of her admiration for the gentleman. Eventually their paths would part. He would return to town and she would need to either return to her father's house, or find a position as a companion; she hoped Lady Catherine would give her a good reference.

It was just after midday that an express rider arrived at Rosings.

Diplock entered the morning room, silver salver in hand. "I beg your pardon, my Lady, but two expresses have been delivered for Mrs Fitzwilliam and Miss Bennet."

Seeing the young ladies instant distress, Lady Catherine commanded, "Well do not just stand there, Diplock, give the ladies their letters." Her voice soften as she continued, "I do pray it is not bad news, my dears."

Jane had broken the seal on her letter, opening it before Diplock had managed the few steps to Elizabeth's side.

"Oh, thank heavens. Do not worry, Lizzy. I believe your missive will be from Mr Darcy, mine is from Richard."

"Is he well?" her Ladyship enquired.

"Yes, Lady Catherine. He is well. The gentlemen are delayed. Something has occurred at Darcy House. Richard has remained behind to aid Mr Darcy."

"Does he say what has happened to cause their delay?"

"No, my Lady," Jane replied.

Elizabeth let out a gasp. "Oh no," she cried. All eyes turned to towards her.

"Well, what does William say?" Lady Catherine demanded.

Elizabeth moved closer to Georgiana. "He writes: *I deeply regret that I am unable to return to Rosings today. Last night I had an unexpected caller. Mr Wickham, believing the family had removed from town for Pemberley, surreptitiously entered Darcy House with the intent to commit larceny.*" On hearing Elizabeth speak George Wickham's name it took all of Georgiana's fortitude not to gasp aloud, though she could not prevent her complexion from paling considerably. *"Unfortunately, for Mr Wickham, I had not yet retired. I was looking for the book I wished to share with you when I heard a noise coming from my study. He was so intent on opening the lock to an old strong box that he did not hear my approach. A minor fracas ensued, but I can assure you that he is in a much worse condition than I. Wickham is now in the safe hands of the constabulary. Today I must speak with the magistrate and others to ensure that he can do no more harm. I have, for many years, been cleaning up after Wickham. Over the years it has amounted to many hundreds of pounds. I have decided no more. He has had more than enough opportunity to change his ways, now he will pay for his misdemeanours. Last night, during the little sleep I had, my father came to me in a dream. I was taken back to a time when I was but a small boy. I had forgotten all about the unhappy event which brought me before my father, and it was only after I woke that I remembered it. I know, without doubt, that my father would approve of my actions this day.*

"He does not mention what occurred when he was a boy; I wonder what might have transpired." As she finished speaking, Elizabeth discreetly reached for Georgiana's hand.

"I believe I remember," Lady Catherine said, shaking her head slowly as a half-smile formed on her lips. "We were in London for the season. It was nearing its end, but there was still a fortnight before our families would retire to the country. William must have been no more than five or six years old. He and Richard played together whenever possible, that day they were at Darcy House. It had been raining constantly for several days, impossible weather for two little boys."

"Was the viscount not with them?" Elizabeth asked.

"No, Sebastian was at Eton. William and Richard decided to play explorers in my sister's small orangery."

"Surely not, Aunt!"

"I am afraid so, Georgiana. How the boys escaped from their nannies was never discovered. Your poor mother. She was so distressed when she saw what had befallen her favourite blooms. Richard was sent home with a note for his father to mete out any punishment your uncle thought suitable, while William faced his father. I believe William is correct. His father came to him to advise his son in his time of need. George Darcy always was a good man."

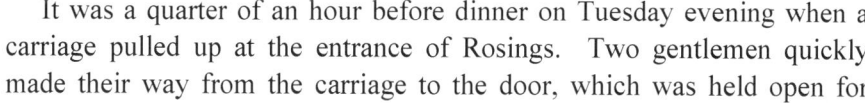

It was a quarter of an hour before dinner on Tuesday evening when a carriage pulled up at the entrance of Rosings. Two gentlemen quickly made their way from the carriage to the door, which was held open for them. The downpour, which had started not two minutes before, ensured, no matter how swift their steps, they were unable to avoid the rain.

"Colonel Fitzwilliam, Mr Darcy, welcome. Please let me relieve you of your wet coats."

"Thank you, Diplock, but I am no longer a colonel. I am now simply Mr Fitzwilliam," replied Fitzwilliam as he removed his greatcoat and handed it to the waiting footman.

"I am delighted to hear it, Sir. Her Ladyship will be so pleased."

Darcy relieved of his coat, smiled as he turned to his cousin. "Come, Fitzwilliam, let us get dry before we greet the ladies." Darcy made his way towards the staircase.

"I will inform Lady Catherine of your safe arrival and that you will join the ladies in the dining room soon."

"My thanks, Diplock," Fitzwilliam replied before hastily following his cousin.

As soon as Darcy and Fitzwilliam were seated for dinner and the first course was served, Lady Catherine demanded to know all. All that had transpired with Wickham, and Fitzwilliam's meeting with the general—everything to the last minutest detail. Dinner was a slow affair while the gentlemen explained the events of the last few days.

"Wickham has been dealt with?"

"Yes, Aunt. Unfortunately there was no cause for him to be charged with larceny, as he was unable to take anything for my home, but the vowels I hold from his debts are great. He was given a choice. He could spend the remainder of his days in Marshalsea, or accept a one-way ticket to Australasia. Wickham, wisely I believe, chose the journey to Sidney. His chances of survival are greater aboard ship than incarcerated in a debtors' prison."

"But what if he returns," Georgiana whispered.

Darcy looked kindly at his sister. "That will never happen. He will be watched. Wickham is aware that this is his final chance to make something of his life. He has been warned. Should he ever set foot in England again debtors' prison will be his fate."

"That is as maybe, William, but you were still longer than I had anticipated." Lady Catherine then turned to her other nephew. "And you, Richard. What is your excuse?"

"As I said, Aunt, my first meeting with the general was postponed. That in turn caused a delay in setting up the sale of my commission. Then there was Wickham to deal with. I assure you, we returned as soon as was possible." The exasperation in Fitzwilliam's tone was evident, as he repeated what had already been said.

Darcy decided it was time to change the subject. He would not repine if he never heard Wickham's name again. "What of Anne, Aunt? How is our cousin?"

"Her health is fair. She now has the Bath chair which allows her, on good days to join us in the morning and sometimes for luncheon. Georgiana, Jane, Miss Bennet and Charlotte all see to Anne's comfort. I know she is grateful for their company. I am sure she will miss Georgiana and Miss Bennet when you return to town, William."

Neither Darcy nor Fitzwilliam wished to be separated from their ladies for any longer so decided to forgo their port. When the meal ended Darcy requested a moment of Elizabeth's time. With Lady Catherine's agreement, Darcy and Elizabeth remained in the dining room when the meal was ended, while the others made their way to the drawing room. The door would remain open and they would re-join the others by the end of five minutes.

Darcy walked over to Elizabeth's side, gently taking her hand in his. "I have missed you greatly, these last four days."

"I have missed you also," she replied softly.

"Elizabeth, I know we planned to marry in town in a month or two, but I wonder how you would feel about marrying sooner."

Elizabeth smiled warmly. "I would be happy to marry whenever you wish."

"I have spoken with your uncle. He is agreeable to an earlier date. The marriage settlement has been signed and I have a special licence in my pocket."

"William, do you think Lady Catherine will allow us to marry here so that Anne might be present? I am sure she would be happy to attend."

"I will ask her this evening. If my aunt is agreeable I will speak with Mr Hunt tomorrow, then we shall be married at our convenience. Once a date is agreed I will write to both your father and your uncle. I hope your family will stay here, but there is a respectable inn near Hunsford that has rooms to let if needs be."

"Let us speak with Lady Catherine, for I wish to be by your side when you speak with your aunt."

Lady Catherine was delighted to host her nephew's wedding. Because of Anne's illness it would be a quiet wedding for close family only, with an announcement posted in the newspaper. She was not so sure about providing accommodation for a tradesman and his family, but both Darcy and Fitzwilliam assured their aunt that the Gardiners were respectable and were sure their aunt would enjoy Mrs Gardiner's company.

When Darcy met with his aunt the following morning he discovered there was another stipulation, one on which Lady Catherine refused to budge—if Mrs Bennet attended she would not be welcome to stay at Rosings. As much as Darcy disliked his future mother for her treatment of his beloved Elizabeth, he did not want their wedding day marred with any unpleasantness. He knew Elizabeth loved her family no matter how certain individuals in that family might treat her. Elizabeth was unaware of Lady Catherine's edict and Darcy did not mention it, for he hoped his aunt could be persuaded to have a change of heart.

Chapter 22

Mr Bennet closed his eyes and sighed. He really needed to thicken the walls with cladding; if he did not need a fire in the colder months he would block the fire place, but that would only lead to further discomfort. Mrs Bennet's cries of disbelief could still be heard all too clearly.

Two days ago Thomas Bennet had informed his wife that guests would be dining at Longbourn the following evening. Including the Bennets, eight persons would dine and one of the guests would be the new heir to Longbourn. Mr Bennet gave no name, but said the young man was a single gentleman. Those words alone were enough to set Mrs Bennet's nerves fluttering. Hindsight revealed that surprising Mrs Bennet had not been beneficial to her husband's peace.

Mrs Bennet had at numerous times during the day sought out cook regarding the meal. There was no tranquillity for anyone at Longbourn that day. Kitty and Lydia were dressed in their best gowns, even Mary, who Mrs Bennet had long given up any hope of attracting a husband, was dressed in her best gown with her hair carefully styled. Mrs Bennet was determined her daughters would be seen in their best light. Part of her also wished that her ungrateful daughter Elizabeth was at Longbourn, for she would make a suitable wife for the heir, but her husband refused to recall their daughter stating it was his wife's desire that Elizabeth had been removed to her brother's house at Cheapside.

The allotted time for the arrival of the guests was upon them and Mrs Bennet was still checking the lace on Lydia's gown when voices could be heard approaching the drawing room.

"Now, girls, remember," Mrs Bennet attempted to whisper. "The young gentleman will be the heir to Longbourn. I am sure he will be attracted to one of you."

"But I want to marry an officer," her youngest daughter wailed.

"And so you should, my love. I am sure Mary or Kitty will be ideal for him."

"But Mama," Kitty cried.

"Shhh child, they are coming, now smile nicely."

Mrs Hill opened the door. "Mr and Mrs Goulding, and Mr Samuel Goulding."

Mr Bennet had barely uttered words of welcome when Kitty blurted out. "I do not want to marry Samuel!"

Samuel Goulding smiled. "That is good, Miss Kitty, as I do not wish to marry you and I have no intention of marrying for many years yet."

Mrs Bennet came over faint. The temptation to call for her smelling salts was great, but she recovered her senses quickly and, with a forced smile, welcomed their guests.

When the Gouldings departed Mr Bennet retreated to his study. Mrs Bennet was close on her husband's heels. Her displeasure evident, as her tirade echoed around the walls of Longbourn.

Mr Bennet had enjoyed seeing the shock on his wife's countenance. Although he did not consider the distress that his few minutes of enjoyment had caused Mrs Bennet, he did realize that any peace he might have hoped for after his evening meal had vanished like the morning mist.

"Mrs Bennet," he cried as his wife took a breath, "there is no need to carry on so. I am sure Samuel has forgotten your ill-treatment of him when he was infatuated with our Jane. He will make a good master of Longbourn when I am gone, although I do not mean to depart this life for a good few years yet. Samuel has assured me that if you should outlive me, you will be welcome to stay at Longbourn for your full mourning period."

"And what of our daughters? What will happen to them?"

"Mrs Bennet, by that time I have no doubt that most of our daughters will be wed. Now please, if you wish to continue with your caterwauling remove yourself from my study!"

Now, a day later, Mrs Bennet's rants were intermingled with stony silence and glares whenever he was within her sight.

Mr Bennet opened his eyes as a knock came at the door. Mrs Hill entered and handed a letter to her master.

"An express, Sir. The rider is resting his horse before returning to Kent, should you wish to send a reply."

Bennet smiled at their long-time housekeeper before turning his attention to the missive in his hand. He broke the seal and unfolded the parchment. Another sigh escaped his lips as his eyes took in the rows of neatly written words; he had known this day would come.

He stood, placed the now refolded letter in his pocket and made his way out of his sanctuary and up the stairs towards his wife's chamber. Passing Hill on his way he requested the rider be given some refreshments as he needed to speak to Mrs Bennet before writing his response.

Darcy looked at the letter in his hand. Not walking away from the servant, he took a deep intake of breath, broke the seal and unfolded it. After reading only a few lines a smile crossed his countenance. Looking at Diplock he asked, "Where might I find Miss Bennet?"

"I believe Miss Bennet is in the music room with Miss Georgiana, Sir."

In a few moments his long strides had him at the door of the room. On opening it his eyes glanced around until they landed on the two women who meant the world to him.

Seated side by side, Elizabeth and Georgiana played a duet. On hearing the sound of the door opening, Elizabeth briefly turned her head to glance in that direction; a sweet smile gracing her countenance before she returned her attention to the music.

Darcy applauded as the ladies hands stilled and the last notes faded away. "That was delightful," he said. "May be you will both delight us this evening with a further rendition of Mozart's Sonata."

Elizabeth, with a gentle smile, bowed her head to Georgiana, indicating it would be her decision. "Of course, brother," she replied, "if that is your wish."

"It is indeed, Georgiana. I thank you." Darcy smiled and then turned his attention to Elizabeth. "I have received a missive from your father."

Elizabeth's smile faded and her colour waned. "What does he say?"

Darcy offered Elizabeth his arm. "Come, sit with me. We will read the letter together."

Georgiana, realising her brother wished to speak privately with Elizabeth, stood up. "I should go to Anne." Georgiana smiled as she curtsied before quickly made her way from the room, leaving the door slightly ajar as she passed out of sight.

Once they were alone Elizabeth asked again, "What does my father say? Is he content with our decision?"

Darcy smiled, but said nothing; instead he simply pressed the letter into her hand.

Elizabeth bit her bottom lip and her hands shook slightly as she unfolded the missive.

Longbourn.

29th Inst.

Dear Mr Darcy,

Thank you for your recent missive. I was sorry to read of your cousin's continued ill health and understand your desire to marry Elizabeth while Miss de Bourgh is still with you and able to join in with your celebration. I have spoken at some length with Mrs Bennet.

Elizabeth looked at Darcy. "Some length!"

"Yes," Darcy replied. "I believe, reading between the lines, that your father has taken a firm stand with your mother." *'And about time,'* he muttered to himself. Not realising he had spoken aloud until Elizabeth spoke.

"Yes, as much as I do not wish to speak ill of my father, I too wish he might have acted on my behalf sooner."

"I believe your mother is now aware that this will be her only chance to improve matters between you."

Elizabeth nodded before letting out a sigh. "Do you think I am silly to hope things will improve?"

"No, my love, she is your mother. It is natural that you love her and hope all will be well between you."

Elizabeth looked back at the letter.

Like all fathers I wish to walk my daughter down the aisle. It will be the most joyous and saddest day of this father's life. Joyous to see my Lizzy married to a gentleman worthy of her who will love and care for her, and sad because I must now resign myself to living forever in a house devoid of any sense.

I will arrive at Hunsford with my family the day before the wedding. I should be most grateful if you could secure accommodation for my family for two nights at the nearest convenient coaching inn. Please explain to Lizzy that I believe this will be for the best. Mrs Bennet is confused as to how her eldest daughter managed to only catch a soldier, even if he is the son of an earl, whereas Lizzy has ensnared such a rich gentleman—her words not mine. I am delighted with both of my new sons and I do not want Lizzy's day spoilt by any thoughtless comments made by my wife. I believe all will be well for the ceremony as Mrs Bennet and my younger daughters are well aware that their pin money will be forfeit for any misdemeanour.

Elizabeth let out a sigh. "Perhaps Mama will not be so disappointed with Jane's choice when she learns that Richard is the new master of Rosings. I do not believe either of my parents is aware of your cousin's good fortune."

"I am sure you are right, my dear, as I am sure your father is right in his decision that your family stay at The Bull."

"Thank you for inviting my family. I am glad Papa will be here to walk me to your side."

"I wanted your family to have the opportunity to share in our day if they so desired."

Elizabeth gave him a gentle smile. *'I am so fortunate to be marrying such a dear man,'* she mused as she gazed into his thoughtful eyes. Elizabeth then thought of Lady Catherine. "I do worry what your aunt will think of my younger sisters, Lydia can be quite loud at times."

"Do not worry, Elizabeth. From your father's letter I have faith that he has everything under control. He appears to have taken all possible steps to avoid any embarrassment."

"At last!" Darcy lifted an eyebrow at Elizabeth's exclamation. "No, you do not need to say it, I know if Papa had taken more interest in the behaviour of his family than comfort in his books there would be no worries of embarrassment." Thinking of the relatives who never caused the slightest embarrassment, she continued, "I wish Uncle Edward and Aunt Madeline could be here."

"I am pleased to hear that. I believe they are arriving with your cousins on Monday." Darcy's words were halted as Elizabeth threw herself into his arms.

"Oh thank you," she cried.

Darcy, delighted in the feeling of holding her close to him, tightened his arms around his beloved.

"Nephew! Unhand Miss Bennet this instant."

Darcy reluctantly released Elizabeth from his embrace on hearing Lady Catherine's demand.

"It was my fault, Lady Catherine." Elizabeth blushed deeply as she lowered her eyes from the Lady's glare. "I was so pleased to hear that my dear Aunt and Uncle will be at our wedding that I forgot all decorum and embraced Mr Darcy. I am sorry, it will not happen again."

Before Elizabeth had finished speaking Darcy spoke, determined to take the greater part of the blame. "No, it was my fault, Aunt. Miss Bennet's gratitude was for the briefest moment, but I encircled her in my arms so she was unable to retreat."

Lady Catherine looked from one to the other. "Well, whoever is to blame, we will have no more of *that* kind of behaviour in my house! You are not married yet, and when you are I sincerely hope you will remember propriety when you are in company. Such open displays of affection are not to be borne!"

The pair, looking suitably chastised, replied in unison. "Of course, Aunt." "Yes, Lady Catherine."

As expected, noon on Monday saw the arrival of the Gardiners and their three eldest; little Faith remained at their home in Russell Square with her nurse. Elizabeth was delighted to see her aunt and uncle and greeted them both warmly.

Patience was brimming with excitement for she had been allotted the important position of flower girl at cousin Lizzy's wedding. She was eager to tell her cousins and Miss Darcy of the pretty new dress she had for the occasion.

The ladies watched with amusement as Patience's pale blue eyes sparkled with delight as she spoke of her new dress. "...and Mama said it matches my eyes. Lizzy, it is a shame your new dress will not match your eyes, but it is very pretty," she concluded.

Her excitement was contagious and Elizabeth, Jane and Georgiana soon found themselves escorting Mrs Gardiner and Patience to the Gardiners' chambers, while Mr Gardiner joined the gentlemen in the library. Lady Catherine was taken with the enthusiasm of Elizabeth's little cousin, it had been many years since the passages of Rosings had echoed with the sounds of children's happy voices, and so she found herself following the ladies and Patience up the stairs.

When her wedding dress was unwrapped Elizabeth gasped. "Oh, it is beautiful."

Madeline Gardiner smiled. "Now, my dear, I suggest you try the gown on. I believe it will fit but it might need a tuck or two."

Elizabeth slipped into the bedroom with Jane. With her sister's help, she was quickly relieved of her day gown and clothed in a beautiful ivory silk gown. Delicate lace covered the bodice, while silk embroidered Sweet William flowers, in various shades of blue, covered the hem, cuffs and neckline.

"Oh Lizzy, you are beautiful. Mr Darcy will be speechless when he sees you."

"I do hope he will not be totally speechless. I sincerely hope he will be able to say his vows!"

The sisters were laughing gaily as they re-entered the small sitting room attached to their aunt's bedroom.

"Oh Lizzy," cried Georgiana, "you will be such a beautiful bride."

"Thank you Georgie." Elizabeth walked up to her aunt, took hold of her hand and pressed a kiss to her cheek. "Thank you so much, Aunt Madeline, this is the most beautiful gown I have ever owned."

"My dear, it is our pleasure. Now let us check to make sure it is a correct fit."

Lady Catherine smiled and gave a nod of approval. "Mrs Gardiner, the gown is delightful and quite befitting for the future Mrs Darcy." Turning to her niece, Lady Catherine continued, "Georgiana, I believe we should spend some time with Anne."

Georgiana wished to stay with Elizabeth and Jane, but she smiled and acquiesced.

Once Mrs Gardiner was alone with her nieces she enquired as to whether they had heard from their parents.

"Yes," replied Elizabeth, "Papa wrote to Mr Darcy. He, Mama and my sisters will arrive in Hunsford tomorrow. Mr Darcy has arranged accommodation for them at The Bull."

"I believe we passed it as we approached Hunsford. Your parents will not stay here?"

"No. Papa did not wish it."

Elizabeth did not elaborate, but her aunt was an intelligent woman and did not need her niece to speak the words to understand Mr Bennet's reasoning. "I am glad to see that your father is thinking of your comfort." The words 'for a change' hung in the air but were not uttered.

"I know this will sound quite terrible, Aunt, but I am glad that Mama and Lydia will not be staying at Rosings." Elizabeth quickly raised her hand and angrily brushed aside a wayward tear. *'I will not cry,'* she silently determined.

Madeline Gardiner gathered Elizabeth into a warm embrace, while trying not to crush the gown. "Jane dear, will you take Patience to her nanny?"

"Of course," she replied with a smile as she looked at her young cousin. "Come, let us see what your brothers are up too."

Patience looked at Elizabeth, a troubled frown marring her small face.

"Lizzy will be just fine," said Mrs Gardiner. "Now go with Jane. I expect there will be some milk and biscuits waiting for you."

Jane smiled encouragingly as she held her hand out to Patience. Taking hold of her cousin, Jane led Patience out of the room. As they walked up some more stairs Patience turned to Jane, her worry still evident. "Are you sure Lizzy will be all right?"

"Yes, sweetheart. She has your Mama with her. All will be well."

"Why will Uncle and Aunt Bennet not be staying here with us?"

Jane sighed, how could she explain to a child the complications caused by her mother, she could not. "It is complicated, Patience. Even I have difficulty understanding the whole." This was quite true; Jane could not understand her mother's behaviour towards her dear sister.

Wednesday 3rd June 1812

A drawing room in the east wing had been prepared for the wedding. The gardens had been raided. An array of pinks and roses adorned the room which had been set out to resemble a church. The flowers had been placed around the room and through the centre, to make an aisle for

Elizabeth to walk down. The sun shone brightly through its large windows, warming the room and encouraging the gentle perfume of the blooms to fill the air.

When Elizabeth woke the sun was just rising. Outside her window she could hear a group of sparrows merrily chirping. She spent the time, before the maid came to attend her, sitting on the window seat, watching the grounds come to life while thinking about the evening before. Lady Catherine had given her a set of half a dozen diamond pins to be arranged in her hair. They were delicate and sparkling so beautifully that Elizabeth had been overcome to receive such a gift.

Lady Catherine's maid had knocked on her bedroom door shortly after Elizabeth's aunt had departed, after telling her niece what she should expect on her wedding night. The blush was still evident on her cheeks as she followed Alice to Lady Catherine's chambers. Elizabeth wondered why William's aunt wished to see her. *'Surely Lady Catherine does not wish to speak of our wedding night!'* Just the thought made the hue on Elizabeth's cheeks grow brighter. As Alice opened the door, Elizabeth took a long, deep breath to steady her nerves before entering. Lady Catherine, who was seated in a comfortable chair, beckoned her closer. As Elizabeth drew nearer she noticed that William's aunt had a small red velvet pouch in her hand.

"When I married Sir Lewis my mother gave me this pouch. I had intended to pass it on to my daughter, but that will never be."

Elizabeth made to speak but Lady Catherine raised her hand. "No, I will have my say. You and your sister have been kindness itself to Anne, and I have enjoyed your company too. I wish for you to have these pins so that you might wear them in your hair at your wedding."

"But Jane…"

"When Jane married she was at your parents' home and I still had not come to terms with the doctor's diagnosis. You are marrying at Rosings so that Anne may share in the joy of your day. I wish you to have them. Perhaps when your eldest daughter weds you might pass them on to her."

Lady Catherine placed the pouch in Elizabeth's hand.

"Thank you, Lady Catherine. I will treasure them. If I am blessed with a daughter she will receive this pouch on the eve of her wedding and be told of your generosity."

When she arrived back in her room she walked to the small occasional table where two candles burnt brightly. Opening the pouch she gently tipped its contents onto the table. She gasped at the sight of the delicate hairpins. Made of tiny diamonds embedded in finely crafted gold, they glistened in the candle light.

Overcome with the gift that Lady Catherine had bestowed on her, a tear slowly made its way down her cheek.

Chapter 23

Elizabeth was lost in thought on the window seat while a maid prepared a bath for her; the water was scented with lavender oil, to match the fragrance of the perfume she preferred. When Jane and Mrs Gardiner entered her chamber Elizabeth was seated at her dressing table, and Georgiana's lady's maid was putting the finishing touches to her hair.

Mrs Gardiner could not help but admire the pins adorning her niece's hair. "Lizzy, what beautiful pins."

"Thank you, Aunt. They are very precious to me. Lady Catherine gave them to me last night. I tried to say that Jane should have them as she will one day be mistress of Rosings. I am sorry, Jane, but Lady Catherine would not be dissuaded. She is pleased that we are to wed here so that Anne may be present."

Jane also admired the gems, but her feelings were nothing but delight that her sister had received such a gift from her future aunt. "Truly, Lizzy, I am delighted you have received such a fine gift. Lady Catherine has been more than generous to me, now it is your turn."

With her aunt and sister's help Elizabeth began to dress with great care, so as not to disturb her elegant coiffure. The process took some time, but in the end was worth the care and attention paid. Elizabeth looked at her reflection in the mirror of her dressing table. She barely recognised the sophisticated young lady looking back at her. A delicate garnet necklace completed her bridal attire. Darcy had given the necklace to Mrs Gardiner early that morning. As Mrs Gardiner fastened it round her niece's neck, she whispered, "I believe you shall have Mr Darcy's passionate devotion for the rest of your life."

Elizabeth's chambers were at the front of the house. Despite the windows being firmly shut, the sounds of a carriage pulling up and its passengers alighting could clearly be heard. Aunt Madeline had just stood back to admire her niece in her finery, when they heard a woman's voice cry, "Oh my!" Elizabeth briefly closed her eyes; Mrs Bennet's voice was unmistakeable.

Mrs Gardiner patted her niece's shoulder. "Do not worry, Lizzy. I am sure your mother will behave. After all is said and done, her pin money depends on her good behaviour."

Jane smiled at her aunt's words. "Aunt Madeline is correct, Lizzy. Mama will not do anything to ostracise herself from my home. I will not allow our family to embarrass you. Mrs Snell will ensure that our mother and sisters are escorted to the drawing room."

Elizabeth looked at her sister with amazement. "Who are you? And what have you done with my meek and mild sister?"

The three ladies chuckled, but even the sound of gay laughter could not totally dissipate the anxiety Elizabeth felt at the thought of seeing her mother again.

Lady Catherine had instructed Elizabeth to wait in her chambers until her father arrived to escort her down the main staircase to the drawing room where the service would take place. Elizabeth waited with bated breath, listening to every sound, so sure was she that her mother would at any moment burst through the door, despite Jane's assurances.

Mr and Mrs Bennet walked into the entrance hall with Mary, Kitty and Lydia following behind. The two youngest girls giggled as they looked at the stern countenance of Rosings' butler.

"Welcome to Rosings, Sir, Mrs Bennet." Indicating to the woman standing next to him he said, "This is Mrs Snell, Rosings' housekeeper."

The housekeeper gave a polite curtsy. "Mrs Bennet, if you and your daughters would care to follow me, I shall escort you to the rose drawing room. It is this way, Ma'am."

Before Mrs Bennet could utter one word, Diplock turned to Mr Bennet. "Sir, I will take you to Miss Bennet."

"But I wish to see Lizzy," Mrs Bennet cried. "I must ensure she is properly attired, as is befitting the wife of Mr Darcy. Not that I can do much about it if her gown is a disgrace at this late time."

"Mrs Bennet!" Her husband's warning tone cut across his wife's lament.

Mrs Bennet closed her mouth firmly and glared at her husband. She was not pleased with Mr Bennet's dictate. With a disparaging look at her husband, she followed the housekeeper. Mary, Kitty and Lydia followed quickly behind. On entering the drawing room Mrs Bennet spied her brother and his sons. Without a word to the housekeeper she quickly made her way to his side.

"Brother, when did you arrive? Where is Madeline? Has she remained in town with the girls?"

Gardiner smiled at his sister. "Good morning, Fanny. It is a pleasure to see you too. We arrived the day before yesterday; Madeline was concerned that Lizzy's wedding gown may need some minor adjustments and so insisted that there was a day to spare for such things."

"Lizzy's gown? I hope Madeline has ensured it has sufficient lace and adornments. A gentleman such as Mr Darcy will be most displeased if his bride's gown is not of the latest fashion. When Miss Bingley was at Netherfield, I believe feathers were all that is fashionable. Has Lizzy sufficient feathers for her hair."

"Do not worry, Fanny. I am sure Mr Darcy will be delighted no matter what Lizzy is wearing."

"Oh, how can you be so flippant? You are just like my husband. You have no compassion for my nerves!" Mrs Bennet shook her head. "How did she do it?"

"How did who do what?" Gardiner asked, pretending not to understand his sister.

"How did my disobedient, impertinent daughter, who has not a touch on my dear Jane, manage to ensnare a gentleman of such wealth and standing when my beautiful, sweet Jane married a mere soldier? Why Mr Darcy must be the richest man in Derbyshire."

Gardiner shook his head at his sister's ignorance. "No, Fanny. I believe that honour would most likely go to the Duke of Devonshire. And Darcy does not see Lizzy in the same light as you. I believe in those thoughts you are alone. Darcy sees a beautiful, intelligent young lady who will be his partner in life. She is witty and kind, and will make an excellent mistress of Darcy's homes. Both Jane and Lizzy have found love, which is a rare and precious thing, especially in the top circles of the ton. You should be happy for them both."

"But my dear Jane will have to follow the drum or be left behind while the colonel goes into unknown dangers."

"No, Mrs Bennet." Richard's deep voice spared his uncle from having to reply. Richard had heard nearly all of the conversation. He loved his dear Jane but could not like Mrs Bennet, so would not grant her the pleasure of calling her mother. "I have resigned my commission and am now simply Mr Fitzwilliam."

"Where will you live? Will you buy a house in Meryton? Oh how I would dearly love to have my sweet Jane close by. And do call me mother, my dear boy," she said with a broad smile.

"I am afraid I must disappoint you, Mrs Bennet," Richard replied. "Jane and I will remain at Rosings."

"Rosings? You are Lady Catherine's heir? This is Jane's home?" Mrs Bennet's excitement was growing.

"It is one of Jane's homes. We also have a house in town, not far from your brother's new residence, and a small estate in Staffordshire, but we will remain at Rosings for the foreseeable future." Richard turned his attention from his wife's mother to the door.

Mrs Bennet looked to see who had taken her new son's attention from her. An elegantly dressed older lady entered the room. *That must be Lady Catherine,'* she thought. She then spied a wan young lady in a Bath chair. A gentleman pushed the chair, while Charlotte Collins walked beside her and Miss Darcy followed behind. Mrs Bennet frowned at Charlotte; she had not forgiven her for taking Longbourn's heir away from one of her daughters.

"I must see to my cousin. Mrs Bennet, Uncle, pray excuse me." He gave a quick bow and walked towards his aunt.

Mrs Bennet silently watched as Richard spoke softly to his cousin. Then to her surprise she saw the former colonel scoop the young lady out of the Bath chair and up into his arms; he then made his way to a comfortable chair that had been placed in position for her. A footman removed the bath chair while Charlotte and the gentleman followed Fitzwilliam, but once she was settled with her mother and Miss Darcy either side of her, Charlotte, with her hand on the gentleman's arm, made her way to the row behind.

Fanny Bennet turned again to her brother. "I assume the sickly young lady is Miss de Bough, but who is the gentleman Charlotte Collins walks with?" she whispered.

Mr Gardiner raised his eye brows, for surely his sister's whisper was loud enough for the servants in the passage to hear. "The gentleman is Dr

Morgan," he replied quietly. "He is Miss de Bourgh's physician. Now come, Fanny, sit here." Edward Gardiner directed his sister to a seat in the front row, with her daughters in the row behind. When Mrs Bennet began to complain, he told her that Thomas, Jane and Patience would join her and there was no room for the other girls as well.

On hearing her uncle's words, Mary immediately ushered her sisters into the row of seats behind her mother.

As Mr Gardiner was attempting to get his sister and nieces settled, Darcy entered the room. Despite his outward appearance of calm he was in fact a bundle of nerves. This was to him the most important day of his life—Elizabeth would be his at last. He barely noticed those gathered in the room, as he walked up the wide aisle to the makeshift altar. He stood, facing the altar, with his back ramrod straight as he breathed deeply in an attempt to calm himself. He felt his Cousin Richard's presence beside him, while Mr Hunt stood to the side.

After what felt like an eternity of waiting, the vicar moved to stand before him with his eyes firmly looking at the end of the room. Darcy turned and look towards the door.

Mr Bennet was pleased and proud as he escorted his daughter. Mrs Gardiner had made her way down the stairs ahead of them and had now entered the drawing room.

"You look lovely my dear," he said as he placed Elizabeth's hand on his arm.

"Thank you, Papa," she replied. Elizabeth was aware how very different this wedding was to Jane's. She was not at Longbourn being married in the church she had been christened in. There were no friends and neighbours in attendance, except for Charlotte. And thirdly, her mother had no influence on the design of her wedding gown, a loss she could not repine. She smiled at her father. *'If you had stood up to Mama's rants, Papa, how different this day might be.'* But she kept her thoughts to herself as they began the short walk which would take her to Darcy's side.

Jane led the way, followed by Patience who held a basket brimming with Sweet William blooms. Darcy watched as his beautiful bride walked towards him. He was overcome with happiness and could not take his eyes off her.

"Breathe!" Richard whispered in his ear. "Darcy, you will be no good to her if you faint from lack of air."

Darcy took a deep breath but otherwise ignored Fitzwilliam's gibe. He could not look away from her, *'Soon, so very soon, she will be my wife and we shall be one for the rest of our days.'*

As he received Elizabeth's hand from her father, he held it firmly and raised it to his lips, while he silently made a vow. *'We will be together for eternity, my love. Not even death shall part us.'*

Elizabeth looked up at Darcy. His eyes, dark pools full of love, held her tight as the warmth of his love enveloped her.

It took a couple of gentle coughs from the vicar to regain their attention so that the ceremony could begin.

The wedding breakfast passed without incident. Lydia and Kitty, mindful of their pin money and their attendance at the next Meryton Assembly, said little to any others. They sat next to each other, whispering and giggling together. Mrs Bennet, still recovering from the shock that Jane was to be mistress of such a grand estate, said little to anyone. When she had tried to share her joy with Jane at her good fortune, Jane had refused to speak of it. Mrs Bennet wondered when the influence of her second daughter had held sway on her eldest. *'Surely, the colonel cannot approve of such behaviour.'*

Anne spent some time at the wedding breakfast before fatigue over took her, it was then that Dr Morgan and Charlotte assisted her back to her chambers. Darcy and Elizabeth, before they departed for town, promised Lady Catherine that they would return in a fortnight. Lady Catherine in turn had insisted that Georgiana remain at Rosings to allow her nephew and his bride some time to themselves. Georgiana had not been at all keen to begin with, when the idea of her remaining behind had first been mentioned, but Jane had quickly allayed any concerns she may have had. Jane persuaded her new sister that Mr Darcy and Elizabeth would need time alone to become accustomed to life as man and wife.

Once Darcy and Elizabeth had departed for town, the Bennets travelled the two miles to the inn on other side of Hunsford where they would remain for a second night.

No sooner had the carriage door been closed, and the horses begun their trot down the driveway, than Mrs Bennet started her bitter tirade. She was most displeased that they did not stay at Rosings. "My brother and his family are there so why not us, the parents of the bride? It is disgraceful to be treated so." The whine in Mrs Bennet's voice was almost more than her husband could bear. "After all our daughter will soon be mistress of that estate. I overheard the maids talking. Apparently when Miss de Bourgh is no longer with them, which, looking at the girl, must be soon, Lady Catherine will remove to the dower house and my Jane will be mistress. I cannot understand why Lizzy did not want us there."

"Mrs Bennet, please desist." Mr Bennet ignored the venomous look given to him by his wife. "Lizzy has nothing to do with any of this. I was the one to decide where we would stay. If I had replied to Mr Darcy's invitation requesting accommodation, I have no doubt it would have been granted. But I did not. Edward and Madeline have every right to accept an invitation to stay at Rosings. They have cared for Lizzy since you, Mrs Bennet, sent her from our home. It is only right that they should be with her in the days leading up to her marriage. You must remember, my dear, Jane and Lizzy have always been close. If one is upset it affects the other. Jane was deeply hurt by your actions, and my inactions, to Lizzy. If we wish to see either of our daughters again we will need to earn their forgiveness.

"Mr Darcy and Mr Fitzwilliam are cousins, and close as any brothers. Darcy was angered by your treatment of Lizzy, Fitzwilliam shares that anger. So you will have a long and challenging path before you, not only do you have to gain your daughters' forgiveness but also that of their husbands."

Not waiting for his wife to make any response Bennet looked to his daughters. "Girls, if you are to have any hope of securing decent young gentlemen as husbands, it is time you learnt how to be sensible young ladies. I have spoken to your brother Darcy and courted his advice. Kitty and Lydia, you will go to school."

"No!" cried Lydia.

"Silence! Once schools are found for you both, I shall see to your enrolment. Mary, in September you shall join Miss Darcy in town, where you will share her companion, Mrs Annesley, and be tutored by her masters." Mr Bennet looked at each of his daughters. "I shall not be dissuaded from my decision. By my inaction I have failed your sisters, but I will not fail you too."

———————⌁———————

It was barely three months after Darcy and Elizabeth had wed that an express arrived from Rosings. Anne was failing. They had planned to depart for London in a few days, but the missive from Fitzwilliam caused them to change their plans. Elizabeth was determined they would depart immediately. With long days in the carriage she hoped they would arrive at Rosings late on the third day. A separate carriage, escorted by outriders, would take Georgiana, Mrs Annesley and Georgiana's maid to town; on the way they would call at Longbourn for Miss Bennet. An express was quickly despatched to Hertfordshire to inform Mr Bennet and Mary of the change of plans.

They arrived at Rosings early on the morning of the fourth day. Both were tired but not as exhausted as their horses. They had tried to complete the journey in three days but twenty miles from Rosings the driver had told his master that the horses needed rest. Darcy immediately agreed and they put up at the first inn they came upon. It was not up to the usual Darcy standards, but the beds were clean and the food wholesome.

The first thing to catch their eye was the black wreath on the door. Anne had passed; they were too late. Elizabeth was devastated when she learnt that Miss de Bourgh had passed just a few hours before. Darcy had taken his wife to their rooms, where he held her close while she cried.

They remained at Rosings for a se'nnight. During that time both the Fitzwilliams and the Darcys attempted to persuade Lady Catherine to delay her removal to the dower house, but their aunt was unyielding in her decision. "I shall not be dissuaded," she adamantly informed them. "Rosings can have but one mistress, Jane, and now that is you. If I were to remain the staff would look to me when they should look to you. Though I hope you will invite me to dine occasionally or take tea with you." Both Jane and Richard assured her that she would always be welcome.

Elizabeth asked Jane if she thought Charlotte might enjoy a stay in town before returning to Meryton, Jane's response surprised her. "I do not believe Charlotte will be returning to Lucas Lodge." When Elizabeth asked why, her sister replied that she had noticed Charlotte and Dr Morgan when neither thought they were being watched. Jane was sure that Dr Morgan held a tendre for Charlotte which was reciprocated. A short time later, Charlotte spoke to Elizabeth of departing Rosings with Dr Morgan, and how they had booked lodgings for her in a respectable boarding house for young ladies until her yearlong mourning period came to an end. Elizabeth insisted that Charlotte stay at Darcy House for as long as needs be; Darcy was quick to agree with his wife.

One Year Later – 10th September 1813

Fitzwilliam Darcy stood at the window of his study and looked out into the dimness as dawn approached. Before him was the rose garden, which had been originally planted by his grandmother. During the summer months, the arbour in its centre had been Elizabeth's favourite place to read during clement weather.

His cousin Richard was supposedly keeping him company, but Darcy did not need to turn around to know his cousin still slept like a baby in a large comfortable chair by the fire; the occasional snort and snore confirmed it was so.

Fitzwilliam had succumbed to sleep a couple of hours ago. At the first sound of a snore, Darcy had made his way to the family chapel where he had spent an hour on his knees praying to God for Elizabeth's safe deliverance.

Darcy was grateful for his cousin's company, and knowing that Elizabeth had her sister and their aunt to comfort her brought him some small relief.

They had been wed for fifteen months; those months had been the happiest in his life. There had been sad times, the death of dear Anne had been one, but they had each other to help and guide them through any stormy waters.

"Is that a smile I see on your face, Darcy?"

Darcy was brought back from his ponderings by the sound of his cousin's voice.

"I was thinking of my wife," he replied, as he turned and walked back towards Fitzwilliam. Worry now etched on his unshaven face.

Fitzwilliam rubbed a hand over his eyes, before peering at the tall clock in the corner. "It cannot be much longer, Darcy. It must be close on a day now that Lizzy has laboured."

"Yes, I pray…" Anything further Darcy might have said regarding his prayers was lost as the door to the study opened and Lady Catherine de Bourgh walked in. Darcy held his breath while he waited for his aunt to speak, but seeing her smile relieved his anxiety.

"She is well?"

"They are both well, William. Elizabeth wishes to see you. Richard, Jane has gone to the nursery to check on Henry. I suggest you follow her there and then you both get some rest."

By the time Lady Catherine finished speaking Darcy was halfway up the stairway. All weariness gone, he took the stairs two at a time as he rushed to the mistress' chamber.

Elizabeth sat in her bed, her damp hair braided, her skin still glistening from exertion. In her arms lay a small bundle swaddled in a sheet. Tiredness filled her eyes but they still shone with undiluted happiness. "Have you come to meet your daughter, Mr Darcy?"

Darcy had not cared what the child was so long as its mother was safe. Elizabeth was his world; he did not want to even imagine life without her. He looked down at the dark haired bundle securely held in her mother's arms; a broad smile caressed his lips. "You are well?" Despite his joy, his main concern was always for Elizabeth.

"Yes, my love. Tired, but well. Mrs Whitcher informs me it should be easier next time."

Darcy let out a sigh of relief, his wife was well, and gave blessing for the midwife who had cared so diligently for Elizabeth over the past months. He leant forward, placing a gentle kiss on his wife's lips. As he straightened slightly Darcy whispered, "I love you, my darling Lizzy. Thank you for my daughter." Bending he kissed the sleeping child's forehead. "What shall we name her?"

"I wish to call her Catherine Anne."

Darcy was surprised; he had assumed she would wish to name a daughter after her sister Jane.

Elizabeth gave a tired smile. "Your aunt has been most kind to me. The hairpins I wore at my wedding, which your aunt gave me, will one day adorn our daughter's locks. I believe it is only fitting that she be named Catherine."

Darcy smiled at his wife and then looked at his daughter. "Welcome to the world, Catherine Anne Darcy."

Elizabeth passed Catherine to her father, who held her safely to his chest while he made himself comfortable in the chair next to the bed. When he was securely seated with his precious daughter in his arms, he looked up at his wife and smiled. Elizabeth had drifted off to sleep.

Holding Catherine close while gently stroking her cheek with his forefinger, Darcy knew that his good fortune today, his sweet daughter and loving wife, was all due to a budding friendship formed in Hyde Park between Elizabeth and Georgiana.

Epilogue

Over the years the friendship between Darcy, Fitzwilliam and Dr Morgan, which started at Rosings, grew. Daniel and Charlotte Morgan were blessed with four children. Three sons, all of whom followed their father and became eminent physicians, and one much loved daughter who was also named Catherine. During the summer months, the Morgan children could often be found at Pemberley or Rosings, while their parents continued their life-saving work in the poorer parts of London.

Lady Catherine's life was also cut short; she only survived her daughter by six years. Fitzwilliam had summoned Morgan when a trifling cold worsened. Despite Daniel Morgan's best efforts, Lady Catherine passed. She knew Rosings was in good hands. She even appeared to be happy that she would soon be joining her husband and daughter, so the doctor knew there was no hope. The heir to Rosings, Henry de Bourgh Fitzwilliam, and his cousin Catherine Anne Darcy, brought Lady Catherine great joy in her final years.

As time passed, the passages of Rosings rang with the sound of children's laughter. After Henry, Jane and Fitzwilliam were blessed with five more children. Their daughters, Elizabeth and Gwendolen, took after their mother in their looks, although Elizabeth was well named as she had her aunt's lively character. Their second son, William, inherited Longenaire, while their third son, Thomas, who was the image of his father, joined the 10th Hussars. His military career was long and distinguished. A year after promotion to the rank of general, Thomas Fitzwilliam was knighted by the Queen for his heroic efforts in the Crimean War. The Fitzwilliam's youngest son, named after his father, took after his mother in both looks and temperament; young Richard Fitzwilliam thought well of everyone. Neither of his parents was surprised when he announced he wished to take Holy Orders.

With Elizabeth as her sister, Georgiana's confidence grew. When she made her come out the following year she was greatly sought after.

At his mother's insistence, Viscount Tansley returned again to town for the little season of 1812, searching for a wife among the debutants of the haut ton. This fact was well broadcast and many mothers pushed their daughters, willingly or unwillingly, at the young man who would one day be an earl. As in previous seasons his search was in vain; he found no one that he could imagine spending the rest of his life with. No matter how rare and unfashionable as it was, Tansley wanted what his brother and cousin had—a marriage that was a partnership, and filled with love and devotion.

It was the season of 1813 when Sebastian eventually found his bride. He was spellbound when he saw Georgiana at her come out ball. She was radiant. He could not understand how he had been so blind. Admittedly it had been a while since he had spent much time in her company. When he agreed to partner Georgiana for the supper dance at her ball he had just looked on it as a duty to his cousins, but now, as he wondered when she had transformed into a beautiful woman, he was glad that dance would be his. A fortnight later, after spending as much time as possible in Georgiana's company, Sebastian knew he had found his future wife.

At Darcy's request Tansley patiently waited, well as patiently as a gentleman in love can, until the end of Georgiana's first season. It was then that he offered her his hand and his heart. Georgiana, who had secretly loved Sebastian all her life, swiftly accepted him. They married at the start of the Little Season, at St George's Mayfair.

Despite Tansley's and Darcy's fears, Georgiana was stronger than her mother. She gave her husband three fine children, two sons and a daughter. Elizabeth Anne was the apple of her father's eye and took after her mother in looks and temperament.

The relationship between Mrs Bennet and her second daughter continued to be fragile for some time. Darcy likened it to a dance; at times it was one step forward and two steps back. The Darcys' first visit to Longbourn after their marriage was in the December of 1812. They stayed at Longbourn for three days to break their journey to Kent. The visit was a success and Mrs Bennet made them all feel most welcome, but the next time they were together it did not go so well. The Bennets' first visit to Pemberley coincided with Catherine's baptism. Mrs Bennet could not hide her disappointment in the girl child. Much to Darcy's annoyance she had told Elizabeth that she must follow her sister's example and produce an heir, for no gentleman of standing would be content with daughters. On hearing of Mrs Bennet's words from his emotional wife, a furious Darcy had spoken with Mr Bennet. Mr and Mrs Bennet had departed for Longbourn the following morning.

On his marriage to Elizabeth, Darcy had been determined to help his new sisters. The three remaining sisters each would receive a dowry of five thousand pounds, as long as their father or guardian approved of their marriage partner. He also paid for Kitty's and Lydia's schooling, and Mary's tutorage with masters at Darcy House. Bennet, grateful for Darcy's help, amended his will. Darcy would be guardian to the three sisters until they reached the age of thirty; he was not as hopeful as Darcy that schooling would improve his silliest daughter. Darcy's faith in education proved correct, though it did take two years before there was any improvement with his wife's youngest sister. Darcy began to fear that Mr Bennet's prediction that he was wasting his money would come true in the case of Lydia.

Mary bloomed while under Mrs Annesley's care. Gone was the sombre girl who took little delight in anything that she considered frivolous, and spent her days with her nose in a book—usually Fordyce's Sermons. In her place was an elegant young lady who was well read and could join in any conversation, be it the latest fashion or discussing a book. Elizabeth was delighted with the change in Mary and when that sister caught the eye of the eldest son of Sir Nathaniel Trubridge, a baronet with a goodly sized estate about twenty miles south of Pemberley, Elizabeth was overjoyed at her sister's good fortune.

Edmund Trubridge had inherited the baronetcy and the estate a year after their marriage. Like Elizabeth and Darcy, their first child, born just before the death of his father, had been a girl. Marianne was a sweet child and loved by all. They had two more daughters, Elizabeth and Alice, and Mary was beginning to fear that she might, like her mother, only birth girls. Mary's fears were proved unfounded when, four years after the birth of Alice, she gave birth to a healthy boy, Nathaniel Thomas Trubridge, who was adored by all his older sisters.

Kitty attended Miss Barclay's school for young ladies in Surrey. Away from the influence of her younger sister, Kitty was eager to learn. Drawing was her talent and she too, like Mary, bloomed. The first friend she made at Miss Barclay's school was a young lady named Sarah Bentley. Miss Bentley was the only daughter of a country gentleman, whose estate was in Berkshire. Being very close in age to each other and both finding a common interest in drawing, the two girls became close friends. They became such good friends that when it was time to return to their respective homes for the holidays, Kitty, instead of returning to Longbourn, was invited to stay with the Bentleys. This became a tradition as Kitty was quite happy to spend every holiday, no matter how long, with the parents of her dear friend. Sarah, not wishing to be parted from Kitty when they left Miss Barclay's school, persuaded her parents that Kitty should stay with them during the summer of 1813 and then accompany them to town in the autumn, so that Sarah and Kitty could enjoy their first season together. Mr and Mrs Bentley, who were taken with their daughter's friend, readily agreed with Sarah's request; both were totally unaware that Miss Kitty Bennet had been 'out' since her fifteenth birthday.

Timothy Bentley shared the same initials as Thomas Bennet, he also had no sons and his humble estate was also entailed to a cousin, but that was where any similarity between the two gentlemen ended. Unlike Thomas Bennet, Mr Bentley had ensured his small estate thrived. Each year any extra money had been invested to go towards dowries for any daughters he and his wife were blessed with. As they only had the one child, Miss Bentley's dowry was a very respectable sixteen thousand pounds.

On hearing that Kitty would have a season in town, Darcy wrote to his aunt, Lady Matlock, requesting her assistance as neither Darcy nor Fitzwilliam would be partaking in the little season. Lady Matlock was happy to assist Kitty and Sarah with their come out. Before coming to town, Mrs Bentley hoped her daughter would do well, but to have Lady Matlock take an interest in Sarah as well as Kitty was beyond her wildest expectations. She was sure the girls' futures would be secure.

Sarah and Kitty did do well. By the beginning of 1814 they had both received and accepted offers from two very eligible gentlemen. Kitty became Mrs Simon Hardy, while Sarah married his close friend Randolph Goadby. The gentlemen were heirs to neighbouring estates, of modest proportions, in Leicestershire; this allowed for the continuing friendship between Kitty and Sarah without any inconvenience of travelling too far.

Lydia was most put out to see all her sisters marry before her. She hated school, though she did make one friend who was so like her in character that other girls believed they were related. The two friends repeatedly found themselves in trouble with the headmistress, Mrs Blake. The school was in Hampshire and quite often the red-coated officers of the militia or the blue coats of naval officers would be seen in the area. It was at those times when Susannah Hardy and Lydia Bennet got into the most trouble for flirting with officers. Mrs Blake, deciding the girls were a bad influence, wrote to both fathers demanding that they be removed immediately.

Mr Bennet contacted Darcy, informing him of the school's edict and saying he knew any money spent trying to educate his youngest daughter was a waste. Darcy, determined that all Lydia needed was a firm hand, removed her from Mrs Blake's school and enrolled her in a school for troubled girls in the north of England. This arrangement worked.

Sixteen months after arriving at Miss Rogers' school in the wilds of Northumberland a very different Lydia entered Derbyshire society. She was still lively, but the wild recklessness was gone. Darcy and Elizabeth both agreed it would be best for Lydia to spend her holidays with them. Although the distance from Northumberland to Derbyshire was great, and would take three long days, it was nothing compare to the distance to Hertfordshire which would easily have taken a se'nnight.

During her first holiday at Pemberley Lydia received a shock, a shock so great that Darcy believed it paved the way for the change in her character. Darcy had requested his solicitor to make enquiries as to the whereabouts of Miss Susannah Hardy, former pupil of Mrs Blake's school of girls in Hampshire. The solicitor had employed two Bow Street runners to look into the case. What they found shocked Lydia Bennet to her bones. Miss Hardy had eloped with an officer of the Hampshire militia, but instead of taking her to Gretna Green he had gone as far as London. With her reputation in ruins, her parents had disowned her in an attempt to try and spare the reputation of her older sister who was still unwed, and now likely to remain so. Susannah Hardy's last known residence was a house of ill repute in Islington.

Darcy had looked gravely at Lydia as tears poured down her cheeks on to the letter in her hands. "That could easily have been your fate, Lydia. You have a second chance with Miss Rogers, use it wisely." Darcy had then left his sister to her sorrow.

When Lydia eventually returned to Longbourn, Samuel Goulding found that he quite liked the changed Miss Lydia. It was not long before that like turned to love and he asked Lydia to marry him. Mrs Bennet had been so shocked as to be rendered speechless for a whole two minutes when she learnt that her dear Lydia was to be the next mistress of Longbourn.

Any fears Mrs Bennet may have had of being thrown into the hedgerows at the demise of her husband did not come to pass. Mr Bennet lived a long and, mostly, contented life. The marriage of Mary, the daughter Mrs Bennet thought least likely to wed, calmed her nerves considerably. Although she never completely understood why Elizabeth had refused Mr Collins, as the years progressed mother and daughter came to an understanding which ensured harmony—if not total tranquillity—whenever they were together. Mrs Bennet was four and fifty when, with no warning, she suffered a severe apoplexy. The seizure paralysed her right side and the doctor feared she would not survive the night. Much to the doctor's and her husband's surprise, Mrs Bennet lingered long enough for all her family to gather at her bedside before the Lord took pity on her pain.

Catherine Darcy was the first of seven children born to the Darcys. After the birth of their fifth daughter, Darcy and Elizabeth resigned themselves to the fact that they would never be blessed with a son. Elizabeth was disturbed by this, but Darcy was not as he felt blessed to have such beautiful daughters. With no entail Catherine's first son would take the name of Darcy and Pemberley would be his.

Elizabeth and Darcy adored their daughters, Catherine, Jane, Madeline, Elizabeth and Amelia, and took great joy in watching them as they grew. It was just before Amelia's fifth birthday that Elizabeth discovered she was with child again. Preparing for another daughter, they decided to call the infant Rosalind Frederica. So sure was Elizabeth that she again carried a daughter that she had diligently embroidered the little one's initials on to a new blanket. Their surprise was great when their son and heir made his way into the world; they named him Richard Fitzwilliam Darcy. Three years later, just six months before Catherine was to make her come out, Elizabeth gave birth to their last child, William Edward Darcy.

Pemberley was a happy home and the halls were filled with much laughter and gaiety. The Darcy children grew up content and well aware of the love and friendship that their parents had for each other and for each of their children.

The End

26547475R00140

Printed in Great Britain
by Amazon